"THE ANUBIS GATES ... together wonderful extravaganza—the sort of thing to be expected of Tim Powers."

—*Poul Anderson*

"Dizzying pace and nonstop invention . . . Powers is into history, as was aptly demonstrated by his last novel, THE DRAWING OF THE DARK . . . he uses historical characters, events, and places with absolute *verismo* and then weaves them into totally wacko situations, somehow keeping the conviction factor afloat."

—*Baird Searles*
ISACC ASIMOV'S SCIENCE FICTION MAGAZINE

"Humorous without being a comedy, dramatic without being tragic, moving without being sappy —THE ANUBIS GATES is the best book of the year . . . buy it as soon as you see a copy, and cast your Hugo votes along with me for THE ANUBIS GATES."

—*C. J. Henderson*
WHISPERS

The old man sighed, ran his fingers through his thinning hair, and then gave Doyle a hard stare. "Time," he said solemnly, "is comparable to a river flowing under a layer of ice. It stretches us out like water weeds, from root to tip, from birth to death, curled around whatever rocks or snags happen to lie in our path; and no one can get out of the river because of the ice roof, and no one can turn back against the current for an instant.

"Picture it, now: if you could stand outside the time river, on some kind of bank, say, and see through the ice, why then you could walk upstream and see Rome and Nineveh in their heydays, or downstream and see whatever the future holds. Now—pay attention, this is the important part—sometime, something happened to punch holes in the metaphorical ice cover. Don't ask me how it happened, but spread out across roughly six hundred years there's a shotgun pattern of gaps . . . and if there happens to be a gap *when* and *where* you are, it is possible to get out of the time stream at that point, and reenter at any other gap.

"I have discovered how to do it."

TIM POWERS
THE

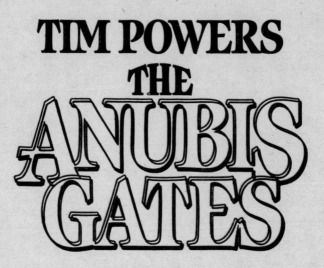

ACE SCIENCE FICTION BOOKS
NEW YORK

THE ANUBIS GATES

An Ace Science Fiction Book / published by arrangement with
the author

PRINTING HISTORY
Ace Original / December 1983

ISBN: 0-441-02380-0

Ace Science Fiction Books are published by
The Berkley Publishing Group,
200 Madison Avenue, New York, New York 10016.
PRINTED IN THE UNITED STATES OF AMERICA

To my wife, Serena

"No man can step into the same river twice,
for the second time it's not the same river,
and he's not the same man."

—Heraclitus

"... They move in dark, old places of the world:
Like mariners, once healthy and clear-eyed,
Who, when their ship was holed, could not admit
Ruin and the necessity of flight,
But chose instead to ride their cherished wreck
Down into darkness; there not quite to drown,
But ever on continue plying sails
Against the midnight currents of the depths,
Moving from pit to pit to lightless crag
In hopeless search for some ascent to shore;
And who, in their decayed, slow voyaging
Do presently lose all desire for light
And air and living company—from here
Their search is only for the deepest groves,
Those farthest from the nigh-forgotten sun ..."

—From "The Twelve Hours of the Night"
by William Ashbless

BOOK ONE

The Face Under the Fur

PROLOGUE: FEBRUARY 2, 1802

"Tho' much is taken, much abides; and tho'
We are not now that strength which in old days
Moved earth and heaven, that which we are, we
    are. . . ."

—Alfred, Lord Tennyson

FROM BETWEEN TWO trees at the crest of the hill a very old man watched, with a nostalgic longing he thought he'd lost all capacity for, as the last group of picnickers packed up their baskets, mounted their horses, and rode away south—they moved a little hastily, for it was a good six miles back to London, and the red sun was already silhouetting the branches of the trees along the River Brent, two miles to the west.

When they'd gone the old man turned around to watch the sun's slow descent. The Boat of Millions of Years, he thought; the boat of the dying sungod Ra, tacking down the western sky to the source of the dark river that runs through the underworld from west to east, through the twelve hours of the night, at the far eastern end of which the boat will tomorrow reappear, bearing a once again youthful, newly reignited sun.

Or, he thought bitterly, removed from us by a distance the universe shouldn't even be able to encompass, it's a vast motionless globe of burning gas, around which this little ball of a planet rolls like a pellet of dung propelled by a kephera beetle.

3

Take your pick, he told himself as he started slowly down the
hill. . . . But be willing to die for your choice.

He had to walk carefully, for his Japanese clogs were
awkward on the uneven dirt and grass.

Fires were already lit among the tents and wagons, and a
weaving of wild odors whirled up to him on the cool evening
breeze: a sharp, earthy reek from the tethered donkeys, wood
smoke, and the aroma of roasting hedgehog, a dish his people
particularly relished. Faintly, too, he thought he caught a
whiff of stale breath from the crate that had arrived that afternoon—a musty fetor, as of perverse spices meant to elicit aversion rather than appetite, almost shockingly incongruous
when carried on the clean breezes of Hampstead Heath. As he
approached the cluster of tents he was met by a couple of the
camp dogs; as always, they backed away from him when they
recognized him, and one turned around and loped purposefully to the nearest tent; the other, with evident reluctance,
escorted Amenophis Fikee into the camp.

Responding to the dog's summons, a dark man in a striped
corduroy coat stepped out of the tent and strode across the
grass toward Fikee. Like the dogs, he halted well short of the
old man. "Good evening, *rya*," he said. "Will you eat some
dinner? They've got a *hotchewitchi* on the fire, smells very
kushto."

"As *kushto* as *hotchewitchi* ever does smell, I suppose,"
Fikee muttered absently. "But no, thank you. You all help
yourselves."

"Not I, *rya*—my Bessie always loved cooked *hotchewitchi*;
so since she *mullered* I don't eat it anymore."

Fikee nodded, though he obviously hadn't been listening.
"Very well, Richard." He paused as though hoping for an interruption, but none came. "When the sun is all the way
down, have some of the *chals* carry that crate down the bank
to the tent of Doctor Romany."

The gypsy scratched his oiled moustache and shifted doubtfully. "The crate that the sailor *chal* brought today?"

"Which crate did you think I meant, Richard? Yes, that
one."

"The *chals* don't like it, *rya*. They say there's something in
it *mullo dusta beshes*, dead many years."

Amenophis Fikee frowned and pulled his cloak closer about
himself. He had left the last rays of sunlight behind him at
the top of the hill, and among these shadows his craggy face

seemed to possess no more vitality than a stone or tree trunk. At last he spoke: "Well, what's in it has seen *dusta beshes*, certainly—many many years." He gave the timorous gypsy a smile that was like a section of hillside falling away to expose old white stone. "But it's not *mullo*, I'm . . . I hope. Not quite *mullo*."

This did nothing to reassure the gypsy, who opened his mouth to voice another respectful objection; but Fikee had turned away and was stalking through the clearing toward the riverbank, his cloak flapping behind him in the wind like the wing-case of some gigantic insect.

The gypsy sighed and slouched away toward one of the tents, practicing a limp that would, he hoped, earn him a dispensation from actually having to help carry the dreadful crate.

Fikee slowly picked his way along the darkening riverbank toward Doctor Romany's tent. Except for the hoarse sighing of the breeze the evening was oddly silent. The gypsies seemed to realize that something momentous was in the wind tonight, and were slinking about as silently as their dogs, and even the lizards had stopped hopping and splashing among the riverside reeds.

The tent stood in a clearing, at the focus of enough lines and rigging—slung from every nearby tree—for a good-sized ship. The angling ropes, assisted by a dozen upright poles, supported the flapping, bulging, many-layered randomness of Romany's tent. It looked, thought Fikee, like some huge nun in a particularly cold-weather habit, crouched beside the river in obscure devotion.

Ducking under a couple of ropes, he made his way to the entrance and lifted aside the curtain, and stepped through into the central room, blinking in the brightness that the dozen lamps cast on the draped carpets which formed the walls, floor and ceiling.

Doctor Romany stood up from a table, and Fikee felt a wave of hopeless envy. Why, Fikee asked venomously, hadn't it been Romanelli who picked that short straw in Cairo last September? Fikee pulled off his drab cloak and hat and flung them in a corner. His bald head gleamed like imperfectly polished ivory in the lamplight.

Romany crossed the room, bobbing grotesquely on his high, spring-soled shoes, and gripped him by the hand. "It's a great thing we—you—attempt tonight," he said in a deep muted voice. "I only wish I could be here with you in person."

Fikee shrugged, a little impatiently. "We are both servants. My post is England, yours is Turkey. I completely understand why it is that you can be present tonight only"—he waved vaguely—"in replica."

"Needless to say," Romany intoned, his voice becoming deeper as though trying to wring an echo out of the surrounding carpets, "if it happens that you die tonight, rest assured you will be embalmed and entombed with all the proper ceremonies and prayers."

"If I fail," Fikee answered, "there won't be anybody to pray to."

"I didn't say *fail*. It could be that you will succeed in opening the gates, but die in accomplishing it," the unruffled Romany pointed out. "In such a case you'd want the proper actions taken."

"Very well," said Fikee with a weary nod. "Good," he added.

There was a sound of shuffling feet from the entry, and then an anxious voice. "Rya? Where would you like the crate? Hurry, I think spirits are coming out of the river to see what's in it!"

"Not at all unlikely," muttered Doctor Romany as Fikee instructed the gypsies to carry the thing inside and set it down on the floor. This they hastily did, making their exit as quickly as respectful deportment would permit.

The two very old men stared at the crate in silence for a time, then Fikee stirred and spoke. "I've instructed my gypsies that in my . . . absence, they are to regard you as their chief."

Romany nodded, then bent over the crate and began wrenching the top boards away. After tossing aside some handfuls of crumpled paper he carefully lifted out a little wooden box tied up with string. He set it on the table. Turning back to the crate, he knocked away the rest of the loosened boards and, grunting with effort, lifted out a paper-wrapped package which he laid on the floor. It was roughly square, three feet on each side and six inches thick.

He looked up and said, "The Book," unnecessarily, for Amenophis Fikee knew what it was.

"If only *he* could do it, in Cairo," he whispered.

"Heart of the British kingdom," Doctor Romany reminded him. "Or maybe you imagine he could *travel*?"

Fikee shook his head, and, crouched beside the table, lifted from under it a glass globe with a slide-away section in its side. He set it on the table and then began undoing the knots on the small wooden box. Romany meanwhile had stripped away the package's paper covering, exposing a black wooden box with bits of ivory inlaid to form hundreds of Old Kingdom Egyptian hieroglyphics. The latch was leather, and so brittle that it crumbled to dust when Romany tried to unfasten it. Inside was a blackened silver box with similar hieroglyphic characters in relief; and when he'd lifted away the lid of that one a gold box lay exposed to view, its finely worked surface blazing in the lamplight.

Fikee had gotten the little wooden box open, and held up a cork-stoppered glass vial that had been nested in cotton inside. The vial contained perhaps an ounce of a thick black fluid that seemed to have sediment in it.

Doctor Romany took a deep breath, then lifted back the lid of the gold box.

At first Doctor Romany thought all the lamps had been simultaneously extinguished, but when he glanced at them he saw that their flames stood as tall as before. But nearly all the light was gone—it was as though he now viewed the room through many layers of smoked glass. He pulled his coat closer about his throat; the warmth had diminished too.

For the first time that night he felt afraid. He forced himself to look down at the book that lay in the box, the book that had absorbed the room's light and warmth. Hieroglyphic figures shone from ancient papyrus—shone not with light but with an intense blackness that seemed about to suck out his soul through his eyes. And the meanings of the figures darted clearly and forcefully into his mind, as they would have done even to someone who couldn't read the primeval Egyptian script, for they were written here in the world's youth by the god Thoth, the father and spirit of language itself. He tore his gaze fearfully away, for he could feel the words burning marks on his soul like a baptism.

"The blood," he rasped, and even the capacity of the air to carry sounds seemed weakened. "Our Master's blood," he repeated to the dimly seen figure that was Amenophis Fikee. "Put it into the sphere."

He could just see Fikee thumb aside the hatch in the side of the globe and hold the vial to the opening before uncorking it; the black fluid spilled inside, falling upward, staining the top of the glass globe. The moon must be up, Romany realized. A drop fell up onto Fikee's palm, and must have burned, for he hissed sharply between his teeth.

"You're . . . on your own," croaked Doctor Romany, and lurched blindly out of the tent into the clearing, where the evening air felt warm by comparison. He blundered away up the riverbank, yawing and pitching on his peculiar shoes, and finally crouched, panting and bobbing, on a slight rise fifty yards upstream and looked back at the tent.

As his breathing and heartbeat decelerated he thought about his glimpse of the Book of Thoth, and shuddered. If any evidence were needed to document the inversion of sorcery during the last eighteen centuries, that prehistoric book provided it; for though he'd never actually seen it before, Romany knew that when the Prince Setnau Kha-em-Uast had, thousands of years ago, descended into the tomb of Ptah-nefer-ka at Memphis to recover it, he had found the burial chamber brightly illuminated by the light that radiated from the book.

And this spell, he thought unhappily, this tremendous effort tonight, would have been almost prohibitively dangerous even in those days, before sorcery became so much more difficult and personally costly to the sorcerer, and, despite the most rigid control, unpredictable and twisted in its results. Even in those days, he thought, none but the bravest and most transcendently competent priest would have dared to employ the *hekau*, the words of power, that Fikee was going to speak tonight: the words which were an invocation and an *invitation to possession* addressed to the dog-headed deity Anubis—or whatever might remain of him now—who, in the time of Egypt's power, presided over the underworld and the gates from this world to the other.

Doctor Romany let his gaze break away from the tent and drift across the river to the heathery landscape that rolled beyond it up to another rise crested with trees that seemed to him too tall for their girth, waving their emaciated branches in the breeze. A northern landscape, he thought, stirred by a wind that's like flowing gin, sharp and clean and smelling of berries.

Reacting to the alien qualities of these things, he thought of the voyage to Cairo he and Fikee had taken four months before, summoned by their Master to assist in the new crisis.

Though prevented by a startling disorder from ever leaving

his house, their Master had for quite a while been using a secret army of agents, and an unchartably vast fortune, in an effort to purge Egypt of the Moslem and Christian taints and, even more difficult, to throw out the governing Turkish Pasha and his foreign mercenaries, restoring Egypt as an independent world power. It was the Battle of the Pyramids four years ago that provided the first real breakthrough for him, though at the time it had seemed the final defeat—for it had let the French into Egypt. Romany narrowed his eyes, remembering the rippling crackle of the French muskets echoing from the Nile on that hot July afternoon, underscored by the drum-roll of the charging Mameluke cavalry . . . by nightfall the armies of the Egyptian governors Ibraheem and Murad Bey had been broken, and the French, under the young general Napoleon, were in possession.

A wild and agonized howl brought Doctor Romany to his feet; the sound rebounded among the trees by the river for several seconds, and when it had died he could hear a gypsy fearfully muttering protective cantrips. No further sounds issued from the tent, and Romany let out his breath and resumed his crouching position. Good luck, Amenophis, he thought—I'd say "may the gods be with you," but that's what you're deciding right now. He shook his head uneasily.

When the French came into power it had seemed like the end of any hope of restoring the old order, and their Master had, by hard-wrought sorcerous manipulation of wind and tides, lent subtle aid to the British admiral Nelson when he destroyed the French fleet less than two weeks later. But then the French occupation turned to their Master's advantage; the French curtailed the arrogant power of the Mameluke Beys, and in 1800 drove out the Turkish mercenaries who'd been strangling the country. And the general who took command of Cairo when Napoleon returned to France, Kleber, didn't interfere with their Master's political intrigues and his efforts to lure the Moslem and Coptic population back into the old pantheist worship of Osiris, Isis, Horus and Ra. It looked, in fact, as though the French occupation would do for Egypt what Jenner's cowpox was evidently doing now for human bodies: substituting a manageable infection, which could be easily eliminated after a while, for a deadly one that would relent only upon the death of the host.

Then, of course, it began to go wrong. Some lunatic from Aleppo stabbed Kleber to death in a Cairo street, and in the ensuing months of confusion the British took up the slack; by September of 1801 Kleber's inept successor had capitulated to the British in Cairo and Alexandria. The British were in, and a single week saw the arrest of a dozen of the Master's agents. The new British governor even found reason to close the temples to the old gods that the Master had had erected outside the city.

In desperation their Master sent for his two oldest and most powerful lieutenants, Amenophis Fikee from England and Doctor Monboddo Romanelli from Turkey, and unveiled to them the plan that, though fantastic to a degree that suggested senility in the ancient man, was, he insisted, the only way to scorch England from the world picture and restore Egypt's eons-lost ascendancy.

They had met him in the huge chamber in which he lived, alone except for his *ushabtis*, four life-size wax statues of men. From his peculiar ceiling perch he had begun by pointing out that Christianity, the harsh sun that had steamed the life-juices out of the now all but dry husk of sorcery, was at present veiled by clouds of doubt arising from the writings of people like Voltaire and Diderot and Godwin.

Romanelli, as impatient with the antique magician's extended metaphors as he was with most things, broke in to ask bluntly how all this might aid in evicting the British from Egypt.

"There is a magical procedure—" the Master began.

"Magic!" Romanelli had interrupted, as scornfully as he dared. "These days we'd get headaches and double vision—not to mention losing about five pounds—if we tried to charm a pack of street dogs out of our way; and even then as likely as not it'd go awry and they'd all simply drop dead where they stood. It's easier to shout and wave a stick at them. I'm sure you haven't forgotten how you suffered after playing with the weather at the Bay of Aboukeer three years ago. Your eyes withered up like dates left too long in the sun, and your legs—!"

"As you say, I haven't forgotten," said the Master coldly, turning those partially recovered eyes on Romanelli, who involuntarily shivered, as always, before the almost imbecilic hatred that burned in them. "As it happens, although I'll be present by proxy, one of you must perform this spell, for it has to be sited very near the heart of the British Empire, which would be the city of London, and my condition forbids travel. Though I'll provide you with all the strongest remaining wards and protective amulets, the working of it will, as you suggest, consume quite a bit of the sorcerer. You will draw straws from the cloth on that table, and the man with the short straw will be the one to do it."

Fikee and Romanelli stared at the two stubs of straw protruding from beneath a scarf, then at each other.

"What is the spell?" queried Fikee.

"You know our gods are gone. They reside now in the Tuaut, the underworld, the gates of which have been held shut for eighteen centuries by some pressure I do not understand but which I am sure is linked with Christianity. Anubis is the god of that world and the gates, but has no longer any form in which to appear here." His couch shifted a little, and the Master closed his eyes for a moment in pain. "There is a spell," he rasped finally, "in the Book of Thoth, which is an invocation to Anubis to take possession of the sorcerer. This will allow the god to take physical form—yours. And as you are speaking that spell you will simultaneously be writing another, a magic I myself have composed that is calculated to open new gates between the two worlds—gates that shall pierce not only the wall of death but also the wall of time, for if it succeeds they will open out from the Tuaut of forty-three centuries ago, when the gods—and I—were in our prime."

There was a silence long enough for the Master's couch to move another painful couple of inches. At last Fikee spoke. "And what will happen then?"

"Then," said the Master in a whisper that echoed round the spherical chamber, "the gods of Egypt will burst out in modern England. The living Osiris and the Ra of the morning sky will dash the Christian churches to rubble, Horus and Khonsu will disperse all current wars by their own transcendent force, and the monsters Set and Sebek will devour all who resist! Egypt will be restored to supremacy and the world will be made clean and new again."

And what role could you, or we, thought Romanelli bitterly, play in a clean new world?

"Is," Fikee said hesitantly, "is it still possible, you're certain? After all, the world already was young that way once, and an old man can't be made into a boy again any more than wine can go back to grape juice." The Master was getting very angry, but he pressed on desperately, "Would it be completely out of the question to . . . adapt to the new ways and new gods? What if we're clinging to a sinking ship?"

The Master had gone into a fit of rage, drooling and gabbling helplessly, and so one of the wax *ushabti* statues twitched and began working its jaws. "*Adapt?*" shouted the Master's voice out of the wax throat. "You want to get baptized? Do you know what a Christian baptism would do to you? Negate you—unmake you—salt on a snail, moth in a fire!" The furious speaking was causing the wax lips to crack. "A sinking ship? You stinking, fearful body-vermin of a diseased whore! What if it *should* sink, is sinking, *has* sunk! We'll ride it down. I'd rather be at the helm of this sunken ship than in the . . . cattle pen! . . . of that new one! Shall I—*ack* . . . *ack* . . . *kha*—" The tongue and lips of the wax statue broke off and were spat out by the still driving breath.

For several moments Master and *ushabti* gibbered together, then the Master regained control of himself and the statue fell silent. "Shall I," asked the Master, "release you, Amenophis?"

Romanelli remembered, with unwelcome clarity, once seeing another of the Master's very old servants suddenly made independent of the Master's magical bonds; the man had, within the space of a few minutes, withered and broken down and dried and split apart and finally shaken himself to dust; but worse than the fact of death and dissolution was his memory that the man had retained consciousness through the entire process. . . . And it had seemed to be an agony worse than burning.

The silence in the chamber lengthened, unbroken except for the faint slapping sound of the *ushabti*'s tongue on the floor tiles. "No," said Fikee at last. "No."

"Then you are one of my crew, and will obey." The Master waved one of his crippled, driftwood arms. "Choose a straw."

Fikee looked at Romanelli, who just bowed and waved *after you* toward the table. Fikee stepped over to it and drew out one of the straws. It was, of course, the short one.

The Master sent them to the ruins of Memphis to copy from a hidden stone the hieroglyphic characters that were his real name, and here too a shock awaited them, for they had seen the Master's name stone once before, many centuries ago, and

the characters carved on it were two symbols like a fire in a
dish followed by an owl and the looped cross: *Tchatcha-em-
Ankh*, it spelled, Strengths in Life; but now different
characters were incised in the ancient stone—now there were
three umbrella shapes, a small bird, an owl, a foot, the bird
again and a fish over a slug. *Khaibitu-em-Betu-Tuf*, he read,
and mentally translated it: Shadows of Abomination.

Despite the baking desert heat the pit of his stomach went
cold, but he remembered a thing that had whimpered and
rolled about as it fell apart into dust, and so he only pursed his
lips as he obediently copied down the name.

Upon their return to Cairo the Master delayed Romanelli's
return to Turkey long enough to fashion a duplicate of him
out of the magical fluid paut. The animated duplicate, or ka,
was ostensibly made to travel to England with Fikee and assist
him in performing the Anubis summoning, but all three knew
that its main task would be to serve as a guard over Fikee and
prevent any dereliction of duty. Since the odd pair would be
living with Fikee's tribe of gypsies until the arrival of the Book
and the vial of their Master's blood, Fikee dubbed the ka Doctor Romany, after the word the gypsies used for their language
and culture.

Another howl broke from the tent downstream, this one
sounding more like pieces of metal being violined against each
other than an issue from any organic throat. The sound rose in
volume and pitch, drawing the air as taut as a bowstring, and
for a moment, during which Romany numbly noted that the
river was holding still like a pane of rippled glass, the ringing,
grating peak note held, filling the dark countryside. Then
something seemed to break, as if a vast bubble over them had
popped, silently but palpably. The ghastly howl broke too,
and as the shattered bits of sound tumbled away in a mad,
despairing sobbing, Romany could feel the air spring back to
its usual pressure; and as though the molecules of the black
fabric had all abruptly relaxed even their usual clench, the tent
burst into bright yellow flame.

Romany sprinted down the bank, picking his footing with
ease in the glare of the fire, and with scorching fingers flicked
the burning entry curtain aside, and bounded into the smoky
interior. Fikee was a huddled, sobbing bulk in the corner.
Romany slammed the Book of Thoth shut and put it in the
gold box, tucked that under his arm and stumbled outside
again.

Just as he got away from the intense heat, he heard a barking, whimpering sound behind him, and turned. Fikee had crawled out of the tent and was rolling on the ground, presumably to put out his smoldering clothes.

"Amenophis!" Romany called over the roaring of the fire.

Fikee stood up and turned on Romany a glance devoid of recognition, then threw his head back and howled like a jackal at the moon.

Instantly Romany reached into his coat with both hands and drew out two flintlock pistols. He aimed one and fired it, and Fikee folded up in midair and sat down hard several feet behind where he'd been standing; but a moment later he had rolled back up on his hands and knees and was scuttling away into the darkness, now on two legs, now on all fours.

Romany aimed the other pistol as well as he could and fired again, but the loping shape didn't seem to falter and soon he lost sight of it. "Damn," he whispered. "Die out there, Amenophis. You do owe us that."

He looked up at the sky—there was no sign of any gods breaking through; he stared toward the west long enough to satisfy himself that the sun wasn't going to reappear. He shook his head in profound weariness.

Like most modern magics, he thought bitterly, while it probably did *something*, it didn't accomplish what it was supposed to.

Finally he tucked the pistols away, picked up the Book and bobbed slowly back to the gypsy camp. Even the dogs had hidden, and Romany met no one as he made his way to Fikee's tent. Once inside, he put down the gold box, lit a lamp, and then far into the night, with pendulum, level, a telescope and a tuning fork and reams of complicated calculations geometrical and alchemical, worked at determining to what extent, if any, the spell had succeeded.

CHAPTER 1

> "In this flowing stream, then, on which there is
> no abiding, what is there of the things which
> hurry by on which a man would set a high price?
> It would be just as if a man should fall in love
> with one of the sparrows which fly by, but it has
> already passed out of sight."
>
> —Marcus Aurelius

WHEN THE DRIVER swung the BMW in to the curb, braked to a
quick but smooth stop and clicked off the headlights, Brendan
Doyle hunched forward on the back seat and stared at the rub-
bled, fenced-in lot they'd arrived at. It was glaringly lit by
electric lights on poles, and he could hear heavy machinery at
work close by.

"Why are we stopping here?" he asked, a little hopelessly.

The driver hopped nimbly out of the car and opened
Doyle's door. The night air was cold. "This is where Mr. Darrow is," the man explained. "Here, I'll carry that," he added,
taking Doyle's suitcase.

Doyle hadn't spoken during the ten-minute ride from
Heathrow airport, but now nervousness overcame his reluctance to admit how little he knew about his situation. "I, uh,
gathered from the two men who originally approached me in
Fullerton—California, that is—that this job has something to
do with Samuel Taylor Coleridge," he said diffidently as the

two of them plodded toward the gate in the chain link fence. "Do you know . . . what it is, exactly?"

"Mr. Darrow will explain it fully, I'm sure," said the driver, who seemed much more relaxed now that his own part in the relay race was almost over. "Something to do with a lecture, I believe."

Doyle stopped. "A *lecture*? He rushed me six thousand miles overnight, to London"—and offered me twenty thousand dollars, he added mentally—"just to give a *lecture*?"

"I really don't know, Mr. Doyle. As I say, he will explain—"

"Do you know if it has anything to do with the position he recently hired Steerforth Benner for?" pressed Doyle.

"I don't know of Mr. Benner," said the driver cheerfully. "Do come along now, sir, this is all scheduled rather tightly, you know."

Doyle sighed and resumed walking, and he wasn't reassured when he noticed the coils of barbed wire strung along the top of the fence. Looking more closely, he saw little scraps of scribbled-on paper, and sprigs of what might have been mistletoe, tied on at intervals along the wire strands. It was beginning to seem likely that the rumors he'd read about Darrow Interdisciplinary Research Enterprises—DIRE—were true. "I probably should have mentioned it before," he called, only half joking, to the driver, "but I can't work a Ouija board."

The man put the suitcase down on the dirt and pressed a button on the gatepost. "I don't think that will be necessary, sir," he said.

On the other side of the fence a uniformed guard was hurrying toward them. Well, you're in it now, Doyle told himself. At least you get to keep the five thousand dollar retainer check even if you decline his offer . . . whatever it turns out to be.

Doyle had been grateful, an hour earlier, when the stewardess woke him to tell him to fasten his seat belt, for he'd been dreaming about Rebecca's death again. Always in the first part of the dream he was a stranger with foreknowledge, trying desperately to find Brendan and Rebecca Doyle before they got on the bike, or at least before Doyle could gun the old Honda up the curling onramp from Beach Boulevard onto the Santa Ana Freeway—and always he was unsuccessful, screeching his car around the last corner only in time, tormentingly, to see the old bike speed up, lean into the curve and disappear around the landscaped bend. Generally he was able to force himself awake at that point, but he'd had several scotches earlier, and this time he might not have been.

He sat up and blinked around at the spacious cabin and the people in the other seats. The lights were on, and only speckled blackness showed beyond the little window—it was night again, though he remembered seeing dawn over icy plains only a few hours ago. Jet air travel was disorienting enough, it seemed to Doyle, without doing it in over the pole jumps that left you unable to guess what day it was. The last time he'd been to England there had been a stopover in New York, but of course DIRE was in too much of a hurry for that.

He stretched as well as he could in his seat, and a book and some papers slid off the fold-down tray in front of him and thump-fluttered to the floor. A lady across the aisle jumped, and he smiled in embarrassed apology as he leaned over to pick the stuff up. Sorting it out and noting the many blanks and question marks he'd scrawled, he wondered bleakly if even in England—for he was certainly going to take advantage of this free trip to try and pursue his own researches—he would be able to dig up some data on the poet whose definitive biography he'd been trying to write for two years. Coleridge was easy, he thought as he tucked the papers back into the briefcase between his feet; William Ashbless 'is a goddamn cipher.

The book that had fallen was Bailey's *Life of William Ashbless*. It had landed open and several of the age-browned pages were broken. He laid them back in carefully, closed the book gently and brushed dust off his fingers, then stared at the unhelpful volume.

It would be an understatement, he reflected disconsolately, to say that Ashbless' life was scantily documented. William Hazlitt had written a brief evaluation of his work in 1825, and incidentally provided a few details about the man, and Ashbless' close friend James Bailey had written the cautious biography that was, for lack of anything else, considered the standard account. Doyle had managed to supplement the narrative with a few illuminating letters and journals and police reports, but the poet's recorded life was still flawed by many gaps.

Which town in Virginia was it, for example, that Ashbless lived in from his birth until 1810? Ashbless at one time claimed Richmond and at another Norfolk, but no records of him had so far turned up at either place. Doyle was going on the assumption that the troublesome poet had changed his name when he arrived in London, and he had unearthed the names of several Virginians who disappeared in the summer of 1810 at about the age of twenty-five. Ashbless' years in London were fairly easy to trace—though the Bailey biography, being Ashbless' own version, was of dubious value—and his brief trip to Cairo in 1811, while inexplicable, was at least a matter of record.

What's missing, Doyle thought, is all the details—and some of the undetailed areas tormented Doyle's curiosity. There was, for example, his possible connection with what Sheridan had lastingly dubbed the Dancing Ape Madness: the surprising number—by sober accounts six, by extravagant three hundred—of fur-covered creatures that appeared one at a time in and around London during the decade between 1800 and 1810; evidently human beings, they outdid even the shock of their sudden, agonizedly capering appearances by falling quickly to the ground and dying in violent convulsions. Madame de Stael noted that Ashbless once, when drunk, told her that he knew more about the peculiar plague than he'd ever dare say, and it was fairly certain that he had killed one of the creatures in a coffee house near Threadneedle Street a week after his arrival in London. . . . But there, to Doyle's chagrin, the trail ended. Ashbless apparently never got drunk enough to tell de Stael the story—for she'd certainly have passed it on if he had—and of course the Bailey biography didn't refer to the matter at all.

And what, precisely, were the circumstances of his death? God knows, Doyle thought, the man made many enemies during his lifetime, but which one was it that caught up with him on, probably, the twelfth of April in 1846? His body was found in the marshes in May, decomposed but verifiably his, also verifiably killed by a sword thrust through the belly.

Hell, thought Doyle, dejectedly staring at the book in his lap, more is known about the life of *Shakespeare*. And Ashbless was a contemporary of such appallingly thoroughly chronicled people as Lord Byron! Granted, the man was a minor poet, whose scanty and difficult work would, if not for some derogatory remarks made about it by Hazlitt and Wordsworth, be absolutely forgotten instead of just reprinted rarely in notably complete anthologies—still, the man's life ought to have left more marks.

Across the aisle, through the windows on that side of the plane, he saw the twinkling lights of London rise as the huge plane banked, and he decided the stewardess wouldn't bring him another drink so near disembarking time. He glanced around, then surreptitiously drew his flask out of his inside jacket pocket, unscrewed the top and poured an inch of Laphroaig into the plastic cup his last drink had arrived in. He put the flask away and relaxed, wishing he could also clip and light one of the Upmann cigars waiting in the opposite pocket.

He took a sip of the warm scotch and smiled—Laphroaig was still damn good, if not quite the wonder it had been when it was being bottled at 91.4 proof. In fact, he thought, these new Upmann cigars from the Dominican Republic aren't nearly what they were when they were being rolled in the Canary Islands.

And none of the young ladies I've gone with since Rebecca have been interesting at all.

He flipped open the old book and stared at the frontispiece engraving, a portrait done from the Thorwaldsen bust: the sunken-eyed, startlingly bearded poet stared back at him from the picture, his massive height and breadth of shoulder clearly implied by the sculptor's skill. And how was it in your day, William? Doyle thought. Were the cigars and scotch and women any better?

For a moment Doyle imagined that Ashbless' faint sardonic grin was directed at him. . . . Then, in a moment of vertigo so strong that he nearly dropped his cup and grabbed the arms of the seat, it seemed that Ashbless really was looking at him, through a picture and across a hundred and fifty years, in scornful amusement.

Doyle shook his head sharply and closed the book again. That's how you know you're tired, he told himself: when a guy a century dead seems about to wink at you out of a picture. Never happened with Coleridge.

He tucked the book into his briefcase next to the book he'd brought along to serve as his credentials—it was *The Nigh-Related Guest*, a biography of Samuel Taylor Coleridge by Brendan Doyle. He had wanted to follow it with a lengthy study of the Lake Poets, but the reviews of the *Guest*, and its sales, had caused his editor at the Devriess University Press to suggest he pursue, as the editor had put it, "a more uncharted sort of territory. I've admired," the editor had gone on, "your two articles in the PMLA that attempted, with some success, to make sense of the murky verse of William Ashbless. Perhaps a biography of that odd poet would strike the critics—and the college librarians!—as a more ground-breaking piece of work."

Well, thought Doyle as he closed his briefcase, unless I resort to outright fiction, it looks like it will be a damned short piece of work.

The plane was descending, and when he yawned his ears popped. Forget Ashbless for now. Whatever Darrow is paying you twenty thousand for, it has to do with Coleridge.

He had another sip of the scotch, and hoped fervently that the job didn't also have to do with planchettes or Ouija boards or any such stuff. He'd once seen a book of poems supposed to have been dictated by the ghost of Shelley, through a medium, and he half-suspected that this DIRE job might be a similar enterprise. He wondered, too, whether twenty thousand dollars might be enough to make him abandon his professional integrity and participate. He drained the cup, as the plane seemed to be about to touch down.

It was certainly an odd coincidence to be hearing so much of DIRE lately. A month ago they'd offered a job to Steerforth Benner, the most brilliant English Literature graduate student Doyle had ever had. Doyle remembered being mildly surprised to hear from Benner that DIRE was still in existence. Doyle knew of the company, of course—from small beginnings in the 1930s, it had become, under the shrewd guidance of its colorful founder, a pillar of American scientific industry rivalling IBM and Honeywell. They'd been very big in things like the space program and undersea exploration, and during the 60s, Doyle recalled, they were always sponsoring Shakespeare plays on television without commercial interruptions. But the company had withdrawn from the public eye during the 70s, and Doyle had read somewhere—in the *National Enquirer*, he believed it was—that J. Cochran Darrow had learned he had cancer, and after exhausting all the scientific possibilities of a cure, had tried to turn the resources of DIRE toward the occult, in the hope of finding a cure in the dubious annals of magic. *Newsweek* had only noted that DIRE was laying off most of its personnel and closing down their production centers, and Doyle remembered a *Forbes* article, titled something like "DIRE Straits," about the sudden worthlessness of their stock.

And then Benner was approached by them and offered a high-paying, though unspecified, position. Over a pitcher of beer one night Benner had told Doyle about all the tests he was taking in order to qualify: tests for alertness under fatigue and distraction, physical endurance and agility, quick comprehension of complicated logic problems . . . and even a few tests which struck Doyle as distasteful, the purpose of which seemed to be to measure Benner's capacity for ruthlessness. Benner had passed them all, and though he did tell Doyle afterward that he'd been accepted for the position, he completely, though amiably as ever, evaded all questions about the job itself.

Well, Doyle thought as, sounding distant through the insulation, the wheels yelped against the runway, maybe I'm about to learn what Benner wouldn't tell me.

The guard unlocked the gate and took Doyle's suitcase from the driver, who nodded politely and walked back toward the purring BMW. Doyle took a deep breath and stepped through, and the guard locked the gate behind him.

"Good to have you with us, sir," the man recited, his voice raised to be heard over the roaring of diesel engines. "If you'll follow me, please."

The lot was more expansive than it had looked from the street, and the guard led him on a looping course to stay out of the way of intimidating obstacles. Big yellow earth-moving tractors lurched and shifted from place to place, popping head-sized stones to dust under their mill wheel tires and sending up an unholy clattering roar as they pushed quantities of rubble into big heaps and then pushed these away somewhere out in the darkness; the rubble, Doyle noted, was fresh, the broken edges of stone still white and sharp-smelling. And there were busy people hurrying about on foot, too, laying out thick power cables and peering through surveying instruments and calling numbers to each other over walkie-talkies. The ring of bright spotlights cast a half-dozen shadows from every object.

The guard was six feet tall and taking long strides, and the shorter Doyle, having to jog occasionally to keep up, was soon puffing and wheezing. What's the goddamn hurry, he wondered angrily; though at the same time he promised him-

self that he'd start doing sit-ups and push-ups in the mornings
again.

A battered old aluminum trailer stood at the periphery of
the glare, moored to the activity by cables and telephone lines,
and this proved to be their destination. The guard hopped up
the three steps to the door and knocked, and when someone
inside shouted, "Come in!" he stepped down and waved
Doyle ahead. "Mr. Darrow will speak to you inside."

Doyle walked up the steps, opened the door and went in.
The inside of the trailer was littered with books and charts,
some looking old enough to belong in a museum and others
obviously brand new; all were clearly in use, the charts
covered with penciled notes and colored pins, and the books,
even the oldest and most fragile, propped carelessly open and
marked up with felt-pen ink.

An old man stood up from behind one of the taller book
stacks, and Doyle was impressed in spite of himself to recognize, from a hundred pictures in magazines and newspapers
over the years, J. Cochran Darrow. Doyle had been prepared
to humor a wealthy but sick and almost certainly senile old
man, but all such thoughts evaporated before the man's piercing and frostily humorous gaze.

Though the hair was whiter and scantier than recent photo-
graphs had shown, the cheeks a little hollower, Doyle had no
difficulty in believing that this was the man who had pioneered
more fields of scientific research than Doyle could probably
even spell, and, out of a small-town sheet-metal factory, built
a financial empire that made J. Pierpont Morgan look merely
successful. "You're Doyle, I hope," he said, and the famous
deep voice had not deteriorated at all.

"Yes, sir."

"Good." Darrow stretched and yawned. " 'Scuse me, long
hours. Sit down, any space you can find. Brandy?"

"Sounds fine to me." Doyle sat down on the floor beside a
knee-high stack of books on which Darrow a moment later set
two paper cups and a pear-shaped bottle of Hennessey. The
old man sat down cross-legged on the other side of the stack,
and Doyle was mortified to note that Darrow didn't have to
suppress a grunt in lowering himself to the floor. Lots of push-
ups and sit-ups, he vowed.

"I imagine you've speculated on the nature of this job,"
Darrow said, pouring the cognac, "and I want you to ditch

whatever conclusions you've come up with. It's got nothing to do with any of them. Here." He handed Doyle a cup. "You know about Coleridge, do you?"

"Yes," Doyle answered cautiously.

"And you know about his times? What was going on in London, in England, in the world?"

"Reasonably well, I think."

"And by know, son, I don't mean do you have books at home on these things or would you know where to look 'em up in the UCLA library. I mean know 'em in your head, which is more portable. Answers still yes?"

Doyle nodded.

"Tell me about Mary Wollstonecraft. The mother, not the one who wrote *Frankenstein*."

"Well, she was an early feminist, wrote a book called, let's see, *A Vindication of the Rights of Women*, I think, and—"

"Who'd she marry?"

"Godwin, Shelley's father-in-law. She died in childb—"

"Did Coleridge really plagiarize Schlegel?"

Doyle blinked. "Uh, yes. Obviously. But I think Walter Jackson Bate is right in blaming it more on—"

"When did he start up on the opium?"

"When he was at Cambridge, I think, early 1790s."

"Who was the—" Darrow began, but was interrupted by the ringing of a telephone. The old man swore, got up and went over to the phone and, lifting the receiver, resumed what was obviously an argument in progress about particles and lead sheathing.

Both from politeness and lack of interest, Doyle made a show of being curious about a nearby book stack—and a moment later his interest became wide-eyed genuine, and very carefully he lifted the top volume.

He opened it, and his half-incredulous suspicion was confirmed—it was the Journal of Lord Robb, which Doyle had been vainly begging the British Museum for a xerox copy of for a year. How Darrow could have got actual possession of it was unguessable. Though Doyle had never seen the volume, he'd read descriptions of it and knew what it was. Lord Robb had been an amateur criminologist, and his journal was the only source of some of the most colorful, and in many cases implausible, crime stories of the 1810s and 20s; among its tales of kill-trained rats, revenges from beyond the grave, and secret thief and beggar brotherhoods, it contained the only detailed account of the capture and execution of the semi-legendary London murderer known as Dog-Face Joe, popularly believed to have been a werewolf, who reputedly could exchange bodies with anyone he chose but was unable to leave behind the curse of lycanthropy. Doyle had wanted to link this story somehow with the Dancing Ape Madness, at least to the extent of the kind of speculative footnote that's mainly meant to show how thoroughly the author has done his homework.

When Darrow hung up the phone Doyle closed the book and laid it back on the stack, making a mental note to ask the old man later for a copy of the thing.

Darrow sat down again beside the book stack with the cups and bottle on it, and picked up right where he'd left off. For the next twenty minutes he fired questions at Doyle, hopping from subject to subject and rarely allowing him time to amplify—though occasionally he would demand every detail Doyle knew about some point; questions on the causes and effects of the French Revolution, the love life of the British Prince Regent, fine points of dress and architecture, differences in regional dialects. And what with Doyle's good memory and his recent Ashbless researches, he managed to answer nearly all of them.

Finally Darrow leaned back and fished a pack of unfiltered cigarettes out of his pocket. "Now," he said as he lit one and drew deeply on it, "I want you to fake an answer."

"Fake one?"

"Right. We're in a roomful of people, let's say, and several of 'em probably know more about literature than you do, but you're being billed as the resident expert, so you've got to at least look like you know everything. So somebody asks you, uh, 'Mr. Doyle, to what extent, in your opinion, was Wordsworth influenced by the philosophy expressed in the verse plays of, I don't know, Sir Arky Malarkey?' Quick!"

Doyle cocked an eyebrow. "Well, it's a mistake, I think, to try to simplify Malarkey's work that way; several philosophies emerge as one traces the maturing of his thought. Only his very late efforts could possibly have appealed to Wordsworth, and as Fletcher and Cunningham point out in their *Concordium* there is no concrete evidence that Wordsworth ever actually read Malarkey. I think when trying to determine the philosophies that affected Wordsworth it would be more productive to consider—'' He stopped, and grinned uncertainly at Darrow. "And then I could ramble indefinitely about how much he was influenced by the Rights of Man business in the French Revolution."

Darrow nodded, squinting through the curling smoke. "Not too bad," he allowed. "Had a guy in here this afternoon— Nostrand from Oxford, he's editing a new edition of Coleridge's letters—and he was insulted at the very idea of faking an answer."

"Nostrand's evidently more ethical than I am," said Doyle a little stiffly.

"Evidently. Would you call yourself cynical?"

"No." Doyle was beginning to get annoyed. "Look, you asked me if I could bluff my way out of a question, and so off the top of my head I had a try at it. I'm not in the habit, though, of claiming to know things I don't. In print, or in class, I'm always willing to admit—''

Darrow laughed and raised a hand. "Easy, son, I didn't mean that. Nostrand's a fool, and I liked your bluff. What I meant was, are you cynical? Do you tend to reject new ideas if they resemble ideas you've already decided are nonsense?"

Here come the Ouija boards, Doyle thought. "I don't think so," he said slowly.

"What if somebody claimed to have incontrovertible proof that astrology works, or that there's a lost world inside the earth, or that any of the other things every intelligent person knows are impossible, was possible? Would you listen?"

Doyle frowned. "It'd depend on who was claiming it. Probably not, though." Oh well, he thought—I still get five thousand and a return ticket.

Darrow nodded, seemingly pleased. "You say what you think, that's good. One old fraud I talked to yesterday would have agreed that the moon is one of God's stray golf balls if I'd said it was. Hot for the twenty grand, he was. Well, let's give you a shot. Time is short, and I'm afraid you're the likeliest-looking Coleridge authority we're going to get."

The old man sighed, ran his fingers through his thinning hair, and then gave Doyle a hard stare. "Time," he said solemnly, "is comparable to a river flowing under a layer of ice. It stretches us out like water weeds, from root to tip, from birth to death, curled around whatever rocks or snags happen to lie in our path; and no one can get out of the river because of the ice roof, and no one can turn back against the current for an instant.'' He paused to grind his cigarette out on an antique Moroccan binding.

Doyle was distinctly disappointed to get vague platitudes when he'd expected to have his credulity strained by wild revelations. Apparently there were a few stripped gears in the old man's head after all. "Uh," he said, feeling that some response was expected from him, "an interesting notion, sir."

"Notion?" Now it was Darrow that was annoyed. "I don't deal in *notions*, boy." He lit another cigarette and spoke quietly but angrily, almost to himself. "My God, *first* I exhaust the entire structure of modern science—try to grasp that!—and then I spend years wringing the drops of truth out of . . . certain ancient writings, and testing the results and systematizing them, and *then* I have to browbeat, coerce, and in two cases even blackmail the boys at my chrono labs in Denver—the Quantum Theory lads, for God's sake, supposed to be the most radically brilliant and elastic-minded scientists at work today—I have to *force* them to even consider the weird but dammit empirical evidence, and get them to whip it up into some practical shape—they did it, finally, and it required the synthesis of a whole new language, part non-Euclidean geometry, part tensor calculus and part alchemical symbols—and I get the findings, the goddamn most important discovery of my career, or anyone's since 1916, I get the whole thing boiled down to one sentence of plain English . . . and do some pissant college teacher the favor of letting him hear it . . . and he thinks I've said 'Life is but a dream,' or 'Love conquers all.' " He exhaled a lungfull of smoke in a long, disgusted hiss.

Doyle could feel his face getting red. "I've been trying to be polite, Mr. Darrow, and—"

"You're right, Doyle, you're not cynical. You're just stupid."

"Why don't you just go to hell, sir?" said Doyle in a tone he forced to be conversational. "Skate there on your goddamn ice river, okay?" He got to his feet and tossed back the last of his brandy. "And you can keep your five thousand, but I'll take the return ticket and a ride to the airport. Now." Darrow was still frowning, but the parchment skin around his eyes was beginning to crinkle. Doyle, though, was too angry to sit down again. "Get old Nostrand back here and tell *him* about the water weeds and the rest of your crap."

Darrow stared up at him. "Nostrand would be certain I was insane."

"Then do it by all means—it'll be the first time he was correct about anything."

The old man was grinning. "He advised me against approaching you, by the way. Said all you were good for was rearranging other people's research."

Doyle opened his mouth to riposte furiously, then just sighed. "Oh, hell," he said. "So calling you crazy would be his second correct statement."

Darrow laughed delightedly. "I knew I wasn't wrong about you, Doyle. Sit down, please."

It would have been too rude to leave now that Darrow was refilling Doyle's paper cup, so he complied, grinning a little sheepishly. "You do manage to keep a person off balance," he remarked.

"I'm an old man who hasn't slept in three days. You should have met me thirty years ago." He lit still another cigarette. "Try to picture it, now; if you could stand outside the time river, on some kind of bank, say, and see through the ice, why then you could walk upstream and see Rome and Nineveh in their heydays, or downstream and see whatever the future holds."

Doyle nodded. "So ten miles upstream you'd see Caesar being knifed, and eleven miles up you'd see him being born."

"Right! Just as, swimming up a river, you come to the tips of trailing weeds before you come to their roots. Now—pay attention, this is the important part—sometime something happened to punch holes in the metaphorical ice cover. Don't ask me how it happened, but spread out across roughly six hundred years there's a . . . shotgun pattern of gaps, in which certain normal chemical reactions don't occur, complex machinery doesn't work. . . . But the old systems we call magic do." He gave Doyle a belligerent stare. "Try, Doyle, just try."

Doyle nodded. "Go on."

"So in one of these gaps a television won't work, but a properly concocted love potion will. You get me?"

"Oh, I follow you. But wouldn't these gaps have been noticed?"

"Of course. Those binders by the window are full of newspaper clippings and journal entries, dating back as far as 1624, that mention occasions when magic has seemed actually, documentably, to work; and since the turn of the century there's usually some note, in the same day's issue, of a power failure or blanket radio interference in the same area. Why, man, there's a street in Soho that some people still call the Auto Graveyard, because for six days in 1954 every car that drove into it conked out and had to be towed away—by horses!—and then started up fine in the next street. And a third-rate part-time medium that lived there staged the last of her Saturday afternoon tea and seance sessions during that week—no one will ever know what happened, but the ladies were all found dead, ice cold after having been dead less than an hour in a warm room, and stamped on every face was, I understand, the most astonishing expression of dismayed terror. The story was downplayed in the press, and the stalling of the cars was blamed on a, quote, accumulation of static electricity, unquote. And there are hundreds of similar examples.

"Now I came across these when I was . . . well, trying to accomplish something science had failed to do, and I was trying to find out if, when and where magic might work. I found that these magic-yes-machinery-no fields are all in or around London and are scattered through history in a bell curve pattern whose peak extends roughly from 1800 to 1805; there were evidently a lot of them during those years, though they tended to be very brief in duration and small in area. They become wider and less frequent farther away from the peak years. Still with me?"

"Yes," said Doyle judiciously. "As far back as the sixteen hundreds, you say? So the gaps then would have been rare, but long when they did show up. And they quickened and shortened until they must have been banging by like clicks from a geiger counter in 1802, say, and then they slowed down and broadened out again. Do they seem to damp out entirely at either end of the curve?"

"Good question. Yes. The equations indicate that the earliest one occurred in 1504, so the curve reaches about three hundred years in each direction, call it six hundred years all told. So anyway, when I began to notice this pattern, I nearly forgot about my original purpose, I was so fascinated by this thing. I tried to get my research boys to work on the puzzle. Hah! They knew senility when they saw it, and there were a couple of attempts to have me committed. But I ducked out of the net and forced them to continue, to program their computers with principles from Bessonus and Midorgius and

Ernestus Burgravius; and in the end I did learn what the gaps were. They were—are—gaps in the wall of time."

"Holes in the ice that covers the river." Doyle nodded.

"Right—picture holes in that ice roof; now if part of your lifetime, some section of the seventy-year-long trailing weed that's you, should happen to be under one of the holes, it's possible to get out of the time stream at that point."

"To where?" Doyle asked guardedly, trying to keep any tone of pity or derision out of his voice. Why, to Oz, he thought, or Heaven, or the Pure Vegetable Kingdom.

"Nowhere," answered Darrow impatiently. "Nowhen. All you can do is enter again through another gap."

"And wind up in the Roman Senate watching Caesar being assassinated. No, sorry, that's right, the holes only extend as far back as 1500; okay, watching London burn down in 1666."

"Right—if there happens to be a gap then. And there. You can't reenter at arbitrary points, only through an existing gap. And," he said with a note of discoverer's pride, "it is possible to aim for one gap rather than another—it depends on the amount of . . . propulsion used in exiting from your own gap. And it is possible to pinpoint the locations of the gaps in time and space. They radiate out in a mathematically predictable pattern from their source—whatever *that* can have been—in early 1802."

Doyle was embarrassed to realize that his palms were damp. "This propulsion you mention," he said thoughtfully, "is it something you can produce?"

Darrow grinned ferociously. "Yes."

Doyle was beginning to see a purpose in the demolished lot outside, all these books, and perhaps even his own presence. "So you're able to go voyaging through history." He smiled uneasily at the old man, trying to imagine J. Cochran Darrow, even old and sick, at large in some previous century. "I fear thee, ancient mariner."

"Yes, that does bring us to Coleridge—and you. Do you know where Coleridge was on the evening of Saturday, the first of September, in 1810?"

"Good Lord, no. William Ashbless arrived in London only . . . about a week later. But Coleridge? I know he was living in London then. . . . "

"Yes. Well, on the Saturday evening I mentioned, Coleridge gave a lecture on Milton's *Aereopagitica* at the Crown and Anchor Tavern in the Strand.''

"Oh, that's right. But it was *Lycidas*, wasn't it?"

"No. Montagu wasn't present, and he got it wrong."

"But the Montagu letter is the only mention anywhere of that lecture." Doyle cocked his head. "Uh . . . isn't it?"

The old man smiled. "When DIRE undertakes to do a job of research, son, we're thorough. No, two of the men who attended, a publisher's clerk and a schoolmaster, left journals which have come into my hands. It was the *Aereopagitica*. The schoolteacher even managed to get a fair amount of the lecture down in shorthand."

"When did you find this?" Doyle asked quickly. An unpublished Coleridge lecture! My God, he thought with a surge of bitter envy, if I'd had that two years ago, my *Nigh-Related Guest* would have got a different sort of review.

"A month or so ago. It was only in February that I got concrete results from the Denver crew, and since then DIRE has been obtaining every available book or journal concerning London in 1810."

Doyle spread his hands. "Why?"

"Because one of these time gaps is just outside Kensington, five miles from the Strand, on the evening of the first of September, 1810. And unlike most gaps that close to the 1802 source, this one is four hours long."

Doyle leaned forward to help himself to another cupful of the brandy. The excitement building in him was so big that he tried to stifle it by reminding himself that what was being discussed here was, though fascinating, impossible. Stick with it for the twenty thousand, he advised himself, and maybe the possibility of getting your hands on Robb's journal or that schoolteacher's notebook. But he wasn't fooling himself—he wanted to participate in this. "And there's another gap here and now, of course."

"Here, all right, but not quite now. We're"—Darrow looked at his watch—"still several hours upstream of it. It's of a typical size for one this far from the source—the upstream edge is tonight, the downstream edge at about dawn of the day after tomorrow. As soon as Denver pinpointed this gap I bought the entire area the field would cover, and got busy levelling it. We don't want to take any buildings back with us, do we?"

Doyle realized his own grin must have looked as conspiratorial as Darrow's. "No, we don't."

Darrow sighed with relief and satisfaction. He picked up the phone just as it started to ring. "Yes? . . . Get off this line and get me Lamont. Quick." He drained his cup and refilled it. "Been living for three days on coffee, brandy and candy bars," he remarked to Doyle. "Not bad, once your stomach gets—Tim? Drop the efforts for Newnan and Sandoval. Well, radio Delmotte and tell him to turn around and take him right back to the airport. We've got our Coleridge man."

He replaced the phone. "I've sold ten tickets, at one million dollars apiece, to attend the Coleridge lecture. We'll make the jump tomorrow evening at eight. There'll be a catered briefing session at six-thirty for our ten guests, and naturally for that we ought to have a recognized Coleridge authority."

"Me."

"You. You'll give a brief speech on Coleridge and answer any questions the guests may have concerning him or his contemporaries or his times, and then you'll accompany the party through the jump and to the Crown and Anchor Tavern—along with a few competent guards who'll make sure no romantic soul attempts to go AWOL—take notes during the lecture and then, back home again in 1983, comment on it and answer any further questions." He cocked an eyebrow sternly at Doyle. "You're being paid twenty thousand dollars to see and hear what ten other people are paying a million apiece for. You should be grateful that all our efforts to get one of the more prominent Coleridge authorities failed."

Not too flatteringly phrased, Doyle thought, but "Yes," he said. Then a thought struck him. "But what about your . . . original purpose, the thing science failed to do, the reason you found these gaps in the first place? Have you abandoned that?"

"Oh." Darrow didn't seem to want to discuss it. "No, I haven't abandoned it. I'm working on it from a couple of angles these days. Nothing to do with this project."

Doyle nodded thoughtfully. "Are there any gaps, uh, downstream of us?"

For no reason Doyle could see the old man was beginning to get angry again. "Doyle, I don't see—oh, what the hell. Yes. There's one, it's forty-seven hours long in the summer of 2116, and that's the last one, chronologically."

"Well." Doyle didn't mean to provoke him, but he wanted to know why Darrow apparently didn't intend to do what seemed to Doyle the obvious thing. "But couldn't this . . .

thing you want done . . . be done very easily, probably, in that year? I mean, if science could *almost* do it in 1983, why by 2116 . . .''

"It's very annoying, Doyle, to give someone a cursory glance at a project you've been working hard at for a long time, and then have them brightly suggest courses which, as a matter of fact, you considered and dismissed as unworkable long ago." He blew smoke out between clenched teeth. "How could I know, before I got there, whether or not the world in 2116 is a radioactive cinder? Hah? Or what sort of awful police state might exist then?" Exhaustion and brandy must have undermined a lot of Darrow's reserve, for there was a glisten in his eyes when he added, "And even if they could and would do it, what would they think of a man from more than a century in the past?" He crumpled his paper cup, and a trickle of brandy ran down his wrist. "What if they treated me like a child?"

Embarrassed, Doyle instantly changed the subject back to Coleridge. But that's it, of course, he thought—Darrow's been the captain of his own ship for so long that he'd rather sink with it than accept the condescension of a life preserver tossed from some Good Samaritan vessel, especially a grander one than his own.

Darrow too seemed eager to steer the conversation back to business.

The sky had begun to pale in the east when Doyle was chauffeured by another driver to a hotel nearby, and he slept until, late in the afternoon, a third driver arrived to take him back to the site.

The lot was now planed flat as a griddle, and all the tractors were gone; several men were at work with shovels and brooms cleaning up horse dung. The trailer was still there, looking adrift now that its telephone and power cables had been removed. Another trailer, big enough to be called a mobile home, was pulled up alongside it. As Doyle got out of the car he noticed pulleys and lines at intervals along the fence top and a collapsed tarpaulin lying at the base of the fence all around the perimeter. He grinned. The old man's shy, he thought.

A guard opened the gate for him and led him to the new trailer, the door of which stood open. Doyle went inside. At the far end of the walnut-panelled and carpeted room Darrow, looking no more tired than he had last night, was talking to a tall blond man. Both men were dressed in the pre-Regency style: frockcoats, tight trousers and boots; they wore them so naturally that Doyle momentarily felt ridiculous in his polyester-cotton suit.

"Ah, Doyle," said Darrow. "I think you already know our chief of security."

The blond man turned around and after a moment Doyle recognized Steerforth Benner. The young man's once-long hair had been cut short and curled, and his wispy moustache, never very evident, was now shaved off.

"Benner!" Doyle exclaimed, pleased, as he crossed the room. "I suspected you must be connected with this project." His friendship with the young man had cooled off in the last month or two, since Benner's DIRE recruitment, but he was delighted to see a familiar face here.

"Colleagues at last, Brendan," said Benner with his characteristic wide smile.

"We jump in a little less than four hours," resumed Darrow, "and there are a lot of things to get done first. Doyle, we've got a period suit for you, and those doors at that end are changing rooms. I'm afraid you'll be supervised, but it's important that everyone dress the role from the skin out."

"We're only going to be staying four hours, aren't we?" Doyle asked.

"It's always in the realm of possibility, Doyle, that one of our guests might run off, despite the efforts of Benner and his boys. If one does, we don't want him to be carrying any evidence that he's from another century." Darrow snapped his hand up, as though physically fielding Doyle's next question. "And no, son, our hypothetical escapee wouldn't be able to tell people how the war will turn out or how to build a Cadillac or anything. Each guest will swallow a capsule, just before we go, of something I think I'll call Anti-Transchrono Trauma. ATCT. What it will actually be, and please don't start yelling yet, Doyle, is a fatal dose of strychnine in a capsule set to dissolve after six hours. Now when we get back they'll have their entire GI tracts pumped full of an activated charcoal solution." He smiled frostily. "Staff is exempt, of course, or I wouldn't be telling you this. Each guest has agreed to these conditions, and I think most of them have guessed what they mean."

And maybe they haven't, Doyle thought. Suddenly the

whole project looked like lunacy again, and he imagined himself in court, some day soon, trying to explain why he hadn't informed the police about Darrow's intentions.

"And here's a speech you can make at the briefing," Darrow went on, handing Doyle a sheet of paper. "Feel free to change it or rewrite it entirely—and if you could have it memorized by then I'd be very pleased. Now I imagine you two would like to compare notes, so I'll get busy in my trailer. Staff won't be permitted to drink at the briefing, but I don't see any harm if you have a couple right now." He smiled and strode out, looking piratically handsome in the archaic clothes.

When he was gone Benner opened a cupboard that proved to be a liquor cabinet. "Aha," he said, "they were ready for you." He pulled down a bottle of Laphroaig, and in spite of his worries Doyle was pleased to see that it was the old 91.4 proof kind, in the clear glass bottle.

"God, pour me some. Neat."

Benner handed him a glass of it and mixed a Kahlua and milk for himself. He sipped it and grinned at Doyle. "I think a bit of liquor is as essential as the lead sheathing; you wouldn't catch me standing in the path of all that radiation without some hooch under my belt."

Doyle had been about to demand a phone to call the police with, but this brought him up short. "What?"

"The tachyon conversion process. Didn't he explain how the jump will work?"

Doyle felt hollow. "No."

"Do you know anything about Quantum Theory? Or subatomic physics?"

Without conscious volition Doyle's hand lifted the glass and poured some scotch into his mouth. "No."

"Well, I don't know nearly enough about it myself. But basically what's going to happen is we'll all be lined up in the path of a blast of insanely high frequency radiation, way up above gamma ray frequencies—photons haven't got any mass, you know, so you can send one phalanx of 'em out right after another without them stepping on each other's heels—and when it hits us, the odd properties of the gap field will prevent whatever would ordinarily occur. I'm not sure what would ordinarily happen, though it'd certainly trash us." He sipped his drink cheerfully. "Anyway, since we'll be in the gap, what will happen—the only way nature can reconcile the inequities involved—is that we'll become, in effect, honorary tachyons."

"Christ," exclaimed Doyle hoarsely, "we'll become ghosts. We'll see Coleridge, all right—we'll see him in Heaven." A car horn blared past on the street, sounding more distant than Doyle knew it must be, and he wondered where some innocent soul was driving to, and what trivial difficulty had made him honk his horn. "Benner, listen to me—we've got to get out of here and get to the police. My God, man—"

"It really is perfectly safe," Benner interrupted, still smiling.

"How can you possibly know that? The man is probably a certifiable lunatic, and—"

"Take it easy, Brendan, and listen. Do I look all right? Is the fence still standing? Then stop worrying, because I made a solo jump to a brief gap in 1805 two hours ago."

Doyle stared at him suspiciously. "You did?"

"Cross my heart and hope to die. They dressed me up like—oh, picture a Ku Klux Klansman who favors metallic robes and doesn't need eyeholes—and then had me stand on a platform by the fence while they lined up their infernal machinery on the other side of the fence. And then whoosh!—one minute I was here and today, the next I was in a tent in a field near Islington in 1805."

"In a tent?"

Benner's smile took on a puzzled quirk. "Yeah, it was weird, I landed in some kind of gypsy camp. The first thing I saw when I ripped off the hood was the inside of this tent, and it was all fumy with incense and full of Egyptian-looking stuff, and there was a cadaverous old bald-headed guy staring at me in extreme surprise. I got scared and ran outside, which wasn't easy in that robe, and it was English countryside I saw, and no highways or telephone poles, so I guess it really was 1805. There were a lot of horses and tents and gypsy types around, and all the gypsies were staring at me, but the gap came to its end just then—thank God I hadn't run outside the field—and the mobile hook snatched me back to here and now." He chuckled. "I wonder what the gypsies thought when I just disappeared, and the robe fell empty without me in it."

Doyle stared at him for several long seconds. Though always amiable, Benner had never been trustworthy—but this wasn't how he lied. The man wasn't a good actor, and this story, especially the note of puzzlement about the old man in the tent, had been told with effortless conviction. He realized dizzily that he believed it.

"My God," he said in an envious near-whisper, "what did the air smell like? What did the ground feel like?"

Benner shrugged. "Fresh air and grassy ground. And the horses looked like horses. The gypsies were all fairly short, but maybe gypsies always are." He clapped Doyle on the back. "So stop worrying. The charcoal enemas will keep the guests healthy, and I'm not going to let any of them get away. You still want to call the cops?"

"No." No indeed, Doyle thought fervently. I want to see Coleridge. "Excuse me," he said, "I've got to get busy on this speech."

At twenty after six Doyle decided he had his new speech memorized. He stood up in the little office Darrow had let him use, sighed, and opened the door to the main room.

A number of well-dressed people were milling around at the far end of the room, separated from him by a dozen or so empty chairs and a big central table. The hundreds of candles in the chandeliers were lit, and the sof , gracious illumination gleamed off the polished panelling and the rows of glasses on the table; faintly on the warm air he caught a smell of bell peppers and grilling steak.

"Benner," he called softly, seeing the tall young man lean tiredly against a wall near the table and, in perfect harmony with the way he was dressed, flip open a snuffbox and bring a pinch of brown powder up to his nose.

Benner looked up. "Damn it, Brendan—*hatchoo!*—damn it, staff's supposed to be all dressed by now. Never mind, the guests are in the dressing rooms, you can change in a few minutes." Benner put away his snuffbox and frowned impatiently at Doyle's clothes as he walked over. "You've got your mobile hook on, at least?"

"Sure." Doyle pulled back his shirt sleeve to show him the leather band, drawn tight and secured with a little lock, around his shaven forearm. "Darrow himself put it on an hour ago. Come listen to my speech, will you? You know enough about—"

"I don't have time, Brendan, but I'm sure it's fine. These damn people, each one of them thinks he's the maharajah of the world."

A man hurried up to them, dressed, like Benner, in the early nineteenth century style. "It's Treff again, chief," he said quietly. "We finally did get him to strip, but he's got an Ace bandage on his leg and he won't take it off, and it's obvious he's got something under it."

"Hell, I knew one of them would pull this. Rich people! Come along, Doyle, you've got to head in this direction anyway."

As they strode across the room the imposing figure of Darrow entered through the main door and their paths converged just as a stout, hairy man wearing nothing but an elastic bandage around his thigh stormed out of one of the dressing rooms.

"Mr. Treff," said Darrow, raising his thick white eyebrows, and his deep voice undercut and silenced all the others, "you have evidently misunderstood the dress requirements."

At this several people laughed, and Treff's face went from red to dark red. "Darrow, this bandage stays on, understand? It's my doctor's orders, and I'm paying you a *goddamn million dollars*, and no fugitive from a nut hatch is going to—"

Only because he happened to smile nervously just then at Benner did Doyle see him whip a thin knife out of his sleeve; but everyone saw him when he kicked forward in a graceful full-extension fencer's lunge and slipped the flat of the blade under the disputed bandage, paused for a theatrical moment, and then flicked it out sideways, cleanly slicing the layers of cloth through from top to bottom.

A good fistful of heavy, gleaming metallic objects thudded onto the carpet. In a quick glance Doyle recognized among them a Colibri Beam Sensor lighter, a Seiko quartz watch, a tiny notebook, a .25 caliber automatic pistol and at least three one-ounce plates of solid gold.

"Planning on buying the natives with glass beads, were you?" Darrow said, with a nod of thanks to Benner, who had straightened back up to his position beside Doyle and slipped the knife away. "As you know, this violates the terms of our agreement—you'll be getting a fifty percent refund, and right now the guards will escort you to a trailer outside the lot, where you'll be held in luxurious captivity until dawn. And in a spirit of friendly concern," he added, with the coldest smile Doyle had ever seen, "I do strongly advise you to leave here quietly."

"Well, one good result of all that," said Benner lightly as

Treff was led, naked, out the door, "is that a dressing room is now free. In you go, Brendan."

Doyle stepped forward and, muttering "Excuse me" to several people, went into the newly vacated dressing room. There was a guard on a stool inside, and he looked relieved that this wasn't Treff coming back in.

"Doyle, aren't you?" the man said, standing up.

"Yes."

"Right, then, off with your clothes."

Sucking in his belly a little, Doyle obediently shed his clothes and hung his suit carefully on a hanger the guard handed him. There was a door in the back of the dressing room, and the guard bustled away through it, taking Doyle's things with him.

Doyle leaned against the wall, hoping they wouldn't forget about him. He tried to scratch under the leather band on his forearm, but it was drawn too tight for him to get a finger under it. He gave up, resolving just to ignore the way the carved bit of green stone under the leather made his shaved skin itch. A mobile hook, Darrow had called it, and he'd let Doyle look at the thing before it was covered by the strap that would hold it tightly against him. Doyle had turned the small lozenge of green stone in his fingers, noting the symbols carved on it—they seemed to be a mix of hieroglyphics and astrological notations.

"Don't look at it so disapprovingly, Doyle," Darrow had said. "It's what will bring you back to 1983. When the 1810 gap comes to an end, this thing will pop back to the gap it came from, which is here and now, and as long as it's in contact with your flesh it'll take you back with it. If you were to lose it, you'd see us all disappear and you'd be marooned in 1810; which is why it's to be locked onto you."

"So we'll all just disappear from there after four hours?" Doyle had asked as Darrow soaped and shaved his forearm. "What if you've miscalculated the length of the gap, and we all disappear in the middle of the lecture?"

"We wouldn't," Darrow had said. "You've got to be within the gap as well as touching the hook, and the gap is five miles away from the tavern we're going to." He laid the stone on Doyle's arm and wrapped the wide leather band around it. "But we haven't miscalculated, and we have a comfortable margin of time to get back to the gap field after the lecture, and we're bringing two carriages, so," he had said as he drew the strap tight and snapped the little lock onto it, "don't worry."

Now, leaning naked against the wall of the dressing room, Doyle smiled at himself in the mirror. What, me worry?

The guard came back and gave Doyle a set of clothes that presumably wouldn't raise any eyebrows in 1810; he also gave him directions on how to put them on, and had actually to assist him in tying the little bow at the front of the cravat. "Your hair doesn't need cutting, sir, the fashion in length is about the same again, but I will just brush it down a bit in front here, so; a bald spot's nothing to be ashamed of. That's it precisely, semi-Brutus style. Have a look at yourself now."

Doyle turned to the mirror, cocked his head and then laughed. "Not bad," he said. He was wearing a brown frock-coat with two rows of buttons; in the front it came down only to belt level, but in back it swept in a long tail that reached to the backs of his knees. He had on tight tan trousers and knee-high Hessian boots with tassels, and the white silk cravat visible between the high wings of the coat's collar gave him, he thought, if not an air of rakish handsomeness, at least one of dignity. The clothes had none of the stiffness of brand new garments; though clean, they had clearly been worn before, and this had the effect of making Doyle feel relaxed and comfortable in them, and not as though he'd been shoehorned into some costume for a party.

When he stepped back into the main room the guests were ambling toward the table, on which a colorful profusion of plates and platters and bottles had appeared. Doyle filled a plate and, remembering that he was "staff," forced himself not to look at the selection of wines and beers but to grab a cup of coffee instead.

"Here you go, Doyle," spoke up Darrow, indicating an empty chair next to himself. "Doyle," he explained to the nearest several people, "is our Coleridge expert."

They nodded and smiled as Doyle sat down, and one white-haired man with humorous eyes said, "I enjoyed *The Nigh-Related Guest*, Mr. Doyle."

"Thank you." Doyle smiled, pleased for the few seconds it took him to realize that the man was Jim Thibodeau, whose massive, multi-volume *History of Mankind*—written with his wife, who Doyle now noticed sitting on the other side of him—had reflected even just in the chapter on the English Romantic poets a depth of research and a relaxed style Doyle

could only admire and envy. But their presence here reinforced the hopeful excitement he'd been feeling ever since
hearing Benner describe jumping to 1805. If the Thibodeaus
are taking it seriously, he thought, there's got to be a good
chance of it working.

The table and food had been cleared away and the ten chairs
were now arranged in a semicircle before a podium. Doyle em-
barrassedly told Benner to take the podium away, and he
replaced it with the chair Treff would have got.

Doyle sat down in it and met the gaze of each guest in turn.
Of the nine of them, he recognized five: three, including the
Thibodeaus, were prominent historians, one was a distinguished British stage actor, and one, he was fairly sure, was a
famous spiritualist and medium. She'd better watch her tricks
here in the gap, he thought uneasily, remembering Darrow's
story about the seance on Auto Graveyard Street in 1954.

He took a deep breath and began. "You are probably
familiar with the life and works of the man who was the father
of the Romantic movement in English poetry, but our outing
this evening certainly calls for a review. Born in Devonshire on
October 21, 1772, Coleridge early on exhibited the precocity
and wide range of reading that he maintained all his life and
that made him, among so many other things, the most
fascinating conversationalist of an age that included such people as Byron and Sheridan. . . ."

As he went on, touching on the poet's scholastic career, his
addiction to opium in the form of laudanum, his unfortunate
marriage, his friendship with William and Dorothy Wordsworth, and the extended trips abroad occasioned by his horror
of his wife, Doyle carefully watched his audience's response.
They seemed satisfied on the whole, frowning doubtfully or
nodding from time to time, and he realized that his presence
here was a gracious detail, like the fine china dishes on which
the food had been served when paper plates would have done
just as well. Darrow could probably have delivered a talk on
Coleridge at least as effectively, but the old man had wanted a
sure enough Coleridge *authority* to do it.

After about fifteen minutes he drew it to a close. Questions
followed, all of which Doyle managed to answer confidently,
and at last Darrow stood up and walked over to stand beside
Doyle's chair, effortlessly replacing him as the focus of attention. He was carrying a lantern, and he waved it in the direc-

tion of the door. "Ladies and gentlemen," he said, "it is now five minutes to eight, and our coaches await us outside."

In a tense silence everyone got to their feet and put on hats and bonnets and greatcoats. *A hundred and seventy years,* Doyle thought, *is the distance to 1810. Can I get there by candlelight? Yes, and back again.* He noted almost disinterestedly that his heart was pounding and that he didn't seem able to take a deep breath.

They all filed out onto the packed dirt of the lot. Two broughams, each with two horses harnessed to it, had been drawn up to within a few yards of the trailer, and by the light of the flickering coach lamps Doyle could see that the vehicles, like the period clothes they were all wearing, were clean and in good repair but obviously not new.

"There's room for five in each vehicle with a bit of crowding," Darrow said, "and since Treff couldn't attend, I'll take his place inside. Staff rides up top."

Benner took Doyle by the elbow as the guests, with a good deal of hat dropping and shawl tangling, began climbing in. "We've got the back of the second coach," he said. They walked around to the rear of the farther coach and climbed up to two little seats that projected from the back at the same height as the driver's. The night air was chilly, and Doyle was glad of the heat from the left rear lamp below his elbow. From his perch he could see more horses being led in from the north end of the lot.

The carriage rocked on its springs when two of the guards hoisted themselves up onto the driver's seat, and hearing metal clink close by, Doyle glanced toward Benner and saw the butts of two pistols sticking out of a leather pouch slung near Benner's left hand.

He heard reins snap and hooves clop on the dirt as the first carriage got moving. "Where are we going?" he asked as their own carriage got under way. "Spatially speaking, I mean."

"Over to the fence there, that section where the curtain isn't up. Do you see that low wooden platform? There's a truck pulled up right to the edge of the fence just outside."

"Ah," said Doyle, trying not to sound as nervous as he felt. Looking back, he saw that the horses he'd noticed being led up were now harnessed to the two trailers and were pulling them away toward the north end.

Benner followed his glance. "The lot, the gap field, has to be completely cleared for every jump," he explained.

"Anything that's within it goes back with us."

"So why didn't your tents and gypsies come back here?"

"The whole field doesn't come back on the return, just the hooks and whatever they're touching. The hook works like the rubber band on one of those paddleball things—energy's required to swat the ball away, and if a fly's in the way he'll go too, but only the ball comes back. Even these coaches will stay there. In fact," he added, and there was enough light from the lamps for Doyle to see his grin, "I noted on my own jaunt that even one's clothes stay there, though hair and fingernails somehow stay attached. So Treff got in on at least part of the fun." He laughed. "That's probably why he's only getting a fifty percent refund."

Doyle was glad now of the tarpaulin curtain around the lot.

The two coaches drew up to the fence, and through the chain links Doyle could see the truck, its wide side panel slid all the way open. A wooden stage, only about a foot high but more than a dozen yards long and wide, had been set up on the patch of dirt next to the truck but just inside the fence, and it boomed and rattled like a dozen drums when the drivers goaded the horses to pull the coaches up onto it. A number of men, already looking anachronistic in 1983 jumpsuits, quickly set up aluminum poles and draped a stiff and evidently heavy cloth over them, so that the two coaches were in a large cubical tent. The fabric of the tent gleamed dully in the contained lamplight, and Doyle leaned way out of his seat to brush it with his fingers.

"A mesh of woven steel strands sheathed in lead," Benner said, his voice sounding louder in the enclosed space. "The same stuff my robe and hood were made of this afternoon," he added more quietly. "The truck's tented too, on three sides."

Doyle was trying not to let Benner see his hands trembling. "Is there an actual blast?" he asked, forcing his voice not to quaver. "Will we feel any concussion?"

"No, you don't really feel anything. Just . . . dislocation."

Doyle could hear people whispering in the carriage below him, and from the other one he heard Darrow's laugh. One of the horses echoingly stamped a hoof.

"What are they waiting for?" Doyle whispered.

"Got to give those men time to make it to the gate and get outside."

Even though the coaches were halted, Doyle still felt sick,

and the oil and metal smell of the peculiar tent was becoming unbearable. "I hate to say it," he whispered, "but that smell is—".

Abruptly something shifted, violently but without motion, and the sense of depth and space was extinguished from everything he could see, leaving only a flat dimness in front of his eyes splashed with patches of meaningless light; the roof rail he was clutching was the only bearing he had—there was no north and south, or up and down, and he found himself back in the dream the stewardess had awakened him from last night, feeling the old Honda shift horrifyingly sideways on the wet pavement and then spill him into a horizontal tumble of shocking velocity, hearing Rebecca's scream end instantly at the first punching impact of the asphalt. . . .

The wooden platform had dropped away from beneath them a short distance, and it shattered when the four horses and two coaches came down on it. The ground was no longer flat, and the poles toppled inward, burying everything a moment later under the heavy folds of the lead-sheathed fabric.

Doyle welcomed the pain when one of the falling poles rebounded from the coach roof and banged his shoulder, for it established the here and now for him. If it hurts it's got to be the real world, he thought dazedly, and he shook off the vivid memory of the motorcycle crash. The smell he so disliked was very intense, for a section of the collapsed tent was pressing his head down onto the coach roof. And, he thought, probably nothing unites you with surrounding reality more thoroughly than being wringingly sick.

Just when he thought he had gathered the energy, though, the lead curtain was hauled off him, and the fresh night air he found himself breathing made the whole idea of vomiting seem self-indulgent and affected. He looked around at the moonlit field the coaches stood in, bordered by tall trees.

"You okay, Brendan?" Benner said for, Doyle realized, the second time.

"Yeah, sure, I'm fine. Jesus, what a jump, huh? Is everybody else okay? How about the horses?" Doyle was proud of himself for asking such unruffled, businesslike questions, though he wished he could talk more quietly and stop bobbing his head.

"Take it easy, will you?" Benner said. "Everything's fine. Here—drink." He unscrewed the top of a flask and handed it to Doyle.

A moment later Doyle was reflecting that liquor was even more effective than pain—or, probably, throwing up—in reconciling one to reality. "Thanks," he said more quietly, handing it back.

Benner nodded, pocketed the flask, vaulted to the broken platform, and strode off it to where four of the six other guards were spading up a patch of earth and, with gloved hands, folding up the lead tent cloth; in so short a time that Doyle knew they must have practiced it they had buried the folded-up bale of fabric and scrambled back up to their places on the coaches.

"You should see the platform," Benner remarked, hardly panting. "A good three inches was sheared off the bottom of it when we jumped. If we hadn't been up on it the horses would have lost their hooves and the wheels would each have a section gone."

The drivers snapped the reins and the coaches moved unevenly forward off the crumpled boards and onto the grass. At a slow pace they began to make their way across the field.

In a few minutes they had reached a stand of willows that screened them from the road, and one of the guards jumped to the ground and sprinted ahead. Crouching, he glanced right and left, and made a patting, keep-your-head-down gesture; a few moments later an open carriage rattled past from left to right, headed for the city. Doyle stared after it in fascination, awed to think that the cheery-looking couple he'd glimpsed through the willow branches would very likely be dead a century before he was born.

The reins flapped and harnesses jingled as the horses advanced to the ditch and, with some effort and backsliding, pulled the coaches across it and onto the road. Wheeling around to the right they set off, and in a minute were rocking along at a good speed east, toward London. The coach lamps, which had fluttered and flickered during the jiggling passage across the ditch, settled down now to a regular back and forth sway on their hooks, casting yellow highlights on the horses' backs and the brightwork on the coaches, but otherwise dimmed by the moonlight that frosted the trees and made the road glow like a track of palest ashes.

If your heels be nimble and light, Doyle thought, *you may get there by candle-light.*

CHAPTER 2

"I am borne darkly, fearfully afar . . ."
                              —Percy Bysshe Shelley

ABOVE THE CROWDED sidewalks the windows of the stately, balconied buildings of Oxford Street were all aglow with lamplight on this young Saturday evening; elegantly dressed men and women were to be seen everywhere, wandering arm in arm, silhouetted by shop windows and open doorways, stepping into or alighting from the hansom cabs that jostled one another for positions at the curb. The air was clamorous with the shouting of the cab drivers, the whirring clatter of hundreds of coach wheels on the cobblestones, and, a little more pleasantly, the rhythmic chanting of street vendors who had strayed west from the weekly fair in Tottenham Court Road. From his perch Doyle could smell horses, cigar smoke, hot sausages and perfume on the chilly night breeze.

When they turned right onto Broad Street Benner pulled one of his pistols—a four-barrelled thing, looking all spidery with its multiple flintcocks and flashpan covers—completely out of the leather sack and leaned his elbow on the coach roof with the gun very evident, pointed at the sky. Looking up front, Doyle saw that all the guards had done the same.

"We're entering the St. Giles rookery," Benner explained. "Some very rough types about, but they won't interfere with a body of armed men."

Doyle looked around with a wary interest at the narrow alleys and courts that snaked away from the street, most of them dark, but a few lit by reflections of some smoky light around a corner. There was much more street-selling here, on the main street at least, and the coaches passed dozens of coffee stalls, old clothes stands, and crates of vegetables watched over by formidable old women who puffed clay pipes and watched the crowd through narrowed eyes. A number of people shouted things at the two coaches, in so thick an accent that Doyle could catch only an occasional "damn" or "bloody," but their tone seemed more jocular than threatening.

He looked behind, and then touched Benner's arm. "Didn't mean to startle you," he said quickly. "That wagon back there—behind the potato cart—the thing that looks like a Conestoga wagon. It's been behind us ever since we got onto the Bayswater Road."

"For God's sake, Brendan, we've only made one turn since then," Benner hissed impatiently. He did turn around, though. "Hell, that's just . . ." Suddenly he looked thoughtful. "I believe it's a gypsy wagon."

"Gypsies again," said Doyle. "They didn't use to—I mean they don't usually come into big cities much, do they?"

"I don't know," Benner said slowly. "I'm not even sure it is a gypsy wagon, but I'll mention it to Darrow."

The street narrowed and darkened as they rattled down St. Martin's Lane and passed the tall old church, and the groups of men that watched their passage from low, dimly lit doorways made Doyle glad of Benner's weapons; then it broadened out into light and festivity again when they came to the wide boulevard that was the Strand. Benner worked his complicated gun back into its sack.

"The Crown and Anchor's just around the corner," he said. "And I haven't seen your gypsy wagon for the last several blocks."

Between two buildings Doyle got a quick view of the river Thames, glittering in the moonlight. It seemed to him that a bridge wasn't there that he'd seen there on his 1979 visit, but before he had time really to orient himself they'd turned into a little street and squeaked to a halt in front of a two-storied half-timbered building with a sign swinging over the open doorway. *The Crown and Anchor,* Doyle read.

Drops of rain began pattering down as the guests stepped

out of the coaches. Darrow moved to the front, his hands buried in a furry muff. "You," he said, nodding at the man who'd driven the forward coach, "park the cars. The rest of us'll be inside. Come on, all." He led the party of seventeen into the warmth of the tavern.

"Good God, sir," exclaimed the boy who hurried up to them, "all of you for dinner? Should have let us know in advance, they'd have opened the back banquet room. But see if there's enough chairs to settle on in the taproom, and—"

"We haven't come for dinner," said Darrow impatiently. "We've come to hear Mr. Coleridge speak."

"Have ye?" The boy turned and shouted down a hall, "Mr. Lawrence! Here's a whole lot more people that thought it was this Saturday that the poet fellow was to speak here!"

Every bit of color left Darrow's face, and suddenly he was a very old man dressed up in ludicrous clothes. The muff fell off his hands and thumped on the hardwood floor. No one spoke, though Doyle, beneath his shock and disappointment, could feel a fit of hysterical laughter building up to critical mass inside himself.

A harried-looking man, followed by a pudgy old fellow with long gray hair, hurried up to them. "I'm Lawrence, the manager," he said. "Mr. Montagu set up the lecture for next Saturday, the eighth of October, and I can't help it that you've all come tonight. Mr. Montagu isn't here, and he'd be upset if—"

Doyle had glanced, and was now staring, at the chubby, ill-seeming man beside Lawrence, who blinked at them all apologetically while the manager was speaking. In his mounting excitement Doyle raised a hand so quickly that the manager halted in mid-sentence, and he leaned forward and said to the man beside Lawrence, "Mr. Coleridge, I believe?"

"Yes," the man said, "and I do apologize to you all for—"

"Excuse me." Doyle turned to Lawrence. "The boy indicated that there is a banquet room not in use."

"Well, yes, that's true, but it hasn't been swept and there's no fire . . . and besides, Mr. Montagu—"

"Montagu won't mind." He turned to Darrow, who was recovering his color. "I'm sure you must have brought suitable cash to cover emergencies, Mr. Darrow," he said. "And I imagine that if you give this fellow enough of it he'll have a fire built and provisions brought to us in this banquet room. After all, Mr. Coleridge clearly thought it was to be this evening, and so did we, so why should we listen to him out on the street when there are taverns about with unused rooms? I'm sure," he said to Lawrence, "even Mr. Montagu can't fault the logic of that."

"Well," said the manager reluctantly, "it will mean taking several of our people away from their proper duties . . . we will all have to take extra pains . . . "

"A hundred gold sovereigns!" cried Darrow wildly.

"Done," choked Lawrence. "But keep your voice down, please."

Coleridge looked horrified. "Sir, I couldn't permit—"

"I'm a disgustingly wealthy man," Darrow said, his poise regained. "Money is nothing to me. Benner, fetch it from the coach while Mr. Lawrence here shows us to the banquet room." He clapped one arm around Coleridge's shoulders and the other around Doyle's and followed the bustling, eager figure of the manager.

"By your accents I surmise you are American?" said Coleridge, a little bewildered. Doyle noted that the man pronounced his r's; it must be the Devonshire accent, he thought, still present after all these years. Somehow that added to the impression of vulnerability Coleridge projected.

"Yes," Darrow answered. "We're from Virginia. Richmond."

"Ah. I've always wished to visit the United States. Some friends and I planned to, at one time."

The banquet room, on the far side of the building, was dark and very cold. "Never mind sweeping," said Darrow, energetically flipping chairs off the long table and setting them upright on the floor. "Get some light in here, and a fire, and a lot of wine and brandy, and we'll be fine."

"At once, Mr. Darrow," said Lawrence, and rushed out of the room.

Coleridge had another sip of the brandy and got to his feet. He looked around at the company, which now numbered twenty-one, for three men who'd been dining in one of the other rooms had heard what was going on and decided to join the group. One had flipped open a notebook and held a pencil expectantly.

"As you all know doubtless at least as well as I," the poet began, "the entire tone of English literature was altered, dropped into a minor and somber key, at the accession of

Cromwell's Parliament party, when the popularly styled Roundheads succeeded, despite the 'divine right of kings,' in beheading Charles the First. The Athenian splendors of Elizabeth's reign, or rather her age, for her years embraced a combined glory of all disciplines that our nation has not at any other time seen, gave way to the austerity of the Puritans, who eschewed alike the extravagances and the bright insights of their historical predecessors. Now John Milton was already thirty-four years old when Cromwell came into power, and thus, although he supported the Parliament party and welcomed the new emphasis on stern discipline and self-control, his modes of thought had been formed during the twilight of the previous period . . . ''

As Coleridge went on, losing his apologetic tone and beginning to speak more authoritatively as he warmed to his subject, Doyle found himself glancing around at the company. The stranger with the notebook was busily scribbling away in some sort of shorthand, and Doyle realized that he must be the schoolteacher Darrow mentioned last night. He stared enviously at the notebook; if luck's with me, he thought, I may be able to get my hands on that, a hundred and seventy years from now. The man looked up and caught Doyle's eye, and smiled. Doyle nodded and quickly looked away. Don't be looking around, he thought furiously—keep writing.

The Thibodeaus were both staring at Coleridge through half-closed eyes, and for a moment Doyle feared the old couple was dozing off; then he recognized their blank expression as intense concentration, and he knew they were recording the lecture, in their own minds, as completely as any videotape machine could.

Darrow was watching the poet with a quiet, pleased smile, and Doyle guessed that he wasn't even listening to the lecture, but was simply glad that the audience seemed satisfied with the show.

Benner was staring down at his hands, as though this was just an interlude, a rest period before some great effort to come. Could he be worrying, Doyle wondered, about the return trip through that slum area? He didn't seem very concerned on the ride down.

"Thus Milton refines the question down to a matter of faith," said Coleridge, bringing the lecture to a close, "and a kind of faith more independent, autonomous—more truly strong, as a matter of fact—than the Puritans really sought.

Faith, he tells us, is not an exotic bloom to be laboriously
maintained by the exclusion of most aspects of the day to day
world, nor a useful delusion to be supported by sophistries
and half-truths like a child's belief in Father Christmas—not,
in short, a prudently unregarded adherence to a constructed
creed; but rather must be, if anything, a clear-eyed *recognition*
of the patterns and tendencies, to be found in every piece of
the world's fabric, which are the lineaments of God. This is
why religion can only be advice and clarification, and cannot
carry any spurs of enforcement—for only belief and behavior
that is independently arrived at, and then chosen, can be
praised or blamed. This being the case, it can be seen as a
criminal abridgment of a person's rights willfully to keep him
in ignorance of *any* facts or opinions—no piece can be judged
inadmissible, for the more stones, both bright and dark, that
are added to the mosaic, the clearer is our picture of God.''

He paused and looked over his audience; then, ''Thank
you,'' he said, and sat down. ''Are there any questions or
amplifications or disagreements?'' Doyle noticed that as the
fire of oratory left him he became again the plump, modest
old fellow they had met in the entry hall—during the lecture
he'd been a more impressive figure.

Percy Thibodeau genially accused Coleridge of having read
his own convictions into Milton's essay, quoting in support
some of his own essays, and the obviously flattered poet
replied at some length, pointing out the many points on which
he differed with Milton; ''But when dealing with a man of
Milton's stature,'' he said with a smile, ''vanity prompts me to
dwell upon the opinions I share with him.''

Darrow fished a watch from his waistcoat pocket, glanced
at it and got to his feet. ''I'm afraid our party will have to be
on our way now,'' he said. ''Time and tide wait for no man,
and we've got a long voyage ahead of us.''

Chairs rutched noisily back from the table and people got to
their feet and began fumbling arms through coat-sleeves.
Nearly everyone, including Doyle, made a point of shaking
hands with Coleridge, and Percy Thibodeau kissed him on the
cheek. ''Your Sara could hardly object to a kiss from a
woman my age,'' she said.

The woman Doyle suspected to be a celebrity spiritualist
had, sure enough, begun to go into some kind of trance, and
Benner hurried over and, smiling, whispered something to her.

She came out of it instantly, and allowed herself to be led by the elbow out of the room.

"Benner," said Darrow. "Oh, sorry, carry on. Mr. Doyle —would you please go tell Clitheroe to bring the coaches around front?"

"Certainly." Doyle paused in the doorway to take a last look at Coleridge—he was afraid he hadn't paid enough attention, hadn't got as much out of the evening as, say, the Thibodeaus—and then he sighed and turned away.

The hall was dark, and the floor uneven, and Benner and the unhappy medium were not in sight. Doyle groped his way around a corner, but instead of the entry hall found himself at the foot of a staircase, the bottom few steps of which were lit by a candle in a wall cresset. It must be the other way, he thought, and turned around.

He started violently, for a very tall man was standing directly behind him; his face was craggy and unpleasantly lined, as if from a long lifetime of disagreeable expressions, and his head was as bald as a vulture's.

"God, you startled me," Doyle exclaimed. "Excuse me, I seem to have—"

With surprising strength the man seized Doyle's hand and, whirling him about, wrenched it up between his shoulder blades, and just as Doyle gasped at the sudden pain a wet cloth was pressed over his face so that instead of air he inhaled the sharply aromatic fumes of ether. He was off balance anyway, so he kicked backward with the strength of total panic, and he felt the heel of his boot collide hard with bone, but the powerful arms that held him didn't even flinch. His struggles made him gulp in more of the fumes in spite of his efforts to hold his breath. He could feel a warm bulk of unconsciousness swelling in the back of his head, and he wondered frantically why someone, Darrow, Benner, Coleridge even, didn't round the corner and shout an alarm.

With his last flicker of bewildered consciousness it occurred to him that this must be the "cadaverous old bald-headed guy" that Benner had startled in his tent in Islington in 1805, five years or a few hours ago.

The evening's ride, which Damnable Richard had been enjoying as a respite from the sweaty labor of melting down more of an apparently endless supply of Britannia metal

spoons, had now been spoiled for him by Wilbur's description
of how their quarry had appeared in that field. "I sneaked out
and followed the old man," Wilbur had whispered to him as
they waited on the driver's bench of the wagon for their chief
to return, "and he went through the woods slow, by stops and
starts, carrying a couple of his weird toys—he had that clay
pot with acid and lead in it, you know, that stings you if you
touch the two metal buttons on top? He kept stopping to
touch it, the Beng only knows why, and I could see his hand
jump back every time when it stung him. And he had that
telescope thing with rutter pictures in it." Richard knew he
meant the sextant; Wilbur could never understand that it was
not called the sex-tent, and so he'd always assumed the chief
was looking at dirty pictures when he peered through it. "And
he stopped a lot of times to look through it—to keep his blood
flowing quick, I judge. So I watched him from behind a tree as
he started out across that field, looking at his tit pictures and
then stinging himself, like maybe he was sorry. Then one time
he touched the pot and his hand didn't jump back. He looked
at it and shook it and touched it again, and he didn't jerk, so I
knew it was broken. Right after that he ran back to the trees
quick, no stops this time, and I flattened out, afraid he'd see
me. He didn't, though, and when I peeked up he was behind
a tree maybe fifty yards away from me, staring hard at the
empty field. So I did too, more than a little scared, because
whatever he was up to had even *him* acting jumpy."

As Wilbur paused for breath, Richard had reached into his
shirt and held his finger and thumb over the ears of his little
wooden monkey, for he always suspected scary talk would
upset it. "Well," Wilbur had gone on, "we stayed there for a
few minutes, and I didn't dare leave for fear he'd hear me.
And, all of a sudden there was a loud thump sound, and a
quick gust of wind in the treetops, and I looked out just in
time to see a big black tent collapsing in the middle of the
field." He had squeezed Damnable Richard's shoulder at this
point. "And it wasn't there when I peeked out a few seconds
before! It just *appeared* there, you see? I made warding signs
and said 'Garlic!' about a dozen times, for anybody could see
this was the Beng's work. Then a couple of fancy-dressed
chals come crawling out from under the tent and pull it away,
and what do you think? There were two coaches inside, with
their lamps burning and all! And people in both of them, and
horses harnessed up all ready to go. And one of these *bengo*

chals says, real loud, 'What a jump! Is everybody all right? How about the horses?' Another one shushed him. Then a couple of them folded up their tent and buried it, and the two coaches headed for the road. That's when the chief ran back to camp, me right behind, and got us into this wagon to follow them.''

Wilbur had now retired to the back of the wagon and was, to judge by his loud, slow breathing, seizing the opportunity to take a short nap. Damnable Richard envied him the ability simply to stop thinking about upsetting things. The old gypsy shifted uneasily on the driver's bench and stared at the back door of the Crown and Anchor. Even being in the city made him nervous, what with all the gorgios staring at him, and the *prastamengros* always eager to clap a Romany *chal* into prison, but to learn that there was sorcery afoot too made his head ache with the danger of it all. Richard had an ungypsylike ability to compare past and present situations, and he wished forlornly that old Amenophis Fikee hadn't disappeared, eight years ago; the picking had been rich enough when he was their chief, and life had been a lot less stressful. He put his hand into his shirt again and petted the monkey's head reassuringly with his thumb.

The tavern's back door squeaked open and Doctor Romany, carrying a limp body over his shoulder, bobbed across the alley toward the wagon. "Up, Wilbur," Richard hissed, a moment before their chief appeared at the back opening.

"Help me get this fellow in, Wilbur," said Romany softly.

"*Avo, rya*," said the instantly alert Wilbur.

"Carefully, you idiot. Don't bang his head—I need what's in it. *Avo*, on the blankets, that's *kushto*. Now bind and gag him." The old chief drew the back opening shut, laced it up, and then, surprisingly agile in his spring-soled shoes, hurried around and climbed up on the driver's bench beside Richard. "They're evidently about to leave here," he said. "I netted one, but let's follow the rest."

"*Avo, rya*," acknowledged Richard. He clicked his tongue at the horses and the wagon surged forward, the canvas cover flapping as the high iron hoops rocked back and forth. They turned onto the Strand two blocks east of the Crown and Anchor, and then drew in to the curb.

They waited nearly half an hour, during which time a number of pedestrians wandered up, attracted by the ornately painted letters that spelled out DOCTOR ROMANY'S TRAVELLING EGYPCIAN FAIR across the canvas sides of the wagon. Then Romany's eyes narrowed. "Richard! There they go at last—after them."

The reins snapped and the wagon swung out into traffic. The street was crowded with carriages and hansoms, the two coaches were receding quickly, and the old gypsy had to stand up on the foot board and use every bit of his horse-handling skill even to keep their quarry in sight.

Doctor Romany pulled a watch from his pocket as they careened to the right into St. Martin's Lane, amid angry and scared yells from other drivers, and he eyed it and then thrust it away. "They must intend to get back to the gate before it closes," Richard heard him say to himself.

The three hastening vehicles, two together and one trailing, retraced the course they'd followed earlier in the evening, and by the time they were clattering west on Oxford Street Richard was sure that the lone man perched at the rear of the second coach had noticed that there was a wagon behind them matching their speed. And as soon as Hyde Park had swung past on the left and they were surrounded by dark fields, there was a muzzle flash and a hollow knocking sound from the second coach, and a pistol ball spanged off the iron hoop over Richard's head.

"*Pre my mullo dadas!*" the old gypsy exclaimed, instinctively reining in a little. "The bugger's shooting at us!"

"Damn your dead father and speed up!" shouted Romany. "I've got a bullet-deflecting spell working."

Richard gritted his teeth and, shielding his poor wooden monkey with one arm, whipped the horses up to their former speed again. The air was damp and chilly, and he wished unhappily that he was back in his tent, laboring over the hot molds and melting pots.

"They're definitely going back to that field on the road side of the trees," Romany told him. "Pull off on this next path and we'll loop around to our camp."

"Is that why you had us set up where we did, *rya*?" asked Richard as he gratefully reined in and let the two speeding coaches recede along the road. "Did you know these people would be coming?"

"I knew somebody might come," Romany muttered.

The wagon lurched and rocked along the rutted track that led away from the Bayswater Road and around to the south of the belt of trees. There was no one standing by the tents and smoldering campfires, but the wagon was met by several dogs, who stared at the new arrivals and then trotted to the tents to let their masters know, by tail-wagging and prancing, that the arrivals were fellow gypsies. A moment later a couple of men appeared and approached the halted wagon.

Romany jumped to the ground, wincing as the springs on the bottoms of his shoes clacked shut and the ground jarred him. "Take our prisoner to your tent, Richard," he said, "and make sure he's neither hurt nor allowed any opportunity to escape."

"Avo, rya," the old gypsy called as their chief sprinted away, springing and bobbing crazily, toward the trees that divided this field from the one where, according to Wilbur, the murderous strangers had materialized.

Recalling Wilbur's bold spying, Richard suddenly resolved not to be outdone. "Take him to my tent, Wilbur," he said, "and bind him up like an old shoe—I'll be back." He gave the gratifyingly goggle-eyed gypsy a big wink, and then set off in pursuit of the chief.

He slanted a bit to the left, so as to reach the trees a few hundred feet west of where Romany had—he could hear the old man picking his way quietly, though not as quietly as a gypsy, between the trees off to his right, and by the time Romany had positioned himself behind a wide trunk at the edge of the field Richard was already prone behind a hummock, having made no noise at all.

The coaches were huddled next to each other in the middle of the field, and everyone had got out of them and gathered in a group a few yards away. Richard counted seventeen of them, and several were women.

"Will you listen to me?" one old man said loudly, clearly upset. "We couldn't have looked for him any longer. As it is we cut our safety margin dangerously slim. Hell, we've only just got here, and there are only a few seconds left until the gap closes. Doyle evidently decided—"

There was a muted thump, and they all fell limply to the ground. Then Richard noticed that the huddled piles were just clothes—the people who'd worn them were gone. The horses and coaches stood unattended in the empty moonlit field.

"They were *mullo chals*," Richard whispered, horrified. "Ghosts! Garlic garlic *garlic*." He could see Doctor Romany hurrying out across the field, so he got to his feet and pulled the monkey out of his shirt. "You don't even have to tell me," he whispered to it. "We're going." He hurried back through the trees to the camp.

Though Doyle couldn't work up the strength to open his eyes at first, the awful antiseptic taste and smell that filled his head let him know he was back at the dental surgeon's office, in the recovery room. He felt around the inside of his mouth with his tongue, trying to figure out which teeth they'd pulled this time. It occurred to him that it was a damn lumpy couch they'd laid him on—and where, he wondered petulantly, is the nurse with my hot chocolate?

He opened his eyes and was annoyed to see that he wasn't in the dental office at all, and therefore probably wouldn't be getting any hot chocolate. He was in a tent, and by the light of a lantern on a nearby table he could see two dark men with moustaches and earrings staring at him, for some reason, fearfully. One of them, the one with a good deal of gray in his curly hair, was panting as if he'd just run a distance.

Doyle couldn't seem to work his arms and legs, but he suddenly remembered that he was in England, to give a lecture on Coleridge for mad old J. Cochran Darrow. *And he told me there was a hotel room for me,* he thought angrily. *Is that what he calls this goddamn tent? And who are these clowns?*

"Where is he?" he croaked. "Where's Darrow?" The two men just stepped back a pace, still staring rudely. Conceivably they didn't work for Darrow. "The old man I was with," he said impatiently. "Where is he?"

"Gone," said the one who'd been panting.

"Well *call him up*," Doyle said. "The number's probably in the book."

The men gasped, and one yanked a little wooden monkey out of a pocket and apparently squeezed its head between thumb and forefinger. "We'll be calling up no gorgio ghosts for you, you *chal* of the *Beng!*" he hissed. "Aye, though the number of the beast is indeed in the gorgio Bible!"

At that moment a dog came into the tent, walked in a quick circle with its tail between its legs, and scuttled out.

"The *rya* is back," said the one with the monkey. "Go out through the back, Wilbur."

"*Avo*," said Wilbur heartily, and crawled out under a flap of the tent.

Doyle was staring at the tent flap. When the dog had

knocked it aside coming in, he'd glimpsed open night outside, and there had been a breath of cold air scented with trees and grass. His memory had at last shaken off the ether fumes and clicked into gear, and he was anxiously replaying the evening in his head. Yes, the jump had worked, and then the city, and that slum area, and yes, Coleridge! And Mrs. Thibodeau kissed him . . . suddenly Doyle's abdomen went hollow and cold, and he could feel cold sweat pop out on his forehead, for he remembered the bald man seizing him. Oh my God, he thought in horror, I missed the return jump, I was outside the field when the gap ended!

The flap was pulled open, and the bald man who'd abducted him from the Crown and Anchor entered the tent, bouncing wildly as he moved. He took a cigar out of a pocket and crossed to the table, bent down over the lantern and puffed it alight. Moving to the cot, he grabbed Doyle's head in one powerful hand and held the lit end of the cigar toward Doyle's left eye. In panic Doyle arched his body and thumped his bound heels up and down, but in spite of the most strenuous struggling his head was held motionless. He could feel the heat on his eye through his clenched shut eyelid; the coal couldn't have been more than a half inch away. "Oh my God, stop it!" he burst out. "Help, stop it, get him away from me!"

After a moment the heat went away and his head was released. He rolled his head from side to side, blinking tears out of his left eye. When he could look at things again he saw the bald man standing over the cot, puffing thoughtfully on the cigar.

"I will know it all," the bald man remarked. "You will tell me where you people came from, how you use the gates for travel, how you discovered the gates—I will know all of it. Do I make myself plain?"

"Yes," wailed Doyle. God damn J. Cochran Darrow, he thought furiously, and may his cancer eat him alive. It wasn't my job to go fetch the coaches! "Yes, I'll tell you everything. In fact, I'll make you a wealthy man if you'll do me a favor."

"A favor," repeated the old man wonderingly.

"Yes." Doyle's cheek itched where tears had run across it, and it was driving him mad that he couldn't scratch it. "And I'm not kidding about making you wealthy. I can tell you property to buy, things to invest in . . . I can probably even tell you where to find hidden treasure if I can have time to think

about it . . . gold in California . . . the tomb of Tutankhamen . . .''

Doctor Romany clutched a couple of the loops of rope over
Doyle's chest and lifted him half off the cot, bending down so
that his face was only inches from Doyle's. "You people know
that?'' he whispered. "Where it is?''

Doyle's half dangling position was making the rope bite into
his sides and shoulders so painfully that he felt near losing
consciousness again, but he could see that he had somehow
displeased this murderous old man. "What," he choked,
"where King Tut's tomb is? Yes—put me down, I can't
breathe!"

Romany opened his hand and Doyle slammed back onto the
cot, his already dizzy head rebounding from the canvas.
"Where is it, then?" asked Romany in a dangerously quiet
voice.

Doyle looked around wildly. The only other person in the
tent was the old gypsy with the monkey, and he was staring at
Doyle fearfully and muttering some word over and over again.
"Well," Doyle said uncertainly, "I'll make a bargain with—"

A few moments later he realized that the reason his ear was
ringing and his cheek felt both hot and numb was that the old
man had given him a hard open-handed blow to the side of the
head.

"Where is it, then?" Romany repeated gently.

"Jesus, man, take it easy!" Suddenly he was certain that his
tormentor somehow already knew where it was, and was in effect calling his bluff. He saw Romany's hand draw back
again. "In the Valley of Kings!" he blurted, "under the huts
of the workmen who built some other pharaoh's tomb!
Ramses or somebody."

The old man scowled, and for several long seconds did
nothing but puff on his cigar. Then, "You will tell me
everything," he said. He dragged a chair over and sat down,
but at that moment the dog trotted in again and, turning
around toward the tent opening, growled softly.

"*Gorgios*," whispered the old gypsy. He peered through the
tent flap. "*Duvel save us, rya, it's prastamengros!*"

Doyle took a deep breath, feeling like someone about to
jump from a dangerous height, and shouted, "*He-e-e-elp!*"
with all the volume he could wring out of his lungs and throat.

Instantly the old gypsy whirled and launched a flying kick at
the lantern, which shattered and sprayed burning oil across

one wall of the tent; Romany had simultaneously clapped a hand over Doyle's mouth and wrenched his head around so that he was staring at the dirt floor; and Doyle heard the old gypsy yell, "Help! Fire!" a moment before Doctor Romany's fist landed just behind his left ear, propelling him once again into unconsciousness.

A couple of tents were burning, and it annoyed Doyle that he couldn't get his eyes to focus; he wanted to postpone worrying about the wooly-tasting gag stuffed in his mouth and the ropes that pressed his wrists against his hips, and these fires seemed like they'd be a first-rate distraction if he could just manage to see them. He vaguely remembered being propped in a sitting position at the base of this tree by the alarming bald man, who had paused to take Doyle's pulse and thumb open his eyelids to peer intently into each eye before hurrying back to where all the fire and shouting were. That was what had really awakened him—the pain of the man's callused thumb on his burned eyelid.

Tilting his head back, he was startled to see two moons in the sky. His brain was working like a car that badly needs a tune-up, but he quickly deduced that this meant he was seeing double, and that therefore there was only one tent burning. With a physical effort he made the two moons coalesce into one. He brought his head back down, and saw one fire. A wave of cool air seemed to sluice through the hot murkiness of his mind, and he was suddenly aware of things—the grass and pebbles under him, the rough treetrunk against his back and the painful constriction of the ropes.

With no warning, a surge of nausea brought Darrow's elegant snacks up to the back of his throat, and he rigidly overrode the reflex and swallowed them back down. The night breeze was chilly on the sweat that had suddenly misted his face and hands, and he forced himself not to think about what would have happened if he'd thrown up while still unconscious with the gag in his mouth. He set to work on getting rid of it, tonguing it forward and then holding it between his teeth so that his tongue could move back and push again. At last he had forced it out of his mouth, under the leather loop that had held it in place, and he shook his head until it spun away onto the grass. He breathed deeply through his open mouth and tried to collect his thoughts. He couldn't remember what had led up to him being dumped out here to watch the fire, but he

did remember the old man's cigar, and one good belt across
the face. Almost without conscious decision he hiked himself
away from the tree, flopped flat on the ground, and began
rolling away.

He was getting dizzy and losing his new-won clarity of
thought, but he kept it up across the dark grass, pressing himself up with one heel, rocking himself over with a heave of his
shoulder, and then letting the momentum of the roll help set
him up for the next one. He had to stop twice to be violently
sick, and he was profoundly thankful that he'd managed to
get rid of the gag. After a while he'd completely forgotten why
he was engaging in this peculiar form of locomotion, and he
imagined he was a pencil rolling toward the edge of a desk, or
a lit cigar rolling off the arm of a chair—but he didn't want to
think about cigars.

Suddenly he was rolling in midair, and he tensed convulsively a moment before plunging into icy rushing water. He
bobbed up to the surface but couldn't make his cold-shocked
lungs take in any air, and then he was under again, his arms
and legs straining uselessly against the ropes. Here's where I
die, he thought—but he kept kicking, and the next time his
head was out of water he gasped a deep breath.

After he got his initial panic under control he discovered
that it wasn't too difficult to float along feet foremost and
jackknife up every half minute or so to take a breath. This
stream probably shallows out sometime before it reaches the
Thames, he thought, and when it does I'll somehow flop my
way to shore.

His heel caught against something, swinging him around to
thump his shoulder against a rock, and he yelped in pain. The
next rock caught him across the middle, and he forced his tortured stomach muscles to keep him curled around it while he
got his breath back. The flowing water at his back was helping
him stay on the rock, but he could feel himself slipping off—
the nails of one hand scrabbled ineffectually against the wet
stone—and all at once he had lost confidence in his ability to
get to shore unaided.

"He-e-elp!" he yelled, and the effort of yelling both
loosened his grip on the rock and brought back the other time
that night that he'd shouted the same thing. *Duvel save us,
rya, it's prastamengros!* he thought as he bobbed away
downstream again, nearly all of his strength gone.

He shouted for help twice more as he was carried along,

spinning helplessly now, his head to the front as often as his feet, and when he'd despairingly realized that he could manage only one more yell, and porpoised himself well out of the water, lungs filled to make it a good loud one, something cold and sharp nipped through his coat and yanked him back against the current.

He expelled the breath in a wild ululating scream of surprise.

"Good Lord, man," exclaimed a startled voice from nearby, "give o'er, you're being rescued!"

"I think you broke his spine, Dad," said a girl's voice eagerly.

"Sit down, Sheila, I've done nothing of the sort. Over on the far side, there, we don't want the boat to capsize when I drag this wretch aboard."

Doyle was being pulled jerkily backward through the water, and looking over his shoulder he saw several people in a rowboat with bulging sides; an older man was drawing in the long, hooked pole that he'd snagged him with. Doyle gave his weight to the hook and let himself relax totally, leaning his head back in the water and staring at the moon while he gasped great, unhindered lungfuls of the cool night air.

"My God, Meg, will you look at this," said the man's voice as the pole clattered on the gunwales and two hands gripped Doyle's shoulders, "your man's tied up like a bloody top before the string's yanked."

A woman muttered something Doyle didn't hear.

"Well," the man went on, "we can't just let him drift past with a wave and a nod, now, can we? Besides, I'm sure he appreciates the fact that we're poor hard-working merchants, and even a Good Samaritan delay like this is costing us money. Stands to reason." There was a locking click and then a knife blade was sawing and snapping through the ropes with businesslike ease. "That's it, feet up now, may as well get them all. Good, that's got it. Now—damn it, Sheila, didn't I tell you to sit over there?"

"I wanted to see if he'd been tortured," said the girl.

"Torture enough, I'd call it, to be bound hand and foot and pitched into the Chelsea Creek and then be fished out only to have to listen to an idiot girl. Sit down."

The man lifted Doyle up by the collar, then reached out over his shoulder and, flipping the sopping coattails aside and grabbing the waistband of his pants, hauled him over the gunwale and onto the forward thwart. Doyle tried to cooperate, but was too weak to do more than brace his hands against the gunwale as it went by under him. He lay motionless on the thwart, still absorbed with the pleasures of relaxing and breathing. "Thank you," he managed to gasp. "I couldn't have . . . kept afloat . . . sixty more seconds."

"My husband saved your life," said a potato-faced old woman sternly, leaning into his field of vision.

"Now, Meg, he's as aware of that as you are, and I'm certain his gratitude will be handsomely expressed. Now let me get us moving again, we're drifting in toward the bank." He sat down on the center thwart and Doyle heard the oarlocks rattle as he took up the oars. "I'll have to set to rowing with a passion to make up for the time we've lost, Meg," he said, more loudly than necessary. "And we'll still probably be too late to get our usual spot at Billingsgate." He paused a moment, and then the boat shuddered, and surged forward, as he leaned into the work.

The girl Sheila leaned curiously over Doyle. "Gentlemanly nice, those clothes was, before they got spoiled," she remarked.

Doyle nodded. "Put 'em on for the first time tonight," he said hoarsely.

"Who was it tied you up and threw you in the creek?"

Having regained his breath and some of his strength, Doyle sat up dizzily. "Gypsies," he answered. "They, uh, robbed me, too. Didn't leave me a cent—I mean a sixpence."

"Oh God, Chris," the old woman interrupted, "he says he hasn't got any money. And he sounds like some kind of foreigner."

The rhythmic clacking of the oars ceased. "Where do you hail from, sir?" Chris asked.

"Calif—uh, America." The breeze on his soaked clothes had set him shivering, and he clamped his teeth to keep them from chattering.

"Well then, Meg, he's got money for travelling, hasn't he? Stands to reason. Where's your hotel, sir?"

"Actually, I—damn, it's cold, have you got anything I could wrap up in?—actually, I had just arrived. They took everything: all my money, my luggage, my, uh, passport. . . ."

"In other words, he's a shivering pauper," stated Meg. She turned a righteous stare on Doyle. "And just how do you expect to repay our kindness in saving your life?"

Doyle was getting angry. "Why didn't you tell me your rates before you pulled me out of the river? I could have told you then that I can't afford them, and you could have gone on and looked for a more affluent person to rescue. I guess I never read the last part of that parable—the part where the Thrifty Samaritan serves the poor devil with an itemized bill."

"Meg," said Chris, "the poor man's right, and we wouldn't accept money from him even if he had any. I know he'll be happy to work off the debt—for that's what it is, you know, sir, in the eyes of man and God—by helping us set up at the market, and carrying the baskets when Sheila goes the rounds with her bunts." He eyed Doyle's coat and boots. "And now fetch him a blanket to change out of his wet clothes under. We can let him have a suit of Patrick's old work things in exchange for his ruined clothes, which we'll have to try to sell as rags."

Doyle was tossed a blanket that reeked of onions, and from some sort of locker in the bow Meg dug out a heavy coat and a pair of pants, both of worn and much-mended dark corduroy, a once-white shirt, and a pair of old boots that looked like they might have graced old Chris' feet when he was Doyle's age. "Ah!" she exclaimed, producing last a dirty white scarf. "Patrick's third-best kingsman."

The chill made Doyle eager to change into these wretched but dry clothes, and when he'd kicked his wet things out from under the blanket Meg gathered them all and stowed them so carefully that he knew they hoped to get a good price for them.

He scrubbed his hair fairly dry with the blanket, then, feeling warm and restored, moved to the end of the thwart away from the puddle he'd been sitting in. He wished he had a pipe or cigar, or even a cigarette. The boat, he noticed, was filled with lidded wooden tubs and lumpy burlap sacks. "I smell onions and . . . ?"

"Pea soup," said young Sheila. "The fishermen and fishmongers get so cold at Billingsgate that they'll fork out tuppence for a plate of it. Thruppence in winter."

"Onions . . . is the main enterprise," panted Chris. "The soup's just . . . a courtesy, like . . . we scarcely get for it . . . what it costs us to make."

I'll bet, thought Doyle sourly.

The moon was low on the horizon, looking big and gold and blurry, and its faery radiance on the trees and fields and creek

ripples wasn't dimmed when Meg leaned out to unhook the
bow lantern, flint-scratch it alight, and replace it on its hook.

The watercourse widened out, and Chris heeled the boat
around to port. "On the Thames now, we are," he said
quietly.

A couple of other boats, tethered together, were visible out
on the broad expanse of the river; they were ponderous, low-
riding things, each with a huge cubical canvas-covered burden
visible under the tangles of rigging.

"Hay boats," said Sheila, crouched beside Doyle. "We saw
one burning out there once, and men on fire were jumping
from the top of the bale down into the water. *That* was a
show—better than the penny gaffs, and free."

"I hope the . . . performers enjoyed it," said Doyle. He
reflected that this little voyage would make an interesting story
to tell over brandy at the Boodles or White's club some day,
once he'd made his fortune.

For he wasn't in any doubt about that. The first few days
would certainly be difficult, but the advantage of all his twentieth century knowledge couldn't help but turn the scales in his
favor. Hell, he could get a job for a while on a newspaper, and
maybe make some startling predictions about the outcome of
the war, and current literary trends; and Ashbless was due to
arrive in London in only about a week, and he could easily
strike up a friendship with him; and in two years Byron would
be returning to England, and he could get an introduction
before *Childe Harold* made him a superstar. Why, he thought,
and I could invent things—the light bulb, the internal combus-
tion engine, latakia tobacco, flush toilets . . . no, better not do
anything to change the course of recorded history—any such
tampering might cancel the trip I got here by, or even the circumstances under which my mother and father met. I'll have
to be careful . . . but I guess I could give Farraday and Lister
and Pasteur and the gang a few smug *suggestions*. Ho ho.

He remembered asking the portrait of William Ashbless
whether the girls, scotch and cigars had been better in his
day. Well, I'm by God going to find out, he told himself. He
yawned and leaned back against a sack of onions. "Wake me
up when we get to the city," he said, and let the boat rock him
to sleep.

CHAPTER 3

"Shamefast he was to come to Towne,
But meet with no one save a Clowne."
—Old Ballad

THOUGH THE ACTUAL fish market of Billingsgate was the big shed on the river side of Lower Thames Street, the carts of costermongers, heaped with turnips and cabbage and carrots and onions, were jammed wheel hub to wheel hub along the length of Thames Street from the Tower Stairs in the east, by the white medieval castle with flags flying from its four towers, west past the Grecian facade of the Customs House, past the eight crowded quays to Billingsgate Market, and past that to just west of London Bridge; and the clamorous, milling commerce filled the entire street, from the alleys in the north face of Thames Street to where the pavement dropped away to the river ten feet below, and the ranked oyster boats moored to the timbered wharf, with planks laid across their jostling gunwales, formed a narrow, bobbing lane the costermongers called Oyster Street.

Doyle, leaning against an outside corner of the fish barn, was certain he'd walked over every foot of the whole scene during the course of the morning. He looked down with distaste at his basket of scrawny onions, and wished he hadn't tried to allay his considerable hunger by eating one of them. He patted his pocket to make sure he hadn't lost the four pennies he'd earned. *Everything you make above one shilling you can keep*, Chris had told him the last time Doyle and Sheila had stopped by the boat; *by now you must know the way of it, and you can do a few rounds all by yourself.* And then he had handed Doyle a basket filled with what had to be the poorest-looking onions in the whole boatload, and sent him off in one direction and Sheila in another. The morbid girl hadn't been the best company, but he missed her now. And a shilling is twelve pennies, he thought hopelessly; I'll never even make that much with these wretched vegetables, much less any more, any bunt, as they call it, for myself.

He levered himself away from the wooden wall and plodded away in the direction of the Tower again, holding his basket in front of him. "Onions!" he called half-heartedly. "Who'll buy these fine onions?" Sheila had taught him the litany.

A coster's wagon, its bed empty, was rumbling past, and the evidently prosperous old fellow on the driver's seat looked down at Doyle and laughed. "Onions you call those things, mate? I'd call 'em rat turds."

This brought merriment from the nearby members of the crowd, and a tough-faced boy ran up and nimbly kicked the bottom of Doyle's basket so that it flew up out of his hands and the vegetables in question showered down around him. One thumped him on the nose, and the laughter doubled.

The coster on the cart pursed his lips, as though he hadn't quite intended to provoke all this. "You're a pitiful sod, ain't you?" he said to Doyle, who was just standing there dazedly watching the impromptu soccer with onions game the street boys had started up. "Here—take twice what they were worth. Here, damn you, wake up!" He dropped two pennies into the hand Doyle automatically held out, then goaded his horse forward.

Doyle pocketed the coins and looked around. The crowd had lost interest in him. The onions—even the basket—were nowhere to be seen. No point going any further, he thought, and began trudging back toward the river in defeat.

"Ah, there's one of the Dolorous Brethren!" piped a weird high voice like Mickey Mouse's. "Just had his onions stomped into Pavement Soup, haven't you now, sir?"

Startled and embarrassed, Doyle looked up and saw that he was being addressed by a gaudily painted puppet in a tall booth that had even gaudier pictures of dragons and little men all over the front of it. There was a scanty audience of ragged boys and a few old bums squatted in front of it, and they laughed when the puppet crooked its arm beckoningly at Doyle.

"Come over and let old Punch cheer you up," it squeaked. Doyle shook his head, feeling himself blush, and kept walking, but the puppet added, "Maybe I could tell you how to earn some real money, eh?" and Doyle stopped.

Eyes of some kind of gleaming crystal made the puppet actually seem to be staring at him. It beckoned again. "What have you got to lose, yer lordship?" it asked in its bird-whistle voice. "You've already been laughed at—and Punch never tries for an effect somebody else just got."

Doyle strode over to it, careful to keep a sceptical expression. Could the concealed puppeteer really be offering him employment? He couldn't afford not to check. Standing a couple of yards in front of the booth, he crossed his arms. "What have you got in mind, Punch?" he asked loudly.

"Ah!" exclaimed the puppet, clapping its wooden hands, "you're a foreigner! Excellent! But you can't talk to Punch till after the show. Sit down, please, your lordship." It waved at the paving stones. "Your box has been held for you and your companion."

Doyle glanced around. "My companion?" he asked, feeling like the straight man in a comedy routine.

"Oh yes," chirped the thing, "I think I recognize Lady Ruin. Hm?"

Doyle shrugged and sat down, pulling his cap lower over his eyes. What the hell, he thought, I'm not supposed to be back at the boat until eleven, and it can't even be ten-thirty yet.

"Very well then!" exclaimed the puppet, straightening up and darting its lifelike gaze around the sparse and tattered assembly. "Now that his lordship has finally arrived, we will commence The Dominion of Secret Glamor, or Punch's New Opera."

A melancholy crank organ started up inside the narrow booth, wheezing and clattering as it tortuously rendered some tune that might have been a cheery dance step once, and Doyle wondered if there was more than one man in the booth, for now a second puppet had appeared on stage, and presumably a hand was still needed to crank the organ.

The newly arrived puppet was, of course, Judy, and Doyle watched, stupefied with hunger and exhaustion, as the two of them alternately exchanged endearments and cudgel-thumps.

He wondered why this had been called Punch's New Opera, for it seemed to be the same old pointlessly savage story line—here was Punch left to take care of the crying baby, singing to it to quiet it down, and finally just slamming its head against the wall and pitching it out the set's little window. He next confessed the deed to Judy, and then killed her when she hit him for it. Doyle yawned profoundly, and hoped the show wouldn't be too long. The sun had finally burned its way through the gray overcast, and was beginning to bake old fish smells out of his shiny corduroy coat.

The next puppet to appear was Joey the Clown, though in this version his name was something Doyle didn't catch that sounded like "Horrible," and he was on stilts. Topical satire, evidently, thought Doyle—for he'd seen a clown on stilts several times during the course of the morning, here and there around the market, and this puppet was a duplicate of him, right down to the somewhat nightmarish patterns of face paint. The clown, with a sort of mocking sternness, was asking Punch what he intended to do about the murder of his poor wife and child.

"Why, I expect I'll go to the constable and have myself locked up," said Punch sadly. "A murdering blackguard like myself ought to be hanged." What's this, thought Doyle, a Punch with morals? That's an innovation.

"And who says so?" inquired the clown, somehow freeing one arm from a stilt to point at Punch. "Who says you ought to be hanged? The police? A crusher-lover, are you?" Punch shook his head. "The magistrates? Are they anything more than a bunch of fat old fools that want to stop you having your fun?" On reflection Punch had to admit they were not. "Is it God, then? Some bearded giant that lives in the clouds? Have you ever seen Him, or heard Him say you mustn't do as you please?"

"Well—no."

"Then come with me."

The two puppets began walking in place, and after a few moments a beadle puppet appeared, and announced that he had a warrant "to take you up, Mr. Punch." Punch looked abashed, but the clown pulled a tiny gleaming knife out of a sleeve and stuck it into the beadle's eye. The boys sitting around Doyle cheered as the beadle fell.

Punch danced a hornpipe, clearly pleased. "Mr. Horrabin," he said to the clown, "can you get us some dinner?"

The show went back to the standard story line and Punch and the clown stole a string of sausages and a frying pan from a public house landlord, though Doyle didn't remember the landlord being actually killed.

Punch, feeling frolicsome, was doing a whirling dance with the string of sausages when a headless puppet entered, also dancing, the stump of its neck bobbing up and down to the beat of the accelerated organ music. Punch was terrified by this apparition until Horrabin explained that it was only his pal Scaramouche, "and isn't it fun to be pals with things everybody else is afraid of?" Punch pondered this, knob chin on his fist, then laughed, nodded, and resumed his dance. Even the Horrabin puppet was dancing on its stilts, and Doyle was awed to think of the contortions the puppeteer must have been going through to keep three puppets dancing and the music going too.

Now a fourth puppet whirled on stage—it was a woman, with the sort of exaggeratedly voluptuous figure that little boys chalk on walls, but her white face, dark eyes and long white veils made it clear that she was meant to be a ghost. "Judy, my sweet creature!" exclaimed Punch, still dancing, "you're ever so much more beautiful now!"

Punch jigged to the front of the stage, and all at once the music stopped and a curtain dropped behind him, isolating him from the others. He did a few more hesitant steps and then halted, for a new puppet had appeared—a somber figure in a black hood, and it was pushing along a gallows with a little noose swinging from it.

"Jack Ketch!" said Punch.

"Aye, Jack Ketch," said the newcomer, "or Mr. Graball, or the Grimy Reaper. It don't make no difference what you call me, Punch. I've come to execute you, by order of the Law."

Horrabin's head popped out for a moment from the wings. "See if you can kill him," he said, and withdrew.

Punch clapped his hands. Then with a lot of double talk he got Jack Ketch to put the noose around his own neck, just to show how it's done, and Punch pulled the rope, hoisting the executioner puppet into the air, its legs somehow kicking realistically. Punch laughed and turned to the audience with spread, welcoming arms. "Hooray!" he cried in his cartoon character voice. "Now Death is dead, and we can all do as we please!"

The curtain behind him snapped back up and the music came on with a crash, very fast and wild now, and the puppets were all dancing around the gallows, Punch hand in hand with Judy's ghost. A couple of the boys and one of the old men got up from the pavement and walked away, the old man shaking his head in disgust.

Punch and the Judy ghost danced up to the front, so that when the curtain dropped again and the music ceased they were alone at the front of the stage. "That, ladies and gentlemen," piped Punch, "was the new and corrected Punch's Opera." Punch slowly looked round his audience —thinned down to only two old bums, three boys and Doyle. Then he did a quick jig and pinched the ghost puppet obscenely. "Horrabin did your humble servant a good turn or two, lads," he said. "And any of you that's interested can come talk to me backstage." He gave Doyle a stare that was surprisingly intense for glass eyes, and then the outer curtains swept in from the sides. The show was over.

One old man and one boy walked around with Doyle to the back of the narrow booth, and the Punch puppet, looking very small away from the scaled down stage, waved at them from over the top of the curtain that served as a stage door.

"My admirers!" the puppet squeaked. "One at a time— Lord Foreigner last."

Feeling like a fool, Doyle stood behind the evidently imbecilic boy while the old man shuffled into the booth. It's as though we're waiting to get into a confessional, he thought glumly. The image was reinforced by the murmured questions and answers he could hear from inside.

Doyle soon noticed that certain members of the milling market crowd were looking at him in peculiar ways; a well-dressed man leading a child by the hand glanced at him with a mixture of pity and contempt, one stout old fellow stared with obvious envy, and a policeman—to Doyle's alarm—gave him a squinting, tight-lipped stare as though half resolved to arrest him on the spot. Doyle stared down at the sprung, bag-like shoes Chris and Meg had let him have in exchange for his elegant boots. Whatever it is, he thought, if there's money in it and it's not too illegal, I'll take it—for a while, anyway, just till I get on my feet in this damned century.

The old man pushed the curtain aside and walked away without a glance at the boy or Doyle, and Doyle, watching him recede into the crowd, was unable to guess whether the old fellow was pleased or disappointed. The boy had stepped inside, and could soon be heard laughing delightedly. He was outside again in a moment, skipping away with a bright new shilling in his hand—and, Doyle noticed, a chalked cross in a circle, which definitely hadn't been there before, on the back of his oversized coat.

He looked back at the booth and met the cunningly worked gaze of the voluptuous Judy puppet peering around the curtain at him. "Come play in my pint pot," she whispered, and winked.

The kid got a shilling, he reminded himself as he stepped forward—and I'll check my coat afterward for chalk marks.

The puppet disappeared inside a moment before Doyle swept the curtain aside and edged in. The interior was dark, but he could see a little stool, and he sank onto it.

He could just make out the silhouette, a foot or two away, of a head in a tall, pointed hat and an upper torso in a coat with grotesquely padded shoulders; the form moved, leaning forward, and he knew it was his host. "And now the ruined foreigner," came a fluty voice, "trying to look at ease in an alien land. Where do you come from?"

"Uh . . . America. And I am broke—penniless. So if you do have some kind of job offer, I'll be—gaah!"

The sliding panel of a dark lantern had been clanked open, and the silhouette was abruptly revealed to be a clown, its face hideously pied with red and green and white paint, its inflamed eyes wide open and crossed, and a startlingly long tongue protruding from between puffed-out cheeks. It was the same clown he'd seen stumping about the market on stilts earlier, the model of the Horrabin puppet.

The tongue withdrew and the face relaxed, but even in repose the face paint made it impossible to guess its expression, or even much of its form. The clown was perched cross-legged on a stool a little higher than Doyle's. "I perceive you've nearly used up your woodpile," the clown said, "and are about to start shoving the chairs and curtains, even the books, into the fireplace. Lucky I came across you today—tomorrow or the day after I don't think there'd have been much left of you."

Doyle closed his eyes and let his heartbeat slow down. He was alarmed to note that even this scanty sympathy made him feel ready to burst into tears. He sighed deeply and then opened his eyes. "If you have an offer," he said quietly, "state it."

The clown grinned, revealing a set of yellowed teeth that pointed every which way, like tombstones in an old and shifting graveyard. "Haven't quite ripped up the floorboards yet," he noted approvingly. "Good. You have, milord, a sensitive and intelligent face; it's clear that you've been well brought up and that garbage clothes like these aren't what you're accustomed to. Have you ever been interested in the dramatic arts?"

"Well . . . no, not particularly. I was in a play or two in school."

"Do you think you could learn a part, gauge an audience and alter your role to suit their tastes, become whatever sort of character they'd be most sympathetic toward?"

Doyle was mystified, but timidly hopeful. "I suppose so. If I could just get some food and a bed first. I know for a fact that I don't get stage fright, because—"

"The question," interrupted the clown, "is whether you're susceptible to street fright. I'm not talking about caperings in a playhouse."

"Oh? What, then, street performing? Well—"

"Yes," said the clown patiently, "the subtlest of street performances—begging. We'll write you a role, and then depending on what . . . *sacrifices* you're willing to make, you can earn up to a pound a day."

The realization that what he'd thought was flattery was just a clinical evaluation of his ability to evoke pity struck Doyle like a slap across the face. "*Begging?*" Anger made him dizzy. "Well, thank you," he said tightly, getting to his feet, "but I've got *honest* employment, selling onions."

"Yes, I observed your aptitude for the job. On your way, then—but when you change your mind, ask anyone in the East End where Horrabin's Punch show is playing."

"I won't change my mind," said Doyle, leaving the booth. He walked away, and didn't look back until he had reached the edge of the long wharf paralleling the street. Horrabin, once again on stilts, was striding away, pulling behind him a wagon that was apparently the booth itself, collapsed and folded up. He shuddered, and turned away to his left, toward the quays, looking for Chris and Meg's rowboat.

It was gone. There were fewer boats now along the quays that projected out into the river, and the water was dotted with boats sailing away east and west—what's the *problem*, Doyle thought worriedly, the market can't be closing, it's only mid-morning—and he could see a rowboat several hundred yards out that might have been the one with Chris and Meg and Sheila in it.

"Hey!" he tried to yell, and was instantly embarrassed at how weak his voice was—even on the next quay over they couldn't have heard him.

"All right, what's the difficulty?"

Doyle turned around and saw the policeman who'd given him the unfriendly eye a few minutes before. "What's the time, please, sir?" he asked the policeman, trying to swallow his vowels the way everyone else was doing.

The officer yanked a watch on a chain out of his waistcoat pocket, cocked an eyebrow at it and put it away. "Coming hard on eleven. Why?"

"Why are they all leaving?" Doyle waved a hand at the boats scattered across the face of the river.

"It's nearly eleven o'clock, isn't it," the officer answered, speaking very clearly as though he thought Doyle might be drunk. "And it's Sunday, you'll be interested to learn."

"The market closes at eleven on Sundays, is what you're saying?"

"You've stated the case. Where are you from? That's no Surrey or Sussex accent."

Doyle sighed. "I'm from America—Virginia. And though I"—he dragged a hand across his forehead—"though I will be doing fine as soon as a friend of mine arrives in the city, I'm destitute now. Where is there a charitable institution that might give me food and a bed until I can get my . . . affairs in order?"

The policeman frowned. "There's a workhouse by the slaughterhouses in Whitechapel Street; they'll give you food and lodging for helping tan hides and drag out the offal bins."

"A workhouse, you say." Doyle remembered the way Dickens was to portray the places. "Thanks." He started to slouch away.

"Just a moment," called the policeman. "If you've got any money on your person, let me see it."

Doyle dug into his pocket for the six pennies and held them out on his palm.

"Very well, I can't take you up for vagrancy now. But perhaps I'll see you about this evening." He touched his helmet. "Good day."

Returning to Thames Street, Doyle expended half his fortune on a plate of vegetable soup and a trowelful of mashed potatoes. It tasted wonderful, but left him at least as hungry as before, so he spent his last three cents on another order of the same. The vendor even let him have a cup of cold water to wash it down.

Policemen were walking up and down the street, calling, "Close 'em up now, day of rest, eleven o'clock it is, close 'em up," and Doyle, a genuine vagrant now, was careful to stay out of their way.

A man of about his own age was striding along with a bag of fish in one arm and a pretty girl on the other, and Doyle, telling himself *just this once*, forced himself to step into the man's path.

"Excuse me, sir," he said hastily. "I find myself in a distressing—"

"Get to the point, fellow," interrupted the man impatiently. "You're a beggar?"

"No. But I was robbed last night, and I haven't a penny, and—I'm an American, and all my luggage and papers are gone, and . . . I'd like to solicit employment or borrow some money."

The girl looked sympathetic. "Give the poor man something, Charles," she said. "Since we're not going to church."

"What ship did you arrive on?" Charles asked sceptically. "That's no American accent I ever heard."

"The, uh, *Enterprise*," Doyle answered. In his confused fumbling for a name he'd almost said *Starship Enterprise*.

"You see, my dear, he's a fraud," said Charles proudly. "There may be an *Enterprise*, but no such ship has landed here lately. There could conceivably be a stray Yankee still about from the *Blaylock* last week, but then," he said, turning cheerfully to Doyle, "you didn't say the *Blaylock*, did you? You shouldn't try a line like that on a man in the shipping trade." Charles looked around the thinning crowd. "Plenty of constables about. I've half a mind to turn you in."

"Oh, let him be," sighed the girl. "We're late anyway, and he's clearly in *some* sort of distressed circumstances."

Doyle nodded gratefully to her and hurried away. The next

person he approached was an old man, and he was careful to say that he'd arrived on the *Blaylock*. The old man gave him a shilling, and added an admonition that Doyle should be similarly generous to other beggars if he ever found himself with money. Doyle assured him that he would.

A few moments later, when Doyle was leaning against the brick wall of a public house, debating whether he dared drown his embarrassment and apprehension by spending some of his new-won wealth on a glass of beer, he was startled to feel a tug at his pant leg; and he nearly cried out when he looked down and saw a ferociously bearded man, legless and sitting on a little cart, staring up at him.

"What dodge are you working and who are you with?" the man demanded in an operatically deep voice.

Doyle tried to move away, but the man tightened his clutch on the corduroy pants and the cart rolled after Doyle for a pace or two like a little trailer. When Doyle halted—for people were staring—the man repeated his sentence.

"I'm not working any dodge and I'm not with anybody," Doyle whispered furiously, "and if you don't let go of me I'll run off the wharf into the river!"

The bearded man laughed. "Go ahead, I'll wager I can swim farther than you can." Seeing the breadth of shoulder under the man's black coat, Doyle despairingly guessed that was true. "Now I saw you hit up those two, and you got something from the second one. You might be a new recruit of Captain Jack's, or you might be one of Horrabin's crew, or you might be freelance. Which is it?"

"I don't know what you're talking about— Get away from me or I'll shout for a constable." Once again Doyle felt ready to burst into tears, for he could imagine this creature never letting go, but rolling angrily along behind him for the rest of his life. "I'm not with anyone!"

"That's what I thought." The legless man nodded. "You're apparently new to the city, so I'll just give you some advice—freelance beggars can take their chances east or north of here, but Billingsgate and Thames Street and Cheapside are staked out for either Copenhagen Jack's lads or the vermin Horrabin runs. You'll find the same sort of arrangements west of St. Paul's. Now you've been warned off by Skate Benjamin, and if you're seen freelancing in the East End's main streets again you'll be . . . well, frankly, pal," Skate said, not unkindly, "you'll be rendered unfit for any employment save begging. So go on, I saw silver and I should take it from you—and if you say I couldn't I'll be forced to prove I could—but you do look like you need it. Go!''

Doyle hurried away west, toward the Strand, praying that newspaper offices didn't close down as early as Billingsgate market, and that one of them might have a position needing filling, and that he'd be able to shake his dizzy feverishness well enough to convince an editor that he was literate and educated. He rubbed his jaw—he'd shaved less than twenty-four hours ago, so that was no problem, but a comb would have been handy.

Oh, never mind looks, he told himself, a little deliriously —I'll win a position by sheer eloquence and force of personality. He squared his shoulders and put a bit of spring into his step.

CHAPTER 4

"The fruit that was to grow upon this Tree
of Evil would be great, for it should be fit to be
served to *Don Lucifer's* table as a new banqueting
dish, sithence all his other meats, though they
fatted him well, were grown stale."

—Thomas Decker

IT WAS A subterranean grotto formed by the collapse, God
knew how long ago, of roughly twelve levels of sewers, the
debris of which had all long since been carried away by the
scavengers and floods of other seasons. It formed a huge hall,
roofed by the massive beams that supported the paving stones
of Bainbridge Street—for the collapse hadn't extended quite
all the way up to the surface—and floored with stones laid by
the Romans in the days when Londinium was a military outpost in a hostile Celtic wilderness. Hammocks on long ropes
were suspended at various heights across the cathedral dimness, and ragged men were already crawling like spiders out
along the lines to pouch themselves comfortably in the swinging sacks. Lights were beginning to be lit, smoky red grease
lamps hung from the timbers exposed in cross section at the
many open sewer-mouths in the walls. A rill of water ran
steadily from one of the higher mouths, losing its solidity as it
arched down through the dim air to splash in a black pool off
to the side.

A long table was set up on the stone floor, and a misshapen white-haired dwarf was standing on tiptoe to set fine porcelain and silver on the linen cloth; he snarled softly whenever a bit of crumbled shoe-leather or a few spilled drops from a pocket flask fell onto the table from the beggar lords overhead. Chairs were set along the sides of the table, and a large highchair, as if for some huge infant, stood at the foot, but there was no chair at the head of the table—instead there was a sort of harness, at which the dwarf kept darting fearful glances, hung on a long rope from the very top of the vast chamber to swing in the sewer breeze only six feet above the floor.

The thief lords were filing in now, their foppishly elegant clothes striking a macabre note in this setting, and taking their places at the table. One cuffed the dwarf out of his way. "Take it from one who can see the top of the table," he said absently, "you've finished setting it. Go get the food."

"And the wine, Dungy!" called another of the lords to the dwarf. "Quick, quick!"

The dwarf hurried away down a tunnel, clearly glad of an excuse to leave the hall even for a few minutes. The lords produced clay pipes and tinderboxes, and soon a haze of opium and tobacco fumes was whirling up, to the delight of the beggar lords, who set their hammocks swinging back and forth across the abyss to catch as much of the smoke as possible.

The space around the table was beginning to fill up too, with shabbily clad men and boys who called greetings to each other. Beyond them, and studiously ignored by them, were groups of men far gone in poverty and psychic and physical devastation. They squatted on the flagstones in the dark corners, each one alone despite their proximity, muttering and gesturing from habit rather than from any desire to communicate.

The dwarf reappeared, hunching lamely along under the weight of a fishnet sack full of bottles. He set the burden down on the floor and began twisting a corkscrew into their necks and popping out the corks. A spaced knocking, as of wood on stone, became audible from one of the larger tunnels, and he worked faster as the sound echoed louder and closer.

"What's the hurry, Dungy?" asked one of the thief lords, watching the dwarf's haste. "Shy of meeting the host?"

" 'Course not, sir," gasped old Dungy, sweating as he drew the last cork, "just wants to do me work prompt-like."

The knocking sound, having become very loud, now ceased, and two white-painted hands appeared gripping the upper stones of the tunnel mouth's arch, followed a moment later by a painted head that bobbed just under the keystone, twelve feet above the ancient pavement. Horrabin grinned, and even the arrogant thief lords looked away uneasily. "Tardy again, Dungy?" piped the clown merrily. "All the setting-up's supposed to be done by now."

"Y-yes, sir," said old Dungy, nearly dropping a bottle. "It just—just keeps getting harder to get the table set, sir. Me old bones—"

"—Will be fed to the street dogs one of these days," finished Horrabin, skillfully poling his way into the hall on his stilts. His conical hat and colorful coat with high, pointed shoulders lent an air of carnival to the scene. "My somewhat younger bones aren't in the best of shape either, it might interest you to know." He halted, swaying, in front of the dangling harness. "Get my stilts," he commanded.

Dungy hurried over and held the stilts while Horrabin poked his arms through the harness straps and then jackknifed his legs into the two bottom loops. The dwarf carried the stilts to the nearest wall and leaned them against the bricks, leaving the clown swinging free a dozen feet off the ground.

"Ah, that's better," sighed Horrabin. "I think malign vibrations begin to travel up the poles after a few hours. Worse in wet weather, of course. Price of success." He yawned, opening a great red hole in the colorful surface of his face. "*Whew!* Now then! To make it up to the assembled lords for being late with their dinner, perhaps you'd care to sing us a little song."

The dwarf winced. "Please sir—the dress and wig is down in me cell. It'd take—"

"Never mind the props tonight," said the clown expansively. "We won't stand on ceremony. Tonight you can sing it without the costume." He looked up toward the distant ceiling. "Music!"

The dangling beggar lords pulled a variety of instruments, ranging from kazoos and Jew's-harps to, in a couple of cases, violins, out of cloth bags tied to their hammocks, and set up a din that was, if not musical, at least rhythmic. Echoes provided a counterpoint, and the ragged men and boys crouched on the floor around the table commenced keeping time with hand-claps.

"Put an end to this idiocy," spoke a new voice, pitched so deeply that it cut through the cacophony. The music and clapping faltered to a stop as the assembly became aware of the newcomer—a very tall, bald-headed man wrapped in a cloak. He stepped into the hall with a weirdly bouncing gait, as though he were walking across a trampoline instead of the solid stone floor.

"Ah!" exclaimed Horrabin, his voice, at least, expressing delight—his facial expression, as always, was impossible to read under all the paint—"Our wandering chief! Well, this is one meeting in which your honorary chair won't stand empty!"

The newcomer nodded, whirled the cloak off his shoulders and tossed it to Dungy—who gratefully scuttled out of the room with it—and stepped up to the highchair at the foot of the table. Now that the cloak was gone everyone could see the spring-soled shoes that he bobbed up and down on.

"My various lords and commoners," said Horrabin in a ringmaster's voice, "may I present our overlord, the Gypsy King, Doctor Romany!" There were a few half-hearted cheers and whistles. "What business induces you to grace our table, Your Majesty?"

Romany didn't reply until he had climbed up into the highchair and, with a sigh of relief, removed his spring-shoes. "Several matters have brought me to your throne-sewer, Horrabin," he said. "For one thing, I've personally brought this month's coin shipment—gold sovereigns in fifty-pound sacks in the corridor back there, probably still hot from the molds." This news brought on a racket of more sincere cheering from the congregation. "And some new developments in the matter of manhunting." He accepted a glass of red wine from one of the thief lords. "Somehow you still haven't found for me the man you call Dog-Face Joe."

"A goddamn werewolf is a dangerous sort of man to find, mate," came a call, and there were murmurs of assent.

"He's not a werewolf," said Doctor Romany without turning around, "but I'll agree he is very dangerous. That's why I've made the reward so big, and advised you all to bring him to me dead rather than alive. In any case, the reward has increased now to ten thousand pounds cash and passage on one of my merchant ships to any spot on the globe. There is now, though, another man I want you to find for me—and this one *must* be captured alive and undamaged. The reward for bringing me this man will be twenty thousand pounds, and a wife of any description you care for, guaranteed to be as affectionate as you please, and of course passage to anywhere you like." The audience shifted and muttered among themselves, and even one or two of the ruined derelicts, who'd only shambled down the ramps and stairs for the traditional concluding food fight, seemed to be showing interest. "I don't know this man's name," Doctor Romany went on, "but he's about thirty-five years old, with dark hair beginning to go bald, he's tending to fat around his middle, pale, and he speaks with some sort of colonial accent. I lost him last night in a field near Kensington, by the Chelsea Creek. He was tightly bound, but apparently—" Romany paused, for Horrabin had begun swinging back and forth in excitement. "Yes, Horrabin?"

"Was he dressed as a costermonger?" the clown asked.

"Not when last seen, but if he escaped by way of the creek, as I suspect he did, he'd certainly have wanted a change of clothes. You've seen him? Where, man, when?"

"I saw a man just like what you've described, but in a coster's old corduroy, trying to peddle onions in Billingsgate this morning, just before the market closed. He sat for my Punch show, and I offered him a begging job, but he got all insulted and walked away. He said he was American. I did tell him that when he changed his mind—and you never saw a man less able to fend for himself—to ask where Horrabin's Punch show is playing, and to talk to me again."

"I think that is probably him," said Doctor Romany with controlled excitement. "Thank Anubis! I was afraid he might have drowned in the creek. Billingsgate, you say—very well, I want your people to scour the entire area from St. Paul's and Blackfriar's Bridge east to the rookery above London Dock, and from the river north to Christ's Hospital, London Wall and Long Alley. The man who brings him to me alive will live the rest of his life in sunny luxury;" Romany did turn around now, and swept the entire company with his cold gaze, "but if anyone should kill him, his lot will be"—he seemed to search for an appropriate image—"such that he'd bitterly envy old Dungy."

From the crowd came mutters to the effect that there were worse things than setting tables and doing idiot dances for a living, but the men around the table, several of whom had sat there when Dungy was their chief, frowned doubtfully, as though wondering whether capturing this man would be worth the risk.

"Our international affairs," Romany went on, "are proceeding smoothly, and there should be a couple of fairly dramatic results in about a month if all continues going well." He allowed himself a brief smile. "If I didn't know it would be discounted as wild hyperbole, I'd observe that this at present underground parliament may, before winter sets in, be the Parliament that governs this island."

Suddenly a burst of lunatic laughter erupted out of one flock of the shadow-huddling derelicts, and a thing that was evidently a very old man hopped with insect-like nimbleness into the light. His face had long ago suffered some tremendous injury, so that one eye, his nose and half of his jaw were gone, and his tattered clothes were so baggy and flapping that there hardly seemed to be any body inside them. "Not much left," he gasped, trying to control the laughter that pummelled him, "not much left of me, hee hee, but enough to tell you, you—*smug fool!*—what your high-perbolee is worth, Murph!" A loud belch nearly knocked him down, and set the crowd laughing.

Doctor Romany stared angrily at this ruinous intruder. "Can't you put this wretch out of his misery, Horrabin?" he asked quietly.

"You can't because you didn't!" cackled the ancient man.

"With your permission, sir," said Horrabin, "I'll just have him carried out. He's been around forever, and the Surrey-side beggars call him their Luck. He rarely speaks, and when he does there's no more meaning to it than a parrot's chatter."

"Well, do it then," said Romany irritably.

Horrabin nodded, and one of the men who'd been laughing strode over to the Luck of Surrey-side and picked him up, and was visibly startled at how light the old man was.

As he was being briskly carried away, the old man turned and winked his one eye at Doctor Romany. "Look for me later under different circumstances," he stage-whispered, and then was again seized with the crazy laughter, which diminished into weird echoes as his bearer hurried down one of the tunnels.

"Interesting sort of dinner guest you cater to," said Doctor

Romany, still angry, as he pulled his spring-shoes back on.

The clown shrugged—a weird effect with his already toweringly padded shoulders. "Nobody is ever turned away from Horrabin's hall," he said. "Some are never permitted to leave, or they leave by the river, but everybody's welcome. You're leaving already, before dinner?"

"Yes, and by the stairs, if it's all right with you. I've got a lot of things to do—I've got to contact the police and offer *them* a big reward for this man, too. And I've never cared for . . . the kind of pork you serve." The expression on the clown's face could have been a warning look; Romany smiled, then climbed back down to the floor, wincing a little when his odd shoes came in contact with the flagstones. Dungy hurried up with his cloak, which Romany unfolded and put on. Just before striding away down one of the tunnels, he turned to the congregation and let his gaze roll across the uncharacteristically quiet company—he even took in the airborne beggar lords—and every eye was on him. "Find me that American," he said quietly. "Forget about Dog-Face Joe for now—fetch me the American, alive."

The low sun was silhouetting the dome of St. Paul's behind Doyle as he trudged back down Thames Street toward Billingsgate. The pint of beer he'd bought ten minutes before had rid him of most of the bad taste in his mouth and some of his appalling embarrassment.

Though not as crowded as it had been this morning, the street was still amply populated—children were kicking a ball around, an occasional carriage rattled past, and pedestrians had to step around a wagon from which workmen were unloading barrels. Doyle was watching the passersby.

After a few minutes he saw a man walking toward him, whistling, and before he went past Doyle asked him, a little wearily, for this would be the fourth person he'd approached, "Excuse me, sir, but could you tell me where Horrabin's Punch show is playing tonight?"

The man looked Doyle up and down and shook his head wonderingly. "That bad, is it? Well, mate, I've never seen it play at night, but any beggar ought to be able to take you to him. 'Course there's never but a couple of beggars around on Sunday evenings, but I believe I saw one or two down by Billingsgate."

"Thanks." *The vermin Horrabin runs*, he thought as he walked on, a little faster now. On the other hand, *Up to a pound a day if you're willing to make some sacrifices.* What kind of sacrifices, I wonder? He thought about his interview with the editor of the *Morning Post*, and then forced himself not to.

An old man was sitting by a wall at the corner of St.-Mary-at-Hill, and as Doyle drew up to him he saw the placard hung on his chest: ONCE A DILIGENT TAILOR, it read, I AM NOW DISQUALIFIED FOR THAT TRADE BY BLINDNESS, AND I MUST SELL PEPPERMINTS TO SUPPORT MY WIFE AND AILING CHILD. CHRISTIAN, BE GENEROUS. He held a tray of dirty-looking lozenges, and when Doyle paused over him the old man pushed the tray forward, so that if Doyle had not stopped he couldn't have helped spilling them.

The old man looked a little disappointed that Doyle hadn't, and glancing around Doyle guessed why; there were a number of well dressed people out strolling in the early evening, and they'd doubtless have been moved by pity to see the old man's candies spilled on the pavement. "Would ye purchase some fine minties from a poor blind man?" he whined, rolling his eyes imploringly at the sky.

"No, thank you," said Doyle. "I need to find Horrabin. *Horrabin*," he repeated when the beggar cocked his head with a look of earnest inquiry. "I think he's some kind of beggar master."

"I've got minties to sell, sir," the beggar pointed out. "I couldn't turn my attention from them to trying to remember folks without a penny to pay for my time."

Doyle pressed his lips together, but dropped a penny into the old man's hand. Night was coming on, and he desperately needed a place to sleep.

"Horrabin?" said the beggar more quietly. "Aye, I know him. And this being a Sunday evening, he'll be in parliament."

"Parliament? What do you mean?"

"I could take you there and show you, sir, but it'd mean losing at least a shilling's worth of minties sales."

"A shilling?" Doyle said despairingly. "All I've got is ten pennies!"

The beggar's hand darted out, palm up. "You can owe me the tuppence, sir."

Doyle hesitated. "Will he be able to give me food and a bed?"

"Oh, aye, no one is ever turned away from Horrabin's hall."

The trembling palm was still extended, and Doyle sighed, dug in his pocket and carefully laid his sixpence and four pennies in the old man's hand. "Uh . . . lead the way."

The old man swept the coins and peppermints into a pocket and stuffed the tray under his coat, then picked up a stick from the pavement behind him and poled himself up. "Come on, then," he said, and strode away briskly west, the way Doyle had just come, swinging his stick in an almost perfunctory way in front of him. Doyle had to take long steps to keep up.

Dizzy with hunger, for he'd lost his soup and mashed potatoes lunch at the *Morning Post* office, Doyle was blinking against the sunset glare and concentrating on keeping up with the beggar, and so despite being vaguely aware of a loud rattling nearby he didn't notice the person pacing him until a well-remembered hand clutched his pant leg. He was off balance, and went down painfully onto his hands and knees on the cobblestones.

He turned his head angrily and found himself looking up into the bearded face of Skate Benjamin. The legless man's cart had come to a halt by colliding hard with Doyle's ankle. "Damn it," Doyle gasped, "let go. I'm not begging and I need to follow that—"

"Not with Horrabin, man," said Skate, an earnest urgency in his low whisper. "You're not bad enough to thrive with that crew. Come with—"

The old beggar had turned around and was hastening back, staring so directly at Skate that Doyle belatedly realized that his blindness was a fraud. "What are you interferin' for, Benjamin?" the old man hissed. "Captain Jack needs to go recruiting these days?"

"Give it over, Bugs," said Skate. "He ain't your sort. But here's your finder's fee anyway, courtesy of Copenhagen Jack." He fished two sixpences out of his waistcoat pocket and tossed them. Bugs snatched them both out of the air with one hand.

"Very well," he said, dumping them in with his minties. "On a basis like that you can interfere any time." He cackled and set off back toward Billingsgate, beginning to tap his cane ahead of him when he was a hundred feet away. Doyle stood up, gingerly trying his weight on his ankle.

"Before he disappears," Doyle said, "you'd better tell me whether this Copenhagen Jack of yours can give me food and a bed."

"Yes, and a more wholesome sort of each than you'd have got from Horrabin. God, you are a helpless one, aren't you? This way, come along."

The dining room of the beggars' house in Pye Street was longer than it was wide, with eight big windows, each a checkerboard of squares of warped glass leaded together, set at intervals in the long street-side wall. A street lamp out front threw a few trickles of light that were caught in the whirlpool patterns of the little panes, but the room's illumination came from bright oil lamps dangling on chains from the ceiling, and the two candles on each of the eight long tables. The narrow east end of the hall was raised four feet above the floor level and accessible by four steps in the middle of its width; a railing ran to the wall from either side of the steps, giving the room the look of a ship's deck, with the raised area as the forecastle.

The beggars who were assembled at the long wooden tables presented a parody of contemporary dress: there were the formal frockcoats and white gloves, mended but impeccably clean, of the Decayed Gentlemen, the beggars who evoked pity by claiming, sometimes truthfully, to be wellborn aristocrats brought to ruin by financial reverses or alcohol; the blue shirt and trousers, rope belt and black tarpaulin hat, bearing the name of some vessel in faded gold letters, of the Shipwrecked Mariners, who even here spiced their speech with nautical terms learned from dance shows and penny ballads; and there were the turbans and earrings and sandals of Distressed Hindoos; and blackened faces of miners supposedly disabled in subterranean explosions; and of course the anonymous tattered rags of the general practitioner beggars. Doyle noticed as he took a place at the end of one of the benches that there were even several dressed like himself as costermongers.

The most impressive figure of all, though, was the tall man with sandy hair and moustache who had been lounging in a high-backed chair on the raised deck, and now stood up and leaned on the railing, looking out across the company. He was extravagantly—not quite ludicrously—attired in a green satin frockcoat, with clusters of airy lace bursting out at wrist and throat, tight white satin knee breeches and white silk stockings, and little shoes that, if shorn of their gold buckles, would have looked like ballet pumps. The babble of conversation had ceased when he got to his feet.

"That's Copenhagen Jack himself," proudly whispered Skate, who had positioned his cart on the floor beside Doyle, "captain of the Pye Street beggars."

Doyle nodded absently, his attention suddenly caught by the roasting turkey smell on the warm air.

"Good evening, friends," said the captain. He was twirling a long-stemmed wine glass in one hand.

"Evening, captain," chorused the company.

Still looking across the dining hall, he held the glass out to the side, and a boy in a red coat and high boots hurried up and splashed some red wine into it from a decanter. The captain tasted it and then nodded. "A dry Medoc with the roast beef," he announced as the boy scampered away, "and with the fowl we'll probably exhaust the sauternes that arrived last week."

The company applauded, Doyle as energetically as any of them.

"Reports, disciplines and the consideration of new members will be conducted after supper." This announcement too seemed agreeable to the beggars, and as soon as the captain sat down at his own elevated table a door swung open from the kitchen, and nine men issued from it, each carrying a whole roasted turkey on a platter. Each table got one, and the man at the head was given a long knife and fork to carve with. Doyle happened to be sitting at the head of his table, and he managed to summon up enough Christmas and Thanksgiving skill to do an adequate job. When he'd slapped some onto all the plates presented to him, including the one Skate held up from below the table edge, he forked some onto his own and set to it with vigor, washing it down with liberal sips of the chilled sauternes that a small army of kitchen boys kept pouring into any glass less than half full. The turkey was followed by roast beef, charred and chewy at the ends and blood-rare in the middle, and an apparently endless supply of hot rolls and butter, and bottles and bottles of what Doyle had to admit was a wonderfully dry and full-bodied Bordeaux. Dessert was hot plum pudding and a cream sherry.

When the dishes had been cleared away and the diners were sitting back, many of them, to Doyle's envy, stuffing clay pipes and dextrously lighting them from the candles on the tables, Copenhagen Jack dragged his tall chair to the front of the raised section and clapped his hands for attention. "Business," he said. "Where's Fairchild?"

The street-side door opened and a young man hurried inside, and for a moment Doyle thought that this must be Fairchild, but a surly, unshaven man had stood up from one of the rear tables and said, "Here, sir." The boy who'd just entered unlooped a muffler from around his neck and, crossing to the front of the hall, sat down on the steps that led up to the raised deck.

The captain nodded to the new arrival and then looked back at Fairchild, who was nervously wrenching at an old cloth cap in his hands. "You were seen to hide five shillings in a drain-pipe this morning, Fairchild."

Fairchild kept his head down, but looked up at Copenhagen Jack through his bushy eyebrows. "Seen by who, sir?"

"Never mind who. Do you deny hiding them?"

The man considered. "Uh . . . no, sir," he said at last. "Only I wasn't . . . hiding 'em from Marko, see, but there were these kids bothering me and I was afraid they'd rob me."

"Then why did you tell Marko when he came by at one in the afternoon that you'd only made a few pennies?"

"I forgot," said Fairchild. "About them shillings."

The young man perched on the steps was scanning the crowd as though he was expecting to meet someone here. Doyle wondered who he was. He seemed young, less than twenty, in spite of his little moustache, and Doyle reflected that the original owner of that coat he was wearing, who had probably been dead twenty years, had been a much bigger man than its present wearer.

"You're not the only forgetful one around here, Fairchild," said the captain gently. "It seems to me I agreed to forget two similar offences of yours during these past several months."

The young man on the steps had let his gaze stop on Doyle; he stared at him speculatively, then with something like anxiety. Just when Doyle was beginning to be worried by it, the young man looked away.

"I'm afraid," Copenhagen Jack went on, "that we'll have to forget some more things: we'll forget you were ever a member of our company, and you can oblige me by forgetting the way to my house."

"But Cap'n," gasped Fairchild, "I didn't mean it, you can have the five shillings—"

"Keep them. You'll need them. Now go." Fairchild left so quickly that Doyle knew the captain must have had some brisk way of ejecting people that didn't want to leave as they were told. "And now," said Captain Jack, smiling, "to pleasanter tasks. Are there any petitioners for admission?"

Skate waved his hand as high as he could, which was no higher than the candles on the table. "I've brought one, captain," he roared, and his cup-rattlingly deep voice made up for the ineffectiveness of his waving.

The captain peered curiously down at the table. "Let him stand up then."

Doyle got to his feet and faced Copenhagen Jack.

"Well, Skate, he's certainly pitiful-looking enough. What's your name?"

"Brendan Doyle, sir."

When Doyle had voiced no more than the first two syllables of his reply, the young man who'd been staring at him whirled and leaped nimbly to the deck and whispered urgently to the captain.

Captain Jack leaned to the side and cocked his head, and a few moments later straightened up and stared at Doyle somewhat incredulously; then he whispered to the boy a few words which, though inaudible, were obviously something like *Are you sure?* The young man nodded vigorously and told him something more.

Doyle viewed these proceedings with mounting alarm, wondering if this moustached youth could be working for the bald-headed gypsy chief. He eyed the street door, and noticed that it hadn't closed quite all the way. He thought, if they make any attempt to seize me, I'll be out that door before these boys can get up from the tables.

The captain shrugged and turned toward the increasingly curious diners. "Young Jacky tells me that our new friend Brendan Doyle has just arrived in town from Bristol, where he's done very well in the past at pretending to be a simple-minded deaf-mute. Under the name of, uh, Dumb Tom he's milked the sympathy of the folks at Bristol for the last five years, but he's been forced to leave there because—what was it

again, Jacky? Oh, I remember—he saw a friend of his coming
out of a whorehouse, and the girl the chap had been with was
leaning out of an upstairs window with a . . . a solid marble
chamber pot she was going to fling down onto the poor man's
head when he walked by underneath, as he was just about to
do. Seems there'd been a disagreement about the fee, and the
girl felt she'd been cheated. In any case, Doyle called to his pal
from across the street: 'Look out!' yells Doyle. 'Back away,
my friend, the tart's fixing to brain you!' Well, his friend's life
was saved, but poor Doyle was overheard by everyone on the
street, and in no time everyone realized he could talk as well as
any of them, and he had to leave town.''

The beggars near Doyle told him he was a fine fellow, and
Skate said, ''You should have told me your story this morning, lad.''

Doyle, concealing his surprise and suspicion, opened his
mouth to reply to Skate, but the captain raised his hand so
suddenly and imperiously that all eyes were on him again, and
Doyle didn't speak.

''And Jacky points out that since Doyle hopes to take up the
begging trade here in London, and since he prospered so when
he didn't speak and suffered exile the first time he uttered a
word, he ought to get back into the habit of relying on gestures
to communicate with. You need practice at being Dumb Tom
again, Mr. Doyle. Don't you agree?''

Everybody turned to Doyle, and he saw one of the captain's
eyelids flutter slightly. The purpose of all this must be to conceal my accent, Doyle realized. But why? And how did that
boy know I'd have one? He smiled uncertainly and nodded.

''You're a wise man, Dumb Tom,'' said Copenhagen Jack.
''Now Jacky tells me you and he used to be great pals in
Bristol once, so I'll let him rob us of your company for a while
so he can explain our ways to you. And in the meantime I'll
consider the rest of the candidates for recruitment. Stand up,
another of you!''

As a bleary-eyed old man struggled to stand up at another
table, Jacky hopped down from the platform and hurried over
to Doyle, his oversized coat flapping around his thin form like
the wings of a bird. Still wary, Doyle stepped back from him
and glanced again at the door.

''Brendan,'' said Jacky, ''come on now. You know I'm not
one to hold a grudge—and I understand she left you for

another bloke only a week later." Skate let out a rumbling chuckle, and Jacky winked and mouthed something that might have been *trust me*.

Doyle let himself relax. You've got to trust somebody, he thought—and at least these people appreciate a good Bordeaux. He nodded and let himself be led away.

Fairchild gently pushed the door closed, and then stood troubled by thought on the pavement outside the dining room. The air was getting chilly as the last gray light faded out of the sky, and he frowned—then took cheer from the memory of the five shillings in the drainpipe, for that would buy him a couple of days of leisurely living, graced with beer and beef pies and skittles. But—and he frowned again as much at the abstractness as at the bleakness of the thought—there would be days after the five shillings were gone. What would he do then? He could ask the captain what to do . . . no, that's right, the captain had just thrown him out, which was why he had to think of what to do.

He whimpered a little as he hurried down Pye Street, and slapped himself across the face a few times in an effort to rouse his brain to constructive thought.

"You knew I'd have an accent." Doyle pulled the corduroy coat closer about himself, for the little room was cold in spite of the smoldering coals in the grate.

"Obviously," said Jacky as he piled blocks of wood onto the old embers and arranged them to produce a good draft. "I told the captain that you mustn't be allowed to speak, and he improvised a story to arrange for it. Close those windows, will you? And then sit down."

Doyle pulled the windows shut and latched them. "So how did you know? And why shouldn't people hear me?" There were two chairs, one on either side of the small table, and he took the one nearest the door.

Having got the fire going to his satisfaction, Jacky got up and crossed to a cupboard. "I'll tell you as soon as you answer some questions of mine."

Doyle's eyes narrowed with resentment at being talked to so peremptorily by a kid who was younger than most of his students—and his resentment was only slightly appeased by the bottle the young man had lifted down from a shelf.

A muted racket of applause and whistling sounded from downstairs, but neither of them remarked on it.

Jacky sat down, and gave Doyle a look that was both puzzled and stern as he splashed brandy into two snifters and pushed one across the table to him.

"Thanks," Doyle said, picking it up and swirling it under his nose. It smelled as good as any he'd ever had. "You people do live well," he admitted grudgingly.

Jacky shrugged his narrow shoulders. "Begging's a trade like everything else," he said, a little impatiently, "and Copenhagen Jack's the best organizer of it." He took a gulp from his own glass. "Tell me the truth now, Doyle—what have you done to make Doctor Romany so anxious to get hold of you?"

Doyle blinked. "Who's Doctor Romany?"

"He's the chief of the most powerful band of gypsies in England."

Ghost fingers tickled the hair at the back of Doyle's neck. "A tall, bald-headed old guy? That wears spring-shoes?"

"That's the man. He's got every beggar and thief in Horrabin's warren looking for a . . . a man of your description with a foreign, possibly American accent. And he's offering a big reward for your capture."

"Horrabin? That clown? My God, I met him this morning, saw that damn puppet show of his. He didn't seem to—"

"It was only this evening that Doctor Romany told everybody to look for you. Horrabin mentioned having seen you at Billingsgate."

Doyle hesitated, trying to sort out the different interests in all this. If a truce could be enforced, he wouldn't mind talking to Doctor Romany, for the man obviously knew—somehow— the times and places where the gaps would show up; and Doyle still had his mobile hook strapped to his arm. If he could learn the location of a gap and be standing inside its field when it closed, he'd reappear in that lot in London in 1983. He felt a wave of homesick longing when he thought about California, Cal State Fullerton, the Ashbless biography. . . . On the other hand, this Doctor Romany hadn't given the impression of being an accommodating sort of person, what with his cigar and all. And what was this boy's interest in the whole thing? Probably the "big" reward.

Doyle must have given Jacky a wary look, for the boy shook

his head in disgust and said, "And no, I'm not planning on turning you over to him. I wouldn't deliver a mad dog into the hands of that creature . . . even if he kept his word about the reward, which is unlikely. The real reward would probably be the opportunity to check the bottom of the Thames for lost coins."

"Sorry," said Doyle, taking a sip of the brandy. "But it sounded like you had been to a meeting of these people."

"I was. Captain Jack pays me to wander around and keep track of what the . . . competition is doing. Horrabin holds meetings in a sewer under Bainbridge Street, and I'm a frequent visitor. But stop dodging the question—why does he want you?"

"Well . . . " Doyle held his glass up and absently admired the way the flames shone through the dark topaz of the liquor. "I'm not completely sure myself, but I know he wants to learn something from me." It occurred to him that he was beginning to get drunk. "He wants to know . . . how I arrived in a field near Kensington."

"Well? How did you arrive? And why does he care?"

"I'll tell you the truth, Jacky my boy. I traveled by magic."

"Yes, it would have to be something like that. What sort of magic? And where did you come from?"

Doyle was disconcerted. "You don't find that hard to believe?"

"I'd find it hard to believe that Doctor Romany could get this excited by anything that didn't involve magic. And I'm certainly not so . . . inexperienced as to claim it doesn't exist." He smiled with such bitterness that Doyle wondered what sort of thing the boy might have seen. "What sort of magic?" Jacky repeated.

"I don't know, actually. I was just part of a group, and the magical mechanics of the whole thing was somebody else's department. But it was a spell or something that permitted us to jump from one . . . place to another without traversing the distance between."

"And you jumped all the way from America that way?"

Why not, thought Doyle. "That's right. And this Doctor Romany must have seen us appear in that field—I think he was watching the place, for you can't just jump from here to there as you please, you see, you've got to take off and land at certain places, what the man in charge called gaps, and I believe Romany knows where all the gaps are—and he must have followed us from there, because he grabbed me when I was just for a moment away from the others, and he took me to some gypsy camp." Doyle gulped some brandy, for telling the story was reawakening his fear of the bald-headed old man.

"And what happened to the other people, the ones you came with?"

"I don't know. I guess they made it back to the gap and jumped back to, uh, America."

"Why did you all come?"

He laughed. "It's a long story, but what we came for was to hear a lecture."

Jacky cocked an eyebrow. "A lecture? What do you mean?"

"Have you ever heard of Samuel Taylor Coleridge?"

"Of course. He's supposed to speak on Milton at the Crown and Anchor next Saturday."

Doyle raised his eyebrows. This beggar boy was beginning to impress him. "Right. Well, he got the dates mixed up and came to give it last night, and we were all there, so he delivered it then. Very interesting talk, as a matter of fact."

"Oh?" Jacky finished his brandy and thoughtfully poured himself another inch. "And how did you people know he'd get the dates mixed up?"

Doyle spread his hands. "The man in charge knew."

Jacky was silent for a few moments, gingerly scratching under his moustache, then he looked up and grinned. "Were you just a hireling brought along to mind the horses or something, or were you interested in the lecture?"

Doyle was tempted to tell this arrogant boy that he'd published a biography of Coleridge. He contented himself with saying, as loftily as possible, "I was brought along to explain to the guests who Coleridge . . . is, and to answer questions about him after we'd got back home."

Jacky laughed with pleasure. "So you're interested in modern poetry! There's more to you than meets the eye, Doyle."

The door at Doyle's back opened and Copenhagen Jack entered, looking even taller and broader-shouldered in the small room. "Two new members," he said, perching himself on the corner of the table and picking up the brandy bottle.

"A good Decayed Gentleman, and the best shaker I've seen in years—you should have seen the fit he threw to show us his style. Astonishing. And how fares Dumb Tom?"

Doyle winced. "Am I really stuck with that?"

"If you stay you are. What's this story about Horrabin being after you?" The captain tilted the bottle up and took a liberal swig from the neck of it.

Jacky spoke up. "It's Horrabin's master, Doctor Romany. He thinks Dumb Tom here knows a lot of sorcerous stuff, and he's mistaken, but he's offered a huge reward, and so every mongrel from Horrabin's rat-warren will be looking for Brendan Doyle." He turned to Doyle. "Face it, man, your Dumb Tom role is purely a survival tactic."

The captain laughed. "And be grateful I don't conduct my business the way Horrabin's father did."

Jacky laughed too, and then seeing Doyle's uncomprehending look, explained. "The clown's father was a St. Giles beggar master too, and he wouldn't run a fake—all of his blind men really were blind, and his crippled children didn't carry crutches just for effect. All very commendable, one would say, until you learn that he'd recruit healthy people and then alter them for the trade of begging. He had a hospital in reverse under London somewhere, and developed techniques for turning robust men, women and children into creatures tailored to evoke horror and pity." The smile had worn off Jacky's face during his speech.

"So if old Teobaldo Horrabin had decided you ought to be Dumb Tom," said the captain, "why he'd cut out your tongue and then have a game try at making you genuinely simple-minded by knocking in one corner of your head or smothering you just long enough for your brain to die. Like Jacky said, he was an expert at it." He sucked some more brandy out of the bottle's neck. "They even say he went to work on his own son, and that Horrabin wears those baggy clothes and that face paint to conceal the deformities his father gave him."

Doyle shuddered, remembering the startling appearance of the clown's face as he'd seen it in the back of the puppet booth. "So what happened to Horrabin père?"

Jacky shrugged. "It was all before my time."

"Some said he died and then Horrabin fils took over," said the captain. "Others said he killed old Teobaldo in order to take over. I've even heard that old Teobaldo is still alive down there . . . and I'm not sure he wouldn't rather be dead." He caught Doyle's questioning look. "Oh, old Horrabin was very tall, and any tight places, even a crowded corridor, used to upset him."

"One loss we suffer in running this lad as a mute," said Jacky, snagging the bottle from the captain long enough to refill the two glasses, "is that he can read."

The captain glanced at Doyle with more interest than he'd shown in anything all evening. "Can you really? Affluently?"

Guessing that he meant fluently, Doyle nodded.

"Excellent! You can read to me. Literature is perhaps my main interest in life, but I've never been able to wring the sense out of the marks on the pages. Do you know any poems? By heart?"

"Oh, sure."

"Give us one."

"Uh . . . all right." He cleared his throat, and then began,

> "The curfew tolls the knell of parting day,
> The lowing herd winds slowly o'er the lea,
> The plowman homeward plods his weary way,
> And leaves the world to darkness and to me . . ."

The captain and Jacky both sat raptly listening during Doyle's recitation of the entirety of Gray's *Elegy*. When he finished the captain applauded, and himself launched into verse, a section from *Samson Agonistes*.

Jacky was next. "Tell me what you think of this," he said, and then recited,

> "These cold and tangled streets, that once were gay
> With light and drink, now echo to my tread
> As I pass by alone. Night breezes thread
> Through dusty rooms their solitary way
> and carry out, through broken windowpanes,
> Into the street, old thoughts and memories."

Jacky paused, and Doyle automatically completed the octave:

> "The lad is far away who cherished these,
> And nothing of his spirit now remains."

• • •

After he'd recited it Doyle tried to remember where he'd read it. It was in a book about Ashbless, but it wasn't by him . . . Got it, he thought—it's one of the damn few works of Colin Lepovre, who was engaged to Elizabeth Tichy before she became William Ashbless' wife. Lepovre disappeared in, let's see, 1809 it was, a few months before the wedding was to have occurred; he was twenty, and left behind him only a thin book of verses that got few and unsympathetic reviews.

He glanced at Jacky and saw that the young man was staring at him with surprise and, for the first time, something like respect. "My God, Doyle, you've read Lepovre?"

"Oh yes," said Doyle airily. "He disappeared, uh, last year, didn't he?"

Jacky looked grim. "That's the official story. Actually he was killed. I knew him, you see."

"Did you really?" It occurred to Doyle that, if he ever got back to 1983, this story might make a good footnote in the Ashbless biography. "How was he killed?"

The young man drained his brandy again and recklessly poured himself a lot more. "Maybe some day I'll know you well enough to tell you."

Still determined to get something publishable out of the boy, Doyle asked, "Did you know his fiancée, Elizabeth Tichy?"

Jacky looked startled. "If you're from America, how do you know all this?"

Doyle opened his mouth to voice a plausible reply, couldn't think of one, and had to make do with, "Some day, Jacky, I may know you well enough to say."

Jacky raised his eyebrows, as if considering taking offense; then he smiled. "As I said, Doyle, there's certainly more to you than meets the eye. Yes, I knew Beth Tichy—quite well. I knew her years before she met Lepovre. I still keep in touch."

"Evidently I was nearly correct in saying that you two were old pals," said Copenhagen Jack. "Doyle, you come with me. Old Stikeleather has got me halfway through Dallas' *Aubrey*, but the way he reads he'll be at least another year finishing it. Let's see if you can read a little more quickly."

The low-ceilinged kitchen of The Beggar in the Bush was crowded, but most of the people were hanging over the table where a card game was going on, and Fairchild, nursing his cup of gin in a dark corner, had room to lean back and put his feet up against the bricks of the wall. Long ago he'd learned not to gamble, for he could never understand the rules, and regardless of what sort of cards he was dealt, somehow people always took his money away and told him he'd lost.

He had taken only one of the shillings from the drainpipe in the alley off Fleet Street, for he had figured out a plan: he would join Horrabin's beggar army and keep the shillings just for special things like meat and gin and beer and—he gulped some gin when he thought of it—a girl every now and then.

His gin gone, he decided not to have another, for if he missed signing up with the stilted clown tonight he'd have to spend some of his money on mere lodging, and that wasn't part of his plan. He stood up and made his way through the shouting and laughing press to the front door of the place and stepped outside.

The flickering lamplight seemed to fall with reluctance across the overhanging housefronts of Buckeridge Street, laying only the faintest of dry brush touches on the black fabric of the night—here an open window high in one wall was underlit, though the room beyond was in darkness; there the mouth of an alley with another lamp somewhere along it was discernible only by a line of yellowly glistening wet cobblestones, like a procession of toads only momentarily motionless in their slow crossing of the street; and ragged roofs and patches of scaling walls were occasionally visible when the vagrant breeze blew the lamp flame high.

Fairchild groped his way across the street to the opposite corner, and as he hunched along toward the next street he could hear snoring from behind the boards nailed up over the unglassed windows of Mother Dowling's boarding house. He sneered at the oblivious sleepers who, as he knew from experience, had each paid three pennies to share a bed with two or three other people and a room with a dozen more. Paying money to be packed like bats in an old house, he thought, smug in the knowledge that he had other plans.

A moment later, though, he was uneasily wondering just what sort of sleeping arrangements Horrabin might provide. That clown was scary; he might have everybody sleep in coffins or something. The thought made Fairchild halt, gaping and crossing himself. Then he remembered that it was getting late, and whatever he intended to do he'd better do soon. At least Horrabin's is free, he thought, moving forward again. Everybody's welcome at Horrabin's.

The sewer parliament would have adjourned by this time, so instead of turning right on Maynard toward Bainbridge Street he followed the wall that brushed his left shoulder, around the corner to face the north, where on the far side of Ivy Lane stood the dark warehouse-like structure known in the neighborhood as the Horrabin Hotel, or Rat's Castle.

Now he was worrying that they might not take him in. After all, he was not smart. He reassured himself with the reflection that he was a good beggar, at least, and that's what was important here. It also occurred to him that Horrabin might be interested to learn that Copenhagen Jack's newest deaf-mute was a fake, and could be tricked into talking.

Yes, Fairchild decided, I'll have to be sure to put myself on the clown's good side by telling him about that.

Jacky stood for quite a while beside the window Doyle had shut, just looking out over the indistinct rooftops, pinpricked here and there with the smoky red dot of a lantern or the amber lozenge of an uncurtained window. I wonder what he's doing this minute, Jacky thought, what dark court he may be silently treading, in what gin den he may be buying some unsuspecting poor devil a drink. Or is he asleep in some garret out there . . . and what sort of dreams could he have? Does he steal those too, I wonder?

Jacky turned away and sat down at the table where the paper, pen and ink were waiting. Lean fingers picked up the pen, dipped the nib in the ink and, after some hesitation, began to write:

Sept. 2, 1810

My dear Mother—
    While I am still not able to give you an address
at which I can be reached, I can assure you that I
am well, & getting enough to eat, & sleeping with a
roof over my head. I know you consider it a
dangerous and affected Lunacy, but I am making
some progress at finding the man—if he can be
called a man—that killed Colin; and although you

*have told me repeatedly that it is a task for the
police, I will ask you once more to take my word
for it that the police are not equipped to deal
with—even acknowledge the existence of—the sort
of man this is. I intend to kill him with the
Minimum of Risk to myself, as soon as it may be
Feasible, and then return home, where I trust I
shall still find a Welcome. In the meantime I am
among Friends, and am in far less danger than you
probably imagine; and if you will, despite my present very regretful disobedience to your Wishes,
keep for me the warmth and love you have so
bountifully shewn me in the past, you will very
deeply gratify your most loving and affectionate
daughter,*

                              Elizabeth Jacqueline Tichy.

Jacky waved the letter in the air until the ink was dry, then
folded it up, addressed it, and dripped candle wax on it for a
seal. She locked the door, got out of her baggy clothes and,
just before swinging the hinged bed down out of the wall,
peeled the moustache off, scratched her upper lip vigorously,
and then stuck the strip of gummed, canvas-backed hair onto
the wall.

CHAPTER 5

"Most persons break the shells of eggs, after
they have eaten the meat. This was originally
done to prevent their being used as boats by
witches."

—Francis Grose

COVENT GARDEN ON Saturday night displayed an entirely different character than it had shown at dawn—it was nearly as
crowded, and certainly no less noisy, but where twelve hours
ago ranks of coster's wagons had lined the curb, there now
gracefully rolled the finest phaeton coaches, drawn by ponies
carefully matched in size and color, as the West End
aristocracy arrived from their houses in Jermyn Street and St.
James to attend the theatre. The paving stones were now being
frenziedly swept every couple of minutes by ragged crossing
sweepers, each jealously working his hard-won section of
pavement, ahead of any pedestrian ladies and gentlemen that
looked likely to tip; and the Doric portico of the Covent
Garden Theatre, newly rebuilt only last year after burning to
the ground in 1808, reared its grand architecture far more
elegantly by lamplight and the gold glow of its interior
chandeliers than it had in the hard brightness of the sunlight.

The crossing sweepers made at least a token gesture of performing a service for the pence and shillings they received, but
also present were people who simply begged. One of the most

successful was a tubercular wretch who shambled about the square, never soliciting alms, but hopelessly gnawing at a mud-caked chunk of stale bread whenever anyone was watching him. And if a pity-struck lady goaded her escort to ask this unfortunate soul what ailed him, the sunken-eyed derelict would only touch his mouth and ear, indicating that he could neither hear nor speak, and then return his attention to the ghastly piece of bread. His plight seemed more genuine for not being flaunted or explained, and he collected so many coins—including a number of five-shilling crowns and one unprecedented gold sovereign—that he had to go empty his pockets into Marko's bag every ten or twenty minutes.

"Ah, Dumb Tom," exclaimed Marko softly as Doyle once again sidled into the alley where he waited. He held out his sack and Doyle dug handfuls of change out of his pockets and tossed them into it. "Yer doin' splendid, lad. Now listen, I'm movin' over to Malk Alley by Bedford Street this time, and I'll be there for the next half hour. Got it?"

Doyle nodded.

"Keep up the good work. And cough sometimes. You do a stunning cough."

Doyle nodded again, winked, and moved back out into the street.

This was his sixth day of begging, and he was still surprised at how good at it he'd proved to be, and how relaxed a life it was. He was even coming to terms with the idea of getting up at dawn and walking a dozen miles a day—covering both sides of the river west of London Bridge—for the appetite he worked up was always lavishly sated by the dinners at Copenhagen Jack's house in Pye Street, and the captain had no objection to his beggars stopping at public houses for the occasional pint, or taking short naps on disused street to street rooftop bridges or between coal barges on the shore by Blackfriar's Bridge.

The make-up around his eyes was making his skin break out, though. It had been Jacky's idea to exaggerate Doyle's already pale complexion to the point of looking consumptive by having him wear a white cloth around his head like a toothache sling, with a black cap above and a red scarf around his neck—to make his face seem very blanched by contrast—and applying some pink make-up around his eyes. "Makes you look more smitten," Jacky had said as he'd smeared the smelly stuff into Doyle's eye sockets, "and if

Horrabin should happen to see you, let's hope it'll keep him from recognizing you."

Jacky puzzled Doyle. The boy sometimes struck him as effeminate in certain spontaneous gestures and word choices, and he certainly had no apparent interest in young ladies, but Wednesday after dinner, when a floridly handsome Decayed Gentleman beggar had cornered Jacky in the hall, calling him his little hot cross bun and trying to kiss him, Jacky had reacted not just with a firm refusal but with disgust, as if he considered all that sort of thing distasteful. And Doyle couldn't understand why a young man of Jacky's intelligence would settle for begging as a means of earning a living, even in such a relatively pleasant operation as Captain Jack's.

Doyle himself certainly didn't intend to stay with it for very long. Three days from now, on Tuesday the eleventh of September, William Ashbless was going to arrive in London, and Doyle had resolved to meet him, strike up a friendship with the poet and then somehow get Ashbless—who had never been noted as hurting for money—to help set him up with some decent sort of job. He knew that the man would arrive at the London Dock on the frigate *Sandoval* at nine in the morning, and at ten-thirty would write the first draft of his best-known poem, "The Twelve Hours of the Night," in the front room of the Jamaica Coffee House. Doyle intended to save some begging money, buy a passable suit, and meet Ashbless there. Having studied the man so thoroughly Doyle already felt that he knew him pretty well.

He wasn't letting himself consider the possibility that Ashbless might be unable, or unwilling, to help him.

"My God, Stanley, will you look at that poor creature!" said a lady as she stepped to the pavement from a hackney cab. "Give him a shilling."

Acting as if he hadn't heard, Doyle resumed gnawing the piece of dirty bread Captain Jack had equipped him with six days ago; Stanley was complaining that if he gave Doyle a shilling he wouldn't have enough for a drink before the show.

"You value your filthy liquor more than the salvation of your soul, is that it? You make me sick. Here, you with the bread or whatever that thing is! Buy yourself a decent dinner with this."

Doyle was careful to wait until she'd approached closer, and then he looked up sharply as if startled, and touched his mouth and ear. She was holding a bracelet out toward him.

"Oh, will you look at that, Stanley, on top of it all he can't hear nor speak. Low as a dog the poor fellow is."

She waved the bracelet at Doyle, and he took it with a grateful smile. The couple moved on toward the theater, Stanley grumbling, as Doyle dropped the heavy bracelet into his pocket.

And then, he thought as he shambled on, once Ashbless has helped me get on my feet in this damned century, if I decide—as I imagine I will—that I'd rather go home to the time when there are paramedics and anesthetics and health inspectors and movies and flush toilets and telephones, I'll cautiously get in touch with the fearsome Doctor Romany and work out some sort of a deal whereby he'll tell me the location of one of the upcoming time gaps. Hell, I could probably trick him into letting me be within the field when the gap closed! I'd have to be sure he wouldn't find and take away the mobile hook, though. I wonder if it's too big to swallow.

The tickling itch had been building in his throat over the last few minutes, and an elegantly dressed couple was approaching at an unhurried pace, so he unleashed his much admired cough; he tried not to let himself do it too often because it tended quickly to change from a simulated ordeal into a genuine lung-wrenching paroxysm, and in the last few days it had been getting worse. He supposed glumly that he had picked it up from his midnight dip in the chilly Chelsea Creek a week ago.

"Holy Mother of God, James, that walking corpse is about to cough his livers right out onto the pavement. Give him something to buy himself a drink with."

"Be wasted on that sod. He'll be dead before dawn."

"Well . . . perhaps you're right. Yes, you certainly seem to be right."

Two men leaned against the iron palings of the fence that flanked the wings of the theatre. One of them tapped ash from a cigar and then drew on it, making a glowing red dot in the shadows. "I asked somebody," he said softly to his partner, "and this boy is a deaf-mute called Dumb Tom. You're sure it's him?"

"The boss is sure."

The first man stared across the street at Doyle, who had pulled himself together and was lurching away, again pretending to gnaw the bread. "He sure doesn't look like a menace."

"Just the fact of him is a menace, Kaggs. He's not supposed to be here."

"I guess so." Kaggs slipped a long, slim knife from his sleeve, absently tested the edge with his thumb and then slipped it away again. "How do you want to do it?"

The other man thought for a moment. "Shouldn't be hard. I'll bump him and knock him down, and you can act like you're helping him up. Let your coat hang forward so nobody'll see, and then slip the knife all the way in just behind his collarbone, blade perpendicular to the bone, and rock it back and forth a little. There's a big artery down there that you can't miss, and he ought to be dead in a few seconds."

"All right. Let's go." He tossed his cigar onto the street and they both pushed away from the fence and strode after Doyle.

Red-rimmed eyes peered out of the face colorful with grease paint, and Horrabin took two knocking steps forward. "They were watching him, and now they're going after him," he said in a growling whisper quite different from his fluty voice. "You're certain they're not ours?"

"I've never clapped eyes on 'em before, yer Honor," said one of the men standing on the pavement below him.

"Then never mind waiting until this crowd's inside," hissed the clown. "Get Dumb Tom now." As the three men sprinted away after Doyle and his two pursuers, Horrabin pounded a white-gloved fist against the brick wall of the alley and whispered, "Damn you, Fairchild, why couldn't you have remembered yesterday?"

I've got to get back to 1983 before this cough kills me, Doyle thought unhappily. A shot of penicillin or something would clear it up in a couple of days, but if I went to a doctor here the bastard would probably prescribe leeches. He felt the throat tickle building up again, but resolutely resisted it. I wonder if it's developed into full-blown pneumonia yet. Hell, it doesn't even seem to be good for business anymore. Nobody wants to give anything to a beggar who looks like he'll be dead in ten minutes. Maybe the captain would—

Someone thrust a leg in his way and before he could step aside he was heavily shoulder-bumped, and he pitched straight forward onto the cobblestones, abrading the palms of his hands. The person who'd tripped him walked on, but someone else crouched beside him. "Are you all right?" the newcomer asked.

Dizzily Doyle started to make his deaf-mute gesture, but all in an instant the man slapped one hand over Doyle's face, holding his jaw shut with the heel of his hand, and with the other drove a blade down at Doyle's shoulder. Doyle caught a glimpse of the knife and thrashed backward, so that it cut through his coat and skin but was deflected outward by his collarbone. He tried to yell but could only produce a sort of loud hum with his mouth still held shut; his assailant knelt on Doyle's free arm and drew the knife up for another try.

Suddenly something from behind collided hard with the man and he *oomphed!* and did a quick forward somersault as his knife clattered away across the cobbles. Three men now stood above Doyle, and two of them quickly hooked hands under his arms and hoisted him up. "Saved yer life, Tommy," panted one. "Now you come with us."

Doyle allowed himself to be marched at a trot back the way he'd come, for he assumed these were some of Copenhagen Jack's beggars who had come to his rescue; then he saw the upright grasshopper figure of Horrabin waiting in the alley ahead, and realized that Doctor Romany had found him.

He extended one arm and then slammed the elbow back into the stomach of the man who held his left arm, and as the man crumpled Doyle drove his left fist into the throat of the man on his right. He too went down and then Doyle was running south with the boundless energy of pure panic, for he remembered Romany's cigar so well that he could almost feel the heat of it on his eye. He could hear the footsteps of the third man pounding close behind him.

He was off the main street and pelting down an alley now, and the racing pursuer's footsteps echoed terrifyingly close, so when he saw a stack of boxes full of vegetable peelings against one wall he reached out as he ran past and yanked the stack out; Doyle spun with the momentum of the action, lost his footing and fell heavily, skidding on his hip and then on his cut shoulder, but the boxes had toppled directly into the path of Horrabin's man and he had tangled his feet in them and done a resounding belly-flop onto the round stones of the pavement. He lay motionless face down, the wind and maybe the life knocked out of him, and Doyle got to his feet, whimpering, and limped as fast as he could on down the alley.

He crossed two narrow streets and followed his alley through one more block and then found himself on the brightly lamplit sidewalk of the Strand, only a few blocks east of the Crown and Anchor. All the running had started him coughing again, and he made a shilling and fourpence from the awed passersby before he got it under control. When he could get a breath again he began walking west on the Strand, for it had suddenly occurred to him that this was the Saturday night Coleridge had been scheduled to speak, and that Coleridge, while not now in any position to grant substantial aid to anyone, might at least be able to help Doyle get back to Captain Jack's house unseen. Hell, Doyle thought, he might even remember me from a week ago.

Oblivious to the bright store and restaurant windows he passed, he hurried down the sidewalk, hunched over to relieve the pain of the stitch in his side, limping, and breathing with fast asthmatic wheezes. He saw a woman recoil from him in actual fear, and it came to him how grotesque he must look with his make-up, tattered clothes and crippled cockroach gait; abruptly self-conscious, he straightened up and walked more slowly.

The crowd that parted hastily in front of him seemed no more composed of individuals than a plywood theatrical flat representing a bus-line, but he did notice when a startlingly tall figure stepped out of an alley into his path. A white conical hat topped a head like a decorated Easter egg, and Doyle gasped, spun around and ran, hearing the knocking of the pursuing stilts on the pavement.

Horrabin ran easily on the stilts, taking bobbing ten foot strides even as he wove through the sidewalk traffic, and as he ran he emitted a succession of piercing high-low-high-low whistles. To the terrified Doyle it sounded like the Nazi Gestapo sirens in old movies about World War Two.

The whistle was rousing certain beggars and drawing them out of alleys and doorways; they were silent, powerful-looking creatures, and two of them plodded toward Doyle while another was working his way over from across the street.

Looking over his shoulder, Doyle caught a freeze frame glimpse of Horrabin only a giant pace away, his face grinning maniacally like a Chinese dragon and one white claw extended. Doyle leaped sideways into the street; he tumbled, rolling with only inches to spare out from under the hammering hooves of a cab horse, and then he scrambled to his feet and sprang up onto the step of a carriage and braced himself there with one hand on the window sill and one on the roof rail.

The carriage's occupants were an old man and a young girl. "Please speed up," Doyle gasped, "I'm being chased by—"

The old man had angrily picked up and poised a lean walking stick, and now with all the force of the first breaking shot of a pool game drove the blunt end at Doyle's chest. Doyle flew off his perch as if he'd been shot, and though he managed to land on his feet he instantly fell onto his hands and knees and then rolled over a couple of times.

The ruin-faced, one-eyed old creature huddled in a doorway giggled and clapped his papier-mâché hands silently. "Ah, yes yes! Now into the river, Doyle—there's something I want to show you on the other side," chittered the Luck of the Surrey-side beggars.

"God save us, he's been shot!" shouted Horrabin. "Get him while he's still got any breath in him, you dung beetles!"

Doyle was on his feet now, but every breath seemed to spread a crack in his chest, and he thought that if he started coughing now he'd die of it. One of his pursuers was only a few paces away, advancing with a confident smile, so Doyle dug into his pocket, fetched out the heavy bracelet and pitched it with all his strength into the man's face, then without pausing to see what effect it had he turned and hobbled to the far curb, crossed the sidewalk and disappeared into an alley.

"Tomorrow night's dinner you all are unless you bring him to me!" shrilled Horrabin, froth flying from his vermillioned lips as he did a woodpecker tap dance of fury on the north sidewalk.

One of his beggars hurried forward but had misjudged the velocity of a Chaplin Company coach and went down under the hooves, and one of the front wheels had cut across his middle before the driver was able to wrench the horses and vehicle to a halt. By now all traffic had come to a stop in this section of the Strand, and drivers were shouting at each other and, in a few cases, lashing at one another with their whips.

Horrabin stepped off the curb and began poling his way through the confusion toward the opposite side of the street.

●　　　●　　　●

Doyle emerged from between two buildings and clattered
down an ancient set of wooden stairs to a sort of boardwalk
that ran along the top of the glistening riverbank. He hurried
down to the end of one of the piers and crouched behind a
high wooden box, and his breathing gradually slowed to the
point where he could close his mouth. The river air was cold,
and he was glad Copenhagen Jack didn't insist that his beggars appear half-clad in cold weather—though it was an effective touch. He pulled his jacket and shirt away from his collarbone—the knife cut was still bleeding pretty freely, though it
wasn't deep.

I wonder who the hell that was, he thought. It couldn't have
been one of Doctor Romany's people, or Horrabin's, for
Jacky told me they definitely want me alive. Maybe it was
some rival of theirs . . . or even just a solo lunatic hobo-killer,
some prototype Jack the Ripper. Doyle gingerly touched the
long cut. Thank God, he thought, that Horrabin's man
arrived when he did.

He rubbed his chest and then inhaled experimentally, filling
his lungs. Though his breastbone stung, and he was doubt-
lessly developing the major bruise of his life—so far—there
was no grating sensation; the vicious old man's cane had
probably not broken anything. He exhaled and leaned wearily
against the box, letting his feet dangle over the water.

The yellow dots of lanterns on passing boats, and their
reflections, stippled the blackness of the river like a Monet
painting, and the lights of Lambeth were a glowing chain on
the close horizon. The moon, a faint orange crescent, seemed
to be balanced on the railing of Blackfriars Bridge half a mile
east. Behind and above him to his right were the lights of the
Adelphi Terrace, looking like some fantastic pleasure ship
viewed from water level, and he could hear faint music from
there when the breeze slackened.

He could feel another coughing fit building up in his throat
and chest, but fear gave him the strength to suppress it when
he heard a slow, heavy knocking coming his way along the
boardwalk behind him.

Jacky was glad the water was flowing fast enough in the
subterranean canal to make the rudder useless in downstream
travel, for if it was swung very far to port it would hit her in
the head; and if the people in the boat had been exerting any
more control over the craft than just using barge poles to push

it away from the walls whenever the current swung it too close,
they'd have felt the drag of their secret passenger. The water
swirling around her neck was becoming even colder as they approached the river, and it was all she could do to keep her
teeth from chattering. She was careful to keep her head out
of the water, for she had a small flintlock pistol wrapped up
in her turban, and she wanted to keep the flashpan dry. The
torches at bow and stern of the boat flickered in the sulphury
breeze, sometimes casting only a dim red glow and at others
flaring up to illuminate starkly every stone of the arched ceiling passing by close overhead.

Five minutes ago she had been dry and warm, cooking a
panful of sausages over the fire in the kitchen of Horrabin's
Rat's Castle on Maynard Street. She'd been dressed in her
Ahmed the Hindoo Beggar outfit, with a turban, sandals, and
a robe made from a chintz bedspread, with walnut stain on her
face and hands and a false beard supplementing her customary
false moustache, for she'd seen the exiled Fairchild at the
Rat's Castle, and didn't want to be recognized as one of
Copenhagen Jack's people. Doctor Romany had arrived a half
hour earlier, and had perched in one of Horrabin's swings,
taken his weird shoes off and absorbed himself with a stack of
shipping reports.

Then one of Horrabin's beggars, a sturdy red-faced old
fellow, had burst in, out of breath from running but gasping
out a message almost before he was in the room. "Doctor
Romany . . . hurry . . . the Strand, and moving south toward
the river . . . a man's been shot . . ."

"Who? Who's been shot?" Romany hopped down from the
swing without putting his spring-shoes back on, and his old
face twisted with agony; quickly he climbed back into the
swing and pulled the shoes on. "Who, damn you?" he rasped.

"I don't know . . . Simmons saw it and . . . sent me to fetch
you. He said it's the man you've . . . offered a reward for."

Romany had his shoes on and laced by this time, and he had
again jumped down from the swing, and was bobbing agilely
now on the powerful springs. "Which one? But it must be
Dog-Face Joe. They'd never dare to shoot the American.
Well, where is he? The Strand, you say?"

"Yes, sir. And moving south, by the Adelphi. It'd be
quickest, yer Honor, to take a boat down the underground
canal straight to the Adelphi Arches. All the waterways are
running strong, what with the rains . . ."

"Lead the way—and hurry. I knew old Joe for years, and if they haven't outright killed him he'll get away from them."

When the two men hurried down the cellar stairs Ahmed the Hindoo Beggar was only a few paces behind, the sausages forgotten. This sounds like it, Jacky had thought, her heart pounding as she forced herself to hang back far enough so they wouldn't see or hear her following. God, let him be still alive; and let me get close enough to put a pistol ball through his brain. And if I could somehow have a moment to whisper to him first, explain who I am and why I'm going to kill him . . . and then at last, she had thought longingly, I could go home.

When they had reached the old stone dock in the under basement there came a moment when two beggars were untying the boat and lighting the torches, and Doctor Romany was staring impatiently down the dark tunnel, and Jacky had been able to pad across the stone floor and slip noiselessly into the cold black water. The boat, which the two men dragged and bumped alongside the dock for Doctor Romany to get into, had rings along the outside of the gunwale so that a tarpaulin could be lashed over it, and Jacky looped two fingers through one of them and let herself be towed along when the boat was poled out into the strong current.

"Ha *ha!*" came the high, birdy voice of the clown. "Now where's my old pal Dumb Tom?" There was a slow knocking of wood on wood as Horrabin moved back and forth on the boardwalk. The only other sounds were the fitful breeze in the rigging of the fishing boats moored nearby, and the lapping of the water around the pier pilings.

Doyle, sitting behind the box at the end of the pier, didn't even breathe, and he wondered how long he could hold out before leaping to his feet and shouting, *Get it over with, here I am, as you very well know!* For there was a teasing note in the clown's voice, as if it did know.

He heard more slow thumping as the clown moved this way and that. My God, Doyle thought, if that thing starts stumping down this pier toward me I'll be into the water and swimming for Lambeth before he's three steps out. Then he imagined the clown following him into the black water, imagined seeing over his shoulder that grinning painted face moving at him with impossible speed as he tried to swim with his stiffening shoulder. His heartbeat seemed to be shaking him apart, like the impacts of a wrecking ball on an old building.

"Horrabin!" came a cry from away to Doyle's right. "Where is he?" Doyle realized with horror that it was Doctor Romany's voice.

The clown giggled, a sound like a hundred manic crickets, and then called, "Right here." The knocking of the stilts moved out onto the pier.

With an explosive shriek that appalled even himself, Doyle dove off the pier end, barely getting a breath before plunging into the cold water. He thrashed to the surface and began swimming frantically.

"What was that?" Romany's voice carried clearly across the water. "What's going on?"

Horrabin had ladder-walked to the end of the pier. "He's in the river. I'll show you where." He whistled, a shriller and more complicated whistle than the one he'd summoned the beggars with in the Strand, and then he waited, looking up and down the river shore.

As soon as the boat had emerged from the tunnel, and just before it passed through the Adelphi Arches and out into the river, Jacky unhooked her numbing fingers and let the craft recede away from her. Just in time, she had told herself, for a moment later one of the beggars had stepped back and grabbed the tiller and the other had lifted a pair of oars from the bottom of the boat and begun fitting the thole pins into the oarlocks. Doctor Romany had shouted a question, and she'd heard a faint answer, but she'd been swimming half underwater and hadn't caught any of the words. Then there had come a scream, short but so loud that nobody within a mile could have missed it. Faintly she'd heard Horrabin's voice say, afterward, "He's in the river. I'll show you where."

She heard the first clattering stroke of the oars just as she reached the bank and pulled herself out of the water.

Doyle, forty feet out now, calmed down a little and began to dog paddle silently. If anything, he thought, any boat or swimmer comes near me, I'll surface dive and go as far as I can under water, and then try to let my head emerge slow and breathe quietly. Hell, with any luck I should be able to elude them. . . . And, with a good deal more luck, get back to shore somewhere before my strength gives out. The current was carrying him to his left, away from Doctor Romany.

He heard a new sound—oarlocks clacking rhythmically behind him to his right.

Horrabin smiled, for a dim glow had appeared under the second pier to his left, and as it moved out from under the overhang it could be seen to be a shotgun pattern of dozens of tiny lights whirling across the face of the dark water. The clown pointed out toward where he'd last heard Doyle splashing, and the cluster of tiny lights scudded out into the river as quick as the wind-blown petals of some luminous flower.

"Follow the lights, Doctor Romany!" Horrabin called merrily.

What lights? Doyle wondered. The nearest lights are across the river. Sure, Doctor Romany, follow them while I drift east.

He quietly treaded water with his legs and right arm, giving his left shoulder a rest. Staying afloat was no problem; he had discovered that by taking turns with his dog paddle, floating on his back and slowly treading water he was able to keep his face out of water with no strenuous use of any one set of muscles. The current was taking him toward Blackfriars Bridge, and he was cautiously confident that he'd be able to climb up on one of the pilings and, once his pursuers had decided he'd drowned, make a segmented swim from piling to piling to the shore.

Suddenly he learned what lights Horrabin had meant, for what seemed to be a couple of dozen little floating candles were skimming across the surface straight toward him. He yanked his head under water and, with just a kick-splash to mark where he'd been, swam away under water in a direction at right angles to the course the lights had been taking.

His tenuous confidence was gone. This reeked of sorcery—hadn't Jacky said Doctor Romany was a magician? Evidently Horrabin was too—and he felt like a man who, limbering up for a fistfight, sees his opponent snap the loaded cylinder closed on a revolver.

He frog-kicked along as far as he could and still expect to surface without gasping, and then he let his head float up and break the surface of the water. Slowly he lifted a hand and pushed the soaked flap of hair away from his eyes.

For a moment he just hung stunned in the water, for the

lights had followed him and now surrounded him, and staring at the nearest couple he saw that they were eggshell halves, equipped with tiny torches, straw masts and folded paper sails, and—and it didn't even occur to him to ascribe it to fever delirium—a tiny man, no bigger than his little finger, crouched in each one, twisting the toy mast deftly in the breeze to hold his diminutive craft in position.

Doyle screamed and flung his arm around in an arc to capsize them, then without waiting to see the effect drew a sobbing breath and dived again.

When his lungs were heaving at his clenched shut throat and he thought he must be about to crack his head against the stones of the bridge pilings, Doyle again let himself bob to the surface. The tiny eggshell mariners were again grouped in a ring around him when he surfaced. They didn't approach nearer than two arm's lengths, and in spite of the kalunk . . . kalunk . . . kalunk of Doctor Romany's boat drawing ever closer he paused, thrashing weakly in the water, to get his breath back.

Something slapped the water, hard, an inch from his left cheek, and the spray stung his eye. A moment later he heard the boom of a gunshot roll across the water from the shore. It was instantly followed by a shot from Romany's boat, but because the boat was moving the shot was badly aimed and kicked up spray among the lighted eggshells, sending one spinning through the air.

God, I'm being shot at from all sides, Doyle thought despairingly as he once more filled his lungs and pushed himself under. They don't even want me alive anymore.

Horrabin had glanced down to his left when a gunshot went off down there among the fishing boats, then his head snapped back up when there was a shot from Doctor Romany's boat. The clown saw the tiny light spring up from the surface and go out when it came down again, and he realized the gypsy chief was shooting at the man in the water.

Horrabin quickly cupped his hands around his mouth and yelled, "I thought you wanted him alive!"

There was a moment's silence, and then Romany's voice echoed across the water. "Isn't this Dog-Face Joe?"

"It's the American."

"Apep eat me. *Then why did you shoot at him, you doomed sod?*"

Jacky had already snatched a close-mesh fishing net out of a nearby boat, flung it into one of the canoes and was pushing the narrow craft out into the water when she heard Horrabin yell, in a voice made even shriller by fear, "It wasn't me, damn it, your Worship, I swear! It's somebody down among the boats here—there he goes now, in a canoe, heading toward you!"

Jacky handled the single oar with speed and grace, and propelled the canoe rapidly out toward the ring of little lights, which was shifting even further east, toward the bridge. God, she thought as she panted with the effort, I'm sorry Tom—I mean Doyle. I was just too eager to kill Dog-Face Joe. I'm sorry, please don't be killed.

She felt hollow and cold with horror, though, for it had felt like a good shot, and she'd been aiming directly at the center of the dimly seen head.

Her canoe was moving faster than Doctor Romany's larger boat, and she'd started well to the east of him, so when Doyle's head burst up out of the water again—again right in the middle of the infallible ring of lights—she was almost a hundred yards closer to him than Romany was.

"Doyle!" she called, profoundly relieved to see him still alive. "It's Jacky. Wait for me."

Doyle was so exhausted that he was almost annoyed to hear Jacky's voice. He'd resigned himself to being captured, and this rescue attempt of Jacky's sounded as if it would involve further exertions, and likely avail nothing but to anger Doctor Romany.

"Sink straight down as deep as you can, and then come back up," came Jacky's voice again, closer now.

Doyle turned his head and, by the light of the candles of his Lilliputian retinue, saw a bearded man in a canoe.

His eyes widened with surprise, but before he could duck under water again the figure in the canoe said, "Wait!" and, reaching up, yanked off the beard. "It is me, Doyle. Now do what I said, and hurry!"

I guess you can't relax yet, Doyle told himself wearily as he slid under the surface again and obediently let half the air in his lungs bubble out through his nose, so that he sank easily through the cold black water; then he halted his descent with a scissors-kick when it occurred to him that there wasn't going to be a pool floor to kick upward from. What if I've sunk so deep, he thought, that I can't thrash my way back to the surface before my lungs mutiny and suck in river water? He instantly began clawing and kicking his way up, and he felt a rope loop brush the back of his hand a moment before he burst out into the air.

There was a wild chittering nearby, like a cageful of excited birds, and Jacky, leaning out over the side, was bundling up the wet weight of a fishing net, in among the tangles of which a few little lights still burned. "Get in," Jacky snapped. "Clamber over the side up front, I'll balance you from the back. Stay away from that net—those little bastards carry knives. And *hurry*."

Doyle took a moment to look upstream—he could see Romany's boat perhaps fifty yards off, the synchronized knocking of the oars very loud now—and then he heaved himself up and rolled into the canoe. Jacky was crouched in the rear, rigidly holding the oar straight down into the water.

As soon as the canoe had stopped wobbling, Doyle panted, "Step on the gas."

Jacky began plying the oar desperately. Having come to a full stop and taken on more weight, though, the canoe was reluctant to move.

"I've got one more pistol," called Doctor Romany. "Drop the oar and I won't fire it."

"Wouldn't dare," gasped Jacky, her arms quivering as she dragged the oar through the motionless water. "Wants you . . . alive."

"Not anymore," said Doyle, sitting up carefully. "A minute ago they were all shooting at me."

"Thought you . . . were someone else."

The canoe was moving now, but slowly. Doyle could distinguish three heads in silhouette in the boat bearing down on them. "Is there a spare oar?" he asked desperately.

"Ever paddled . . . canoe?"

"No."

"Shut up then."

Doyle noticed a long tear in Jacky's trousers on the outside of the left thigh, exposing a long, rough cut. He opened his mouth to ask about it, then noticed a round hole punched in the fabric of the canoe, toward the stern. "Good God, Jacky, you've been shot!"

"I know." Even by the dim light of the rising crescent moon Jacky's face was visibly dark with effort and glistening with sweat, but the canoe was now matching the speed of Doctor Romany's boat. For a minute or two both craft maintained their interval as they knifed and lumbered through the water, and the oarlocks clacked in the same rhythm as Jacky's desperate panting; then the canoe put on a little more speed and began to leave the clumsier boat behind.

Blackfriars Bridge was looming close in front of them, and when it was clear that they would lose the pursuing boat Jacky sat back and stared ahead at the great stone arches they were being relentlessly propelled toward. "North middle arch," she gasped, and stabbed the oar into the water on the starboard side. The rocketing canoe heeled over and began cutting a wide arc to starboard across the face of the river.

When they were nearly in line with the arch she'd indicated, and so close that Doyle could see the explosive splashing where the river pounded against the stone pilings, she whipped the oar out of the water and plunged it in on the other side; the craft straightened out, and there was an instant of blackness and roaring water and the awareness of hard stone rushing past on all sides—and a fast rise and drop that almost landed Doyle in the water again—and then they were out on the broad river, on the east side of the bridge now, and Jacky was slouched back, eyes shut and hands hanging limp over the sides, devoting her energy to getting her breath back as the canoe gradually lost speed.

Doyle looked back, and realized that Doctor Romany would not have been able to duplicate the sharp turn to the wider middle arch, and would not dare try shooting the bridge through the narrow arch that lay ahead of him. If he wanted to continue the pursuit he'd have to heel around to a halt and then row to the one the canoe had darted through. "You lost 'em, Jacky," he said wonderingly. "By God, you left 'em behind."

"Grew up . . . on a river," Jacky panted after a while. "Handy . . . with boats." After a few more moments of panting, and pushing back sweat-damp hair, Jacky went on, "I thought the Spoonsize Boys were a myth."

Doyle knew that Jacky must be referring to the little egg-shell mariners. "You've heard of them?"

"Oh, sure, there's even a song about 'em. 'And the Spoon-size Boys steal the dollhouse toys when the cat by the fire is curled, then away they floats in their eggshell boats down the drains to the underground world.' Goes on and on, blaming all sorts of things on 'em. People say Horrabin made the creatures—and the things certainly seemed to be obeying him tonight, marking your location all the time. They say he made a bargain with the devil to learn how."

Doyle's eyes widened as a thought struck him. "Did you ever see his Punch show?"

"Of course. He is damned clev—oh! Yes . . . yes, I daresay you're right. Good God. But the Punch puppets are bigger."

"The pocketsize boys."

"And here I was admiring his puppet-working skill." Jacky picked up the oar and began rowing again. "Better keep moving—he wants you badly."

"The way everybody was shooting at me—us—it looked like they just wanted me dead. You saved my life, Jacky. How's your leg?"

"Oh, it stings, but it just tore across the surface. He shot at me three times while you were underwater and I was throwing the net over your little escorts. First time in my life I've been shot at. Don't like it."

Doyle was shivering. "I don't like it either. Horrabin's shot missed my eye by maybe an inch."

"Well . . . that's why I had to row out and get you. You see, it wasn't Horrabin that shot at you. *He* knew who you were. It was me."

Doyle's first impulse was to get angry, but the sight of Jacky's wound extinguished it. "Who did you—and Doctor Romany, I guess—think I was?"

Jacky rowed in silence for a few moments, then answered reluctantly, "I guess at this point you've earned the right to hear the story. We thought you were a man known as Dog-Face Joe. He—"

"Dog-Face Joe? The murderer who's supposed to be a werewolf?"

He could see Jacky's eyes widen in surprise. "Who could have told you about *him*?"

"Oh, I'm just a good listener. So what have you or Romany got against him?"

"He killed a friend of mine. Hell. He—he tricked me into killing a friend of mine. He—I've never . . . talked to anyone about this, Doyle. Not this part of it. God *damn* it all anyway. You've read Colin Lepovre's poetry—well, Colin was . . . a close friend, and . . . do you know how Dog-Face Joe stays alive?''

"I heard he could switch bodies with people."

"You do know lots more than you let on, Doyle. I wouldn't have thought there were a half-dozen people in London who knew that. Yes, that's what he does. I don't know how, but he can switch with anyone he can manage to spend some time with. And he has to do it fairly frequently, because as soon as he gets into a new body it starts to grow fur . . . all over it. So after a few days it's a choice of shave his whole body or go find a fresh one." Jacky took a deep breath. "Last year he took Colin's. I think Dog-Face Joe must have poisoned the old body just before he left it. Colin came to me, evidently in great pain"—Jacky's voice was clearly being controlled only with great effort, and though he was staring toward the dome of St. Paul's, Doyle could see peripherally the sheen of tears on the youthful cheek—"and it was in the middle of the night. I was in my parents' house, reading, when he opened the door and hurried toward me, groaning like, I don't know, a big dog or something, and he was bleeding terribly from the mouth. Damn it, Doyle, he was in the *cast-off* body, the one Joe had just vacated, and it was covered with fur, like an ape! You understand me? In the middle of the goddamn night! How was I to . . . *possibly* . . . know it was Colin? God damn it to *hell!*"

"Jacky," said Doyle helplessly, baffled by the impossible story but recognizing genuine suffering. "You couldn't have known."

London Bridge was less than half a mile ahead, and Doyle could see the hulks of grounded coal barges on the Surrey-side shore to his right. Jacky began angling in that direction. "There was a gun," Jacky went on in a flat voice, "a flintlock pistol—that's it there, by your foot—it was on the mantle, and when this furry thing came rushing into the house, I leaped up, grabbed the pistol and fired right into its chest. The thing dropped, bleeding all over the place. I went and stood over it, not too close, and it . . . *looked* at me for a moment before it sort of shuddered a few times and went limp. There was a mess. But when it looked at me I recognized him—I knew it was Colin. The color of the eyes was different, of course, but I recognized the . . . not expression, exactly . . . I recognized *him* in there.'' Past the easternmost of the barges was a pier below a lighted house, and Jacky seemed to be heading for it. The glow from the narrow windows glittered warm gold on the oily black water. ''After that I just slept through two weeks. Nobody else could—day and night I was screaming, throwing food and jabbering obscenities so foul that my innocent mother didn't even understand most of them . . . but I was asleep. And after I came out of it I set out to kill Dog-Face Joe with the same gun that killed—with which I killed—Colin.'' Jacky grinned sourly. ''Follow all that?''

''Yes.'' Doyle wondered how much of this Lovecraftian fantasy could be true—perhaps one of the mysterious Dancing Ape creatures *had* broken into Jacky's house at roughly the same time that Lepovre decided to hit the road—and he wondered too whether he was correct in suspecting that this was more than grief for the death of a close friend. Could his first suspicions about Jacky have been correct? ''It's trite to say, Jacky, but I mean it—I'm sorry.''

''Thanks.'' Jacky had been slowing the canoe by dragging the oar in the water, and now it slid, hardly moving at all, alongside the pier, and Jacky stopped it by grabbing a rope dangling between the pilings and hanging onto it when the canoe's weight came onto her arm. ''Pull your end around there, Doyle—there's a ladder that starts about four feet over your head.''

When they'd both climbed up to the narrow pier, Jacky said, ''Now we've got to figure out what to do with you. You can't come back to Copenhagen Jack's house—Horrabin will have a dozen spies there watching for you.'' They were walking slowly toward the building, which seemed to be some kind of riverfront inn, and Jacky, feet bare, was picking her way carefully over the ragged old timbers. ''When does this friend of yours arrive in town? What's his name, Ashbin?''

''Ashbless. I'll meet him this Tuesday.''

''Well, the innkeeper here, old Kusiak, has a stable off to the side, and he's always needing help. Can you shovel horse dung?''

''If there are people who can't, I'd hate to think I was one of them.''

Jacky pulled open the inn's dockside door and they stepped into a small room with a fireplace, and Doyle hurried over to it.

A girl in an apron appeared, and her welcoming smile

faltered a little when she noticed that both guests had evidently fallen into the river, and one was still dripping wet.

"It's all right, miss," Jacky said, "we won't sit on the chairs. Would you tell Kusiak, please, that it's Jacky from across the river, and a friend, and we'd like two hot baths—in individual private rooms—"

Doyle grinned. Modest little chap, this Jacky.

"—And some clean dry clothes, it doesn't much matter what sort," Jacky went on. "And after that two pots of your excellent fish chowder in the dining room. Oh, and some hot coffee with rum in it while we wait."

The girl nodded and hurried away to check all this with the innkeeper.

Jacky squatted down beside Doyle at the fireplace. "You're pretty sure this Ashbin character will get you set up in some decent sort of position?"

Doyle wasn't sure, and was trying to convince himself more than Jacky when he said, a little defensively, "He's not hurting for money, I believe. And I do know him pretty damn well."

And he's got friends and influence, Doyle added to himself, and he might just be able to get me an audience—in enforced immunity!—with old Romany, in which we could bargain on *my* terms: I'll let him have certain harmless bits of information—or even outright lies; yes, that would be safer—in exchange for a gap location. If I could have the right sort of friends waiting outside the tent he wouldn't dare do any more things like his cigar in the eye trick. And it would take me months, or years, to build up that kind of influence unaided, and Darrow said the gaps decrease in frequency after 1802, and in any case I don't think I *have* months—this cough was already killing me before tonight's swim. It may now choose to develop into real pneumonia. I've got to get back, soon, to where there are hospitals.

Also, Doyle wanted to interview Ashbless in detail about his early years and then stash the information somewhere where it wouldn't be disturbed until he could "discover" it when he got back to 1983. Schliemann and Troy, he thought fatuously, George Smith and Gilgamesh, Doyle and the Ashbless Documents.

"Well, good luck with him," said Jacky. "Maybe next month at this time you'll have a job at the Exchange and rooms in St. James. And you'll hardly remember your days as

a beggar and a stablehand—'' She smiled. "Oh yes, and your
morning as a less than successful costermonger . . . what else
have you done?''

The rum-laced coffee arrived then; and the girl's smile, and
her assurances that their baths were being drawn even now,
showed that Kusiak had acknowledged Jacky as a good credit
risk. Doyle sipped his coffee gratefully. "Nothing much," he
answered.

The structure known throughout the St. Giles rookery as
Rat's Castle had been constructed on the foundations and
around the remains of a hospital built in the twelfth century;
the hospital's bell-tower still survived, but over the centuries
the various owners of the site had, largely for warehousing
purposes, steadily added new floors and walls around it, until
now its arched Norman windows looked, instead of out across
the city, into narrow rooms fronted right up against them and
moored to the ancient stone; the cap of the tower was the only
bit of the structure still exposed to the open air, and it would
have been hard to find in the rooftop wilderness of chimney
pots, airshafts and wildly uneven architecture.

The bellropes had rotted away centuries ago, and the pulleys
plummeted to the floor to be carted away as scrap metal, but
the ancient cross timbers still spanned the shaft, and new ropes
had been looped over these in order to hoist Horrabin and
Doctor Romany some fifty feet off the floor, roughly three-
quarters of the way up the enclosed tower. Since it allowed
them to converse at a comfortable distance from the ground, it
was their preferred conference chamber. Oil lamps had been
set on the sills of the old stone windows at the very top, and
Damnable Richard attended this evening's council, sitting on
the sill of a window one level down from the lamps, which put
him only a foot or two above the heads of the dangling chiefs.

"I have no idea who those two men were, your Honor,"
Horrabin was saying, and his already weird voice echoed with
a sort of nightmare ululation in the stone shaft. "They were
certainly none of my crew."

"And they really did mean to kill him?"

"Oh, yes. Dennessen says when he knocked the second man
off our American he had already stabbed him once, and was
cocking another thrust."

Doctor Romany swung meditatively for a few moments
back and forth, kicking off gently from the concave

stonework. "I can't understand who they could be. Someone working against me, obviously, who either already knows what the American has to tell . . . or simply doesn't want me to learn any of it. It couldn't be the people he came with, because I saw them all disappear when the gate ceased to exist, and I've monitored all gates since and nobody has come through them. And the Antaeus Brotherhood hasn't been a threat to us for more than a century, I gather."

"They're a bunch of old men," Horrabin agreed, "who have forgotten the original purpose of their organization."

"Well, tell your man Dennessen that if he could recognize the man who tried to kill the American, and bring that man to me alive, the reward will be the same as if he'd killed Dog-Face Joe." He flapped his arms to stop swinging. "The bearded man who shot at the American and then picked him up may be of the same group. You say you recognized the daring canoeist?"

"I believe so, yer Worship. He wasn't wearing his usual turban, but it looked like a beggar who sometimes hangs around here, called Ahmed. A fake Hindoo. I've got an order and reward out now for his capture."

"Good. We'll wring the story out of one of these birds, Set willing, even if we have to peel him down to nothing but lungs and a tongue and a brain."

Damnable Richard carefully reached for his wooden monkey, whom he'd set on the window ledge so as to be able to see the prodigy of two sorcerers hung up like hams in a smokehouse, and put his thumb and forefinger over its ears, for savage talk tended to upset it. And Richard himself wasn't pleased. He'd been in town for a full week now, confined to Rat's Castle and the hall under Bainbridge Street, while Doctor Romany at least got to travel around in order to be at each gate when it appeared, which involved going out into the country a good deal of the time.

"I can't help thinking—wondering whether—this interference may be prompted by my . . . partner's efforts in Turkey," said Doctor Romany.

"But nobody knows what they are," pointed out Horrabin. He added more softly, "Even I know only that your twin brother has found a young British lord, sojourning abroad alone, who you two seem to think you can make some use of. It seems to me I should be more fully acquainted with your plans."

Romany seemed not to have heard him. He said thoughtfully, "I don't believe there's been any breach of secrecy at
this end, simply because I'm the only one that knows anything
important. But I don't know much about what may be going
on at Doctor Romanelli's end of things, back in Turkey; I
understand this young lord is fond of writing letters. I just
hope my . . . brother hasn't allowed some unobtrusively important bit of information to find its way, in one of these
letters, to certain people in this island."

Horrabin looked surprised. "Where'd you say this troublesome young peer is?"

"A few days out of Athens, obediently heading back up the
Gulf of Corinth to Patras; for some reason milord is very
vulnerable psychically when he's in that little area: Patras,
the Gulf of Patras, Missolonghi. So when he was last there, in
July, Romanelli had the imperial consul, an employee of his,
put milord to sleep by having him concentrate on the operation of a musical clock, and while he was asleep my brother
placed a command in milord's mind, under the thinking level
so he wouldn't be aware of it—a command to return to Patras
in mid-September, by which time things should be warmed up
here so that everything will come to a boil at once. And his
lordship is even now carrying out the order, blithely supposing
that the decision to return to Patras is his own."

Horrabin was nodding impatiently. "The reason I asked
was, well, for a letter of his to have incited trouble here, it
would have to have been sent . . . when? Months ago, I should
think. Aren't there about a dozen wars going on between here
and there? So even if he'd written to somebody right at first, in
July, there hasn't been time for the letter to arrive here and for
somebody here to find out who you are and what you want."

Romany raised his eyebrows and nodded. "You're right—I
hadn't considered the slow pace of international mail these
days." He frowned. "Then who in hell were those men, and
why are they interfering with me?"

"I couldn't say," answered the clown, slowly stretching and
bending his limbs like some sort of huge, painted spider. Damnable Richard covered his monkey's eyes. "But," added Horrabin, "they're interfering with me too. Four dozen of my
tiniest homunculi were drowned out there tonight by that
bloody Hindoo. You need to make your Master in Cairo send
more of that stuff—what's it called?"

"Paut," said Doctor Romany. "That's damned hard stuff

to produce nowadays, magic being as strangled as it is." He shook his head dubiously.

Horrabin's painted face clenched in what was probably a scowl, but he continued his slow exercises. "I need it—to work for you I need it—to make more homunculi," he said evenly. "Dwarves and such I can warp down from human stock, but for boys that can overhear conversations while hidden in a teacup, follow a man by crouching in a fold of his hat," the clown's voice was rising, "sneak into a bank through the drains and replace good gold sovereigns with your gypsy fakes—"and he tilted over so that his head was near Romany and his legs pointed away, and he added, in a whisper, "or if you want some lads that can enter a monarch's chamber concealed in a nurse's dress, and put mind-rot drugs in his soup without being seen, and then, dressed up as anything from bugs to the twelve apostles, do dances on a table top out of his reach, just to give his ravings added color—for work like that you need my Spoonsize Boys."

"We won't have to do that very much longer, if things work out as planned in Patras," said Romany quietly. "But your creatures have their uses, I admit. I'll explain the situation to my Master, and let you know tomorrow what he says."

"You communicate by means of something faster than the mail," observed Horrabin, his orange eyebrows inquiringly raised halfway to his hat.

"Oh yes," said Romany with a deprecatory shrug. "By sorcerous means my colleagues and I can converse directly at any time, across any distance, and even send objects through space instantly. Such perfect communication ensures that our stroke, when we deal it, will be flawlessly aimed, timed and coordinated—unanswerable." He permitted himself a smile. "In our hand is the King of Sorcerers, and that beats any of the cards John Bull may have in his hand."

Damnable Richard looked at his monkey and rolled his eyes and shook his head. What a crock, eh, monkey? he thought. He just doesn't want this terrible clown to know how much he needs him. How many times, monkey, have you and I seen him shouting at that silly candle of his with Egypt-writing on it, and after a couple of hours just get a faint voice saying, "What? What?" coming out of the round flame . . . and how *about* the times he's tried to send or get objects from his pals in the far off lands? Remember the time his Master tried to send him a little statue, and all that showed up was a handful of red hot gravel? Hah! This to sorcery!

He spat disgustedly, earning an angry yell from Doctor Romany. "Sorry, *rya*," Richard said hastily. He scowled at the monkey. Don't start me chatting with you, he told it. You see what you did? Got me in trouble.

"In any case," Doctor Romany went on, wiping the top of his bald head, "we flushed the American out of cover, and I want a serious search for him tonight, while he's still running scared. Now the three of us here—are you paying attention, Richard? Very well—the three of us here know him by sight, so each of us should lead a search party. Horrabin, you'll mobilize your wretches and search the area from St. Martin's Lane to St. Paul's Cathedral—and check with all lodging house owners; look into pubs; eye closely all beggars. Richard, you will lead a search of the south shore, from Blackfriars Bridge to past the granaries below Wapping. I'll take some of my dockside boys southeast from St. Paul's through the Clare Market rookery and the Tower and Docks and Whitechapel area. Frankly, that's where I expect to find him; he'll have made friends on the north side of the river, and when we last saw him he was being carried east, away from the area you'll have, Horrabin."

Two hours after dawn Damnable Richard trudged back up the stairs, stepping softly, for he believed the wooden monkey in his pocket was asleep. When he wearily took his place in the window the two sorcerers were already dangling from their ropes, though Doctor Romany was swinging back and forth as if only recently drawn up.

"I presume," said the gypsy chief, turning up toward him a face haggard with exhaustion, "that you had no better luck on the Surrey-side than we did on the north."

"*Kek, rya.*"

"Means no," Romany told Horrabin.

There was a large stone missing from the tower's dome, and as the spot of bright sunlight slid by slow inches down the sunlit wall, and the costermongers in Holborn Street could be faintly heard shouting the virtues of their vegetables, the two sorcerers discussed strategies, and Damnable Richard had tucked his awakened monkey into his shirt collar and was having a long talk with it in the faintest of whispers.

CHAPTER 6

"The other night upon the stair
I met a man who wasn't there . . ."

—Old Rhyme

TUESDAY MORNING, two days later, was overcast and threatening rain—but in the coffee houses around the Royal Exchange the brokers and auctioneers were conducting business as vigorously as ever. Doyle, stupefied by hunger and lack of sleep, sat in a corner of the Jamaica Coffee House and watched a dozen merchants bidding for a shipment of tobacco salvaged from some ship that had managed to founder in the Thames; the auction was by Inch of Candle, whereby the last bid made before a short candle went out was the one taken, and the candle was now very low and the bidding quick and loud. Doyle took another sip of his lukewarm coffee, forcing himself to take only a small one, for if he finished it he'd have to buy another to keep his table, and the purchase of his present set of clothes—brown trousers and jacket, a white shirt and black boots, all secondhand but clean and whole—had left him only a shilling, and he wanted to be able to buy Ashbless a cup of coffee when he arrived.

His shoulder burned with a hot ache, and he was afraid the brandy with which he'd soaked his bandage hadn't killed the infection in the knife cut. I should just have drunk the brandy, he reflected. His eyes were watering and his nose tingled, but it

seemed his body had forgotten how to sneeze. Hurry up,
William, he thought. Your biographer is evidently dying. He
hunched around to glance at the clock on the wall—twenty
minutes after ten. Ashbless was due in ten minutes.

At least I made it to here and now alive, he told himself.
There were moments when it looked like I wouldn't. Knifed,
shot at and nearly drowned on Saturday evening, and then
captured by that gypsy later that night.

He smiled a little bewilderedly into his coffee as he remembered the encounter. He'd thanked Jacky and bidden the boy
farewell—having agreed to meet at high noon on Friday at the
middle of London Bridge—and was being introduced to
Kusiak's stable boss when the gypsy had hurried in, demanding to exchange three spent horses for three fresh ones. The
stable boss had initially refused, but reconsidered when the
gypsy impatiently produced a handful of gold sovereigns from
a pouch and offered to throw them in. Doyle's idle interest
had turned to hollow-bellied fear when he recognized the man
—this was the same gypsy that had watched with no sympathy
when Doctor Romany had tortured him a week ago; Doyle
quietly stepped back out of the circle of lamplight and turned
to leave, but by the time he got to the side door the recognition
had become mutual. Doyle ran down an alley and then dashed
east along a sidewalk toward London Bridge, but the old
gypsy was faster, and the running footsteps behind Doyle
sounded louder and louder until a hand had clamped on his
collar and he'd been thrown to the ground.

"Speak the first word of any spell, dog of the Beng, and I'll
bounce your head off this pavement," the gypsy had said,
crouching over him and hardly panting at all.

"Go ahead," Doyle had gasped. "Christ, why can't you
people leave me alone?" He slowly got his breath back. "And
if I knew any spells do you think I'd have run from you? Hell
no, I'd have conjured up some damn kind of . . . winged
chariot or something. And changed you into a pile of horse
dung so I'd have had the pleasure of shovelling you onto a
manure cart."

To Doyle's surprise the gypsy had grinned. "Hear that,
monkey? Man wants to turn us to horse manure. Most of
these magical *chals* try to turn things to gold, but old Wheezy
here thinks small." He'd yanked Doyle to his feet. "Come on
now, *Bengo*, there's a man wants to talk to you."

A couple of people were leaning out of a back door Doyle

had fled past, and one called an angry question, so the old gypsy had led him down a street away from the river and then turned right again so that they were approaching Kusiak's front entrance. Doyle was walking ahead.

When they were passing the open door of a public house two buildings away from Kusiak's, Doyle stopped. "If you're taking me back to that lunatic who tried to burn my eye out last time," Doyle said, a little unsteadily, "then I need two beers first. At least two. And since you've got all that gold, sport, you can buy 'em."

There was silence behind him for a moment, then the gypsy said, "It's a *kushto* idea. *Adree* we go."

They entered and walked through the high-ceilinged room where the bar was, to a smaller chamber two steps up where a lot of tables were set randomly across the wood floor. The gypsy rolled his dark eyes toward a table in the corner, and Doyle nodded and crossed to it and, sitting down, warmed his hands over the candle that sat on it.

When a girl had appeared and taken their order—beer for Doyle, wine for the gypsy—Doyle's captor said, "They call me Damnable Richard."

"Oh? Well, pleased to—no. Uh, I'm Brendan Doyle."

"And this is my partner," the gypsy said, pulling from his pocket a monkey carved out of wood. Doyle remembered seeing Richard with it last Saturday night. "Monkey, this is Doyle. Doyle is the gorgio the *rya* has been so anxious to find, and the *rya* will be very pleased with us for netting him." He smiled quite cheerfully at Doyle. "And this time we'll take you to someplace where there are no *prastamengros* to hear you yell."

"Listen, uh, Damnable," said Doyle with quiet urgency, "if you'll pretend you didn't catch me, I'll make you a rich man. I give you my word—" He rocked violently back in his seat then, for the gypsy had moved as fast as a striking mousetrap and rapped a knuckle hard against the bridge of Doyle's nose.

"You gorgios all think the Romany, the gypsies, are stupid," Richard remarked.

The wine and beer arrived at this point, and Doyle made the girl wait while he finished his beer in two long, laboring, throat-burning drafts, and then gasped out an order for another pint.

Richard was staring at him. "I guess it's no harm if I bring you to him drunk." He looked after the girl wistfully, "A bit of cool beer would sit well after all that running." He sipped his wine without enthusiasm.

"It's not bad. Have some."

"No—beer was my Bessie's favorite drink, and since she *mullered* I've not had a drop of it." He drained the wine in one long gulp, shuddered, and then when the girl brought Doyle's second beer he ordered another glass of wine.

Doyle gulped some more beer and pondered this. "My Rebecca," he said carefully, "loved nearly every kind of liquor, and since she . . . *mullered*, I've drunk enough for the two of us. At least."

Richard pondered this, frowning, for a few moments, then nodded. "It's the same idea," he pronounced. "It's to keep them from being forgotten." When the girl came to their table this time she demanded some money, got it, and then left a pitcher and a bottle on the table. The two men thoughtfully filled their glasses. "Here's to dead ladies," said Damnable Richard.

Doyle raised his glass. There was a moment of silent gulping, and then both glasses bumped back down on the table empty. They were ceremoniously refilled.

"How long ago . . . did Bessie die?" asked Doyle.

Richard drank half his glassful before answering. "Seventeen years ago," he said quietly. "She was thrown from a horse near Crofton Wood. She was always *kushto* with horses but we were running at night from *prastamengros* and her horse put his foot in a hole. The fall . . . just . . . broke her head."

Doyle refilled his own glass and then reached across to the wine bottle and refilled the gypsy's. "Here's to dead ladies," Doyle said softly. Again they drained the glasses and refilled them.

Doyle found that he could still speak clearly if he spoke slowly and chose his words as carefully as a golfer selecting the right iron to use for a difficult stroke. "Rebecca also had her head broken," he told the gypsy. "In spite of the helmet—the helmet broke too—she hit a freeway pillar head-first. I was riding, she was behind." The gypsy nodded sympathetically. "We were on an old 450 Honda, and the streets were too wet to ride on if you were carrying a passenger. I even knew that then, but we were in a hurry and, hell, she had on a helmet, and I'd been riding bikes for years. I was changing lanes, 'cause when you get onto the Santa Ana Freeway from Beach Boulevard you wind up in the fast lane, and I wanted to get to a slower one; and as I leaned it to the right and went across those lane divider bumps I felt the bike . . . shift sideways. Horrible sensation, like an earthquake, you know? A . . . deadly and unexpected motion. And the old 450's were top-heavy anyway, with those overhead cams, and it—just—went —down." He swallowed a massive gulp of beer. "Rebecca tumbled off to the right and I slid on straight ahead. Burned my leather jacket paper-thin on the pavement—if it had been dry it would have sanded me down to the bare ribs. The cars all managed to stop without running over me, and I got to my feet and hopped back—I'd broken my ankle, among other things—back to where she was. Her . . . head was—"

He was pulled out of his memories by the clink of the pitcher-lip on the rim of his glass. "No need to say it," said Richard, lifting the pitcher away when the glass was full again. "I too saw what you saw." He raised his own glass. "Here's to Rebecca and Bessie."

"May they rest in peace," said Doyle.

When the glasses had clunked to the table again Damnable Richard stared hard at Doyle. "You're not a sorcerer, are you?"

"God, I wish I was."

"Somebody you were with must have been, though—I saw the two carriages disappear from that field like fleas from the back of your hand."

Doyle nodded morosely. "Yes. Left without me."

The gypsy got to his feet and threw a sovereign onto the table. "Take that," he said. "I'll tell them I took off chasing a *chal* that I thought was you, and knocked him down, but it was the wrong man and I had to buy him a drink to keep him from going to the *prastamengros*." He turned to leave.

"You're—" Doyle blurted. The gypsy paused and gave him an unreadable stare. "You're letting me go? After only having a drink with me?" He knew he should just shut up, but he felt he couldn't live with this mystery. "Did you think my offer to make you rich was a bluff?"

"It's you gorgios that are stupid," said Damnable Richard. He smiled, turned and walked out of the room.

The candle flickered out in a puddle of melted wax—the auction was over. The winner stood up to deal with the paperwork, looking a little more surprised than pleased that his last bid had been the last of all.

Doyle glanced at the clock, and felt a tiny cold quiver in his chest—it was thirty-five minutes after ten. His glance darted around the room, but there was no giant blond man present, with or without the fierce beard Ashbless was evidently never without. Damn it, Doyle thought; the son of a bitch is late. Could I have missed him during the last few minutes? No, he's not supposed to just duck in and out; he's supposed to sit down and write the damned "Twelve Hours of the Night." That's what, a couple of hundred lines long?

His face was hot and his mouth tasted feverish. Reasoning that he must at all costs keep from passing out here, he ordered a pint of stout for two precious pennies. When it arrived the clock said twenty minutes of eleven, and though he tried to drink it slowly, as befitted a restorative, when the clock pinged the third quarter-hour his glass was empty, and he could feel the alcohol pressing outward against the walls of his skull—for he hadn't eaten in twenty-four hours—and Ashbless still hadn't arrived.

Get hold of yourself, he thought. Coffee, no more beer. So he's a little late; the accounts of his arrival were more than a century old when you read them—and those were based on Ashbless' recollections, as recorded by Bailey in the 1830s. A bit of inaccuracy is hardly surprising. It might very well have been *eleven*-thirty actually. It *has* to have been eleven-thirty. He settled down to wait. Three carefully nursed cups of coffee later the clock bonged eleven-thirty and there had been no sign of William Ashbless.

The stock and shipping business continued to be lively, and at one point a portly gentleman who'd sold a Bahamian plantation at a tremendous profit ordered up a glass of rum for everyone present, and Doyle gratefully poured the stuff down his feverish throat.

And he began to get angry. This really did, it seemed to him, show a carelessness on the poet's part, a lack of regard for his readers. Arrogant—to claim he'd been here at ten-thirty when actually he hadn't bothered to arrive until at least . . . let's see—getting on for noon. What does he care if he's kept people waiting? thought Doyle blurrily. He's a famous *poet*, a friend of Coleridge and Byron. Doyle visualized him in his mind, and fever and exhaustion gave the picture an almost hallucinatory clarity—the broad shoulders, the craggy face lion-maned and Viking-bearded. Before, that face had seemed, like Hemingway's, basically humorous and sociable in a hard-bitten way, but now it only looked cruel and unapproachable. He's probably outside, Doyle thought, waiting for me to drop dead before he'll condescend to come in and write his damn poem.

An idea struck him, and he stopped a boy and asked him for a pencil and some sheets of paper. And when it arrived he began to write out, from memory, the entire text of "The Twelve Hours of the Night." In composing the original PMLA article on Ashbless' work, and later while writing the biography, he had read the poem hundreds of times, and in spite of his sick dizziness he had no difficulty in remembering every word. By twelve-thirty he was scribbling the somewhat awkward final eight lines:

> He whispered, "And a river lies
> Between the dusk and dawning skies,
> And hours are distance, measured wide
> Along that transnocturnal tide—
> Too doomed to fear, lost to all need,
> These voyagers blackward fast recede
> Where darkness shines like dazzling light
> Throughout the Twelve Hours of the Night."

There, he thought, letting the pencil clatter to the table. Now when the bastard finally gets around to keeping his historical appointments I'll just hand him this—and I'll say, *If you're curious about this, Mr. William Hell-of-a-fellow Ashbless, I can be reached at Kusiak's, Fickling Lane, Southwark.* Ho ho.

He folded up the sheets of paper and sat back smugly, content now to wait.

When the gargling screams started, Jacky broke into a run down the narrow alley toward Kenyon Court, the old flintlock in her shoulder pouch bouncing painfully against her left shoulder blade. She swore, for it certainly sounded like she was too late. Just as she burst out of the alley into the littered court a gunshot echoed between the dilapidated buildings.

"*Damn* it," she panted. Under the ragged curtain of her bangs her eyes darted this way and that, trying to spot anyone—from a toddler to an old woman—leaving the court, especially with a too nonchalant air; but the entire population of the area seemed to be hurrying toward the house from which the shot had sounded, and shouting questions to the people that lived there, and cupping their faces against the dust-frosted windows.

Jacky sprinted, ducked and elbowed her way nimbly through the noisy crowd to the house's front door, and just pressed down the latch, swung the door open and stepped inside. She shut the door behind her and shot the bolt.

"And just who the bloody hell are you?" came a voice with more than a hint of hysteria in it. A heavy-set man in a brewer's apron stood on the first landing of the stairway on the other side of the front room. The smoking gun in his right hand seemed to be something he hadn't noticed yet, like a fleck of mustard on one's moustache, and right now it only served as a weight, keeping that hand from flying about in aimless gestures as the left was doing.

"I know what you just killed," Jacky panted, her voice urgent. "I've killed one myself. But never mind that for now. Are any people, any members of your family, not here? Did anyone leave the house in the last few minutes?"

"*What?* There's a goddamn ape upstairs! I just shot it! My God! None of my family are at home, thank all the saints! My wife will go mad. I may go mad."

"Very well, what was . . . the ape doing? When you shot it?"

"Was it yours? You son of a bitch, I'll have you clapped in jail for letting that thing run wild!" He began clumping down the stairs.

"No, it wasn't mine," Jacky said loudly, "but I've seen another like it. *What was it doing?*"

The man waved with both hands, clanking the gun against the wall. "It was—Jesus!—screaming like somebody on fire, and spitting pints of blood out of its mouth, and trying to crawl into my son Kenny's bed. Damn me, it's still there—the mattress will be—"

"Where is Kenny right now?" Jacky interrupted.

"Oh, he won't be home for hours yet. I'll have to—"

"*God damn it, where's Kenny?*" Jacky shouted. "He's in terrible danger!"

The man gaped at her. "Are the apes after Kenny? I knew something like this would happen." Seeing Jacky open her mouth for another outburst, he said hastily, "At the Barking Ahab, around the corner in the Minories."

As Jacky sped out the door and ran back toward the alley she thought, you poor bastard, it's a blessing you'll never find out that it was probably your Kenny you shot, as, crowbarred into an unfamiliar and fur-covered and poisoned body, he tried to crawl into his bed.

The Minories was blocked by a line of wagons carrying bales of clothing from the Old Clothes Exchange in Cutler Street toward London Dock, and Jacky ran to the nearest one, scrambled up the sideboards and from this vantage point looked up and down the street. There it was—a swinging sign with an Old Testament-looking man painted on it, his head tilted back and his mouth an O. She swung down from the wagon just as the driver behind was beginning to shout about thieves, and she made a beeline for the Barking Ahab.

Though the door was open and a breeze fluttered the smoke-yellowed curtains in the windows, the place smelled strongly of cheap gin and malty beer. The owner looked up irritably from behind the counter when Jacky came clattering and panting in, but changed his expression to a doubtful smile when the pop-eyed, out-of-breath newcomer slapped a half-crown onto the polished wood.

"There's a lad named Kenny drinking here?" Jacky gasped. "Lives over in Kenyon Court." Be here, Joe, she thought. Don't have left yet.

A voice sounded from a table behind her. "You a Charlie, Jack?"

She turned and looked at the four poorly dressed young men around the table. "Do I look like a Charlie, mate? This isn't a law matter—his father's in some trouble, and sent me after him."

"Oh. Well, maybe Kenny heard of it; he got up and dashed out of here five minutes ago like he'd remembered something left on the fire."

"Aye," said another, "I was just coming in, and he shoved by me without a glance, much less a 'hullo' for a chap he's been pals with nigh a decade."

Jacky sagged. "Five minutes ago?" He could be half a mile away by now, she thought, in any direction, and I could never get a good enough description of Kenny to be sure of him even if I found him. And even if I was sure I'd found him, I couldn't shoot him just because I'm almost certain that Kenny was shot in his own bed, and that his body is now occupied by old Dog-Face Joe. I'd have to question him, trick him, somehow get him to betray himself. Maybe once I could have killed him on the almost certainty, but not anymore—not after having almost punched a hole through the skull of poor old Doyle.

She got a fair description of Kenny anyway—short, fat, red hair— and then left the place. Well, that's what he'll look like for the next week or two, she thought. Judging by the areas where the "apes" have tended to show up, he likes the East End—probably because disappearances are not uncommon here, and it's easier to evade pursuit among the mazy alleys and courts and rooftop bridges of the rookeries, and any crazy stories coming out of the area would be more likely to be discounted as products of drink, opium or lunacy—so for the next couple of weeks I'll search the low lodging houses of Whitechapel and Shoreditch and Goodman's Fields for a short, fat, red-haired young man who'll have no close friends, be a bit simple-minded and talk about immortality to anybody who'll listen, and maybe need a shave on his forehead and hands—for evidently the thick fur begins to grow all over a body as soon as he gets into it. I wonder what sort of creature he is, she thought, and where he came from.

She shuddered, and slouched away east toward a public house she knew of in Crutchedfriars Road where she could sit quietly over a double brandy for a while—for this had been the closest she'd ever come to her prey, and the ravings of poor Kenny's father had vividly brought to mind her own encounter with one of Dog-Face Joe's cast-off bodies. This one was bleeding from the mouth too, she noted. I wonder if they all do, and if so, why.

She stopped, suddenly pale. Well of course, she told herself. Old Joe wouldn't want the person he shoves into his discarded body to be able to say anything before the poison finishes him. Before he . . . exits a body he must, in addition to drinking a fatal dose of poison, chew up his tongue to the extent that the new tenant won't be able to speak with it . . .

Jacky, who had read and admired Mary Wollstonecraft, and despised the fashion of fluttery helplessness in women, felt, to her own annoyance, close to fainting.

• • •

The Jamaica Coffee House closed at five o'clock, and Doyle found himself ordered out onto the pavement, and not very politely. He shuffled aimlessly out of the alley and stood for a while on the Threadneedle Street sidewalk, staring absently at the impressive facade of the Bank of England across the still-crowded street, the manuscript pages flapping forgotten in his hand.

Ashbless had not appeared.

A hundred times during the long day Doyle had mentally reviewed the historical sources of his certainty that Ashbless would arrive: the Bailey biography clearly stated that it was the Jamaica Coffee House, at ten-thirty in the morning, Tuesday the eleventh of September 1810—but of course the Bailey biography was based on Ashbless' years-old recollections; but Ashbless submitted the poem to the Courier in early October, and Doyle had not only read but actually handled the cover letter. "I wrote 'The Twelve Hours of the Night' on Tuesday the Eleventh of last month," Ashbless had written, "at the Jamaica off Exchange Alley, and the Motif was occasioned by my recent long voyage. . . ." Damn it, Doyle thought, he might have remembered the date incorrectly ten or twenty years later, but he could hardly have been mistaken after less than a month! Especially when he was so precise about the day and the date!

A portly little red-haired fellow was staring at him from the corner by the Royal Exchange, so Doyle, having developed a wariness of the scrutiny of strangers, walked purposefully away east, toward Gracechurch Street, which would lead him down to London Bridge and across the river to Kusiak's.

Could Ashbless have been intentionally lying? But why on earth should he want to? Doyle looked furtively behind, but the red-haired lad wasn't following him. You'd better relax, he told himself—every time somebody looks at you directly you assume it's one of Horrabin's beggar agents. Well, he thought, resuming the puzzle, the next event I think I'm sure of in the Ashbless chronology is that he's seen to shoot one of the Dancing Apes in one of the Exchange Alley coffee houses on Saturday the twenty-second of this month. But I can't wait a week and a half. I'd be too far gone with pneumonia to benefit from even twentieth century medicine, probably. I'll have to—God help me!—approach Doctor Romany. The thought made him feel sick. Maybe if I, I don't know, strap a pistol around my neck, and keep my finger near the trigger, and tell him, *We bargain or I'll blow my own head off, and you won't learn one thing* . . . Would he dare to call my bluff? Would I dare let it be a bluff?

He was passing a narrow street off Aldgate, and somebody crossing one of the rooftop bridges was whistling. Doyle slowed to listen. It was a familiar tune, and so melancholy and nostalgic that it almost seemed chosen as a fitting accompaniment for his lonely evening walk. What the hell is the name of that, he wondered absently as he walked on. Not *Greensleeves*, not *Londonderry Air*. . . .

He froze and his eyes widened in shock. It was *Yesterday*, the Beatles song by John Lennon and Paul McCartney.

For a moment he just stood there, stunned, like Robinson Crusoe staring at the footprint in the sand.

Then he was running back. "Hey!" he yelled when he was below the little bridge, though there was nobody on it now. "Hey, come back! I'm from the twentieth century too!" A couple of passersby were giving him the warily entertained look people save for street lunatics, but nobody peered down from the rooftop level. "Damn it," Doyle yelled despairingly, "Coca Cola, Clint Eastwood, Cadillac!"

He ran into the building and blundered his way upstairs and even managed to find and open the roof door, but there was no one in sight up there. He crossed the little bridge and then descended through the other building, panting, but singing *Yesterday* as loudly as he could, and shouting the lyrics down all cross corridors. He drew many complaints but didn't get anyone who seemed to know what the song was.

"I'll give you a place to hide away, mate," shouted one furious old man who seemed to think Doyle's behavior had been specifically calculated to upset him, "if you don't get out of here this instant!" He shook both fists at Doyle.

Doyle hurried down the last flight of stairs and opened the door out to the street. By this time he was beginning to doubt that he'd even really heard it. I probably heard something that sounded like it, he thought as he drew the door shut behind him, and wanted so much to believe somebody else had found a way back to 1810 that I convinced myself it was the Beatles tune.

The sky was still a gray luminescence behind the rooftops, but it was darkening. He hurried on southward, toward London Bridge. I don't want to be late for the six-thirty shift at Kusiak's stable, he reflected wearily—I need that job.

The remaining leaves on the trees in Bloomsbury Square shone gold and red in the sunlight on Thursday afternoon as Ahmed the Hindoo Beggar stepped out of Paddy Corvan's, stared with homesickness for a moment at the trees and the grass, then carefully wiped beer-foam from the artificial beard and moustache and turned resolutely to the left, down Buckeridge toward Maynard Street and the Rat's Castle. The breeze was from ahead, out of the heart of the St. Giles rookery, and the smells of sewers, and fires, and things being cooked that ought to be thrown away, shattered the frail sylvan charm of the square.

Jacky hadn't been to Rat's Castle since the night five days ago when she'd hurried down the stairs to the underground dock, right behind Doctor Romany, intent on killing Dog-Face Joe; and she was checking in now to see if anyone else had made any progress toward finding the furry shape-changer.

When she turned right into the dark chasm, narrow at pavement level but narrower still at the top, that was Maynard Street, a little boy leaned out of an imperfectly boarded-up loading dock on the third floor of an abandoned warehouse on the corner. Under a piratical and oversized three-cornered hat his fish-blank eyes followed the shambling figure of Ahmed the Hindoo Beggar, and the nearly toothless slash of a mouth turned up in a smile. "Ahmed," the boy whispered, "you're *mine.*"

A rope still hung from the rusted pulley under the overhanging roof three floors above—only because it hung too far away from the wall to be snagged by leaning out from the docks on each floor and its ends swung too far above the pavement to be reached even by a man on another man's shoulders—and goaded by the immensity of the reward Horrabin had offered, the child hopped up onto the board his hands had been resting on, and then sprang out across two yards of empty space and clutched the old rope.

The pulley had rusted almost to immobility, and fortunately for the boy the rope ran through it haltingly, so that though he collided hard with the brick wall on the way down he didn't break his legs when he landed on the pavement three floors below. He wound up sitting down, with loops of stiff, weathered rope slapping the cobbles around him and thumping his hat down over his eyes. The child sprang to his feet and scurried after Ahmed as a trio of old women emerged from a cellar stairway and began to fight about who'd get the rope. Ahmed was walking beside a low wall, and the boy climbed up onto it, ran along the coping and then sprang onto the Hindoo Beggar's back, screeching like a monkey. "Oi've goat Ahmid!" he shrilled. "Fetch 'Orr'bin!"

Drawn by the echoing racket, several men stepped out of the recessed front doorway of Rat's Castle, stared for a few moments at the prodigy of a lurching Hindoo flapping about with a shrieking child perched on his back and clawing at his throat, then they sprinted up and seized the Hindoo's arms. "Ahmed!" said one, fondly. "The clown is *ever* so anxious to chat with you."

They tried to pry the boy loose, but he only dug his fingernails deeper into Ahmed and bit at every reachable hand. "Hell, Sam," one said finally, "take 'em as is. He won't give the reward to no infant."

Jacky was trying not to panic. She thought, if I could get a hand to my turban I could—maybe—snatch the pistol out and kill one of these men and maybe club this nightmare child off me. The reeling knot of people was only a few steps from the building now, and she reached up under the turban, found the butt of the pistol and yanked it down—the turban came down too, tangled around the barrel—and she pressed it against the ribs of the man on her right and yanked the trigger.

The hammer came down on a fold of cloth, knocking open the flashpan cover but producing no sparks. Desperately she wrenched away the cloth and, as the man was shouting, "Christ, a gun, grab him!" she cocked it one-handed and again pulled the trigger. There was a spray of sparks but all the powder had spilled out of the open pan and the gun didn't fire, and an instant later a hard fist slammed into Jacky's stomach and a nimble boot kicked the gun out of her hand.

The gun clanked on the paving stones, and the piggyback child, evidently deciding to take the cash in hand and waive the rest, hopped to the ground, seized the pistol and scampered away. The two men picked up the jackknifed, gasping Hindoo Beggar—"Lightweight bugger, ain't he?"—and carried her inside.

Horrabin had returned to the Castle only a few minutes

earlier, and he had just relaxed in his swing—Dungy was
wheeling away the folded-up Punch stage—when they carried
Ahmed into the room. "Ah!" exclaimed the clown. "Good
work, my lads! The fugitive Hindoo at last." They set Jacky
down on the floor in front of the swing, and Horrabin leaned
forward and grinned down at her. "Where did you take the
American on Saturday night?"

Jacky could still only gasp.

"He pulled a pistol on us, yer Honor," one of the men explained. "I had to give him a thump in the tum."

"I see. Well, let's—*Dungy! Bring me my stilts!*—let's lock
him up in the dungeon. It's Doctor Romany that'll have the
most questions for him, and," the clown added with a giggle,
"the most *motivating* questioning techniques."

It was an odd little parade that descended four flights of
stairs and walked a hundred yards down a subterranean corridor that could have been pre-Roman—the hunched dwarf
Dungy limping along in the lead, carrying a flaring torch over
his head, followed by the two men who frog-marched between
them the chintz-curtain-robed Ahmed, whose face behind the
false beard and moustache and walnut stain was gray with
fear, and Horrabin, bent way over forward to avoid brushing
his hat against the roof stones, bringing up the rear on his
stilts.

Eventually they passed through an arch into a wide
chamber; Dungy's torch illuminated the ancient, wet stones of
the ceiling and near wall, but the far wall, if indeed there was
one, was lost in the absolute blackness. To judge by the
echoes, the chamber was very large. The procession paused
after a few paces into it, and Jacky could hear water dripping
and, she was certain, faint but excited whispering.

"Dungy," said Horrabin, and even the clown sounded a little uneasy, "the nearest vacant guest room—hoist the lid. And
hurry."

The dwarf limped forward, leaving the others in darkness.
Twenty feet away he stopped and lifted a little metal plate
away from a hole in the floor, and squatted down, trying to
get his head and the torch both next to the hole without setting
his greasy white hair on fire. "Nobody home." He set the
torch upright in a hole between the stones, hooked the fingers
of both hands around a recessed iron bar in the floor, carefully rearranged his feet, and then tugged upward. A whole
stone slab lifted up, evidently on hinges, exposing a circular

hole three feet across. The slab came to rest at a bit more than a ninety degree angle and Dungy stepped back, wiping his brow.

"Your chamber awaits, Ahmed," said Horrabin. "If you hang by your hands and then drop, it's only six feet to the floor. You can do that or be pushed in."

Jacky's captors led her forward and, when she was standing in front of the hole, let go of her and stepped back. She forced herself to smile. "When's dinner? Will I be expected to dress?"

"Make any preparations you please," said Horrabin coldly. "Dungy will drop it in on you at six. Get in now."

Jacky eyed the two men who'd escorted her, calculating whether she could break away between them, but they caught the look and stepped back, moving their arms out from their sides a little. Her gaze fell hopelessly back to the hole at her feet, and to her own humiliation she felt close to tears. "Are—" she choked, "are there rats . . . down there? Or snakes?" *I'm just a girl!* she wanted to yell, but she knew that revealing that would only add to the ordeals in store for her.

"No, no," Horrabin assured her. "Any rats and snakes that make their way down here are devoured by other sorts of creatures. Sam, he doesn't want to do it himself; push him in."

"Wait." Jacky carefully crouched and sat down on the edge of the hole, her sandalled feet dangling in the darkness. She hoped the others wouldn't see how badly her legs were shaking under the chintz robe. "I'm going, I don't need your . . . kind help." She leaned forward and gripped the opposite edge. She paused to take a deep breath, then hiked her rump off the rim and swung down into the hole so that she hung by the grip of her hands. She looked down and could see nothing, just the most solid blackness she'd ever stared into. The floor could believably have been three inches below her toes, or three hundred feet.

"Kick his hands," said Horrabin. She let go before anyone could.

After a long second of free fall she landed on flexed knees on muddy ground, and managed not to let either kneecap clip her chin as she sat down hard. Something scurried away from her across the mud floor. Looking up, she saw the underside of the stone slab appear for one instant lit by the red torchlight, and then, with a shocking, eardrum-battering crash, fall back into place; for a few more moments there was a tiny square of dim red light above her, but then someone replaced the metal plate over the peek-hole and she was in featureless, disorienting darkness.

Though as tense as an over-wound clock, she didn't move, just breathed silently through her open mouth and listened. When she'd dropped in, the close echoes of her fall had convinced her that the sunken room could be no more than fifteen feet across, but after a thousand silent breaths she was certain that it was far wider, in fact not a room at all but a vast subterranean plain. She seemed to hear wind in faraway trees, and every now and then a faint echo of distant singing, some sad chorus wandering far out across the plain. . . . She grew doubtful of her memory of the stone roof above her—surely it was just the eternal black sky, in which any stars seen were—perhaps had always been—just meaningless flashes on the individual retina. . . .

She was just beginning to wonder whether the sound of the surf had always simply been the soft roar of her own breathing projected onto a certain sort of agitation of water—and she knew that there were even more fundamental doubts and losses to be discovered—when an actual noise brought her out of her downward spiralling introspection. The noise, only a tiny grating and a clink, was startlingly loud in that hitherto silent abyss, and it brought the dimensions of her cell back to her original estimate of about fifteen feet across.

It had sounded like the peek-hole cover being removed, but when she looked up she couldn't see anything, not even a square of lesser darkness. After a moment, though, she could hear breathing, and then sibilant but indistinct whispering.

"Who's there?" asked Jacky cautiously. It's got to be only Dungy with my dinner, she insisted to herself.

The whispering became quiet, aspirated giggles. "Let us in, darling," came the whisper clearly. "Let my sister and me in."

Tears were running down Jacky's cheeks and she crawled to a wall and braced her back against it. "No," she sobbed. "Get out of here."

"We've got gifts for you, darling—gold and diamonds that people lost down the sewers since the long ago times. They're all for you, in exchange for two things you won't ever need again, like yer dollies after you growed up into a young lady."

"Your eyes!" came a new, harsher whisper.

"Yes indeed," hissed the first speaker. "Just your eyes, so that my sister and I can each have one, and we'll climb up all the stairs there are and take a ship to the Haymarket and dance right under the sun."

"Soon," croaked the other.

"Oh yes, soon, darling, for the darkness is hardening, like thick mud, and we want to be away when it turns as solid as the stones."

"Not in it," put in the harsh voice.

"No, not in it, we mustn't have my pretty sister and me caught forever in the stones that are hardened night! So open the door."

Jacky crouched in her corner weeping almost silently, and hoping that when the stone slab had fallen into place it had jammed solidly, and couldn't ever be opened.

Then there was a faint shuffling from far away, and the two voices chittered in consternation. "One of your brothers comes," said the first voice. "But we'll be back . . . soon."

"Soon," assented the other gravelly whisper. There followed a sound like leaves scuttering across pavement, and then Jacky could see, through the uncovered peek-hole, a waxing red glow, and she could hear Dungy nervously whistling the idiotic song Horrabin always made him sing.

After a few moments the torch and Dungy's ravaged face appeared in the little hole. "How'd you move the cover aside?" the dwarf asked.

"Oh, Dungy," said Jacky, getting to her feet and standing directly below, for at this point any human company was welcome, "I didn't. Two creatures who claimed to be sisters moved it, and offered me treasures in exchange for my eyes."

She saw the dwarf straighten and peer uneasily around; and remembering the extent of the chamber above, she knew how useless such an inspection was. "Yeah," he said finally, "there are such things down here. Unsuccessful experiments of Horrabin's—hell, there may even be some of mine still around." He looked down into the pit again. "Doctor Romany and Horrabin think you're a member of some group working against them. Is that the case?"

"No."

"I didn't think so. Still, it's enough if Horrabin does." The dwarf hesitated. "If I . . . let you out, will you help me kill him?"

"I'd be delighted to, Dungy," said Jacky sincerely.

"Promise?"

The dwarf could have asked nearly any price and Jacky would have paid it. "I promise, yes."

"Good. But if we're going to work together you've got to stop calling me Dungy. My name is Teobaldo. You call me 'Tay.'" The dwarf's face disappeared, and Jacky heard a grunt of effort and then the stone slab lifted away from above her. He peered down through the wider hole, and she could see that he held a stout stick with a length of rope knotted around the middle of it and trailing away out of sight. "I hope you can climb a rope," said Teobaldo.

"Of course," said Jacky. We're about to find out whether I can or not, she thought.

The dwarf laid the stick across the hole and pushed the rope into the pit. Excess loops piled up on the muddy ground at Jacky's feet. She took a deep breath, stepped up to the dangling rope, locked her hands onto it as high as she could reach, and then began yanking herself up, hand over hand. In two seconds she had one hand, and a moment later both hands, locked on the stick.

"Grab the coping," said Teobaldo, "and then I'll move the stick and you can pull yourself out."

Jacky discovered that she could also chin herself and scramble out of a hole with no footholds. When she'd got to her feet she stared somberly at her rescuer, for she remembered now where she'd heard the name Teobaldo. "You used to be in charge here," she said quietly.

The old dwarf gave her a sharp glance as he hauled up the line and quickly coiled it around his palm and elbow. "That's right."

"I . . . heard you were tall, though."

The dwarf set down the coiled rope and stood on the edge of the hole opposite from the stone lid. He flexed his arms and then said, reluctantly, "Push that down, will you? I'll try to catch it and lower it into place quietly. I'm supposed to be bringing you your dinner, and I'd just have pitched it in through the peek-hole, so if they hear the slab fall they'll all come running."

Jacky braced herself against the block, wedged her sandalled feet into a channel between two paving stones, and heaved.

The dwarf caught it against his outstretched palms and let it fold him down to a low crouch. He took several deep breaths and then heaved it up a little, got out from under it and caught the descending edge in his hands. His lips were drawn back from his teeth in a rictus of extreme effort, and Jacky could see sweat popping out on his forehead as he lowered it, his arms trembling; then he let go and leaped back. The slab dropped into place with a sound like a heavy door slamming.

Tay sat on the floor panting. "That's . . . good," he gasped. "They'll . . . not have heard that." He got painfully to his feet. "I *was* tall once." He pulled the torch out and looked across the slab at Jacky. "Can you do magic?"

"I'm afraid not."

"Well, we'll trick him. I'll go back upstairs now and tell him you want to talk—but not to Doctor Romany, who would only kill you. I'll say you want to buy your freedom by telling Horrabin so much that he'll be equal to—hell, stronger than—Romany. You've got Words of Power, I'll say. He's become a fair sorcerer, Horrabin has, in the eight years he's been Romany's right-hand man, but he's always trying to get the old man to give him a Word of Power or two. Romany's never done it. And we'll say that your group knows all about Romany's plans in Turkey; 'cause that's another thing that bothers Horrabin, that Romany won't tell him anything except stuff he needs to know to run the London end of things. Yeah," said the old man bleakly, "he'll bite that hook. He'll ask why you let yourself get captured if you're such a whizzo witch, but I'll just tell him that you said—I don't know—that the stars are crooked for that stuff right now. Does that sound good?"

"I guess so, but why the complicated story?" Jacky asked nervously, already wishing she hadn't promised to help him in this perilous undertaking.

"To get him down here *alone*," snapped Tay, "without his guards. He wouldn't want them to hear the Words of Power, or even be aware that he was making deals with Doctor Romany's enemies."

"And what will we do when he comes down here? Just kill him?" Though glad to be out of the pit, Jacky was feeling tense and distinctly ill. "Do you have a gun?"

"No, but a gun's no good against him anyway. One of the spells Doctor Romany gave him is a bullet-deflecting charm. I've seen a pistol fired straight into the middle of his chest—but the ball never touched him, just broke a window off to the side. And I've twice seen hard-thrust daggers simply jerk to a stop inches away from him, and shatter, as if he'd been wearing a suit of thick clear glass. The only time I've ever seen him cut was a couple of years ago when he went to Hampstead Heath to explain city ways to the gypsies—for at the time they thought the gypsies might be useful in organized burglary—and a gypsy that didn't fancy the idea said Horrabin was the Beng, they tell me that means devil, and this gypsy leaped up, yanked a tent spike out of the ground and slammed it into the clown's thigh. And it wasn't deflected and it didn't stop inches away from him—it tore right through, and the clown was bleeding like a ripped wineskin and almost fell off his stilts, and if the gypsy'd been able to get a second swing he'd have put Horrabin right out of the picture."

Jacky nodded dubiously. "So what was so special about the stake?"

"The dirt on it, man!" said Tay with impatience. "Before Doctor Romany made Horrabin a magician, the clown didn't have to walk around all day on stilts. But when you cast your lot with magic you . . . forfeit, you forfeit your connection with the earth—the dirt, the soil. Touching the earth is terribly painful for these magical boys, which is why Romany wears those spring-shoes and Horrabin walks on stilts. Their magic can't work on dirt, and so this muddy stake punched through his charms as if they were cobwebs." The dwarf pulled a knife out from under his shapeless coat and handed it to Jacky. "There's plenty of mud between these paving blocks—rub a lot of it on the blade and then go crouch in the shadows. When he bends over to peek into the pit I'll knock him down, and then you run up and just hack away. The underground dock is through that arch there, and we can escape down the river. Got all that?"

"Why don't we just escape? Right now?" said Jacky with a weak smile. "I mean, why bother taking the risk of actually trying to kill him?"

Tay frowned angrily. "Well, for one thing because you promised—but I'll give you some better reasons. It's a good twenty minutes to the Thames by the underground channel, and if I'm not back upstairs pretty quick he'll send men down to see what's going on, and when he learned we were gone he'd send men running south to climb down into the sewers ahead of us and intercept us—but if we kill him, especially if he leaves orders not to be interrupted, and if we hide the body —why nobody'll miss him for hours."

Jacky nodded unhappily and, crouching down, fingered up a lump of mud and smeared it on both sides of the blade.

"Good. You go stand over there." With great reluctance Jacky picked her way over the uneven pavement to a point twenty yards from the dwarf. "No, I can still see you. Farther! Yes, and a bit farther still. That should do it."

Jacky was trembling and darting fearful glances at the impenetrable shadows all around her, and she cried out when the dwarf turned toward the arch. "Wait!" she almost shrieked. "Aren't you going to leave the torch here?"

The dwarf shook his head. "It'd look suspicious. I'm sorry—but it'll only be for a few minutes, and you've got that dagger."

He walked away through the arch. Paralyzed with fear, Jacky could hear his footsteps receding away down the hall beyond as she watched the shape of the arch, the only spot of light, slowly darken. A few seconds after the chamber had reverted to full dark, Jacky heard a harsh whisper from nearby: "*While she's alone.*" And there was a sound like long, stiff starched skirts sweeping across the floor toward her.

Stifling a scream, Jacky ran in the direction in which it seemed to her that the dock archway had stood. After ten pounding paces she rebounded from a brick wall—and though she had struck it first with her knee and shoulder, her head had been the next to collide with it, and she wound up sitting half-stunned on the floor. She shook her head, trying to clear it and stop her ears from ringing. She knew she'd misjudged the direction of the dock arch—but was it left or right of here? Had she done a half turn or a full one when she bounced off the wall? Was the wall a yard or two in front of her, or behind, or to one side?

Suddenly something poked at her eye, and with a sob Jacky lunged upward with the dagger, and felt the point tear through balloon-like resiliencies that popped and bathed her hand and arm in cold fluid; then there was shrill, whispered screaming and the dank air shook with a buzzing like the vibrating wing-cases of some giant insect, and Jacky was on her feet and running again, stumbling over the unevennesses of the floor but never quite falling, sobbing hopelessly and sweeping the dagger back and forth through the darkness in front of her. Abruptly the floor shelved away under her feet, slanted down, and though she managed to maintain her balance for a few tilting, tiptoe steps, finally she tripped, tumbled and came up

onto her skinned hands and knees, winded but still clutching the dagger. All right, come on then, she thought despairingly. At least I know you can be hurt. I suppose I've run right out of that chamber, and down into some tunnel where there never has been and never will be the faintest ray of light, but I'll hack away at you monsters until you kill me.

Cautious rustlings sounded from nearby. A whispering voice muttered something, of which Jacky caught only the words, "Killed her . . ."

Another voice said softly, "It still has its eyes—I can feel the wind of them blinking."

"Take its eyes," whined a voice like an old woman's, "but my children need its blood."

Jacky was suddenly aware that she could smell river water, and faintly she heard water slapping against stone. It seemed to be at her back, and she turned around—and was surprised to find that she could see.

No, not see exactly, for seeing needs light; in the darkness her eyes were aware of a patch of deeper darkness, a blackness that shone with the absence and negation of light, and she knew that if the object approaching on the river should ever appear above ground, even the brightest sunlight would be swallowed up and obscured by its black rays. As it drew slowly closer she could see that it was a boat.

Another piece of the positive darkness arose behind it, defining the opposite bank; it seemed to be the shape of a vast serpent, and Jacky could hear a metallic rasping echo along the watercourse as it slowly uncoiled itself.

The whisperers around Jacky chittered in terror. "Apep!" exclaimed one. "Apep rises!" And Jacky heard a scuttling and pattering as her pursuers fled.

Jacky was right behind them.

There was light—real, red-orange light—visible when the floor levelled out into the main chamber, and Jacky could see the dwarf and the clown on stilts just appearing through the arch a hundred feet away. The two figures, weirdly tall and weirdly short, halted and stared in Jacky's direction. She hunched down, though she knew they couldn't see her that far back in the shadows.

"I wonder what's got them so agitated," said Horrabin.

"Your damned mistakes," said Tay uneasily. "The Hindoo complained that they were speaking to him through the peek-hole."

Horrabin laughed, but his merriment sounded forced. "You object to company, Ahmed? Be grateful we don't render you incapable of being aware of it."

Horrabin and Tay advanced across the warped floor and halted. Jacky knew they must have arrived at the hole in which she'd been incarcerated. Gripping the dagger tightly, she stole forward; her sandals had been lost in the tumble, and her bare feet made no sound on the stone.

When she was fifty feet away, and beginning to tread cobblestones crescented with the orange reflection of the torchlight, Horrabin leaned forward—an odd spectacle, for his stilts had to lean backward—and said, "Step into the light, Ahmed, and make your best offer!"

The dwarf actually crossed himself before placing both hands against Horrabin's stilts and shoving.

With a shrill, fearful cry the clown lurched forward, tried to get his stilts back under himself, failed, and crashed to the floor as Jacky crossed the last few yards at a sprint; the clown rolled over on his back, his head strained back with yellow teeth showing in a grimace of agony, and Jacky sprang onto the arched-up stomach and drove the dagger down at the proffered white-painted throat.

The blade snapped off as if she'd tried to stab one of the paving stones; and as it clanged away across the floor the red-veined eyes rolled down to look at her over the white point of the chin, and though the bared teeth were flecked with blood, and blood was running out of the painted ears, the mouth curled up in what was, unmistakably, a smile.

"Whatcha got in yer 'and, yer Worship?" Horrabin whispered.

Jacky felt something scrabbling strongly in her still poised right fist, and she convulsively flung away what should have been the bladeless dagger hilt, but was a handful of big black bees, as dark and fat as plums. One stung her hand before she could flick it off, and the others swarmed buzzing and clicking around her head as she rolled off the clown and scrambled away across the floor.

Tay was standing in the archway that led to the dock, still holding the torch. "All we can do is run!" he shouted to Jacky. "Come on, before he can get up!"

As Jacky hurried to the arch, pursued by the bees, and joined Tay in a scramble to the end of the dock, they heard Horrabin cry from behind them, "*I'll have you back, Father!*

And I'll make you into something that has to live in a tank!"

The two fugitives had found a raft, crawled onto it, and cast loose. "What happened to the mud on the blade?" Tay asked, in a tone of only mild interest.

"I had to stab one of the creatures down here," gasped Jacky, slapping a persistent bee into a pasty mess against the wood of the raft. "It seemed to have cold water for blood. I guess it washed the mud off."

"Ah, well. Good try, anyway." The dwarf opened a pouch at his belt and took out a pill, which he swallowed. He shuddered, then offered another of the pills to Jacky.

"What is it?"

"Poison," said Tay. "Take it—a much easier death than what he'll give you if he catches you alive."

Jacky was shocked. "No! And you shouldn't have taken one! My God, perhaps you can vomit it up. I think—"

"No, no." Tay wedged the torch between two of the raft timbers and lay down across the rough surface, staring at the passing ceiling. "I decided to die this morning. He told me to get ready for a full-dress performance tonight—skirt, wig, nail polish—and I just decided . . . no. I couldn't do it one more time. I decided to try to kill him, so I'd have died either way, you see; four years ago he set up—what did he call it?—a one-way sustenance link. Magical talk. Means when he dies, I do too. He thought that made him safe from me. It might have, if he hadn't made me do those goddamn song and dance numbers all the time. God, I'm sleepy." He smiled peacefully. "And I can't think of a . . . nicer way to spend my last few minutes than on a boat ride with a young lady."

Jacky blinked. "You . . . know?"

"Ah, I've known all along, lass. You're that Jacky, too. With the false moustache. Oh yes." He closed his eyes.

Jacky stared at the silent dwarf, horrified and fascinated. The raft turned and bumped down the canal. When she judged he was dead, she said softly, "Are you really his father?"

She was startled when he answered. "Yes, lass," he said weakly. "And I can't really blame him for the way he's treated me. I deserved no better. Any man that would . . . alter his own son, just to make the lad a more efficient beggar . . . ah, I had it all coming to me, certainly." A faint smile touched Tay's lips. "Oh, and did that boy repay it in full! He took over my beggar army . . . and then put *me* through the hospital in the basement . . . many, many times . . . yes, I was tall once . . ." He sighed, and his left heel thumped a few times on the wood. Jacky had now seen two people die.

Remembering Tay's prediction that men would be sent ahead to descend into the sewers to intercept them, Jacky didn't wait to arrive at one of the docks further down, but lowered herself into the water. It was cold, but as the subterranean river had slowed and diminished in width since her dip in it Saturday night, it had also lost its sharp chill. For a moment she clung to the raft.

"Rest in peace, Teobaldo," she said, and then pushed off.

Once she'd shucked the sodden Ahmed robe she had no difficulty in swimming against the current, and soon she had left the raft—and the torch—behind, and was swimming upstream in darkness. It wasn't a threatening darkness, though, and Jacky knew instinctively that the deeper river, the one on which she'd "seen" the boat, had no connection with this channel—perhaps not even with the Thames.

Voices were echoing down the watercourse—"Who the hell did he say it was?" "Old Dungy and that Hindoo." "Well, Pete's lads will stop 'em at the dock below Covent Garden." —and yellow light glinted on the water and the wet walls and ceiling ahead of her. Then she rounded a curve, dog paddling silently, and could see, far ahead, the dock from which they'd embarked. There were several men on it, all carrying torches, though Horrabin didn't seem to be present.

"They must be crazy," commented one, his voice carrying clearly down the tunnel. "Or maybe they thought the Hindoo had better magic. It'll be interesting to hear them—ow! Damn it, how did a bee get down here?"

"Jesus, there's another one! Come on, there's nothing to be done here. Let's go upstairs and watch when they bring them in. It ought to be good—the clown ordered the hospital opened."

The men hurried away, and the tunnel went dark; for a moment the archway glowed orange, and then as the torches were carried away up the hall it too faded into the uniform darkness. Jacky paddled steadily toward the after image in her eyes, being careful not to turn her head, even when she felt the false beard peel off and slide past her shoulder. After a few minutes she banged a hand against the timbers of the dock. She pulled herself up onto it and sat there, panting. She was naked except for a pair of shorts, and reaching up to brush her hair back she noticed that her moustache had pulled away with the beard.

This wasn't, she reflected, the sort of costume in which she could slip unnoticed out of Rat's Castle.

She padded timidly through the arch, wishing she still had the dagger. In the silence she could hear a bee buzzing somewhere. The long hallway was evidently empty, and she picked her way down it, pausing frequently to listen for pursuit from either direction, but especially from behind.

She climbed a set of stone steps to a wide landing, and in groping to find the next set of steps she brushed the wooden surface of a door. There was no faintest sliver of light visible around the frame or between the boards, so either the room beyond was as dark as the stairs or this was an unreasonably solid door.

She pressed the latch—it wasn't locked!—and inched the door open. No light spilled out on the stairs, so she hurried inside and closed the door behind her.

She had no way to strike a light even if she'd dared to, so she reconnoitered the room by feel, following the wall around all four sides of the little room back to the door again, and then making a cautious diagonal across the middle of the floor. There was a narrow bed, neatly made, a dresser with a couple of books on it, a table on which Jacky's gently groping hands felt a bottle and a cup—she sniffed the cup: sharp gin—and, in the corner, a chair on which were draped—and Jacky thanked God as she fumblingly identified the objects—a short dress, a wig, a make-up kit, and an ancient pair of ladies' leather slippers.

It's an absolute miracle that these clothes should be laid in my path, she thought. Then she remembered that old Teobaldo had said he'd been ordered to do a full-dress performance tonight—this must be his room, and he must have laid the costume out before, as he'd put it, deciding to die. Though she couldn't see, she glanced curiously around the room, and wished she could know what the books on the dresser were.

Len Carrington sat down right in the front room and had a long sip from his pocket flask, not caring who might see him. Why was it, he'd have liked to know, that *he* was suddenly appointed the clown's second in command, and simultaneously expected to mollify the angry Doctor Romany, evaluate the unsatisfactory reports being run back every few minutes from the team that was trying to catch the two fugitives, and assure the raging Horrabin—who was moaning in a hammock, evidently with bad burns all over himself—that every step was being taken to remedy the situation? Carrington didn't even understand what the situation was. He'd heard that the dancing dwarf had tried to kill the clown and had then fled down the underground river with a Hindoo, for God's sake, but if that was so, why was Doctor Romany only interested in talking to the Hindoo?

Someone was trotting up the stairs from the basement. Carrington considered, and then rejected, the idea of standing up.

It proved to be, of all things, a woman. Her hair looked like some sort of rodent's nest and her dress fit her like a tarpaulin tied around a hatrack, but her face, under a lot of powder and rouge, was pretty.

"They told me to look for Horrabin downstairs," she said, as calmly as if a woman in Rat's Castle was not as unprecedented a thing as a horse in Westminster Cathedral. "I didn't see him."

"No," said Carrington, scrambling to his feet. "He's . . . under the weather. What the devil are you doing here?"

"I'm from Katie Dunnigan, who runs all the accommodation houses around Piccadilly. I'm supposed to arrange a conference—evidently this Horrabin fellow wants to buy in."

Carrington blinked. So far as he knew the clown had not branched out into prostitution, but it was certainly his sort of thing. And it was inconceivable that a young girl would come to this place without some such reason. He relaxed—she certainly had nothing to do with the two fugitives. "Well I'm afraid you can't see him now. You'd better leave—and tell this Dunnigan woman to send a man next time! You'll be lucky if you're raped less than a dozen times before you get out of this building."

"Loan me a knife, then."

"Wha—why should I?"

Jacky winked. "You ever get out to Piccadilly?"

A slow smile built on Carrington's face, and he reached out and slipped an arm around her.

"No no, not me," she said hastily. "I, uh, have—a disease. But we've got clean girls in Piccadilly. Shall I give you the password that'll get you one gratis, or not?"

Carrington had recoiled from her, but now grudgingly

reached under his coat and pulled out a knife in a leather sheath. "Here," he said. "What's the password?"

Jacky said the filthiest compound noun she'd ever heard. "I know it sounds crazy, but that's it. Just walk into any of those places, go up to the bouncer by the front door and whisper that to him."

Jacky walked unhurriedly out of Rat's Castle, ostentatiously cleaning her fingernails with the knife.

CHAPTER 7

"Youth, Nature, and relenting Jove
To keep my *lamp* in strongly strove,
But *Romanelli* was so stout
He beat all three—and *blew* it *out*.—"
                    —Lord Byron, in a letter from Patras,
                                        October 3, 1810

DOYLE AWAKENED ON his straw pallet Saturday morning and realized that he'd come to a decision; the prospect of what he intended to do dried his mouth and set his hands trembling, but it was the clean jumpiness of a difficult course resolved upon, and it came as a relief after a week of murky indecision.

He realized now that it had been a mistake to pin all his hopes on the intervention of Ashbless. Even if he could find the poet, it was a fantasy to imagine that Ashbless would, or *could*, do anything to aid him. The conflict was between himself and Doctor Romany, and a confrontation was the only way to resolve it. The sooner it occurred, the better—for Doyle's health was definitely declining.

He asked Kusiak for the day off, and the old man was happy to give it to him, as Doyle's hacking cough was getting so bad that customers were uneasy around him, as though fearing he carried some plague. Doyle took the meager cash he'd saved and bought what he thought of as insurance: a battered and rusty old flintlock pistol which the marine store

owner had insisted would actually fire, and with which Doyle
would threaten to kill himself if Doctor Romany tried to have
him seized. Yesterday on London Bridge Jacky had told him
about the abortive attempt on Horrabin's life, and Doyle
wished he had the poison pill the dwarf had offered Jacky; it
would be easier to carry that between his teeth than to lug
around a pistol pointed at his head.

Realizing that his arm would get tired if he should have to
keep the heavy pistol pointed at himself for very long, he had
taken off his belt, run the end of it through the gun's trigger
guard, and then re-buckled it around his neck. With his coat
buttoned up over it and his scarf fluffed out to cover the gun's
muzzle, which was now pressing coldly into the soft spot
behind his chin, he avoided being conspicuous and also kept
the pistol in a position where one yank of his thumb between
the second and third buttons of his coat would send a pistol
ball punching up through his mouth, palate, nasal cavity,
brain, and then bursting out into the sunlight right aft of his
widow's peak.

In Bishopsgate Street he met a beggar from Captain Jack's
house, and after exchanging greetings the man told him that
Doctor Romany's gypsy camp was currently in a field up at
the north end of Goswell Road, telling fortunes for aristocrats
from the West End and selling love potions and poisons to the
inhabitants of the Golden Lane rookery.

Doyle thanked him, asked to be remembered to the company, and turned east on London Wall Street. Just as he was
crossing Coleman Street—only a block, he realized, from
Keats' birthplace—he heard a sharp whistle from the north
side of the street.

It was the high-low-low first three notes of *Yesterday*.

And it was answered, from the opposite side of Coleman
Street, by the up and down the scale next nine notes.

This time there was no doubt. He was not the only twentieth
century man in 1810. His heart pounding, he sprinted across
the street and then paused on the north pavement, looking
wildly around. Many people were staring at him, and he
looked earnestly into each amused or disapproving face, hoping to recognize somehow a fellow anachronism; but they all
seemed to be indigenous citizens.

He'd taken a couple of uncertain steps up Coleman Street
before noticing the coach at the opposite curb. Its side window
was open and Doyle could dimly see a passenger within. In the

instant before his feet were yanked off the pavement he saw
the flash of a gun in the carriage, but what he *heard* was the
detonation of the pistol under his shirt as the bullet shattered
the flashpan and hammer and ignited the powder; he'd been
turning quickly, and the muzzle was next to his jaw instead of
under it when the gun went off, and the red-hot ball only
plowed up the side of his face and ripped his right ear off,
instead of exploding his head.

He lay crumpled, unaware of the rattle as the carriage
moved off. He vaguely realized that there had been an explosion, and that he was hurt, and that there was blood all over
him. His chest hurt terribly, but when his numb hands had
brushed aside the powder-burned tatters of his shirt and
knocked the smoking, splintered gun off to the side, there
seemed to be no lethal injury—just a lot of burns and
scratches. His ears were ringing, the right worse than the left;
in fact, that whole side of his head was as dead as though he'd
been given a shot of Novocain. He fumbled at it with his hand
and felt hot, free-flowing blood, and ripped flesh, but no ear.
What in God's name had happened?

He had rolled over and was trying to get to his feet when
several people came over and sympathetically but roughly
dragged him upright. Doyle was dazedly aware of what they
were saying: "Are ye going to live, mate?" "How can you
ask, look, he's shot right through the head." "The man in
that carriage shot him." "Nonsense, I saw it all—his chest exploded. He was carrying a bomb. He's one of the French spies
from Leicester Square."

"Why, look," exclaimed one. "There's a wrecked pistol
tied around his neck." He tilted Doyle's face up toward his
own. "Why in hell were you carrying a pistol that way?"

Doyle wanted to get away from there. "I . . . just bought
it," he mumbled. "Thought it would be a good way to carry it
home. Uh . . . I guess it went off accidentally."

"The man's an idiot," pronounced Doyle's questioner. To
Doyle he added, "It can't have been any good anyway. You
see it flew to bits after being fired only once. Here, now, come
with me and we'll get you to a doctor who'll patch up your
head."

"No!" Doyle couldn't recall whether antiseptics were in
general use in 1810, and though he knew he wasn't thinking
clearly, he also knew he didn't want to pick up some damned

infection from unwashed fingers and stitching thread. "Just
. . . get me some brandy please. Strong brandy. Or whiskey—
anything with a lot of alcohol in it."

"I knew it!" piped up one old man who couldn't really see
what was going on. "It's a dodge. He likely lost his ear years
ago, and goes 'round pretendin' to have blowed it off over and
over again all over London, just so's gullibles will stand him to
a drink."

"Naw," contradicted someone else. "Look, there's part of
his ear over there. Whoops! Look out! He's gettin' sick!"

Doyle was indeed. A few moments later he gathered the
strength to push through the decreasingly solicitous crowd.
Unaware of the wondering stares turned on him from all sides,
he shed his coat, ripped off the remains of his shirt, tied it
tightly around his head to staunch the blood that was pattering
on the pavement and sliming his hands, replaced his coat, and
then, dizzy from shock and loss of blood, he reeled away to
find a grog shop; for though he was certain of very little at the
moment, he took comfort in the knowledge that the purchase
of the gun, which still swung from his neck, had left him with
enough cash for two brandies: one to soak his bandage with
and one to pour, rapidly, down his throat.

Two days later he heard the Beatles tune again.

When he'd gotten back to Kusiak's on Sunday afternoon,
pushed open the front door and lurched into the entry hall, the
old innkeeper had looked up from some bookwork with an expression of alarm that had quickly turned to a tight-lipped
anger. He'd cut through Doyle's incoherent explanations with
a curt order that Doyle be put to bed in a spare room and
watched over "until his soul pops away through the ceiling or
his damn feet can take him out the back door." He had put a
knuckle under Doyle's chin and tilted the pale face up. "I
don't care which way, Doyle, but you leave here as damn soon
as possible—you understanding me, hah?"

Doyle had drawn himself up to his full height and framed a
dignified reply—which he could never recall afterward—and
then abruptly his eyes rolled up out of sight and he toppled
backward like an axed tree; the floor boomed like a drum
when he struck it with the whole length of his body, and his
fingernails, scrabbling for a moment on the polished boards,
sounded like castanets.

Kusiak, with some relief, pronounced him dead and ordered

him taken out back to await the summoning of a constable, but when a couple of the kitchen boys had dragged the limp body as far as the back door, Doyle sat up, looked around urgently, said, "Flight 801 to London—you're supposed to be holding a ticket for me. It's paid for—by Darrow of DIRE. What's the *problem*?" and then passed out again.

Kusiak wearily cursed Doyle, and the absent Jacky, and then ordered the boys to take the delirious and unwelcome guest to the smallest possible vacant room, and check in on him from time to time until he had the grace to die.

For two days Doyle languished on a narrow bed in a windowless and peculiarly shaped room under the main stairs, nourished by Kusiak's excellent fish chowder and dark beer, and sleeping most of the time; on Tuesday evening he stood up and walked out into the hall, where he was seen by the aproned Kusiak, who said that if he was recovered enough to leave the room he was damn well healthy enough to leave the inn altogether.

When Doyle had put on his coat and taken a few wobbly steps down the street, he heard something clatter on the pavement behind him. He turned around and saw that Kusiak had thrown his destroyed pistol out after him. He went back and picked it up, for it might bring a few pennies at one of the ubiquitous junk shops, and as things stood right now the acquisition of three pennies would double his fortune.

It certainly is ruined, he thought as he picked it up. The hammer and flashpan were gone, the stock was splintered, and the twisted corpse of the bullet that had crashed into it was visible, wedged deeply into the wood. Doyle shuddered, remembering that the ball would have drilled straight through his chest if this gun had not been in the way.

He peered at the bullet more closely—it had the flat base of a slug fired from a shell—it wasn't a ball.

Well, that confirms it, he thought nervously. Bullets like this don't come into use until 1850 or so. There *are* other twentieth century men here—I mean now—and for some reason they're hostile. I wonder what the hell they've got against me.

And, he thought, I wonder who the hell they are.

He had reached Borough High Street. To his right was the somber bulk of St. Thomas' Hospital, and to his left London Bridge soared away through the twilight, spanning the broad Thames whose surging, gunmetal-gray face was already beginning to twinkle with the first lights of the evening. There seemed to be more promise across the river, and he turned left.

But why, he asked himself as he walked down toward the river, would time travellers *hang around* in London in 1810? And why, for God's sake, try to kill me? Why not just take me back? Do they think I *want* to be here . . . now?

A thought struck him. Maybe, he told himself, it's because I'm looking for Ashbless. Maybe he *would* have shown up at the Jamaica, but they've abducted him; and since I'm from the future myself, I'd notice his absence, so they've got to prevent me telling anyone about it.

At the gently curving apex of London Bridge he paused and leaned on the still warm stone rail and gazed west along the river toward the darkening sunset that silhouetted the five arches of Blackfriars Bridge half a mile upriver. I guess I'll have to make another attempt to talk to Doctor Romany. It's probably a lost cause, but I've got to *try* to get back to 1983. He sighed, allowing himself a moment of self-pity. If it was just this bronchitis or pneumonia or whatever it is, I might stay and try to beat it and make a living here and now; but when two evidently powerful groups are fighting over you, one wanting to kill you while the other will settle for just torturing you, it's hard to hold a job.

He pushed away from the rail and began walking down the north slope of the bridge. Of course I could just leave the city, he told himself. Just right now get to the shore, steal a boat and push off—let the current take me to Gravesend or somewhere. Begin life anew.

When he came out of his reverie he was off the bridge and crossing Thames Street. He glanced up and down the lamplit street, remembering the day, two and a half weeks ago, that he'd almost allowed himself to be taken to Horrabin by that fake blind beggar, and then had been rescued by Skate Benjamin.

There were few people out on the streets this Tuesday evening, and the pubs and dining rooms along Gracechurch Street spilled light but little noise out across the cobblestones. Doyle was able to hear the whistling when it was still a good distance away. *Yesterday* again.

When the first moment of blind panic had passed, Doyle smiled in grim amusement at how Pavlovian his response to that damned Beatles tune had become—he had instantly leaped into a recessed doorway, yanked the ruined gun out of his coat pocket and raised it like a club over his head. Now, as he realized the sound was coming from at least a block away, he lowered the gun and allowed himself to breathe—though the pounding of his heart didn't slacken. He peered cautiously out of the alcove, not daring to leave it yet for fear of attracting notice. After a few moments the whistler rounded the corner from Eastcheap and began walking down Gracechurch, in Doyle's direction but on the opposite side of the street.

The man was tall, and seemed to be drunk. His wide-brimmed hat was pulled low over his face and he lurched from side to side as he walked, though once for a moment or two he broke into a clumsy parody of tap dancing, whistling the tune fast to accompany himself. Just when he was about to pass Doyle's hiding place he noticed, with an exaggerated jerk of his head, a pub at his right, a narrow, ill-lit place called The Vigilant Rowsby. The man stopped whistling, patted a pocket, and, reassured by the jingle of coins, pushed open the bull's-eye windowed door and disappeared inside.

Doyle started to hurry away south, toward the river and Gravesend, but after a few steps he halted and glanced back at the pub.

Can you walk away from it? he asked himself. This guy certainly seems to be alone, and not particularly dangerous at the moment. Don't be an idiot, objected the fearful part of his mind, get the hell out of here!

He wavered, then hesitantly, almost on tiptoe, he crossed the street and stepped up to the heavy wooden door of The Vigilant Rowsby. The place's old name sign squeaked gently back and forth on its chains over his head as he tried to work up the nerve to take hold of the S-shaped iron door handle.

The decision was taken out of his hands when the door was yanked open from the inside and a tall, burly man stepped out onto the pavement, seeming almost propelled by the burst of warm air, redolent of beef and beer and candle tallow, that billowed out around him. "What's the problem, Jack?" exclaimed the man loudly. "No pence for beer? Here. When Morningstar drinks, everybody drinks." He dropped a handful of copper into Doyle's pocket. "In you go." Morningstar placed a giant hand between Doyle's shoulder blades and shoved him inside.

Keeping his face averted from most of the tables and booths, Doyle hurried to the long counter at one end of the room and bought a beer from the bored-looking publican. Doyle brushed his hair down across his forehead and then tilted the heavy glass beer mug up to his face and, with only his eyes showing, turned his back to the counter and started a slow scan of the room while he took the first long sip.

Halfway through it he froze, and almost choked on his beer. The man who had been whistling was sitting over a beer in a tall-backed booth against the far wall; his hat was set next to his glass, and the candle on the table lit his slack, blear-eyed face clearly. It was Steerforth Benner.

When he had convinced himself that he was neither mistaken nor hallucinating, Doyle gulped some more beer. Why hadn't Benner returned with the rest of the party? Had anyone else missed the boat? Doyle pushed away from the counter and, taking his beer with him, crossed to Benner's table. He slipped his free hand into his coat pocket and gripped the ruined pistol.

The big, sandy-haired man didn't look up when Doyle stood over him, so Doyle lifted the pistol inside his coat until the muzzle showed as a ring against the taut fabric, and then shook him by the shoulder.

Benner looked up, his wheat-colored eyebrows raised in irritable inquiry. "Yes?" he said, and t' :n, carefully, "What is it?"

Doyle was impatient. Why did the man have to be drunk? "It's me, Steerforth. It's Doyle." He sat down on the opposite side of Benner's table, letting the barrel of the concealed gun clank onto the wood. "This is a pistol here," he said, "and it's pointed, as you can see, at your heart. Now I want some answers to some questions."

Benner was staring at him in wide-eyed, slack-jawed horror. He said quickly, the words tumbling out of his mouth, "Christ Brendan don't torture me are you *real*, I mean *there*, good God you're not a ghost or a DT are you? Say something, goddammit!"

Doyle shook his head disgustedly. "I should pretend to be a ghost, just to see you really crack. Get hold of yourself. I'm real. Do ghosts drink beer?" Doyle performed this trick, without taking his eyes off Benner. "Obviously you know I was shot at Sunday. Tell me who did it and why—and who else is going around whistling *Yesterday*."

"They all are, Brendan," said Benner earnestly. "All the boys Darrow brought back here with him. The tune's a recognition signal with them, like that three note thing the Jets whistled to each other in *West Side Story*."

"Darrow? He's back here? I thought the return trip worked."

"The trip you came along on? Sure it worked. Everybody except you got back fine." Benner shook his head ponderously. "I'll never know why you wanted to stay here, Brendan."

"I didn't want to. I was kidnapped by a crazy gypsy. But what are you telling me, then? That Darrow came back again? How could he? Did he find new gaps to jump through?"

"No. Why should he need to? Look, the whole Coleridge speech thing was just a lucky way to finance Darrow's real purpose—which was to move back here to eighteen-goddamnten permanently. He was hiring open-minded, history-savvy lads to be his personal retinue—physician bodyguards—that's the job I got that I wouldn't tell you about, remember? And then he noticed that old Coleridge was giving a speech in London during the period of the gap. He'd been having problems paying for everything, and this was the solution—get a million a head from ten rich culture freaks to go hear Coleridge. And he decided he needed a Coleridge expert for that, and that's when he hired you. But all along, the main . . . objective . . . was to come back again, just him and his hand-picked staff, to live. So when the Coleridge party got back to 1983, he hustled them all off into cars and then set up for another jump back to the same September first gap, and we jumped again. But this time we arrived in the middle of the gap, an hour or so after all of you—us—had driven off to see Coleridge, and we cleaned up the signs of our arrival and were long gone by the time the two coaches came back, minus one Coleridge expert, and waited for the gap to end." Benner grinned. "It would have been fun to drive to the Crown and Anchor and look in on ourselves. Two Benners and two Darrows! Darrow even thought about doing it, and seeing that you didn't go AWOL, but he decided that changing even that small a bit of history would be too risky."

"So why does Darrow want me killed?" demanded Doyle impatiently. "And if Darrow's so damn concerned about the inviolability of history, why has he kidnapped William Ashbless?"

"Ashbless? That jerk poet you were writing about? We haven't messed with him. Why, isn't he around?"

Benner seemed to be sincere. "No," Doyle said. "Now quit ducking the question. Why does Darrow want me dead?"

"I think he wants us all dead, eventually," Benner muttered

into his beer. "He's been promising that his staff will be permitted to return to 1983 through a gap in 1814, but I'm pretty sure he intends to kill us all, one by one, as he stops needing us. He's holding all our mobile hooks, and he's already killed Bain and Kaggs—those were the two who were supposed to do you in a week ago. And then this morning I overheard him order *me* shot on sight. I managed to grab a fair amount of cash and get away, but now I don't dare go near him." Benner looked up unhappily. "You see, Brendan, he doesn't want anyone else here who knows twentieth century things—radio, penicillin, photography, all that kind of stuff. He was worried you'd patent a heavier than air flying machine, or publish 'Dover Beach' under your own name, or something like that. He was very relieved when I—"

There was a pause that lengthened uncomfortably while a hard smile deepened the lines in Doyle's cheeks. "When you reported to him that you'd shot me through the heart."

"Christ," whispered Benner, closing his eyes, "don't shoot me, Brendan. I had to, it was self-defense: he'd have had *me* killed if I didn't. Anyway, it didn't kill you." He opened his eyes. "Where *did* it hit you? I didn't miss."

"No, it was a good shot, square in the center of the chest. But I was carrying something under my jacket, and it stopped your bullet."

"Oh. Well, I'm glad of that." Benner smiled broadly and rocked back in his seat. "You say you *didn't* choose to go AWOL from the Coleridge trip? Then you and I can help each other tremendously."

"How?" Doyle asked sceptically.

"Do you want to get back? To 1983?"

"Well . . . yes."

"Good. So do I. Man, don't know what you got till it's gone, eh? You know what I miss most? My stereo. Christ, back home I could play all nine Beethoven symphonies in one day if I wanted to, and Tchaikovsky the next. And Wagner! And Gershwin! Janis Joplin! Hell, it used to be fun to drive up to the Dorothy Chandler and hear things in concert, but it's lousy if that's the only way you can hear 'em."

"So what's your plan, Benner?"

"Well—here, Brendan, have a cigar—and," he waved at a barmaid, "let me get us another round, and I'll tell you."

Doyle took the cigar, a long Churchill-sized thing with no band or cellophane wrapper, and bit a notch in the end; then, again without taking his eyes off the other man, he lifted the candle and puffed the cigar alight. It didn't taste bad.

"Well," began Benner, lighting one for himself when Doyle put down the candle, "to begin with, the old man's nuts. Crazy. Smart as you could ask for, of course, a very shrewd guy, but he hasn't got both oars in the water anymore. You know what he's had us all doing since we got here? When we could be, I don't know, booking passage for Sutter's Mill and the Klondike? He's bought a damn shop in Leadenhall Street and outfitted it, completely, as a for God's sake depilatory parlor—you know? Where you go to get unwanted hair removed?—and he's had two men staffing it at all times, from nine in the morning until nine-thirty at night!"

Doyle frowned thoughtfully. "Did he . . . say why?"

"He sure did." The beers arrived and Benner took a hearty swig. "He told us all to keep our eyes peeled for a man who'll have five o'clock shadow all over himself and ask for an all-body treatment. Darrow told us to shoot him with a tranquilizer gun, tie him up, and carry him upstairs, and not to hurt him at all beyond the tranquilizer bullet, which damn well better not hit him in the face or throat. And get this, Brendan: I asked him, boss, what does this guy look like? I mean, aside from having whiskers all over himself. You know what Darrow told me? He said, I don't know, and even if I did know, the description would only be good for a week or so. Now—are those the words and actions of a sane man?"

"Maybe, maybe not," said Doyle slowly, eyebrows raised, reflecting that he now knew far more about Darrow's plans than Benner did. "How does all this bear on your plan to get us home?"

"Well—say, do you still have your mobile hook? Good—Darrow knows the times and locations of all the gaps. And they're pretty frequent around now, the 1814 one isn't the closest. So we'll bargain with him, get him to tell us the location of the next one, and we'll go and be standing in its field when it comes to an end, and snap! Back we'll be in that empty lot in modern London."

Doyle took a long puff on the—he had to admit—excellent cigar, and chased it with a sip of beer. "And what are we selling?"

"Hm? Oh, didn't I say? I've found his hairy man. Yesterday he came in, just like the old man said he would. Short, chubby red-haired guy with sure enough five o'clock shadow all over him. When I started edging toward the trank gun he got spooked and ran out, but," Benner smiled proudly, "I followed him to where he lives. So this morning I was listening in on Darrow's room—trying to find out if he was in a mood to be approached with an offer of you give me my hook and tell me where's a gap and I'll tell you where your hairy man lives, and by God, I hear Darrow telling Clitheroe to tell all the boys Benner is to be shot on sight! Seems he doesn't trust me. So after emptying one of the cash boxes, I split, and went and talked to the hairy man myself. Had lunch with him just a few hours ago."

"You did?" Doyle thought he'd rather have lunch with Jack the Ripper than Dog-Face Joe.

"Yeah. Not a bad guy, really—wild-eyed, and talks about immortality and Egyptian gods all the time, but damned well educated. I told him Darrow did have the power to cure his hyperpilosity, but had some questions for him. I hinted that the old man intended to torture him—which, for all I know, he may—and that he'd need a middleman, a mouthpiece, to deal with Darrow through. I said I'd been one of Darrow's boys, but had quit when I heard about the atrocities he planned to commit upon this poor son of a bitch. See? But I still had the problem of the shoot Benner on sight order Darrow had given his men." Benner grinned. "So you become my partner. You talk to Darrow, negotiate the deal, and then you share the payoff—a trip home. I figure you'll say something like this." Benner sat back and cocked an eyebrow at Doyle. "We'll tell old King Kong not to come see you, Darrow, until he gets a letter from us. And we'll give that letter to a friend—I know just the girl for it—with instructions to mail it only if she sees us disappear through one of the gaps. So you give us a hook and the location of a gap, and if our girl sees our empty clothes fall—and you see, she might be a hundred yards away in a treetop or window, so you can't hope to find her—*then* your hairy man will get the go see Darrow message."

Doyle had been trying to interrupt. "But Benner," he said now, "you forget that Darrow's issued a kill Doyle order too. I can't approach him."

"Nobody's after *you*, Brendan," said Benner patiently. "For one thing, everybody thinks I killed you, and for another, they remember you as the chubby, healthy-looking guy who gave the speech on Coleridge. Have you looked in a mirror lately? You're *emaciated*, and pale as a guy in a Fritz Eichenberg engraving, and there's about a hundred new lines in your face—shall I go on? Okay—and now you're *definitely* bald, and to top it all off, your goddamn *ear* seems to be gone. How'd you do that? And I noticed the other day you walk funny. Frankly you look twenty years older. Nobody's going to look at you and think, Aha, Brendan Doyle. So don't worry. You just go into that depilatory parlor and say something like, 'Hi there, a friend of mine grows fur all over his body, let me talk to your boss.' And then when you see Darrow you set up the deal. At that point you can admit you're Doyle—he won't dare hurt his only link with Mighty Joe Young.''

Doyle nodded thoughtfully. "It's not bad, Benner. Complicated, but not bad." Doyle was pretty sure he knew what Darrow was trying to do . . . and, incidentally, why the old man had a copy of Lord Robb's *Journal*. It's his cancer, he told himself. He can't cure it, but as soon as he acquired time travel he also acquired access to a guy that can switch bodies. So he gets a copy of Lord Robb because it contains the only mention of the time, place and circumstances of Dog-Face Joe's vigilante-style execution in 1811. Not a bad bit of knowledge to bargain with!

"Damn it, are you listening to me, Brendan?"

"Sorry. What?"

"Listen to me, this is important. Now today is Tuesday. How about if Saturday I meet you at—do you know Jonathen's, in Exchange Alley up by the bank? Well, let's meet there at about noon. By then I can have set up this letter business with my girl and the hairy man, and you can go see Darrow. Okay?"

"How am I supposed to survive until Saturday? You made me lose my job when you shot me."

"Oh, sorry. Here." Benner dug into his pocket and tossed five crumpled five-pound notes onto the table. "That hold you?"

"It ought to." Doyle stuffed them into his own pocket, and then got to his feet. Benner held out his hand, but Doyle only smiled. "No, Benner. I'll cooperate with you, but I won't shake hands with a guy who'd try to kill an old friend just to get his own ass out of a sling."

Benner closed his hand with a soft clap, and smiled. "Say that again after you've been in the same spot and acted differently, old buddy. Then maybe I'll be ashamed. See you Saturday.''

"Right." Doyle started to leave, then turned back to Benner. "This is a good cigar. Where'd you get it? I've been wondering what the cigars are like in 1810, and now I can afford them."

"Sorry, Brendan. It's an Upmann, vintage 1983. I stole a box of them from Darrow when I left."

"Oh." Doyle walked to the door and stepped outside onto the pavement. The moon was up, and the shadows of racing clouds swept along the street and the housefronts like furtive ghosts in a hurry to get to the river. An old man was hunching along over the gutter in the middle of the street, and as Doyle watched he stooped and picked up a tattered cigar butt.

Doyle walked up to him. "Here," he said, holding out his own lit cigar. "Never mind that trash. Have an Upmann butt."

The old man looked up at him wrathfully. "Up mah what?"

Too weary to explain, Doyle hurried away.

Wealthy enough now to indulge himself, Doyle took a room at the Hospitable Squires in Pancras Lane, for all the sources agreed that this was where William Ashbless stayed during the first couple of weeks after his arrival in London; and though he was surprised to learn that the landlord had never heard of Ashbless, nor ever rented a room to a tall, burly blond man, with or without a beard, the matter of Ashbless' absence was a good deal less urgent to Doyle now that he was in on the deal with Benner.

He spent the next three days simply relaxing. His cough didn't seem to be getting any worse—if anything, it was receding—and the fever he'd been living with for two weeks had evidently been purged from him by Kusiak's spicy fish chowder and beer. For fear of Horrabin's people, or Darrow's, he didn't stray far from his inn, but there was a narrow balcony outside his window from which, he discovered, he could climb up shingled eaves to the roof of the building; and on a flat surface between two chimney pots he found a chair, its wood whitened and split by decades of London weather. Here he sat in the long twilights, looking down across the descending terraces of Fish and Thames streets to the misted river, its boats tacking down the tide with an appearance of unhurried serenity; he would have tobacco and a tinderbox lying on the wide brick collar of the chimney pot at his left, and a bucket of cool beer on the roof below his right hand, and alternately puffing on his pipe and taking sips from his ceramic cup, he would look out across the almost Byzantine tangle of rooftops and towers and columns of smoke, all dominated by the dome of St. Paul's Cathedral way out across the city to his right, and he considered, with the comfortable detachment of one from whom a decision is not immediately required, simply not meeting Benner, and instead living out his life in this half-century that was to be characterized by Napoleon, Wellington, Goethe and Byron.

The three-day rest was marred by only one distasteful event. On Thursday morning as Doyle was returning home from a bookseller's in Cheapside, a shockingly deformed old man hunched and flapped up to Doyle, seeming to propel himself as much by the swimming motions of his driftwood hands as by the use of his feet. The bald head that stuck out from the collection of ancient clothing like a mushroom growing on a compost heap had at one time suffered a tremendous injury, for the nose, the left eye and the left half of the jaw were gone, replaced by deeply guttered, knotted scar tissue. When the old wreck stopped in front of Doyle, Doyle had already dug into his pocket and produced a shilling.

But the creature was not begging. "You, sir," the old man cackled, "look like a man who'd like to go home. And I think," he winked his eye, "your home lies in a direction we couldn't point our finger at, hey?"

Doyle looked around in a sudden panic, but didn't see anyone who seemed to be confederates of this ruinous person. Perhaps he was just one of the ubiquitous street lunatics, whose line of gibberish chanced to have a seeming reference to Doyle's situation. He probably meant Heaven or something. "What do you mean?" Doyle asked cautiously.

"Heh heh! Do you think maybe that Doctor Romany is the only one that knows where the gates of Anubis will open, and when? Think again, Ben! I know 'em, and there's one I could take you to today, Jay." He giggled—an appalling sound, like marbles rolling down metal stairs. "It's just across the river. Want to see?"

Doyle was bewildered. Could this man truly know the location of a gap? He certainly knew about them, at least. And the gaps are supposed to be frequent around now; it's not unlikely that there'd be one open on the Surrey-side. God, what if I could get home today! It would mean ditching Benner . . . but that bastard has no claims on my loyalty. And if this is a trap of Horrabin's or Darrow's, it's needlessly roundabout. "But," he said, "who are you? And what will you get out of showing me the way home?"

"Me? I'm just an old man who happens to know something about magic. As to why I want to do you this service," he giggled again, "it might be that I'm not exactly a *friend* of Doctor Romany's, mightn't it? A case could be made for it being Romany I have to thank for this." He waved at the destroyed side of his face. "So. Interested? Want to come see the gate that will—or has, or is—taking you home?"

Lightheadedly Doyle said, "Yes."

"Come on, then." Doyle's devastated guide set off energetically down the pavement, again seeming to swim as much as walk, and Doyle started to follow but halted when he noticed something.

Dry leaves were clustered in waves along the pavement, and when the old man trod on them they didn't crackle.

He turned his awful face back toward Doyle when he noticed he had stopped. "Hasten, Jason," he said.

Doyle shrugged, resisted a sudden impulse to cross himself, and followed.

They crossed the river by Blackfriars Bridge, neither of them saying much, though the old man seemed to be as pleased as a child on Christmas morning who, now that everybody is home from Mass, is finally allowed to go into the room where the presents are. He led Doyle down Great Surrey Street and then to the left down one of the narrower streets and finally to a high brick wall that completely enclosed one fairly large lot. There was a stout-looking door in the wall, and with a grin and a horrible raising of both eyebrows, the old man held up a brass key.

"The key to the Kingdom," he said.

Doyle hung back. "This gate today just happens to be behind a door you've got a key to?"

"I've known . . . for quite a while! . . . what was here," the old man said, almost solemnly. "And I bought this lot, for I knew you'd be coming."

"So what is it?" Doyle asked nervously. "A long-term gap, is that what you're saying? But it's no good to me until it ends."

"It'll be a gate when you get to it, Doyle, there's no doubt on that score."

"You make it sound like I'm to die in there."

"You won't die today," said his guide. "Nor any day to come."

The old man was turning the key in the lock, and Doyle stepped back, but looked on uneasily. "You think not, huh?"

"I know not." The door was unlocked, and the old man pushed it open.

Whatever Doyle had expected to see, it was not the grassy lot visible through the doorway, with the weak September sunlight shining on the weather-rounded lumps of masonry broken long ago. The old man had scuttled inside, and was picking his way over the green hillocks; Doyle gathered his nerve, clenched his fists and leaped through the doorway.

Aside from the old man and himself and the remains of ancient walls thrusting up through the grass, the walled-in lot was completely empty. The old man was blinking his one eye at him, surprised by the suddenness of Doyle's entrance. "Close the door," he said finally, and returned his attention to whatever he'd been grubbing at in the dirt.

Doyle closed the door without letting it lock and strode over to his peculiar guide. "Where's the gate?" he asked impatiently.

"Look at these bones." The old man had pulled a piece of canvas away from a pile of very old-looking bones, some of them blackened as if by fire. "Here's a skull," he said, holding up a battered ivory sphere on which the cheek and jaw bones clung tenuously.

"My God," said Doyle, a little repelled, "who *cares?* Where's the goddamn *gate?*"

"I bought this place many years ago," said the old man reminiscently, speaking to the skull, "just so I could show you these bones."

Doyle let his breath out in a long hiss. "There is no gate here, is there?" he said wearily.

The old man looked up at him, and if his scarred face bore any expression, it was unreadable. "You'll find a gate here. I hope you're as eager to pass through it then as you are now. Do you want to take this skull with you?"

Just a street lunatic after all, Doyle thought, with some knowledge of the magical hierarchy in London. "No, thank you." He turned and plodded away over the unmowed grass.

"Look for me again under different circumstances!" called the old man.

When, promptly at noon on Saturday, Steerforth Benner strode in through the open doorway of Jonathen's Coffee House, Doyle saw him and waved, and pointed at the empty chair on the other side of the table at which he'd been sitting for half an hour. Benner's boot heels rapped on the wood floor as he crossed the room, pulled out the chair and sat down.

He stared at Doyle with a belligerence that seemed to be masking uncertainty. "Were you early, Doyle, or did I misremember the hour of our appointment?"

Doyle caught the eye of a waiter and pointed at his coffee cup and then at Benner; the waiter nodded as he tapped up the three steps to the main floor. "I was early, Benner. You did say noon." He looked more closely at his table mate—Benner's eyes seemed to be a bit out of focus. "You all right? You look . . . hung over or something."

Benner looked at him suspiciously. "Hung over, you say?"

"Right. Out late drinking last night, were you?"

"Ah! Yes." The waiter arrived with his cup of steaming coffee, and Benner hastily ordered two kidney pies. "No better remedy for the effects of overindulgence than a bit of food, eh?"

"Sure," said Doyle unenthusiastically. "You know, we're both going to have some readjustment to do when we get back—you've not only picked up an accent, you're using archaic phrasing, too."

Benner laughed, but it seemed forced. "Well, of course. It's been my intention to seem . . . indigenous to this ancient period."

"I think you're overdoing it, but never mind. Have you got it all set up?"

"Oh yes, yes of course, no problem at all."

Doyle reflected that Benner must be very hungry, for he kept looking around impatiently for the waiter. "The girl will do it?" Doyle asked.

"Certes the girl will do it, she'll do it splendid. Where in *hell* is that man with our pies?"

"Screw the goddamn pies," said Doyle impatiently. "What's the story? Has there been a hitch? How come you're acting so strangely?"

"No no, no hitch," said Benner. "I'm just hungry."

"So when do I go see Darrow?" Doyle asked. "Today? Tomorrow?"

"Not so soon, must give it a few days. Ah, here are our pies! Thank you. Fall to, Doyle, don't want to let it get cold."

"You have mine," said Doyle, who had never been able to stand the thought of eating kidneys. "So why do we have to wait a few days? Have you lost the hairy man?"

"You eat your damned pie. I ordered it for you."

Doyle rolled his eyes impatiently. "Stop trying to change the subject. Why the wait?"

"Darrow's going to be out of town until, uh, Tuesday night. Would you rather have some soup?"

"Not *anything*, thank you," said Doyle very distinctly. "So let's say I go see him Wednesday morning?"

"Yes. Oh, and also I was concerned about a man who seems to be following me. I can't imagine who he is—a short man with a black beard. I think I eluded him when I came here, but I'd like to be certain. Would you go look outside and see if he's hanging about? If he is, I don't want him to know I'm aware of him."

Doyle sighed, but got up and walked to the door and, stepping out onto the pavement, looked up and down the sunlit expanse of Threadneedle Street. The street was crowded, but Doyle, ducking and *pardon me*-ing and standing on tiptoe, couldn't see any short, black-bearded man. Someone was hoarsely screaming up the street to his right, and heads were craning in that direction, but Doyle wasn't interested in finding out what the commotion was about. He went back inside and returned to the table.

"I didn't see him." Doyle sat down.. Benner was stirring a cup of tea that hadn't been there when Doyle went out. "How long has he been following you? And where did you first notice him?"

"Well . . . " Benner sipped the tea noisily. "Damn, they serve fine tea here. Try some." He held the cup toward Doyle.

The yelling outside was getting louder and more general, and Doyle had to lean forward to be heard. "No, thank you. Will you answer me?"

"Yes, I'll answer. But first, please try some. It's really very good. I'm beginning to think you fancy yourself above eating or drinking with me."

"Oh for God's sake, Benner." Doyle took the cup and

tilted it impatiently to his lips, and just as he opened his mouth for a sip Benner reached out and lifted the bottom of the cup, so that Doyle got a real solid gulp. He only just managed to keep from choking on it. "Damn you," he sputtered when he'd swallowed it, "are you crazy?"

"I simply wanted you to get a good draught of it," Benner said happily. "Isn't it savory?"

Doyle smacked his puckered lips. The stuff had been bitterly spicy and thick with leaves and, like a red wine with a lot of tannin, so dry that it made his teeth feel raspy. "It's horrible," he told Benner, and then a disquieting thought struck him. "You son of a bitch, let me see you drink some."

Benner cupped a hand to his ear. "I beg your pardon? There seems to be—"

"Drink some right now!" Doyle was almost shouting to be heard over the racket that was now just outside.

"Do you suppose I want to poison you? Hah! Watch." To Doyle's considerable relief Benner drained the cup with no hesitation. "You're no connoisseur of tea, Doyle, that's evident."

"I guess not. What in *hell* do you suppose is going on outside? But tell me about this bearded—"

There were some panicky yells in the room behind Doyle, by the front door, and before he could turn around there was an explosive crash and roaring metallic splash as the front window burst inward. The street altercation doubled in volume. As Doyle whirled out of his chair and onto his feet he was peripherally aware of Benner coolly leaping up and drawing a small flintlock pistol from under his coat.

"My God," someone was screaming, "kill it, I think it's going for the kitchen!"

Doyle could see a frantically churning crowd on the street side of the room, and sticks from shattered chairs were being swung as clubs, but for the first tense several seconds he couldn't see who or what was at the center of it; then a waiter was flung tumbling through the air to bowl down half a dozen people, and Doyle saw, in the small central clearing of the riot, a squat ape with fur the color of a red setter. Though shorter than most of its opponents, it managed by sheer, gibbering ferocity to burst through the hole left by the catapulted waiter, and in two bounds it had covered half the distance to Doyle and Benner's table. In the instant before Benner's gun cracked at his ear Doyle had time to notice that the ape's fur was mat-

ted with blood in a number of places, and that it seemed to be
bleeding more profusely through the mouth.

Doyle felt the concussion of the air slap at his cheek and saw
blood jump from the ape's chest as the slug hammered it right
back off its feet. Its shoulders struck the floor ten feet behind
where it had last been, and for one moment before its limp,
rattling collapse the creature was nearly standing on its head.

In the instant of ringing silence that followed, Benner seized
Doyle's arm above the elbow and marched him quickly into
the kitchen and through the back door into a very narrow,
shadowed alley.

"Go," Benner said. "This alley connects with Cornhill."

"Wait a minute!" Doyle nearly tripped over an old broken
cartwheel that had somehow eluded all the scrap scavengers.
"That was one of Dog-F—I mean, the hairy man's cast-offs!
Why did it come—"

"It doesn't matter. Now will you—"

"But it means he's in a new body now! Don't you understand—"

"I understand it better than you do, Doyle, believe me.
Everything's under control and I'll explain later."

"But—oh, okay. Hey, wait! Damn it, when will I meet you
again? You said what, Tuesday?"

"Tuesday's fine," said Benner impatiently. "Trot!"

"*Where* on Tuesday?"

"Don't worry about that—I'll find you. Oh, what the devil.
Tuesday right here at ten in the morning, does that make you
feel better?"

"Okay. But could you loan me some more money? I
don't—"

"Oh aye, aye, mustn't have you starving yourself. Here. I
don't know how much is there, but it's bountiful. Now go,
will you?"

The gray-haired waiter had swept the dustpan full of glass
bits, and with the napkin he'd tied in a turban-like bandage
around his head he looked like some sort of Grand Vizier
looking about for a sultan to present a heap of randomly cut
diamonds to. "I'm sorry, son, but things were too excited just
then for me to really take notes, yes?" He dumped the panful
of glass into the trash barrel and stooped to sweep up another
load.

"But he was heading for two men at a table?"

The waiter sighed. "Heading for them or more likely just making a break in their direction."

"And can you remember *anything* else about the man who shot him?"

"Just what I said, tall and blond. And the guy with him was short and dark and skinny and sick-looking. Now be off home, eh?"

There seemed nothing more to be learned here, so Jacky thanked the man and slouched disconsolately out onto the cobbles of Exchange Alley, where several men were gingerly loading into a wagon the red-pelted corpse of Kenny whatever-his-name-had-been, vacated a week ago by Kenny but only today by Dog-Face Joe.

Damn, Jacky thought. He's moved on, and now I have no idea at all whose body he may be in.

She stuck her hands deep into the pockets of her oversized coat and, picking her way around the wagon and through the pack of gawking spectators, ambled away down Threadneedle Street.

Halfway home Doyle started trembling, and when he'd got to his rooftop perch and downed a first quick beer he lowered his face into his hands and breathed very deeply until the shivering stopped. My God, he thought, so that's what it's like when the damn things appear. No wonder poor Jacky went a little mad after killing one, so that he believed he saw Colin Lepovre's soul staring out of the dying creature's eyes. Or, hell, maybe he did. Doyle poured and drank off another cupful of beer. I sure hope, he thought, that Benner knows what he's doing. I hope he knows what kind of fire he's playing with.

Doyle put down his cup and let his gaze wander to his left. And where is he now, Doyle wondered uneasily, and has the fur begun to whisker out like grime on the new body yet, and has he started looking for another one to take?

On the weathered stone doorstep of a little whitewashed house roughly two thousand miles southeast of Doyle's rooftop eyrie, a bald-headed old man sat stolidly smoking a long clay-bowled pipe and staring down the slope of dusty yellow grass at the pebbled beach and the water. The warm, dry wind was from the west, coming in with long ripples across the otherwise smooth Gulf of Patras, and in the occasional moments of its abatement he could sometimes hear the quiet clatter of sheep's bells among the foothills of the Morea behind him.

For the third time during that long afternoon the boy Nicolo ran out of the house, this time actually kicking the doctor's arm so that he nearly dropped his pipe. And the boy didn't even apologize. The doctor smiled coldly up at the unhappy boy, promising himself that one more piece of rudeness from this Greek catamite would result in an ugly, painful and prolonged death for his beloved "padrone."

"Doctor," gasped Nicolo. "Come now! The *padrone*, he rolls on the bed and speaks to people who are not in the room! I think he will die!"

He won't die until I let him, thought the doctor. He looked at the sky—the sun was well down the western side of the cloudless Grecian sky, and he decided that he could proceed now; not that it really mattered anymore at which hour of the day he did it—but old dead laws hang on as superstitions, and just as he wouldn't dream of pronouncing the name of Set on the twenty-fourth day of the month Pharmuthi, or willingly see a mouse on the twelfth of Tybi, he could not bring himself to perform a work of black magic while Ra the sungod was overhead, and might see.

"Very well," said the doctor, laying aside his pipe and getting laboriously to his feet. "I'll go see him."

"I will come also," declared Nicolo.

"No. I must be alone with him."

"I will come also."

The ridiculous boy had placed his right hand on the hilt of the curved dagger he always carried in his red sash, and the doctor almost laughed. "If you insist. But you will have to leave when I treat him."

"Why?"

"Because," said the doctor, knowing that this excuse would sit well with the boy—though it would have set *milord anglais*, inside, scrabbling for his pistols—"medicine is magic, and the presence of a third soul in the room might change the healing sorceries into malevolent ones."

The boy looked sulky, but muttered, "Very well."

"Come along, then."

They walked into the house and down the hallway to the doorless room at the end, and although the stone walls had kept the inside air cool, the young man lying on the narrow

iron bed was drenched with sweat, and his curly black hair was
plastered to his forehead. As Nicolo had reported, he was tossing fretfully, and though his eyes were closed he was frowning
and muttering.

"You must leave now," the doctor told the boy.

Nicolo went to the doorway, but paused, mistrustfully eyeing the odd collection of things—a lancet and bowl, colored li-
quids in little glass bottles, a metal loop with a wooden bead
halfway along it—on the bedside table. "One thing before I
go," he said. "Many of the people you have treated for this
fever have died. Monday the Englishman George Watson slipped through your fingers. The padrone," he waved at the man
on the bed, "says you are more of a periculo, a danger, than
the fever itself. And so I will tell you this—if he too should be
one of your many failures, you will follow him into death on
the same day. Capeesh?"

Amusement was struggling with annoyance on the doctor's
craggy and eroded face. "Leave us, Nicolo."

"Have a care, Doctor Romanelli," said Nicolo, then turned
and strode away down the hall.

The doctor dipped a cup into the basin of water that stood
on the table and took a few pinches of powder-dry crushed
herbs from a pouch at his belt, sifted them into the cup and
stirred it with a forefinger. Then he slipped one arm under the
delirious man's shoulders, lifted him to a half-sitting position
and put the cup to his still muttering lips.

"Drink up, my lord," he said softly, tilting the cup. The
man in the bed drank it reflexively, though he frowned, and
when Doctor Romanelli took the empty cup away the man
coughed and shook his head like a cat with a noseful of
something it doesn't like. "Yes, it's bitter, isn't it, my lord? I
had to down a cup of it myself eight years ago, and I still
remember the taste."

The doctor stood up and moved quickly to the table, for
time counted now. Romanelli struck sparks to a little pile of
tinder in a dish, got a flame, and held his special candle in it
until the wick wore a corona of round flame, then he wedged it
back into its holder and stared earnestly at it. The flame didn't
trail upward as a normal candle's would have done, but
radiated evenly in all directions so that it was a sphere, like a
little yellow sun, and it cast heat waves down as well as up,
making the hieroglyphic figures on the candle shaft seem to
shift and jitter like race horses waiting in the starting gate.

Now if only his ka in London was doing his part correctly!

He spoke into the flame. "Romany?"

A tiny voice answered. "Ready here. The tub of paut is fresh and warmed to the right temperature."

"Well, I would hope so. The way is paved for him?"

"Yes. The request for an audience with King George was acknowledged and approved earlier this week."

"All right. Let's line up this channel."

Romanelli turned to the metal loop, which was firmly moored to a block of hard wood, and with a little metal wand he struck it. It produced a long, pure note, which was answered a moment later by a note out of the flame.

The answering note was higher, so he slid the wooden bead an inch farther up the loop and struck again; the sounds were similar now, and for a moment the ball of flame seemed to disappear, though it glowed again when the notes diminished away.

"I believe we have it," he said tensely. "Again now."

The two notes, one struck in London and one in Greece, rang out again, very nearly identical—the flame turned to a dim, churning grayness—and as the struck metal was still singing he gingerly touched the bead, moving it a hairbreadth further. The notes were now identical, and where the flame had been was now a hole in the air, through which he could see a tiny section of a dusty floor. As the double ringing faded away to silence the peculiar sphere of flame reappeared.

"Got it," said Romanelli excitedly. "I could see through clearly. Strike again when I tell you, and I will send him through."

He picked up the lancet and a dish, and turning to the unconscious man in the bed he lifted a limp hand, sliced a finger with the blade and caught the quick drops of blood in the dish. When he'd got a couple of spoonfuls he dropped the hand and the scalpel and faced the candle again.

"Now!" he said, and struck the loop with the wand. Once more the note was answered, and as the candle flame again became a hole he dropped the wand, dipped his fingers into the dish of blood and flicked a dozen red drops through.

"Arrived?" he asked, his fingers poised ready to try it again.

"Yes," answered the voice from the other side as the ringing faded out and the flame waxed bright. "Four drops, right in the tub."

"Excellent. I'll let him die as soon as I hear it's succeeded." Romanelli leaned forward and blew the candle out.

He sat back and stared reflectively at the unquiet sleeper on the bed. Finding this young man had been a stroke of luck. He was perfect for their purposes—a peer of the British realm, but with a background of obscurity and near poverty, and—perhaps because of his lameness—shy and introverted, with few friends. And during his days at Harrow he had obligingly published a satire that managed to offend quite a number of influential people in England, including his sponsor, Lord Carlisle—they would all be willing to believe that he had committed the shocking crime that Romanelli and his British ka would make it appear that he had committed.

"Doctor Romany and I are going to propel you out of obscurity," Romanelli said softly. "We're going to make your name famous, my lord Byron."

Under the remarkably placid smile on the face of the severed head of Teobaldo, which had been set in a niche high in the wall, the clown Horrabin and Doctor Romany stared into the coffin-sized tub of dimly glowing paut in which the drops of blood had blackened, solidified, sunk to the mid-level and were now beginning to sprout networks of fine red webs, connecting one to another.

"In twelve hours it will be recognizably a man," said Romany softly, standing so still that he didn't bob at all on his spring-soled shoes. "In twenty-four it should be able to speak to us."

Horrabin rearranged his stilts under himself. "A genuine British lord," he said thoughtfully. "The Rat's Castle has had a number of distinguished visitors, but young Byron here will be the first," and even under his caked make-up Romany could see him sneer, "*peer of the realm.*"

Doctor Romany smiled. "I've led you into elevated circles."

There was silence for a few moments, then, "You're certain we have to do this no-sleep project tomorrow night?" said the clown in a whining tone. "I always have to have ten hours in the hammock or I get terrible back pains, and since my damned father," he waved at the dried head, "knocked me onto the ground, the pains are twice as bad."

"We'll each take turns, getting four hours sleep out of eight," Doctor Romany reminded him wearily. "That ought to be enough to keep you alive. Pity *him*," he added, nodding at the tub of paut. "He'll stay awake and be shouted at the whole time."

Horrabin sighed. "Some time day after tomorrow we'll quit?"

"The evening, probably. We'll hammer at him by turns all tomorrow night and all the day after. By evening he won't have any will of his own left, and after letting him be visible for two days we'll give him his instructions, and that midget pistol, and turn him loose. Then my gypsies and your beggars will go to work, and about an hour after my man in the Treasury announces that a fifth of all the gold sovereigns in the country are counterfeit, my captains will start a run on the Bank of England. And then when our boy Byron does *his* trick, the country should be virtually on its knees. If Napoleon is not in London by Christmas I'll be very surprised." He smiled contentedly.

Horrabin shifted on his stilt-poles. "You . . . *are* certain that'll be an improvement? I don't mind giving the country a whipping, but I still question the wisdom of killing it outright."

"The French are easier to manage," said Romany. "I know—I've dealt with them in Cairo."

"Ah." Horrabin heeled toward the doorway but paused to stare into the tub, where the red threads had now coalesced into a sketch of a human skeleton. "God, that's disgusting," he remarked. "Picture being born out of a tub of slime." Shaking his carnival-tent head, he stumped out of the room.

Doctor Romany too stared into the glowing tub. "Oh," he said quietly, "there are worse things, Horrabin. Tell me in a month whether or not you've found that there are worse things."

On the morning of Tuesday the twenty-fifth of September Doyle stood over the line of tobacco jars at Wassard's Tobacconist Shop, trying to find a smokeable blend in these days before humidification and latakia, and he was slowly becoming aware of the conversation going on next to him.

"Well of course he's a genuine lord," said one of the middle-aged merchants standing nearby. "He's pig-drunk, ain't he?"

His companion chuckled, but replied thoughtfully, "I don't know. He looked more sick—or crazy, yes, that's it."

"He sure do dress dainty."

"Yes, that's what I mean, it's like he's an actor costumed up to play a lord in a penny gaff show." He shook his head. "If it weren't for all those gold sovereigns he's flinging about that's what I'd guess it was—a prank to spark interest in some damned show; and you say you've heard of this Lord . . . what's his name? Brian?"

"Byron. Yes, he wrote a little book making fun of all the modern poets, even Little, who I'm partial to myself. This Byron's one of them university lads."

"Snotty, putting-on-airs little bastards."

"Exactly. Did you see his moustache?"

Doyle, puzzled by all this, leaned forward. "Excuse me, but do you mean to say you've *seen* Lord Byron? Recently?"

"Oh, aye, lad, us and half the business district. He's at The Gimli's Perch in Lombard Street, disgracefully drunk—or crazy," he allowed, nodding to his companion, "and buying round after round of drinks for the house."

"I may have time to go and partake," said Doyle with a smile. "Has either of you a watch?"

One of the men fished a gold turnip from his waistcoat and eyed it. "Half past ten."

"Thank you." Doyle hurried out of the shop. An hour and a half yet before I meet Benner, he thought; that's plenty of time to check out this Byron impostor and try to guess what kind of dodge he's working. Byron's not a bad identity for some con artist to assume, he reflected, for the real Byron is still fairly unknown in 1810—it'll be the publication of *Childe Harold's Pilgrimage*, two years from now, that'll make him famous—and so the man in the street wouldn't know that Byron is touring Greece and Turkey right now. But what kind of dodge is so big that it's worth "flinging about" gold sovereigns just to set it up?

He made his way south to Lombard Street, and had no difficulty picking out the Gimli's Perch—it was the tavern with a crowd of people blocking the street in front of it. Doyle sprinted up to it and tried to see over the heads of the crowd.

"Back off, now, Jack," growled a fat man beside him. "You'll take your turn like everybody else."

Doyle apologized and edged around to one of the windows and, cupping his hands around his eyes, peered inside.

The tavern was packed, and for half a minute all Doyle could see was clamoring drinkers, all busy at either draining filled cups or waving empty ones at the harried waiters and bartenders; then through a chance parting in the crowd he saw a dark, curly-haired young man limp up to the bar and smilingly drop a stack of coins onto the polished surface. A cheer went up that Doyle could hear right through the thick glass, and the young man was lost to view behind a forest of waving arms.

Doyle fought his way back to the street and leaned against a lamppost. Though the surface of his mind was calm, he could feel a chilly pressure expanding deep within him, and he knew that when it nosed like a surfacing submarine up into his consciousness it would be recognizable as panic—so he tried to talk it down. Byron is in Turkey or Greece somewhere, he told himself firmly, and it's only a coincidence that this lad looked—so damnably!—like all the portraits of him. And either this impostor is coincidentally lame too, or he so thoroughly studied his model that he's added the detail of Byron's lameness . . . even though nearly no one in 1810 would know to expect it. But how can I explain the moustache? Byron did grow a moustache when he was abroad—you can see it in the Phillips portrait—but even if an impersonator could somehow know that, he'd hardly use it in deceiving people who, if they'd seen the original Byron at all, had seen him clean-shaven. And if the moustache is just an oversight, something the impersonator didn't know Byron lacked when last seen in England, then why the accurate detail of the limp?

The panic, or whatever it was, was still building. What if that is Byron, he thought, and he isn't in Greece at all, as history will claim? What the hell is going on? Ashbless is supposed to be here but isn't, and Byron isn't supposed to be but is. Did Darrow shoot us back to some alternate 1810, from which history will develop differently?

He was feeling dizzy, and glad of the support of the lamppost, but he knew he had to get into that tavern and find out whether or not that young man was the real Byron or not. He pushed himself out onto the sidewalk and took a couple of steps and he suddenly realized that the fear building up within him was too primal and powerful to be caused by something as abstract as the question of what time stream he was in. Something was happening to him, something his conscious mind couldn't sense, but which was churning up his subconscious like a bomb detonated at the bottom of a well.

The crowd and the building in front of him suddenly lost all their depth and most of their color and clear focus, so that he seemed to be looking at an impressionist painting of the scene done only in shades of yellow and brown. *And someone's snapped the volume knob down,* he thought.

Just before light and sound flickered away altogether and, unsupported now, he fell into unconsciousness like a man falling through the trap door of a gallows, he had an instant in which to wonder if this was how it felt to die.

Sometimes hopping, but more often crawling on one foot and two hands like a half-stomped cockroach because his left leg had a new, grating joint in it, Doyle scuttled retching and gasping across the rain-slick asphalt, not even seeing the oncoming cars bow their front ends down close to the pavement as their brakes took hold and the tires began barking and squealing.

He could see the crumpled figure lying, in the random attitude of carelessly tossed things, on the gravel shoulder, and even though he was torturing himself toward her to see if she was all right, he knew she would not be—for he'd already lived through this event once in real life and several times in dreams; though his mind was incandescent with anxiety and fear and hope, he simultaneously knew what he'd find.

But this time it happened differently. Instead of the remembered porridge of blood and bone and bright-colored helmet fragments exploded across the pavement and freeway pillar, the figure's head was still whole and attached to the shoulders. And it wasn't Becky's face—it was the beggar boy Jacky's.

He sat back in surprise, and then saw, somehow without surprise, that he wasn't on a freeway shoulder at all—he was in a narrow room with filthy curtains flapping stiffly in an unglassed window. The window kept changing its shape; sometimes it was round, swelling and contracting like some architectural sphincter from the size of a peep-hole in a door to the size of the rose window at Chartres Cathedral, and at other times it elected to warp itself through all the shapes that could be called rectangular. The floor too was capricious, at one moment swelling so that he had to crouch to avoid bumping the ceiling, at the next sagging like a dissipirited trampoline, leaving him in a pit, looking up to watch the belly-dancing window. It was an entertaining room, all right.

His mouth was numb, and though the dentist, who wore two surgical face masks so that his glowing eyes were all Doyle could see, ordered him not to touch it, Doyle did surreptitiously drag a furry-gloved hand across his lips, and was terrified to see bright blood matting the golden fur. Some dentist, he thought, and though he forced himself out of that vision and back into the little room, he was still wearing the fur gloves and blood was still dripping energetically from his mouth. When he hunched over, huddling himself against another stomach cramp, the blood spattered the plate and knife and fork that someone had left on the floor.

It made him mad that whoever it was hadn't picked up their dishes, but then he remembered that these were the remains of his own dinner. Had it caused the numbness and bleeding? Had there been broken glass in it? He picked up the fork and stirred the bits of food still on the plate, fearfully watchful for any hard gleamings. After a while he decided there wasn't any glass in it.

But what was it, anyway? It smelled vaguely like curry, but seemed to be some kind of cold stew made of leaves and something that looked like kiwi fruit, but smaller and harder and more furry. His mind stuck on the rhyme of curry and furry—like a coin banging around in the intake hood of a vacuum cleaner, the evident relation of the two words held his attention and prevented consideration of anything else—but he finally got past it and experienced a moment of cold lucidity when he recognized the unusual fruit. He'd seen them before, in the Foster Gardens of Nuuanu in Hawaii, on a tall tree whose scientific name he still remembered: *Strychnos Nux Vomica*, the richest source of raw strychnine.

He'd been eating strychnine.

The water smelled terrible, implying a dead tide clogged with days-old fish corpses and putrid seaweed, but the sidewalk was alive with cheery people in colorful bathing suits, and Doyle was glad to see there wasn't a line at the Yo-Ho Snack Stand. He lurched up to the narrow window and banged his quarter on the wooden counter to get the man's attention. The man turned around, and Doyle was surprised to see that it was J. Cochran Darrow in the apron and white paper hat. He finally did go broke, Doyle realized sadly, and now he has to run a damned frozen banana stand. "I'll have a—" Doyle began.

"All we're serving today is activated charcoal shakes," Darrow interrupted. He cocked his head. "I told you that, Doyle."

"Oh yeah. I'll have one of those, then."

"You've got to make it yourself. I've got a boat to catch—it's due to sink in ten minutes." Darrow reached out through the window, grabbed Doyle by the collar and with a powerful heave pulled him in through the window until his shoulders jammed against the sides.

There was no light inside, and a cloud of ashes swirled up and set Doyle choking. He unwedged himself and fell back on the floor and saw that he'd wedged himself head first into the room's little fireplace. My God, he thought, I'm hallucinating up one side and down the other. Does strychnine cause delirium? Or have I managed to ingest a couple of poisons?

Darrow was right, though, he thought. What I need is charcoal, a massive dose of it—and *fast*. I remember reading about a guy who ate a ten times over fatal dose of strychnine, and chased it with powdered charcoal and felt no ill effects at all. What was his name? Touery, that was it. So where am I going to get some? Call room service and ask 'em to send up about fifteen hundred cartons of that cigarette with the activated charcoal filter.

Wait a moment, he thought. Here I am staring at a fair quantity of it. All these burned-up blocks of wood in the fireplace here. It may not be activated, but it'll still have billions of microscopic pores, the better to absorb you with, my dear strychnine.

In a moment he had found a bowl and a little round-headed statuette of some dog-headed Egyptian god or other, and was using them as a mortar and pestle to pulverize the black chunks of crunchy incinerated wood. While doing this he noticed that his hands and forearms appeared to have grown a pelt of glossy yellow fur, and this he ascribed, a little nervously, to the hallucinations.

Another explanation of the phenomenon patiently awaited consideration on a back burner of his mind.

Through it all the blood kept dripping from his mouth, often falling into the mound of grainy black powder, but it was tapering off, and he had more important things to worry about. How the devil, he wondered as he sifted the gritty black stuff between his furry fingers, am I going to consume this?

He began by swallowing all the charcoal pieces that were relatively pill-sized. Then, using water from a basin in the corner, he made little balls of the black powder and managed to force down several dozen of these.

Mixed with a little water the stuff was adequately malleable, and after a while he stopped eating the black lumps and began pushing them together to make a little man-shaped figure. His skill surprised him, and he resolved to get some modelling clay at the first opportunity and begin life anew as a sculptor—for he'd only rolled the limb columns between his fingers for a few moments before pinching them onto the trunk lump, but now he noticed that the swell of thigh and bicep and the angularity of knee and elbow were faultlessly done, and the few quick thumbnail scratches he'd made on the front of the head had somehow produced a face like Michelangelo's Adam on the Sistine Chapel ceiling. He'd have to save this little statue —sometime it would be reverently exhibited at the Louvre or someplace: Doyle's First Work.

But how could he have thought the face looked like Adam? It was the face of an old, a hideously old man. And the limbs were twisted, shrunken travesties, like the dried worms you find on the sidewalks on a sunny day after rain. Horrified, he was about to crush it when it opened its eyes and gave him a big smile. "Ah, Doyle!" it croaked in a loud, harsh whisper. "You and I have a lot to discuss!"

Doyle screamed and scrabbled back across the floor away from the gleeful thing—with difficulty, for the floor had again begun its rising and falling tricks. He heard a slow, tooth-jarring drumbeat from somewhere, and as huge drops of acid began to form on the walls, break surface tension and trickle down, he realized too late that the entire house was one living organism, and was about to digest him.

He woke up on the floor, profoundly exhausted and depressed, staring with no interest at the drops of dried blood spattered in front of his eyes. His tongue ached like a split tooth, but he didn't think it was anything urgent. He knew that he had survived the poisoning and the hallucinations, and he knew that eventually he'd be glad of it.

His face itched, and he brought a hand across to scratch it—then halted. Though the hallucinations had passed, the hand was still covered with golden fur.

Instantly the explanation, the explanation of all this, that had been in the back of his mind came to him, and he knew it was true. It increased his depression a little, for it meant more work for him when he gathered the energy to get up and begin dealing with things. Just to confirm it formally he felt his face. Yes, as he'd suspected, his face too was bushily pelted. All I needed, he thought sourly.

Obviously he was in the latest of Dog-Face Joe's cast-off bodies; and Joe himself was off God knew where in Doyle's own.

And whose body, he wondered, was this one I'm in? Why, Steerforth Benner's, of course. Benner mentioned that he had lunch with old Joe a week ago, and Joe must have fed him whatever mixture of alchemical herbs it is that unscrews the hinges of people's souls, and then on Saturday made the switch.

So, Doyle reasoned, it was Dog-Face Joe, in Benner's pirated body, that I met Saturday at Jonathen's. No wonder he . . . didn't seem to be himself. And of course that's why he was so anxious to have me eat or drink something there—so he could give *me* a dose of the soul-switch stuff; and when I didn't want anything, he had to send me outside to look for a doubtless fictitious man so that he could get a cup of tea, fling his filthy leaves into it, and harass me into drinking it.

Despite his weary apathy, Doyle shuddered when it came to him that the red ape that he had seen shot that day had been Benner himself, the poor bastard, carelessly shoehorned into Dog-Face Joe's last body.

So now, Doyle thought, he's got my body and is free to go see Darrow and make the deal, without having to cut Benner or me in at all.

Doyle sat up, permitting himself a loud groan. His mouth and nose and throat were crusted and rusty-tasting with dried blood, and he realized with a dull sort of amusement that good old Joe the Ape Man must chew the hell out of his own tongue just before vacating the body, to make sure its new tenant wouldn't be able, in the short time before the poison hammered him down, to say anything that might make people wonder.

He stood up—a little dizzily because of his new, increased height—and looked around. He was not surprised to find scissors, a brush and straight razor and a cake of gray soap on a shelf by the bed—Dog-Face Joe probably bought a new razor every week. There was also a mirror lying face down on the shelf, and Doyle picked it up and, apprehensively, looked into it.

My God, he thought, as much awed as frightened, I look like the wolf man—or Chewbacca—or the guy in that French movie of *Beauty and the Beast*—or no, I've got it, the Cowardly Lion of Oz.

Thick golden fur billowed in waves down over his chin, and outward across his cheeks to become exaggerated sideburns, and snaked upward along his nose to join the upside down waterfall of luxuriant golden fur that began at the eyebrow ridges and swept in a wild mane right up over the top of his head and hung down shaggily to his broad shoulders. Even his neck and the area under his jaw were thickly furred.

Well, he thought, picking up the scissors and stretching out a lock of his forehead hair, no point in delaying. Snip. There's one handful of it gone. I hope I still remember how to use a straight razor.

An hour later he had clipped and shaved his forehead—being careful to leave eyebrows—and his nose and cheeks, and he decided, before moving on to the tricky task of shaving his hands, to see how he looked. He leaned the mirror up against the wall at a different angle, stepped back and cocked an eyebrow at it.

His chest was suddenly hollow, so that his quickening heartbeat echoed in there like thumps on a drum. After the initial shock he began reasoning it out, and he almost wanted to laugh at the neatness of it. For of course I did go to the Jamaica Coffee House on Tuesday the eleventh, he marveled, and as a matter of fact I did write—or at least copy from memory—"The Twelve Hours of the Night" there. And I did stay at the Hospitable Squires in Pancras Lane. And this body did shoot one of the Dancing Apes in Jonathen's Saturday. It hasn't been an abduction or an alternate 1810 at all.

For Doyle recognized the face in the mirror. It was Benner's, of course, but with the wild mane of hair and the Old Testament prophet beard, the new, haggard lines in the cheeks and forehead and the somewhat haunted expression of the eyes, it was also, beyond any doubt, the face of William Ashbless.

BOOK TWO

The Twelve Hours of the Night

CHAPTER 8

"He told me that in 1810 he met me as he thought
in St. James Street, but we passed without speaking.—He mentioned this—and it was denied as
impossible—I being then in Turkey—A day or
two after he pointed out to his brother a person
on the opposite side of the way—"there"—said
he "is the man I took for Byron"—his brother instantly answered "why it is Byron & no one
else."—But this is not all—I was *seen* by
somebody to *write down my name* amongst the
Enquirers after the King's health—then attacked
by insanity.—Now—at this very period, as nearly
as I could make out—I was ill of a strong fever at
Patras. . . ."

—Lord Byron, in a letter to John Murray,
October 6, 1820

THOUGH IT HAD been difficult to find all the little motors and
get them correctly wound, and to adjust the air vents around
the dozens of concealed candles, the chest-high village *Bavarois*,
as Monsieur Diderac had described the appallingly
expensive toy, seemed to be ready to perform. All it needed
was for the candles to be lit and the master switch, disguised as
a miniature tree stump, to be clicked over to the right.

Doctor Romany sat back and stared morosely at the con-

traption. Damnable Richard had wanted to start it up so his
monkey could see it work before the yags arrived, but Romany
was afraid that a thing so complicated mightn't work more
than once, and he refused. He now reached out and gently
touched the head of a tiny carved woodsman, and gasped in
dismay when the little figure marched several inches down his
painted path, swinging his toothpick-hafted axe and making a
sound like a clock clearing its throat.

Apep eat me, he thought fretfully, I hope I haven't broken
it. Why have we all had to decline so, anyway? I remember
when the yags demanded fine chess sets and sextants and
telescopes for their services. And now what? Damn toys.

And they were never as respectful as they ought to be, he
reflected ruefully, but now they're downright rude.

He stood up and shook his head. The tent was murky with
incense smoke and he crossed bobbingly to the entrance flap,
lifted it away and hooked it to the side, and blinked in the sudden brightness at the heather fields of Islington.

It wasn't so far from here, he reflected, that, eight years
ago, poor old Amenophis Fikee gave himself to the dog-
headed god of the gates, lost most of his mind and all of his
magic—except that damned body-switching spell—and ran off
with a pistol ball in his belly and the mark of Anubis whisker-
ing out all over him . . . ran off to a dubious career as Dog-
Face Joe, the "werewolf" that London mothers threatened
badly behaving children with . . . leaving Romany, a ka that
should have been retired long ago, in charge of Fikee's post,
the entire United Kingdom.

Well, Romany thought complacently, the Master obviously
did a good job of drawing this ka; I don't think Fikee—or
even Romanelli!—could have done any better at the task of
maintaining and protecting the Master's British interests. I
suppose he'll retire me—render me back down to the primal
paut—after our coup here this week. I won't be sorry to go.
Eight years is long enough for a ka.

I do just wish, though, he thought with a narrowing of his
predatory eyes, that I could have solved the mystery of that
alarmingly well-educated group of magicians that made use of
Fikee's haphazard gates for travel. That one I had, that Doyle,
seemed like he would have cracked open nicely if I could have
had a little time with him. I wonder where on earth they came
from.

He cocked an eyebrow. But that should be easy to tell, he realized. Just calculate what other gate was open at the same time as the Kensington one. It was obviously one of those that exist in pairs, one big, long gate here and a little quick one over there during the period of the big one. They're not common, and in such cases I've always chosen to monitor the larger one, but they do occur, and this was obviously an instance of it. It would be easy to calculate where they embarked from, and it might be a useful bit of research to leave to my successor.

Turning away from the sunlight, he sat down at his table and began shuffling through the more recent stacks of gate locus calculations. He found the one for the first of September, and frowningly scrutinized it.

After a few moments he bit his lip impatiently, dipped a pen in an inkwell, crossed out a whole section of figures and began laboriously re-working them. "Shouldn't trust a ka to do high-level mathematics," he muttered. "Lucky I even plotted the Kensington one accurately. . . . "

His face went blank when he arrived at an answer, though, for the fresh calculations were identical to the ones he'd crossed out. He hadn't made an error—there really had been only one gap open that evening. The September first gap had *not* been one of the infrequent twinned ones.

So where, he wondered, did they come from? And the answer came to him so quickly that he grimaced with self-disgust at not having thought of it sooner.

Certainly, the people in the coaches had jumped from one gate to another—but why had he assumed that the two gates had to exist at the same time?

Doyle's crew of sorcerers had come to September first, 1810, from a gate in another time.

And if they can do that trick, thought Romany excitedly, then so can we. Fikee, your sacrifice may not have been in vain after all! Ra and Osiris, what could we—what couldn't we do? Jump back and prevent the British from taking Cairo. . . . Or further back, and undermine England so that by this century it isn't a nation of any consequence! And to think, all Doyle's party did with this power was come to hear a poet give a speech. We'll use it more . . . purposefully, he thought as a rare wolfish grin slowly split his face.

But, he thought as he reached out and drew closer the Candle of Far Speaking, this is too big a thing to keep to myself. He lit it with the flame of the oil lamp on the table, and the lamp's teardrop-shaped flame fluttered and seemed to recoil, when the little spherical fire bloomed at the tip of the magical candle's wick.

To the minimal, insect-reflex extent that he was able to be glad about anything, the smiling young man was glad that Doctor Romany's domination of him had not only removed his perceptibly burdensome free will, but also made an abstraction of physical discomfort. He was distantly aware of hunger, and cramped pains in his feet, and, much more distantly, of a voice that seemed to be howling in horror in the deepest cellar of his mind, but the fire of his consciousness had been doused with water so that the resulting steam could power some unimaginable engine; the few coals that still glowed could feel nothing but an anesthetized kind of satisfaction that the engine seemed to be working well.

Like a coachman instructed to ride around and around a certain block until his fare, ready at last, shall emerge from a house and hail him, the smiling young man began again at the top of the memorized page: "Good morning, my good man," he said. "I am Lord Byron. May I buy you a pint of something?" The ever-smiling young man didn't really hear the man's answer—it seemed muffled, as if spoken on the other side of a partition—but some part of his brain, or perhaps the engine, recognized it as calling for reply number three: "I certainly am, my friend—sixth baron Byron of Rochdale; I inherited the title in 1798, when I was ten years old. If you're wondering why a peer of the realm should be in a place like this, drinking with common laborers, well, it's because I think it's the common laborers that *are* this country, not the lords and royalty. I say—" There was the usual interruption that called for reply number one: "Innkeeper! A pint of whatever this gentleman will drink!" The young man's hand, like a precision machine, fished a coin from his waistcoat pocket and dropped it onto the nearest level surface, and then his mouth picked up the number three response exactly where it had left off: "—to hell with these men who are supposed to govern us just because of the womb they happened to issue from! I say the King, and you, and me, are none of us better than the others, and it's not right that some eat off silver and never work a day in their lives, while others just as good work backbreakingly hard every day and hardly taste real meat once in a week! The Americans rid themselves of that kind of artificial society, and the French tried to, and I say that we—''

He realized that the man he'd been reciting to was gone. When had he left? No matter—another would be along presently. He sat back, his blank smile returning to his face like something dead floating to the surface of a pond.

After a time he became aware that someone else had sat down next to him, and he started up again. "Good morning, my good man. I am Lord Byron. May I buy you a pint of something?"

He was answered with one of the sentences he had been warned he might get, and with an unfocussed uneasiness he responded with reply number eight: "Yes, my friend, I was travelling abroad until recently. I had to come home due to an illness, a brain fever, which still clouds my mind at times. Please excuse the uncertainty this infirmity plagues me with—do we know each other?"

After a long pause during which the still-smiling young man was aware of a vicarious sort of worry in himself, the man answered in the negative, and so with relief he went on. "If you're wondering why a peer of the realm should be in a place like this, drinking with common—''

The newcomer interrupted the recital with a question that, frighteningly, was not muffled: "How are you coming with *Childe Harold's Pilgrimage*?" the stranger asked. "Oh, sorry, it's *Childe Buron's Pilgrimage* at this point, isn't it? Ah—'Whilome in Albion's isle there dwelt a youth, who ne in virtue's ways did take delight . . . ' How does it go from there?"

For some reason these sentences hit the young man like a splash of ice water, and as they forced his hearing into clarity they did the same for his sight; his surroundings leaped from a congeries of comfortable blurs into awful focus, and for the first time in four days he saw a face clearly.

And the face of the man who had spoken to him was one that would attract attention—perched on impressively broad shoulders and a rope-muscled neck, and framed by a thick golden mane and beard, it was haggard, lined and mad-eyed as if with fabulous and harrowing secrets.

The no longer smiling young man knew that he'd been briefed on what to do in this situation—"If things become

close *up*, and *louder*," Romany had repeatedly told him, "and
you lose the veil of protection my guidance give you, return to
the camp here *instantly*, before the people in the streets tear
you to bits like a crippled dog in a ratting pit. . . ." —But this
bearded man's words had triggered something else, something
more important than Romany's command. Byron could hear
himself speaking: " 'But spent his days in riot most uncouth,
and vexed with mirth the drowsy ear of night.' " A swarm of
astringent memories seemed to be loosed by these somehow
very familiar phrases, and they stung like circulation returning
to a suddenly unconstricted limb; he remembered being
aboard the brig *Spider* with Fletcher and Hobhouse . . . the
Albanians at Tepaleen with their white kilts and gold-trimmed
capes, their belts bristling with ornate pistols and daggers . . .
the dry yellow hills and deep blue sky of the Morea . . . and
something about a fever, and . . . a doctor? His brain shut
down with an almost audible slam on that line of recollection,
but his voice continued, " 'Ah me! in sooth he was a
shameless wight, sore given to revel and ungodly glee; he
cheered the bad and did the good affright . . . ' "

A hand seemed to squeeze his throat shut, and he knew it
was Doctor Romany. In his head he heard the bald-headed
doctor's order: "Return to the camp here *instantly*."

He stood up, darting bewildered glances around at the other
drinkers in the low-ceilinged taproom, and then, muttering
apologies, limped across to the door and out onto the street.

Doyle leaped to his feet, but his new height made him dizzy
and he grabbed the table for support. My God, he thought as
he took a deep breath and then reeled off in pursuit of the
young man, it really is Byron—he knew *Childe Harold*, which
no one in England will see for two years. But what's wrong
with him? And what's wrong with history? How can he be
here?

He lurched to the door and hung onto the wooden frame as
he stepped down to the pavement. He could see Byron's curly-
topped head bobbing through the crowd to his right, and he
followed unsteadily, wishing he could make this admittedly
superior body work as gracefully as Benner had.

The people in the street seemed eager to get out of the way
of the lurching, mad-eyed, lion-headed giant, and he caught
up with Byron at the next tavern; grabbing his elbow, he
steered him forcefully inside. "Beer for me and my friend,"

he said carefully to the barmaid who was blinking up at him. Damn this cut-up tongue, he thought. He marched the ineffectually resisting young man to a table and sat him down, then leaned over him with one hand gripping the back of the chair so that his muscled arm barred any escape. "Now then," Doyle rumbled sternly, "what's the matter with you? Aren't you curious about how I happened to know those lines?"

"I—I have an illness, a brain fever," said Byron nervously, his smile seeming imbecilic when coupled with his evident anxiety. "I . . . must go, please, I . . . have an illness—" The words seemed to be jerked out of him one at a time, as if they'd been knotted along a piece of string that Doyle was pulling out of his throat.

Abruptly Doyle realized where he'd seen this mindless smile before—on the faces of the cultists who he used to see begging for change in airports and out in front of all-night restaurants. I'll be damned, he thought—Byron acts like he's been programmed.

"What do you think of this weather we're having?" Doyle asked him.

"Please, I've got to go. My illness—"

"What day is it?"

"—a brain fever, which still clouds my mind at times—"

"What's your name?"

The young man blinked. "Lord Byron, sixth baron of Rochdale. May I buy you a pint of something?"

Doyle sat down in the other chair. "Yes, thanks," he said. "Here comes the girl with it now."

Byron took a gold coin from his pocket and paid for the beers, though he didn't touch his. "If you're wondering why a peer of the realm—"

" 'For he through sin's long labyrinth had run,' " interrupted Doyle, " 'nor made atonement when he did amiss—' Who wrote that?"

Again Byron's smile disappeared, and he pushed his chair back, but Doyle stood up and blocked his exit again.

"Who wrote that?" he repeated.

"Uh . . . " Sweat broke out on Byron's pale brow, and when he finally answered, it was in a whisper. "I . . . I did."

"When?"

"Last year. In Tepaleen."

"How long have you been in England?"

"I don't—four days? I think I've been sick . . . "

"How did you get here?"

"How did I . . . "

Doyle nodded his shaggy head. "Get here. On a ship? What ship? Overland?"

"Oh! Oh, of course, I came back . . . " Byron frowned. "I can't recall."

"You can't? Doesn't that seem peculiar to you, that you don't know that? And how do you think I knew those verses of yours?" I wish I had Ted Patrick here, he thought.

"You've read my poetry?" said Byron, his weird smile returning. "You gratify me. But it all seems childish to me now; now I am pursuing the poetry of action, the well-placed sword rather than the well-chosen word. My goal is to strike the blow that shall sever the—"

"Stop it," said Doyle.

"—chains that restrict us from—"

"Stop it. Look, I don't have lots of time, and my mind isn't firing on all cylinders either, but your presence here—I need to know what you're doing here, I need to know . . . oh, hell, lots of things . . . " Doyle's voice was becoming a distracted whisper as he picked up his beer mug. "Whether this is the real 1810 or some fake one . . ."

Byron stared at him for a moment, then reached uncertainly for the other mug and brought it halfway to his mouth. "He told me not to drink," he said.

"To hell with him," muttered Doyle, wiping foam from his bushy moustache. "You going to let him tell you when you can have a drink?"

"To . . . to hell with him," agreed Byron, though speaking with some difficulty. He took a long, deep sip, and when he lowered the mug his eyes seemed more focussed. "To hell with him."

"Who is he?" asked Doyle.

"Who?"

"Damn it, the man who has programmed—sorry, harnessed, blinkered and saddled you?" Byron frowned in puzzlement, the new clarity in his eyes fading, so Doyle said quickly, " 'Good morning, my good man. I am Lord Byron. May I buy you a pint of something? If you're wondering why a peer of the realm should be in a place like this'—who said all that?"

"I did."

"But who said it to you, who made you memorize it? Those

aren't your words, are they? Try to remember who said all that to you."

"I don't—"

"Close your eyes. Now hear those words, but in a different voice. What's the voice like?"

Byron obediently shut his eyes, and after a long pause, said, "Deeper. An old man."

"What else is he saying?"

" 'My lord,' " and Byron's voice even went an octave deeper as he quoted it, " 'these statements and replies should be sufficient to get you through these two days. But if things become close up, and louder, and you lose the veil of protection my guidance gives you, return to the camp here instantly, before the people in the streets tear you to bits like a crippled dog in a ratting pit. Now Richard will drive you to town in the wagon, and he'll pick you up at six o'clock this evening at the corner of Fish and Bread streets. Here's Richard now. Come in. Ready to go? Avo, rya. Rya, that toy the foreign chal brought—let's start it up, my monkey would like to see it move. We'll talk about that later, if you please, Richard. Right now take milord here to town.' " Byron opened his eyes wonderingly. "And then," he added, in his own voice again, "I was in a wagon."

Doyle kept his face impassive, but his mind was racing. God help us, it's Romany again, he realized. What in hell is the man up to here? What can he hope to gain by brainwashing Lord Byron and turning him loose to make semi-treasonous speeches? He's certainly making the man visible—all I had to do to find him today was follow the rumors of the lunatic lord who's buying everybody drinks. Is he responsible for Byron being in England now? Anyway, I've got to hang onto this poor devil.

"Listen," he said, "you've got some high-octane memories to retrieve, and we can't do it here. I've got a room a few streets away—inherited it, sort of—and the people that live there aren't inclined to be nosy. Let's go there."

Still dazed, Byron got to his feet. "Very well, I suppose, Mr. . . . ?"

Doyle started to answer, then sighed. "Oh hell. I guess you can call me William Ashbless. For now. But I'm damned if I'll stay William Ashbless for the whole ride. All right?"

Byron shrugged bewilderedly. "That's fine with me."

Doyle had to remind him to pay for the beers, and during

the brief walk to the lodging house Byron kept craning his neck at the buildings and the crowds of busy people. "I really *am* in England again," he muttered. His dark eyebrows lowered in a frown that he wore for the rest of the walk.

When they'd reached the shabby building and picked their way up the stairs—which several families seemed to consider their personal chamber, swearing at the two young men and jealously hiding bits of horrible food as they climbed past—and reached the room that had once been Dog-Face Joe's, and when they'd filled two cups from the coffee pot that was still warm over the coals in the fireplace, Byron fixed on Doyle his first alert glance of the day.

"What's today's date, Mr. Ashbless?"

"Let's see . . . the twenty-sixth." Byron's expression didn't change, so after taking a cautious sip of the coffee, he added, "Of September."

"That's not possible," Byron stated. "I was in Greece . . . I remember being in Greece on Saturday the, uh, twenty-second." He shifted on his chair and bent down to pull off his shoes. "Damn, these shoes hurt," he began, then picked one of them up and stared at it. "Where on earth did I get these? Not only are they too small, they're about a century out of fashion. Red heels, of all things, and these buckles—! And how in God's name could I ever have put on this coat?" He dropped the shoe and said, in a voice so tightly controlled that Doyle knew he was scared, "Please tell me the true date, Mr. Ashbless, and as much as you know of what has happened to me since I left Greece. I gather I've been ill. But why am I not with my friends, or my mother?"

"It is the twenty-sixth of September," Doyle said carefully, "and all I know about your recent actions is that for the past couple of days you've been buying drinks for half the population of London. But I know who *can* tell you what's been happening."

"Then let's go to him immediately. I can't bear this—"

"He's here. It's you. No, listen—you were recalling verbatim conversations a few minutes ago. Do it again, and listen to yourself. Let's see . . . try 'Avo, rya.' Remember hearing that, in a different voice."

"*Avo, rya,*" said Byron, and the alertness fell out of his expression. " '*Avo, rya. He's very kushto with it. Handled guns before, it's clear. That's good, Wilbur. Though he won't need much skill—he should be only a few feet away from him when* he'll use it. Does he seem to be able to draw it with sufficient speed? I'd like to just have it in his pocket, but I'm afraid even a lord might have to submit to a search before entering the royal presence. *Oh, avo, rya, the little holster under his arm gives him no problem. You should see him—it's in his hand quick as a snake.* And he's shooting with no hesitation? It's got to be automatic. *Avo, the dummy is all shot to bits, he's done it so often—'* "

Byron leaped out of the chair. "Good God, man," he exclaimed in his own voice, "I was to go kill King George! What abomination is this? I was a puppet, sleep-walking, taking these diabolical instructions as . . . docilely as a maid would agree to serve dinner! By God, I'll get satisfaction for this . . . atrocious *affront!* Matthews or Davies will convey my challenge to . . . to . . . " He slammed his right fist into his left palm and then pointed at Doyle. "I think you know who."

Doyle nodded. "I think I do. But don't go off half-cocked here. You may as well inventory what you know before you rush into it. Tell you what—try 'Yes, Horrabin,' in the same voice that was asking the questions in that last conversation. Do you get anything from that?"

Though still frowning, Byron sat down again. "Yes, Horrabin." Again his face went blank. " 'Yes, Horrabin, I'd have that one killed too. This has got to run like clockwork, and it's conceivable he may know enough to obstruct it at some point. Better to err on the side of excessive thoroughness, eh? Incidentally, is the Antaeus Brotherhood still actually in existence? I mean, do they meet and all? If so, I say we destroy them too. They were evidently quite a thorn in our side at one time. *A hundred years ago they might have been, your Worship, but it's nothing but an old men's club these days. I've heard the old stories, and it certainly sounds as if they were formidable once; they're relics now, though, and obliterating them would only call possibly harmful attention to their history.* That's a point . . . very well, but post some of your people at wherever it is that these old men congregate—*Off Bedford Street, your Worship, rooms above a confectioner's—* and have them report back here if they see any . . . oh, never mind. I'm firing at shadows. Why don't you take his lordship here outside and run him through his lines again.' " Focus and intensity returned into Byron's eyes and he clicked his tongue impatiently. "This is worthless, Ashbless. I get nothing but incomprehensible dialogues, and I still can't recall one detail of how I got from Greece to here. I do remember being taught the route back to this man's camp, though, and I'll return, sure enough—but I'll bring a set of duelling pistols." He stood up lithely and padded to the window—which Doyle still half-feared would recommence its contortions—and stood with his arms crossed, staring vengefully out across the roof-tops.

Doyle shook his head in exasperation. "This man isn't a *gentleman*, my lord. He'd probably accept your challenge and then signal one of his men to blow your brains out from behind."

Byron turned and squinted at him. "Who is he? I can't recall hearing a name applied to him. What does he look like?"

Doyle raised his shaggy eyebrows. "Why don't you just remember? Hear the voice: 'Yes, Horrabin, I'd have that one killed too.' But don't just hear it—*see* it, too."

Byron closed his eyes, and almost immediately said wonder-ingly, "I'm in a tent all full of Egyptian antiquities, and the most hideous clown in the world is sitting on top of a birdcage. He's talking to a bald-headed old—good heavens, it's my Greek doctor, Romanelli!"

"Romany," Doyle corrected him. "He's Greek?"

"It's Romanelli. Well, no, I expect he's Italian; but he's the doctor that was treating me when I was in Patras. How is it that I didn't recognize him until now? I wonder if he and I came back here together . . . but why should Romanelli want the king killed? And why bring *me* all the way back from *Patras* to do it?" He sat down again and stared hard, even belligerently, at Doyle. "No joking now, fellow—I need to know the true date."

"It's one of the few things I'm sure of," said Doyle evenly. "Today is Wednesday the twenty-sixth of September, 1810. And you say you were in Greece only four *days* ago?"

"Damn me," whispered Byron, sitting back, "I think you're serious! And do you know, my recollections of lying sick in Patras don't seem more than a week old. Yes, I was in Patras Saturday last, and so was this Romanelli villain." He grinned. "Ah, there's sorcery in this, Ashbless! Not even . . . *cannons*, arranged in a relay system across the continent, could have got me from there to here in time to have been buy-ing drinks for people in London yesterday. Julius Obsequens wrote about such things in his book of prodigies. Romanelli evidently has command of aerial spirits!"

This is getting murky, thought Doyle. "Maybe," he said cautiously. "But if Romanelli was your doctor out there, then he's—well he's probably still there. Because this Doctor Romany, who's apparently a twin of him, has been here all along."

"Twins, is it? Well, I'm going to get the full account from the London twin—at gunpoint, if necessary." He stood up purposefully, then glanced down at his clothes and stockinged feet. "Damn! I can't challenge a man while I'm dressed so. I'll stop first at a haberdasher's."

"You're going to threaten a sorcerer with pistols?" Doyle inquired sarcastically. "His . . . aerial spirits will drop a bucket over your head so you can't see to aim. I say we pay a visit to this Antaeus Brotherhood first—if they were once a threat to Romany and his people, they may still know some effective defenses against them, mightn't they?"

Byron snapped his fingers impatiently. "I suppose you're right. We, you say? You have matters to settle with him yourself?"

"There's something I need to learn from him," said Doyle, standing up, "that he won't . . . willingly . . . tell me."

"Very well. Why don't we investigate this Antaeus Brotherhood while my boots and clothes are being prepared. Antaeus, eh? I daresay they all walk around barefoot on dirt floors."

This reminded Doyle of something, but before he could track it down Byron had struggled back into his despised shoes and opened the door.

"You are coming?"

"Oh, sure," Doyle said, picking up Benner's coat. But remember that remark about bare feet and dirt floors, he told himself. That reminds me of something that seems important.

The sweat drops were rolling like miniature crystal snails down Doctor Romany's bald temples, and his concentration was shattered by physical exhaustion, but he resolved to try once more to contact the Master in Cairo. The trouble, he realized, was that the ether was for once too receptive, and within probably ten miles the beam of his message became a cone that widened out and extended its energy in lateral spread rather than motion forward toward the candle that was always burning in the Master's chamber; and then the message shuddered to a halt, and rebounded back to Romany's candle, producing the loud, warped echoes that infuriated Doctor Romany and terrified the gypsies.

Again he held the lamp flame to the black curl of candle wick, and because this was the twelfth attempt, he could feel the energy drain out of him at the instant the round flame appeared.

"Master," he rasped into it. "Can you hear me? This is the Romanelli ka in England. It is urgent that I speak to you. I have news that may cause you to want to abort the present enterprise. I—"

"Gorble geermee?" His own voice, distorted and slowed, came back at him so loudly that he jerked away from the candle. "Dizza Rubberbelly kadingle. Idda zurjee . . ." Abruptly the idiot echo faded out, leaving only a sound like distant wind, waxing and waning as if heard through a flapping curtain. Romanelli leaned forward again. This wasn't the sharpening that indicated successful contact, but at least it was something different. "Master?" he said hopefully.

Without becoming a voice or seeming to be anything more than the sound of vast emptiness, the distant sussuration began to form words. "Kes ku sekher ser sat," the void whispered, "tuk kemhu a pet . . ."

The peculiar flame went out when the candle, propelled by Romany's fist, thumped into the side of the tent. He stood up and, sweating and trembling and bobbing unevenly, strode out of the tent.

"Richard!" he yelled angrily. "Damn it, where are you? Get your—"

"Acai, rya," said the gypsy, hastening up to him.

Doctor Romany glanced around. The sun was low in the west, throwing long shadows across the darkening heath, and was doubtless too concerned with its imminent entry into the Tuaut, and its boat trip through the twelve hours of the night, to glance back at what might be transpiring in this field. The rack of wood was laid out on the grass, looking like a twenty-foot section of a bridge, and the sharp aromatic fumes of brandy were so pungent on the evening breeze that he knew his threats had worked, and that the gypsies had used the entire keg to douse the wood and hadn't saved any for drinking.

"When did you splash it on?" he asked.

"Only a minute or so ago, *rya*," answered Richard. "We were drawing lots to see who'd go fetch you."

"Very well." Romany rubbed his eyes and sighed deeply, trying to thrust out of his mind the whisper he'd heard. "Bring me the brazier of coals and the lancet," he said finally. "And we'll have a try at summoning these fire elementals."

"*Avo.*" Richard hurried away, audibly muttering garlic, and Romany again turned toward the sun, which was now poised on the edge of entering the darkness, and while his guard was down the words he'd heard came rushing back to him: *Kes ku sekher ser sat, tuk kemhu a pet. . . .* Your bones will fall upon the earth, and you will not see the heavens. . . .

He heard Richard's feet swishing through the long grass behind him, and he shrugged fatalistically and began prodding his left arm with the claw fingers of his right hand, trying to find a good bountiful vein.

I hope they'll settle for ka blood, he thought.

The elderly man in the threadbare dressing gown lowered his white brows and widened his eyes in an almost ape-like expression of astonished disapproval when Doyle ventured to refill his tiny glass from the decanter of mediocre sherry, even though he'd only nodded and smiled and said, "Help yourself, my lord," when Byron had refilled his for the *second* time.

"Ah, hmm, what were we discussing, before . . . ?" the man quavered. "Yes, aside from . . . ah . . . *fellowship*, yes, promoting the . . . quiet joys of sensible company, our main purpose is to prevent the . . . pollution of good old honest British stock by . . . inferior strains." One trembling hand shook an incautiously large mound of snuff onto a lumpy knuckle of the opposite hand and then the old man snorted the powder up a nostril and seemed, to Doyle at least, almost to die of the resulting sneezing fit.

Byron made a silent snarl of exasperation and bolted his sherry.

"Mercy! I—*kooshwah!*—I beg your pardon, my lord." The old man dabbed at his streaming eyes with a handkerchief.

Doyle leaned forward and rumbled impatiently, "And just how do you go about preventing this, as you call it, pollution, Mr. Moss?" He glanced around at the dusty curtains, tapestries, paintings and books that insulated the rooms of the Antaeus Brotherhood from the fresh autumn breeze outside. The smells of candle wax, Scottish snuff and deteriorating leather book bindings and upholstery was beginning to make him feel ill.

"Eh? Oh, why we . . . write letters. To the newspapers. Protesting the, ah, leniency in the immigration laws, and proposing statutes to . . . ban gypsies and Negroes and, uh, Irishmen from the larger towns. And we print and distribute pamphlets, which," he said with an ingratiating grimace toward Byron, "tends, as you might imagine, to deplete the club kitty—ah, treasury. And we sponsor morality plays—"

"Why the *Antaeus* Brotherhood?" interrupted Doyle, angry that the vague hope he'd felt on hearing the name seemed to be proving so unfounded.

"—which . . . what? Oh! Yes, well we feel that England's strength, like that of Antaeus in, as it were, classical mythology, is based on . . . maintaining contact with the earth, the soil . . . you know, the solid native British . . . uh . . . "

"Soil," said Byron, nodding fiercely as he pushed his chair back and stood up. "Excellent. Thank you, Mr. Moss, it's been inspiring. Ashbless, you may stay and glean more *valuable information*, in case we should be attacked by savage Negroes or Irishmen. I'd sooner wait at my haberdasher's. *There* I shall simply be *bored*." He turned on his heel, visibly suppressing a wince as his shoe pinched his foot, and limped out to the hall. His irregular footsteps thumped and knocked down the patchily carpeted stairs, and then the street door could be heard to slam.

"I beg your pardon," Doyle said to the dumbstruck Moss. "Lord Byron is a man of tumultuous passions."

"I . . . well, youth," Moss muttered.

"But listen," said Doyle earnestly, hunching forward in his chair, to Moss' evident alarm, "didn't you people used to be more . . . militant? I mean like a hundred years or so ago—weren't things more . . . I don't know . . . serious in their consequences than a letter to the *Times* would be?"

"Well, there do seem to have been . . . excesses, yes, incidents of a violent nature," Moss allowed cautiously, "back when the Brotherhood had its quarters on London Bridge, down on the Southwark end of it. There are mentions in our archives of some rather—"

"Archives? Could I examine them, please? Uh, Lord Byron indicated he'd want to know the history of the Brotherhood before he decided to join," he added hastily, seeing the simian frown reforming on Moss' features. "After all, before he invests his fortune in an organization of this nature he'd like to check it out."

"Oh? Well, yes of course. Irregular, you realize," Moss said, precariously poling himself up out of his chair with a cane, "but I suppose in this case we may make an exception to the members only rule. . . ." Erect at last, he tottered toward the door behind him. "If you'd bring the lamp and step this way," he said, and the reference to a fortune earned Doyle the addition of a grudging "sir."

The door swung inward with such creaking that Doyle knew it hadn't been opened in quite some time, and when he'd stepped inside behind Moss, and the lamp illuminated the narrow room beyond, he could see why.

Stacks of mildewed, leather-bound journals filled the place from floor to ceiling, and had in places collapsed, spilling crumbled fragments of age-browned paper across the damp floor. Doyle reached for the top volume of a stalagmite stack that only came up chest-high, but rain had leaked into the room at some time and melted or germinated the ancient bindings into one solid mass. Doyle's prying was exciting to madness a nation of spiders, so he stopped and looked at a shelf that contained several pairs of mummified boots. Catching a glitter by the heel of one, he looked closer and saw a three-inch length of fine gold chain trailing from the ancient leather. All the boots proved to have chains, though most were copper long since gone green.

"Why chains?"

"Mm? Oh, it's . . . traditional, in our formal functions, to wear a chain attached to the heel of the right boot. I don't know how the custom got started, just one of those peculiarities, I expect, like cuff buttons that don't—"

"What do you know about the origins of the custom?" Doyle growled, for like Byron's remark about bare feet and dirt floors, this seemed to remind him of something. "Think!"

"Now see here, sir . . . no need to . . . wrathful tones . . . but let's see, I believe members wore the chains at all times during the reign of Charles the Second . . . oh, of course, and they didn't just staple it to the heel as they do now, the chain actually entered the boot through a hole and passed through the stocking and was knotted around the ankle. God knows why. Over the years it's been simplified . . . prevent chafing . . ."

Doyle had begun dismantling one of the drier and older-looking book stacks. He found that they were roughly chronological, arranged in the same pattern as geological strata, and that the journal entries from the eighteenth century chronicled nothing but a dwindling involvement in social affairs—a dinner at which Samuel Johnson was expected but didn't show, a complaint against adulterated port wines, a protest against gold and silver galloon, whatever that might be, adorning men's hats—but when he had unearthed the upper volumes of the seventeenth century the notes abruptly became sparser and more cryptic, and were generally slips of paper glued or laid into the books rather than written on the pages. He was unable to follow any gist of these older records, which consisted of lists, in some code, or maps with incomprehensibly abbreviated street names; but at length he found one volume that seemed to be entirely devoted to the occurrences of one night, that of February the fourth, 1684. The pieces of paper laid in it were generally hastily scrawled and in plain English, as if there hadn't been time to use a cipher.

The writers of them did, though, seem to take it for granted that any reader would be familiar with the situation, and interested only in the details.

". . . Then we followed him and his hellish retinue back a-crosse the ice from the Pork-Chopp Lane stayres to the Southwark side," Doyle read on one slip, "our party dex-'trously in a *Boat* with *wheeles*, piloted by B. and our unnam'd Informant, and although we took care to avoid any clear conflict while on the water, onely endeav'ring to drive them onto the land . . . the Connexion of course being no good upon the frozen water . . . there ensu'd Troubles." Another fragment read, " . . . destroied entirely, and their leader kill'd by a pistol-ball in the face . . . " Toward the front of the book there was an entry actually written on a page: "As wee were about to set about dynynge upon sawfages and a rare chine of beef, in hee burst, and sadlie call'd us away from what was to bee one of the fine dinners."

So what the hell happened, gang? Doyle thought. The "hellish retinue" sounds ominous . . . and what do you mean by "the Connexion"? He flipped hopelessly to the back of the book, and his eye was caught by a very short note written clearly on the endpaper.

He read it, and for the first time during all his adventures and mishaps he actually doubted his sanity.

The note read: "IHAY, ENDANBRAY. ANCAY OUYAY IGITDAY?"—and it was in his own handwriting, though the ink was as faded with age as every other notation in the book.

Suddenly dizzy, he sat down on a stack of books, which exploded to dust under his weight, spilling him backward against another pile, which toppled down upon him, burying him in damp, disintegrating parchment and showers of panicked spiders and silverfish.

The appalled Moss actually fled when the incoherently shouting giant, now garlanded with bugs and rotting paper, rose from the ruin like a Fifth Horseman of the Apocalypse embodying Decay.

The man who at this point didn't know whether he was Doyle or Ashbless or some long-dead member of the Antaeus Brotherhood got his feet under him and, still shouting, and slapping bugs out of his beard, ran out of the archive closet and through the sitting room into the hall. A cuckoo clock hung on the wall, and impelled by an impulse he didn't pause to question he seized one of the dangling pendulum chains, yanked the brass pinecone-shaped weight off the end of it, and then drew the end of the chain up through the clock's works and out free. He stumbled away down the stairs, clutching the length of chain and leaving the clock stopped forever behind him.

The heat of the burning platform was intense, and when Doctor Romany turned and took several steps away, the night air was frigid on his sweaty face. He clenched his fist and opened it, grimacing at the stickiness of the blood that had run down his arm during the repeated lancetings. He sighed deeply and wished he could sit down on the grass. At that moment it seemed to him that the freedom to just sit down on the ground must be the dearest of the countless things he'd had to forfeit in order to pursue sorcery.

Wearily, still facing out beyond the wheel of red firelight into the darkness that was connected to him by his long shadow, he took the stained lancet and the sticky bowl out of his pocket for one more try.

Before he could once more prod the exhausted vein in his arm, though, a voice like the drawing of a violin bow across a choked-up E string sang from behind him. "I see shoes." There was merry savagery in the inhuman voice.

"I do, too," replied another like it.

Romany breathed a sigh of thanks to dead gods, then braced himself for the always disconcerting sight of the yags, and turned around.

The awakened columns of flame had assumed roughly human outlines, so that at a quick glance they looked like burning giants waving their hands over their heads.

"*The shoes face us now,*" rang another voice over the crackling of the flames. "*I believe they must belong to our indistinct summoner.*"

Romany licked his lips, annoyed as always that the elementals couldn't really see him. "These shoes do indeed belong to your summoner," he said sternly.

"*I hear a dog barking,*" sang one of the fire giants.

"Oh, a dog, is it?" said Romany, angry now. "Well, fine. A dog couldn't unveil for you the excellent toy under the sheet behind me, now could he?"

"*You've got a toy? What does it do?*"

"What are you asking a dog for?" said Romany.

For a few moments the bright figures waved their arms without speaking, then one said, "*We beg your pardon, sir sorcerer. Show us the toy.*"

"I'll show it to you," Romany said, bobbing on his spring-shoes over to the shrouded shape, "but I won't turn it on until you've promised to do something for me." He drew the sheet off the *village Bavarois*, pleased to see that the candles all still glowed in their proper places behind the windows of the miniature houses. "As you can see," he said, trying to appear confident that the thing would work, and that the yags would keep any promise they might make, "it's a Bavarian village. When it's working, all the little men you see there walk around, and these sleds move, pulled by these horses, whose legs actually bend! And these girls dance to a, uh, refreshing accordion tune."

The tall flames were arched over toward him as if by a strong wind, and their outlines were no longer so carefully human, an indication that they were getting excited. "*T-t-tuuurn . . . it on,*" stuttered one of them.

Very carefully, Doctor Romany reached for the switch. "I will let you see it move for a moment only," he said. "Then we will discuss what I want of you." He clicked the switch over.

The machine inhaled deeply, then began cranking out jolly music as the tiny figures danced and marched and moved around. He clicked it off again and glanced nervously at the yags.

They were just columns of roiling flame now, with bursts of fire shooting out in random directions. "*Yaaah!*" a couple of them were roaring. "*Yaaah! Yaaaaah!*"

"It's turned off!" Romany shouted. "Look, it's off, it's stopped! Do you want me to turn it on again?"

The flames gradually settled down and reassumed their roughly human shapes. "*Turn it on again,*" spoke one.

"When you've done what I want done," said Doctor Romany, mopping his forehead with his sleeve, "I will."

"*What do you want?*"

"I want you all to appear in London tomorrow night—the blood and brandy fires will be set for beacons—and then I want you to remember this toy, and imagine what it will be like when you can watch it go for as long as you please."

"*London? You asked us to do this once before.*"

"The time in 1666, yes." Romany nodded. "But it wasn't me asking you then. It was Amenophis F—"

"*It was a pair of shoes. How should we distinguish?*"

"I guess it's not important," Doctor Romany muttered, feeling vaguely defeated. "But it's to be tomorrow night, do you understand? If you do it at the wrong time, or at the wrong place, you won't get to have this toy, or even see it again."

The flames swayed restlessly; the yags weren't inclined toward punctuality. "*N-never see it again?*" sang one, in a voice half pleading and half threatening.

"Never," affirmed Romany.

"*We want to see the toy work.*"

"Very well. Then when you become aware of the beacon fires, come quickly and animate them. I want you to go wild then."

"*We will go wild then,*" echoed a yag in tones of satisfaction.

Romany let his shoulders slump with relief, for the hard part was over. All that was necessary now was to wait politely until the yags departed, and the fire was once again just a fire. The only sounds were the flutter of flames, the occasional explosive snap of a splitting board, and, when the breeze was from the north, the muttered conversation of tree frogs.

Abruptly a shout sounded from the dark periphery of the camp: "Where are you hiding, Romany or whatever your name is? Step forward, you son of a bitch, unless the price of sorcery has left you a cowering eunuch!''

"*Yaaah!*" exclaimed one of the yags, simultaneously brightening and relaxing its human shape. "*Shoes is a cowering eunuch!*" A burst of billowing flame shot out, roaring like laughter.

"*Ho ho!*" the next one yelled. "*Young curly-head wants to extinguish our host! Can't you taste his wrath?*"

"*Perhaps he'll work the toy for us!*" yipped another, losing all consistency of form in its extreme excitement.

Doctor Romany cast a panicky glance toward the unseen intruder, agonizedly aware that the fire elementals were on the brink of going totally and disastrously out of control. "Richard!" he shouted. "Wilbur! Damn it, get that man at the south end of camp and shut him up!"

"*Avo, rya,*" wailed an unhappy gypsy's voice from the darkness.

"If you'll all just calm down," Romany roared at the yags, who by this time were exploding fiery pseudopods in all directions, "I'll turn on the toy one more time." In addition to being scared, Romany was angry, and it was not so much the intrusion that irritated him as the fact that the yags could *see* the intruder—and even read his mind to a limited extent.

"*Wait a moment,*" commanded one of the flame columns to the others. "*Shoes is going to work the toy again.*" The flames slowly and reluctantly resumed their human template.

There came no more shouting from the edge of camp, and Romany relaxed a little, light-headed in the aftermath of the crisis. His confidence was almost fully restored as he turned once again toward the *village Bavarois.*

Richard hurried up just as Romany was reaching for the master switch. The old gypsy's teeth were bared in a rictus of fear at being this close to the yags, but he walked right up next to Doctor Romany and spoke into the sorcerer's ear. "The m-man shouting, *rya,* it was your *gorgio* lord, come home early."

Romany sagged, his tenuous confidence abruptly eradicated like fresh ink washed from a page by a gush of ice water. "Byron?" he whispered, wanting to be absolutely sure of defeat.

"*Avo,* Byron," Richard muttered quickly. "He's wearing different clothes now, and he's got two pistols in a case. Wanted to fight a duel with you, but we've got him tied up."

The gypsy bowed and then sprinted wildly back into the darkness toward the tents.

That's torn it, Romany thought, dazed, as he automatically continued the motion of reaching for the master switch. He must have met someone who knew the real Byron; and whoever it was awakened him, broke my control.

He pushed the switch into the on position, held it there for a few moments while the mannikins moved and the music jingled and honked incongruously away across the nighttime fields, and the yags began billowing and roaring, then he clicked it off.

"I've changed my mind!" he shouted. "I've decided you can have the toy tonight—never mind London." The Master, he remembered ruefully, had said that the burning of London alone, if not coupled with both the ruin of the British money *and* the scandalous regicide, would be an inconclusive blow at best, and a waste of a lot of valuable preparation. "Wait until my men can load it on a cart, and then we'll carry it way out across the heath to the edge of the woods so you can enjoy it with, uh, a lot of elbow room."

Romany's voice was flat with disappointment, though the yags were flaring like powder keg detonations. "Take it easy now," he told them, "here in camp. Wait till you get to the woods before you cut loose. Listen to me, damn it, or you can't have the toy!"

At least there's the time traveling possibility to explore, he told himself as he turned to go fetch Richard and Wilbur. At least I don't have to report a *total* failure.

"They'll be shut down for the night," said the cab driver for the third time. "I'm certain of it. But see here, I can take you to a palm-reading lady I know in Long Alley."

"No thank you," said Doyle, pushing open the little door of the cab. He unfolded his tall frame out and stepped to the ground carefully, for the half-drunk driver hadn't secured the brake. The air was chilly, and the sight of flames flickering in the distance beyond the dark gypsy tents made the prospect of going in there at least a little more attractive.

"I'd best wait anyway, sir," the driver said. "It's a long way back to Fleet Street, and you'll not get another cab way out here." The horse stamped a hoof in the dirt impatiently.

"No, you go, I'll walk back."

"If you're sure. Good night then." The driver snapped his

long whip and the cab rocked and thumped away. A few seconds later Doyle heard the wheels rolling on the pavement of Hackney Road, moving back toward the dim glow in the southwest that was the city.

Faintly he could hear voices from the direction of Romany's camp. I suppose Byron must already be here, he thought. The haberdasher had said he'd left his shop a good half hour before Doyle arrived there, and had paused after getting his boots and clothes only long enough to ask where the nearest gunsmith was; and by the time Doyle had found the gunsmith shop, Byron had moved on from there too, having purchased, with more of the gold sovereigns Romany had given him, a set of duelling pistols. And then Doyle had had to stop a police-man to ask where Doctor Romany's gypsy camp was currently set up, while Byron already knew the way.

The damn fool, Doyle thought. I told him pistols wouldn't daunt the likes of Romany.

He took two steps toward the flame-silhouetted tents, then stopped. What exactly do you hope to do here? he asked himself. Rescue Byron, if he's still alive? The police are the ones for that. Make some kind of deal with Doctor Romany? Oh, right; sure, it would be useful to learn the location of the 1814 gap that Darrow's employees will jump back to 1983 through, so that I could be there and run up and grab one of them by the hand an instant before the gap closed—but if Romany thought I knew anything he wanted, he'd just seize me, not bargain with me.

Doyle rolled his shoulders back and gripped his hands together hard, feeling the flexed muscles strain against the fabric of his shirt. Though this time, he thought with cautious satisfaction, he might not find me quite so easy to overpower. I wonder how Dog-Face Joe is doing with my old body. I guess he's not one to worry about going bald, at least.

He could feel the vertigo coming on again, so he shook his head sharply, took several breaths of the chilly night air and strode forward through the grass. I'll just sneak around and reconnoiter, he told himself. Snoop. I needn't even get close to the tents.

A thought struck him and he paused. Then he grinned de-precatingly and kept walking, but a moment later he stopped again. Why not? he asked himself. Enough insane things are proving to be true for it to be worth a try.

He sat down in the grass, pulled his right boot off and,

with Dog-Face Joe's—or possibly Benner's—pocketknife he hacked a hole through the stitching of the back seam. Then he pulled down his stocking, fished the length of clock chain out of his pocket, tied one end of it around his bare ankle and put the boot back on. With the blade of the knife it wasn't difficult to draw the trailing end of the chain out through the hole so that the end of it dangled a foot and a half from his heel. He stood up and continued walking toward the tents.

The yags brightened and leaned over south, toward the tents. "Look at the confused man," chimed one. "Coming here without knowing what he wants."

"Or even who he is," added another with lively interest.

Doctor Romany glanced to the south, where he could dimly see Wilbur and Richard harnessing a horse to a wagon. It can't be either of them the yags are reading, he thought. It must be the Byron ka, his head full of contradictory memories and instructions, radiating confusion. If his emotions continue to excite the yags, I'll have Wilbur knock him out—or even kill him; he's of no use anymore.

Doyle could feel the bright flickering intrusions in his mind, like the hands and eyes of frisky children who, finding the library door unlocked, dart inside to feel the bindings and gape at the dust jackets.

He shook his head again, trying to clear it. What was I doing now? he thought. Oh, of course—scouting the camp to see where the fine toy is . . . no! Byron and Romany. Why, he wondered uneasily, did I think of a toy just then? A wonderful intricate toy with little men and horses running cleverly down little paths . . . his heart was pounding with excitement, and he wanted to shoot huge fireballs glaring out across the dark fields . . .

"Yaaah!" came a weird, roaring shout from ahead of him, and at the same time the flames beyond the tents flared up.

Distantly he heard a more normal voice yelling, "Richard! Hurry up with that!"

Whatever's going on over there, Doyle thought, it's certainly holding everyone's attention. He hurried forward, hunched over and keeping a broad tent between himself and the fires, and in a few moments he was crouched behind the tent, pleased to see that he was not panting at all.

The fluttering aliennesses brushed his mind again, and he

heard a wild, roaring voice say, "*His new body runs better!*"

My God, Doyle thought, his palms suddenly damp, something over there is reading my mind!

"Never mind him!" shouted the voice that Doyle now realized differed from the roaring ones in that it was human. "He's tied up! If you want the toy you've got to calm down!"

"*Shoes is no fun at all,*" sang another of the inhuman voices.

I've got to get out of here, Doyle thought, standing up straight and turning back toward the road.

"Richard!" called the voice Doyle now suspected was Doctor Romany's. "Tell Wilbur to stay with the—with Byron, and be ready to kill him when I give the word."

Doyle hesitated. I don't owe him anything, he thought. Well, he did buy me lunch and give me a couple of his sovereigns. . . . But hell, they were Romany's to begin with. . . . Still, he didn't have to help me. . . . But I *did* warn him not to come back here. . . . Oh, he'll be all right—he doesn't die until 1824 . . . in the history *I* remember, that is—of course in that history Byron wasn't *in* London in 1810. . . . Oh well, I guess I can at least keep an eye on things.

A lush old horse chestnut tree stood a few yards to his right, serving as a mooring for several of the tent ropes, and he quickly tiptoed over behind it. Looking up, he saw a branch that seemed likely to support him, and he leaped and caught it.

The chain that trailed from his right heel was suddenly swinging free in the air, and not touching the ground.

"*He is disappeared!*" exclaimed one of the yags, its voice screechy with astonishment.

"Wilbur!" yelled Romany. "Is Byron still there, and conscious?"

"*Avo, rya!*"

Then what, Romany wondered, is the yag talking about? Could there have been a stranger hanging about? If so, I guess he's gone.

Richard had cringingly drawn the wagon up beside the village *Bavarois*, and now stepped down from the driver's bench and approached the toy.

"Can you lift that into the wagon by yourself?" barked Romany tensely.

"I d-don't think so, *rya*," Richard quavered, keeping his eyes averted from the restless fire giants.

"We've got to get them out of the camp at once. Wilbur!
Kill Byron and come here!"

Richard winced. He'd killed several men during the course
of his life, but it had each time been a desperate, hot-blooded
and roughly equal contest, and only the reflection that he'd
have been killed himself if he'd held back had sustained him
during the subsequent hours of horrified trembling and
nausea; this cold throat-cutting of a bound man was not only
beyond his capacity to perform, but even, he realized unhappily, beyond his capacity to stand by and observe.

"Wait, Wilbur!" he yelled, and when Romany turned
wrathfully toward him he deliberately reached out and shoved
the master switch of the *village Bavarois* into the on position
—and then broke it off.

As soon as he'd heard Doctor Romany order Wilbur to kill
Byron, Doyle had crawled out along a nearly horizontal
branch, hoping to be able to see this Wilbur and pitch
something down at him, but he had not yet learned to allow
for the greater weight of his new body—the branch, which
would only have flexed under his old body's weight, bowed,
gave a groan that went up the scale to a screech, and then with
a rapid fire burst of cracks and snappings, tore right off the
trunk.

The heavy limb and its rider plunged through the top of the
tent below, demolishing what had served as the gypsies' kitchen; kettles, spoons, pots and pans added a wild percussive
clatter to the ripping and crashing and the ground-shaking
thump, and then very quickly the billowed out, slowly settling
tent fabric was illuminated from within by fire.

Doyle rolled off the collapsing tent onto his hands and
knees on the grass. The tall fires beyond the tents were billowing and roaring like a gasoline dump going up, and he decided
he must have been imagining things when, while still in the
tree, he'd thought the flames were shaped like men.

He hopped to his feet, wary and ready to run in any direction, and as soon as his chained foot touched the ground he
felt again the inquisitive flutter-touches in his mind, and he
heard one of the inhuman voices shout, "*There he is again!*"

"Hello!" came a similar voice. "*Brendan Doyle! Come see
our toy!*"

"Doyle is *here*?" he heard Romany cry.

"*Yaaah!*" something roared in a tooth-rattling bass, and a

horizontal column of flame lashed out an incredible thirty yards and made a torch of one of the tents. Over the screams of the gypsies who scrambled out of it, Doyle thought he could hear, somehow, a tinkly piano and an accordion playing merrily.

Bouncing as agile as a bug on his spring-shoes, Doctor Romany came high-stepping away from the fires, glancing wildly around, but he jolted to a stop when he saw Doyle standing by the burning kitchen tent. "And who are you?" he gasped. Then he snarled, "Never mind." The panting, sweaty-faced sorcerer reached one spread-fingered hand back toward the greater glare, as though drawing energy from it, and then jabbed the pointing finger of his other hand at Doyle. "Die," he commanded.

Doyle felt a cold grittiness strike him and freeze his heart and stomach, but a moment later it had drained away in an icy rush down through his right leg and out through his foot into the ground.

Romany stared at him in astonishment. "Who the hell *are* you?" he muttered as he stepped back. He reached to his belt and drew from it a long-barrelled flintlock pistol.

Doyle's body seemed to react of its own accord—he sprang up and forward and straightened his leg hard, driving his heel like a piston into Romany's chest; the wizard catapulted backward and landed on his back six feet to the rear. Doyle relaxed in midair and hit the ground in a crouch, and his left hand picked the falling pistol out of the air.

"Rya?" came a voice from behind him. "Do you want me to kill Byron or not?"

Doyle whirled and saw a gypsy with a bared knife standing and peering about at the entrance to a nearby tent. The man finally noticed the sorcerer rolling and flopping on the ground, and he turned quickly and re-entered the tent.

In two long, running strides Doyle covered the distance to the tent, and he tore the flap aside just in time to see the gypsy cock the knife back over the throat of Byron, who lay on a cot tightly bound and gagged. Doyle's arm was kicked upward by the gun's recoil before he even decided to shoot, and through the plume of smoke he saw the gypsy spin away to the rear of the tent with blood spattering from a hole in his temple.

His ears ringing with the bang of the shot, Doyle lunged forward, pried the knife out of the dead hand and, straightening up, sawed the blade up through the ropes around Byron's ankles and wrists.

The young lord reached up and pulled the gag away from his mouth. "Ashbless, I owe you my life—"

"Here," Doyle said, pressing the knife hilt into Byron's hand. "Be careful, there's wild things abroad tonight." Doyle rushed out of the tent, hoping to seize Romany while he was still rolling helpless and unattended on the ground—but the sorcerer was gone.

Most of the tents were blazing now, and Doyle hesitated, trying to decide which direction of escape would be safest. Then his eyes were strained with trying to focus on what he was seeing, for unless he was somehow grossly misjudging the perspective, he'd just glimpsed two—and now a third!— completely burning men, each at least thirty feet tall, running and bounding energetically, even joyfully, across the grass between the tents and the road. Two more ran past a moment later, as fast, it seemed to Doyle, as comets.

It looks like we leave, and damn quick, by the north end of camp, Doyle thought, but as he turned that way he saw the fiery runners lap the north side, too. My God, he thought, whatever they are, they're running in a circle around the camp!

He whirled to the south again, and in an instant two things were clear: there were now too many of them, racing far too fast, for anyone to hope to dart out of the circle between them; and the blazing wheel was growing perceptibly smaller with every second.

Romany called these things up, thought Doyle desperately, and if it turns out he can't send 'em back, it won't be for lack of me twisting his arm—or his neck. He's got to be in one of these tents.

Doyle sprinted toward the nearest one, his shadow fragmenting and whirling around him.

CHAPTER 9

"... through thine arm
The sons of earth had conquer'd; now vouchsafe
To place us down beneath, where numbing cold
Locks up Cocytus."
—Virgil addressing Antaeus
in Dante's *Inferno*

THE REQUISITE ENERGY will present no problem, thought Doctor Romany as he hunched over the papers on his desk and tried not to hear the screams of the gypsies who hadn't escaped, and the roaring of the now solid wall of fire spinning out of control around the camp; and by the degree of the angle at which I lay the glass rods I can decide how far I'll jump. But how can I get *back*? I'll need a vitalized talisman linked to this time ... a piece of green schist inscribed with this time's coordinates would be perfect ... he glanced speculatively at a statue of Anubis, in use as a paperweight, carved from that stone.

Over the calamitous noise outside he heard a crashing in the next tent, and a voice shouting, "Where's Romany, damn you? Are you hiding him in here?"

It must be that hairy giant who was somehow immune to my cold-cast, Romany thought. He's after me. There's no time to be carving stones. I'll have to do it on paper and rely on some of my blood—some *more* of it—to vitalize it.

As he rapidly scrawled Old Kingdom hieroglyphics across a sheet of white paper, he wondered who the bearded man could be. And where was Brendan Doyle?

The pen paused in midair as a possible answer occurred to him. Why, I'll bet that's it, he thought almost with awe. Of course—didn't the yags say: *His new body works better?* But he seemed so genuinely helpless when I had him. Was all that just an *act?* By Set, it must have been! Anyone who can get Amenophis Fikee to switch him into a superior body without poison in it, and can not only survive my best cold-cast but an instant later physically *disarm* me, is . . . well, not helpless.

As Romany continued drawing the ancient figures he tried to decide what time to jump to. Sometime in the future? No, not when it meant leaving tonight's debacle as established history. Better to jump into the past, fix things up so that the situation tonight's aborted effort was supposed to remedy never would have arisen in the first place. When had the Master's troubles with England really started? Certainly far earlier than the sea-fight in Aboukeer Harbor in 1798, after which anyone could see that the British were destined to control Egypt; even if that battle had fallen out the other way, and the French general Kleber had not been assassinated, England still would have been running things by now. No, as long as he was going to go back, he may as well go *way* back, to when England got its first toe-hold in the African continent. That would have been in . . . about 1660, when Charles II was restored to the throne of England and married the Portuguese princess Catherine of Braganza, part of whose dowry was the city of Tangier.

Romany did some rapid calculations . . . then scowled when he realized that there was no gap within twenty years of Charles' wedding. There was one in 1684, though, on the—he scribbled furiously—on the fourth of February. That was one year before Charles' death, during the Cairene Master's first attempt to establish the foolish and malleable royal bastard James, Duke of Monmouth, as successor to the strong-willed Charles. Fikee had been, for almost two decades, holding in abeyance the Newtonian recoil of the yag conjuring of 1666, and had been instructed to let the equilibrium spring back—in the form of a tremendous freeze—in coordination with the poisoning of the sovereign, the forging of a "newly discovered" marriage certificate between Charles Stuart and

Lucy Walter, Monmouth's mother, and the secret return of Monmouth himself from Holland.

As he hurriedly took out the well-used lancet for one more dig into a vein, Romany remembered what had gone wrong with that plan. The fatal dose of mercury wound up in the stomach of one of Charles' spaniels . . . and the Great Freeze, which was supposed to end with Monmouth's triumphal arrival in Folkestone, proved to be more forceful than Fikee had anticipated, and continued well on into March . . . and the forged marriage certificate in its locked black box had somehow been lost. The Master had not been pleased.

The tent walls were orange with the glare of the spinning ring of frenzied yags outside, and drops of sweat diluted the thick blood that he now carefully smeared around the paper's margins.

Yes, Romány thought, getting quickly to his feet and moving the glass rods on the desk top, that's where—sorry, when—I'll jump to. And I'll tell Fikee and the Master what their future holds, and tell them to forget about trying to control England, but rather to devote their energies to destroying her: work to make the frost continue and intensify rather than cease, pit Catholic against Protestant against Jew, murder the upcoming leaders while they're still children. . . .

He smiled as he caressed the glass poles into the perfect angle and then reached an open hand out toward the ring of racing fire elementals outside, to draw off from them the tremendous energy that would be needed to fuel and propel his jump through time.

Doyle slammed the clothes trunk shut and, ignoring the cowering gypsies who lay on the floor panting, ran outside. The blazing wheel around the camp shone as white as the sun, impossible to look at, and he was gasping in the depleted air, feeling the sweat steam away as fast as it appeared on him. Tents around the periphery were all ablaze, and even the inner ones near him had begun to smoke. My God, he thought fearfully, why doesn't he stop them? If the temperature in here goes up a few more degrees we'll all torch off like matches on a griddle.

He ran to the next tent, the fringe of which burst into a trim of blue fire just as he struck the flap aside and stumbled in. Doctor Romany stood inside, next to a desk, with one hand flung out toward Doyle and the other clutching a piece of paper. Doyle sprang at him—

—and was swept up on an incandescent wind. For several seconds he just hunched, waiting for a shattering impact, and then he was free falling through a silent and lightless void . . . until without warning light and sound abruptly crashed back at him.

He got a quick, bewildered impression of a large room lit by candles in crude wooden chandeliers, and then he was falling again, through air that felt shockingly cold, and a second later his boots crashed onto a table, one exploding a cooked, stuffed duck and the other splashing in all directions nearly the entire contents of a bowl of soup—his legs skidded away and he sat down jarringly in a platter of baked ham.

Spattered diners along both sides of the table yelled in astonishment and reared back, and Doyle saw Doctor Romany sprawled face down among the plates on the next table over.

"Excuse me . . . I beg your pardon," Doyle muttered in confusion, scrambling down off the table.

"Damn me!" exclaimed one pop-eyed old fellow, mopping at his shirt with a napkin. "What is this damnable trick?" Everyone, in the aftermath of surprise, seemed to be angry, and Doyle heard someone say, "Stinking witchery it is. Let's have them arrested."

Romany too had attained the floor, and spread his arms so authoritatively that the people who had leaped to their feet near him now stepped back obediently. "There was an explosion," he gasped, managing to sound stern as well as breathless. "Get out of my way, I must—" Then he noticed Doyle.

And despite his total disorientation Doyle was surprised and gratified to see the sorcerer turn pale and then whirl, and punch and curse his way to the nearest door, which he wrenched open. He shot Doyle one last fearful look before disappearing into the night outside.

"After him, Sammy, and bring him back here," spoke a calm voice from behind Doyle. He turned and met the suspicious gaze of a heavyset man wearing an apron and holding a cleaver with relaxed familiarity. "I heered no explosion," he said to Doyle as a burly young man hurried out after Romany. "You'll bide here until we determine at least who's to pay for the spoilt dinners."

"No," said Doyle, forcing his new voice to sound reasonable—which wasn't easy, for he'd noticed several men wearing wide-cuffed jackboots, knee-length vests and short wigs, and the accents he was hearing were nearly incomprehensible, and he was pretty sure he knew what had somehow happened. "I'm getting out of here, you understand. Now you can try to stop me with that thing, but I'm so scared that I'll make a real try at taking it away from you, and I imagine we'll both get hurt, and this looks like a lousy year to be injured in."

To emphasize his words he reached out and lifted an empty pewter beer mug from a table. Benner, he thought as he hefted it and got a good grip on it, I hope you were capable of this. He squeezed the mug hard, hard enough to whiten his knuckles—the chatter had subsided, and everyone, even the innkeeper, was watching with interest—and then he redoubled the pressure, feeling every little nick and pit on the surface of the cup biting into the insides of his fingers; his arm was aching all the way back to his shoulder, and trembling violently . . . but the cup didn't give at all.

After several more moments of useless straining he let off the pressure and gently set the cup back down on the table. "Very solid workmanship," he muttered.

Several people near him were grinning, and there was open laughter from the farther tables. A grudged grin was even breaking through the innkeeper's stolid frown. As Doyle turned to leave everyone began laughing, and like cracks starring a stretch of ice it broke the tension, so that he was able to thread his way, red-faced but unhindered, through the merriment to the door.

When he opened the door and stepped outside, the cold instantly burned his face and hands into numbness. His lungs retreated from the first breath he took, and he thought his nose must start bleeding just from the passage of the savagely frigid air. Jesus, he screamed in his mind as the door banged shut behind him, what is this? This can't be England—the son of a bitch must have jumped us to some damned outpost in Tierra del Fuego or somewhere.

If everyone in the inn hadn't been laughing at him he'd have turned around and gone back inside; as it was he pressed on, his stinging hands thrust into the pockets of his too-thin coat, and sprinted forward along the narrow, dark street, vaguely hoping to catch up with Romany and terrify the wizard into finding a warm place where he could just sit down for a while.

He didn't find Romany, but Sammy did, and Doyle came upon Sammy curled up in a narrow alley mouth about a block and a half from the inn; in the ashy moonlight Doyle might not have seen him, but he heard his hopeless sobbing. Frozen tears had attached Sammy's cheek to the brick wall, and there was a faint crackling when Doyle crouched and gently lifted the young man's head up.

"Sammy!" said Doyle, loudly so as to break through the boy's obsessive grief. "Where did he go?" Getting no answer, he shook him. "Which way, man?" The steam of his breath plumed away upward like smoke.

"He . . . " the young man gasped, "he showed me the . . . *snakes* inside me. He told me, 'Look at yourself,' and I did, and I seen all them snakes." Sammy began sobbing again. "I can't go back yonder, or home either. They'd get inside of everyone."

"They're gone," Doyle told him firmly. "You understand me? They're gone. They can't stand the cold, I saw every one of them crawling away to die when I got here. Now where did the bastard go?"

Sammy sniffed. "Be they gone? And dead? Certes?" He glanced fearfully down at himself.

"Yes, damn it. Did you see where he went?"

After patting and prying at his clothes with diminishing dread, the young man began shivering. "I m-must get back," he said, getting stiffly to his feet. "Devilish cold. Oh, aye, ye wanted to know where he went."

"Yes." Doyle was almost tap-dancing on the cobblestones in a fit of shivering. His right ankle was numb, and he was afraid that the trailing chain would freeze solid with his skin.

Sammy sniffed again. "He leapt over the house there into the next street."

Doyle cocked his head to hear better. "What?"

"He jumped over that house, like a grasshopper." Sniff. "He had metal coils on the bottoms of his shoes," Sammy added by way of explanation.

"Ah. Well . . . thank you." Obviously Romany hypnotized this boy with both barrels, Doyle reflected. And in only seconds! Better not let the fact that he seems to be afraid of you make you overconfident if you run into him. "Oh, by the way," he said as the boy began shuffling away, "where are we? I'm lost."

"Borough High Street. Southwark."

Doyle raised his eyebrows. "London?"

"Well of course London," the boy said, beginning to jog in place impatiently.

"Uh, and what's the year? The date?"

"Lord, mister, I don't know. It's winter, that's certain." He turned and hurried away back toward the inn.

"Who is king?" Doyle called after him.

"Charles!" came the over the shoulder reply.

Charles the whichth, thought Doyle. "Who was king before him?" he shouted after the disappearing figure.

Sammy chose not to hear him, but there was the snap and creak of a window being pushed open above him. "Oliver the Blessed," called a man's voice irritably, "and when he ruled, there beed not such street clamors at night."

"I beg your pardon, sir," said Doyle hastily, turning his cold-stung eyes upward and trying to spot which one of the dozen small paned windows was slightly open. "I'm suffering from a," why not, he thought, "from a brain fever, and I've lost my memory. I have nowhere to go. Could you let me sleep until dawn in the kitchen, or toss me down a more substantial coat? I—"

He heard the window bang closed, and the latch scritch tight, though he still hadn't spotted which one it was. Typical Cromwellian, he thought, heaving a sigh that sailed away as a small cloud. So, he thought as he slouched onward, I'm somewhere between, uh, 1660 and—what? When did Charles II die? Around 1690, I think. This is worse still. At least in 1810 I had the chance of finding Darrow's men and going home with them, or, failing that, to accept what fate seemed to have groomed me for and live out my life in fair comfort as William Ashbless. (Damnation, it's cold.) You idiot—why didn't you do that? Just write out Ashbless' poems from memory, visit Egypt, and let the modest fame and fortune—and pretty wife, even—roll in. But no, instead you had to go bothering sorcerers, and so now history's deprived of William Ashbless, and you're stuck in a damn century when nobody brushed their teeth or took baths, and a man is middle-aged at thirty.

He happened to be glancing up when a bizarre figure swooped diagonally across the narrow strip of sky visible between the overhanging rooftops—it was silhouetted for an instant against the nearly full moon—and he leaped backward

out of the street, huddling against the stones of the nearest
wall, though he knew he must be invisible down among the
shadows, for the impossibly high-bounding figure had been
Doctor Romany, unmistakable even for a moment and at a
distance with his bald head, flapping robe and the bottom sole
of each shoe flying two feet behind him on the fully extended
springs.

As his upward momentum disappeared and he felt gravity's
first faint cobweb net begin to coax him back down, and as the
nearer rooftops began to rise again, blotting out the frosted
splendor of the tall houses along the length of London Bridge
and the motionless white river that lay under it, Doctor
Romany realized that his leaps were not as high now as they
had been several minutes ago, and his envelope of agitated air
was losing its integrity and letting the intense chill in at him.
This was not really an increase in his powers, but just his usual
magical strength extending farther in the more archaic, and
therefore more conducive to sorcery, environment—and
already the effect was beginning to wear off. This is like, he
thought as he flexed his legs against an outcropping gable and
did a slow somersault down toward the cobblestones, a man
finding his customary sword light after practicing for hours
with a very heavy one: the sword is actually as heavy as ever,
and the delusion of new strength soon disappears. This apparent increase in my powers probably won't last the night . . .
and the gate at that inn we disrupted will close at about dawn.

Therefore, he thought as he arrested his slow fall by draping
an arm around the shoulder of an inn sign shaped like a dancing blackamoor, I shall have to get word to Fikee and the
Master as soon as possible, tell them who I am and why I'm
here.

One of the fine dinners this will be, thought Ezra Longwell,
who always relished the excellent food the Brotherhood provided for its members. He refilled his glass of port from the
bottle near the hearth—in this grim winter even champagnes
had to sit for half an hour by the fire before they were served,
and clarets and fortified wines needed a full hour and a half.
As he sipped the still chilly wine he crossed to the little Tudor
window, which the kitchen heat had kept unfrosted. He wiped
the steam off it with his sleeve and peered out.

West of the bridge, lights twinkled among the clustered
booths and tents of the frost fair that stretched across the
iced-over river from the Temple Stairs to the Surrey shore.
Skaters whirling lanterns raced merrily across the ice like
rockets or shooting stars, but Longwell was glad to be indoors
and looking forward to a hot meal.

He stepped away from the window and with one last affectionate look at the steaming pots—"Deal gently with those admirable sawfages!" he told the stout kitchen mistress—he
walked out through the hall to the dining room, the fine chain
on his ankle rattling faintly on the boards of the floor.

Owen Burghard looked up and smiled as Longwell entered
the room. "And how is the 'sixty-eight bearing up, Ezra?"

Longwell reddened as he crossed to his customary chair,
aware of the amused glances he was getting from the other
members. "Not too badly," he said gruffly as the chair
creaked under his weight, "though too damn cold."

"The better to temper your sanguine humors, Ezra," said
Burghard, returning his attention to the chart on the table. He
tapped the right-hand edge with the stem of his clay pipe and
said, in his not quite pedantic manner, "So you see, gentlemen, that these periods of increased activity on the part of
Fikee's band of gypsies—"

He was interrupted by a heavy pounding on the door.

In an instant all of them were on their feet, hands on sword
hilts and pistol butts, and each one of them had automatically
flicked the chain trailing from his right boot before standing
up, as though the free play of the chain was as vital as a
weapon.

Burghard crossed to the door, drew the bolt and stepped
back. "It's not locked," he said.

The door opened, and all eyebrows went up as what would
appear to be a giant from Norse mythology lurched into the
room. He was shockingly tall, more so even than the King,
who stood a full two yards, and his peculiarly cut and unsea-
sonably thin coat did nothing to conceal his broad shoulders
and muscular arms. His ice-crusted beard made him look ancient. "If you've got a fire," this frost apparition croaked in a
barbarous accent, "and any kind of hot drink . . ." He
swayed, and Longwell feared that the books would be shaken
from their shelves if this monster were to topple over.

Then Burghard had gasped, pointing at the intruder's right

boot—from which an ice-clogged length of chain trailed across the floor—and rushed to support him. "Beasley!" he snapped. "Help me with him. Ezra, coffee and brandy, haste!" Burghard and Beasley helped the faltering, half-frozen man across the floor to the bench in front of the dining room fire. When Longwell brought a big mug of fortified coffee, the giant just inhaled the pungent steam for a while before taking a sip.

"Ah," he breathed at last, putting the coffee down beside him and spreading his hands before the blaze. "I thought I was going to die out there. Are your winters always this bad?"

Burghard frowned and glanced at the others. "Who are you, sir, and how did you come here?"

"I heard you used to—that you meet in a house on the south end of the bridge. At the first place I knocked they wouldn't let me in, but they gave me directions to get here. As to who I am, you can call me—well hell, I can't think of a name that would do. But I came here," and a smile split the haggard face, "because I knew I would. I think you're the hounds I need to help me catch my fox. There's a sorcerer called Doctor Romany—"

"Do you mean Doctor Romanelli?" asked Burghard. "We know of him."

"You do? This far upstream? Good God. Well, Romanelli has a twin, called Romany, who has jumped—I think I may say by sorcerous means?—to your London. He must be caught and induced to return to . . . where he belongs. And with any luck he can be made to take me back with him."

"A twin? A ka I'll wager you mean," said Longwell, tonging up a coal from the grate and setting it carefully into the newly packed bowl of his pipe. "Would you like a pipe?"

"Lord, yes," said Doyle, accepting from him a fragile white clay pipe and a bag of tobacco. "What do you mean, a ka?"

Burghard squinted at Doyle. "You're a damn puzzling mix of knowledge and ignorance, sir, and sometime I would relish hearing your own story. For example, you are wearing a connection chain but don't seem to know much about us, and you know of Doctor Romanelli but don't know what a ka is or how it happens that this winter is so savage." He smiled, though a calculating glint remained in his deceptively mild-looking eyes. He ran his fingers through his short-cropped, thinning hair. "In any case, a ka is a duplicate of a human, grown, in a vat full of a special solution, from as little as a few drops of the original person's blood. If the procedure be done rightly, the duplicate will not only resemble the original in every particular, but will have, too, all the knowledge that the original had."

Doyle had stuffed his pipe with the dry tobacco and now lit it the same way Longwell had. "Yes, I suppose Romany might be such a thing," he said, puffing smoke and letting the fire melt the ice out of his beard. His eyes widened. "Ah, and I believe I know another man who is probably a . . . ka, also. Poor devil. I'm sure he doesn't know."

"Do you know of Amenophis Fikee?" asked Burghard.

Doyle looked around at the company, wondering how much he dared disclose. "He is, will be or has been the chief of a band of gypsies."

"Aye, he is. Why all the was's and shall-be's?"

"Never mind. Anyway, gentlemen, this ka of Doctor Romanelli is here in London tonight, and he's armed with knowledge no one here should have, and he needs to be found and driven back to where he belongs."

"And you want to go back with him," said Burghard.

"Right."

"Why employ such a perilous, albeit quick, means of travel?" asked Burghard. "By ship and horse or donkey you could be anywhere in six months."

Doyle sighed. "I gather that you function as a sort of . . . magical police force," he began.

Burghard smiled and winced at the same time. "Not precisely, sir. What we're paid by certain wealthy and savvy lords to do is prevent sorcerous treason. We employ not magic but the negation of magic."

"I see." Doyle laid down his pipe on the hearth. "If I tell you the story," he said carefully, "and you agree that this Romany creature is a—let's say direly powerful—menace to London and England and the world, will you help me catch him and then not hinder my return—if it's even possible—to where I belong?"

"You have my word," said Burghard quietly.

Doyle stared at the man for several seconds while the fire popped and crackled in the silence. "Very well," he rumbled at last. "I'll make it quick, for we must act soon, and I believe I know where he'll be for the next hour or so. He and I jumped here by some magical process or other, but not from another place, such as Turkey. We jumped from . . . another time. The last morning I saw was that of September the twenty-sixth, in the year 1810.''

Longwell burst into a gale of laughter which ceased when Burghard raised his hand. ''Go on,'' he said.

''Well, it seems that something has—'' He paused, for he'd noticed a leather-bound book on the table, and though now it was new, and the 1684 stamped in gold on the spine gleamed brightly, he recognized it and stood up and crossed to it. A pen lay beside an inkwell ready to hand, and, grinning, he dipped the pen in the ink, flipped to the last page and scrawled across it, ''IHAY, ENDANBRAY. ANCAY OUYAY IGITDAY?''

''What did you write?'' asked Burghard.

Doyle dismissed the question with an impatient wave. ''Gentlemen, something has broken holes in the structure of time . . . ''

Only fifteen minutes later a band of a dozen men, bundled up against the extreme cold, filed out of the old building's street door and hurried away south down the narrow bridge street toward the Surrey shore. There was room between the ancient houses to walk two abreast, but they moved in single file. Doyle was the second man in line, right behind the cloaked figure of Burghard, whose stride Doyle was able to match easily, even with the unaccustomed angular bulk of a sheathed sword bumping his right thigh. The thin streak of yellow light thrown by Burghard's dark lantern was the only illumination, for the darkness was absolute in the dark defile of the street, though several storeys overhead the moonlight frosted the ragged roofs and the web of stout crossbeams meant to keep the unsteady old buildings from falling against each other. The bridge was silent except for the occasional rattle of an ankle chain against a cobblestone, and from away to his right Doyle could faintly hear music and shouted laughter.

''Here,'' whispered Burghard, stepping into an alley and turning his light on a wooden framework that Doyle realized was a stairway leading down. ''No sense announcing our coming by marching through the south gate.''

Doyle followed him down the dark stairs, and after a long winding descent through a well cut into the stonework of the bridge they emerged into open air again below the underside of the vast span, and Doyle noticed for the first time that the river, visible beyond the lumber of the stairs and between the arches of the bridge, was a white, unmoving expanse of moon-lit ice.

A party could be seen moving across the ice toward the north shore, and after glancing at them once casually Doyle found his gaze drawn back to the distant figures. What was it about them that had caught his eye? The awkward, hunchback look of several of them? The prancing, bounding gait of the one in front?

Doyle closed his big, gloved hand on Burghard's shoulder. "Your telescope," he growled quietly as Longwell collided with him from behind, not jarring him at all.

"Certes." Burghard fumbled under his coat and passed a collapsible telescope up to Doyle.

Doyle click-click-clicked the thing out to its full extent and trained it on the distant group. He was unable to focus, but he could see clearly enough to be sure the lightfooted leader was Doctor Romany; the other five—no, six—figures seemed to be misshapen men dressed in furs.

"That's our man," Doyle said quietly, handing the telescope back to Burghard.

"Ah. And so long as he be on the ice we daren't confront him."

"Why is that?" Doyle asked.

"The connection, man, the chains are no good on water," hissed Burghard impatiently.

"Aye," muttered Longwell from the darkness behind and above Doyle, "were we to confront him upon the ice, he'd set all the devils of hell on us in an instant, and our souls'd not be moored against the onslaught."

A gust of Arctic wind battered the old stairway, making it sway like the bridge of a beleaguered ship.

"Still, we can follow 'em to the north shore, can't we," mused Burghard, "and call 'em halt yonder. Aye, come along."

They resumed their downward course, and after a few more minutes of cramped shuffling arrived at a split, buckled and snow-dusted dock, and stepped off it onto the ice.

"They're bearing more west now, after a fair northward stint," said Burghard quietly, his eyes on the seven moving

figures way out on the ice field. "We'll come out from under
the bridge on the west side and then curve north, and meet
them ashore at the culmination of the circumbendibus."

When they walked out through one of the high arches onto
the ice, Doyle saw bobbing lights ahead, and heard again,
louder, the laughter and music. There were tents and booths
out on the river, and big swings with torches attached to the
sides, and a large boat on axles and wheels tacking slowly back
and forth across the face of the ice, with garish faces painted
on its sail and wheels, and ribbons and banners streaming
from the rigging. The silent procession of the Antaeus
Brotherhood skirted the festivities on the east side, plodding
north.

When they were still a hundred yards from shore Doctor
Romany's party emerged from the blackness under the north-
ernmost arch of the bridge and made for a set of steps below
Thames Street. The tall, spry figure that was Doctor Romany
turned around as they started up the stairs, and even as he'd
begun to turn Burghard twisted himself to the side and turned
a nimble cartwheel, finishing it up with a double-fisted push
against Doyle's chest; Doyle's feet skated out from under
him and he sat down heavily on the ice as Burghard laughed
uproariously. Longwell began to do a grotesquely dainty
ballet twirling, and for an instant Doyle was certain that
Romany had fired a lunacy-inducing spell at them, and that
at any moment he himself would begin barking like a dog or
eating his hat.

Romany turned back toward the north and he and his surprisingly agile retinue bounded up the stairs. Then a ragged
cloud sailed across the face of the moon, dimming the scene
like a scrim.

Burghard and Longwell, both sober-faced now, helped
Doyle to his feet. "My apologies," said Burghard. " 'Twas
essential they think us but drunken roisterers. Quick now, let's
get 'em."

The dozen men on the ice began running toward shore—
Doyle quickly got the hang of the half-sliding step necessary to
maintain balance—and in a couple of minutes they were at the
base of the stairs, climbing over a sunken boat's mast, which
projected at an angle from the solid ice.

They followed a narrow lane up to Thames Street, then
paused in that wider boulevard, looking left and right for their
vanished quarry.

"There," said Burghard tensely, pointing at a snowy stretch in the middle of the street. "They've gone straight across into that alley."

The twelve men followed, though Doyle couldn't see how Burghard had deduced Romany's course; all he saw when he passed the patch of snow were the tracks of a couple of very large dogs.

They ran into the alley, and Doyle's body reacted to a faint, fast scratching sound before his mind had even properly heard it—his left hand whirled his sword out of the sheath and snapped it into line just as one of the things leaped at him and impaled itself on the point. He was jolted back by the solid impact and he heard a deep-throated growling and the clatter of teeth against steel in the instant before his left foot kicked the dying monster off his blade.

"Ware monsters!" he heard Burghard yell in front of him, and then the lantern clanged to the iced cobblestones and its sliding panel fell open, splashing the narrow alley with yellow light.

The scene Doyle found himself confronted with was like some lunatic painting Goya never quite worked himself up to: Burghard was rolling on the ground in a savage wrestling match with some inhumanly muscular thing that seemed to be both man and wolf, and several more of the creatures crouched ready beyond the desperately struggling pair; their shoulders were hunched, as though walking on their hind legs was a novelty, and their snouts extended out dog-like from their receding foreheads, and their wide mouths bristled with teeth that looked to Doyle like ivory cutlass blades. . . . But intelligence glittered in their tiny eyes, and they stepped back warily as Doyle, without taking his eyes off them, drove his sword through the torso of the hairy creature struggling with Burghard at his feet.

"Sorls, Rowary!" barked one of the things over its shoulder as Burghard kicked his slain assailant aside and stood up, cuffing blood away from his eyes and drawing his sword with his right hand; his blood-stained dagger was already gripped in his left fist. The two contorted, thick-pelted corpses had quit shaking and now sprawled motionless between the two groups.

"Longwell, Tyson," Burghard said quietly, "around these houses, fast, and stop up the other end of the alley." There was a clatter and jingling as the two obediently hurried away.

Romany had turned and strode back, and now shouldered his way between two of his wolfish attendants and confronted his attackers. His lean face, weirdly underlit by the lantern, was contorted with rage as he opened his mouth and began to pronounce syllables that warped and shrivelled the very air that carried them—Doyle felt the chain around his ankle vibrate and grow warm—and then he noticed Doyle standing in the forefront with a bared and bloody sword in his hand, obviously immune to his magic and not even bothering to try to prevent it. The chant faltered and stopped, though Romany's mouth stayed open in a dismayed gape.

Doyle crouched to pick up the lantern, then straightened, grinned at the wizard and pointed his sword at him. "I'm afraid you'll have to come with us, Doctor Romany," he said.

The magician made a prodigious leap backward over the heads of the wolf men. He bounded away down the alley, and his creatures loped after him, cautiously followed by Doyle and Burghard and the others.

The loud bang of a pistol shot sounded from some point ahead of them, and an instant later a shrill howl echoed between the close stone walls, and as it died away into choked panting Doyle heard Longwell shout, "Halt, ye monsters— there be primed pistols enough here to send all of ye home."

Doyle, running forward ahead of Burghard, raised the lantern just in time to glimpse a robed figure flying straight upward. "He's jumped for the roof, get him quick!" he roared, and two more gunshots flared and banged ahead of him, the muzzle flashes angled upward, and then he was nearly deafened as Burghard's pistol went off beside his ear.

"Them things is going up the walls like spiders!" yelled Longwell. "Shoot 'em off!"

A window squeaked open somewhere overhead, and what could only be a chamber pot burst against the opposite wall, showering Doyle. "Begone from here, ye thieves and murderers!" shrieked a woman's voice.

Shingles and bits of stone blown loose by the gunshots clattered back down onto the alley floor. "Don't shoot!" called Burghard, his voice harsh with disappointment, "You'll hit that damned woman."

"They're gone, chief," said Longwell, hurrying up to where Doyle and Burghard and the others stood. "Fled over the roof fast as rats."

"Back to Thames Street," rasped Burghard. "We've lost Romany—he could go in any direction across the roofs."

"Aye, let us go back to our dinner," suggested Longwell fervently as they sheathed their swords, thrust away their pistols and picked their way back over the two hirsute corpses to the moonlit pavement of Thames Street.

"I know where he's going," said Doyle quietly. "He's heading back to the place where I originally said he'd be—the place where his magic will work best—the gap field, that inn in Borough High Street."

"I'm not delighted with the idea of crossing the ice, now that he knows we oppose him," spoke up a gangly, curly-haired member. "If he was to turn on us out there . . . "

"It wouldn't necessarily doom us," said Burghard, leading the way forward. "Don't let yourself rely so heavily on your armor. Right now we'll reconnoiter and make no incautious moves."

They hurried back down the cross lane to the stairs below Thames Street, and leaning out over the railing at the top step they stared out across the ice at the torches and tents of the frost fair.

"Too many people about to be knowing if any is them," grumbled Longwell.

"Perhaps," muttered Burghard, who had pulled out his telescope and was inching it by slow degrees across the scene. "I see them," he whispered finally. "They're just making a straight line across, not even bothering to avoid people—ho, you should see some of these people recoil!" He turned to the towering figure of Doyle. "How much more powerful will he be when he gets to that inn?"

"I don't know the precise amps or anything," Doyle said; "let's just say vastly. He must have had something pretty urgent in mind to have left it before."

"I'm afraid we'll have to follow right on his heels then," said Burghard reluctantly, starting down the stairs. "Come along smartly—we've got some catching up to do."

Oriental clog shoes knocked on frost-split cobblestones as another company of furtive men rounded the corner from Gracechurch into Thames Street. The peculiarly shod leader scanned the empty street for a moment and then resumed his determined stride.

"Wait one moment, alchemist," said one of his company. "I'll go no farther without an explanation. That was gunfire we heard, was it not?"

"Aye," said the leader impatiently. "But 'twasn't aimed at thee."

"But what *was* it aimed at? I think that was no man that screamed." The breeze blew the man's long brown curls, unconfined by a wig, forward across his somewhat pudgy and petulant face. He pushed his hat down more firmly on his head. "I'm in command here, though without official sanction, as much as was my father in France. I say all we need is what you carry in yonder box—we need no advice from another damned sorcerer."

Amenophis Fikee walked back to where the man stood and, able to look down at him by virtue of his stilted shoes, hissed, "Listen to me, you posturing clown. If your damned backside is ever to rest on the throne it will be because of *my* efforts, and in spite of yours. Or do you imagine that the idiot assassination attempt you and Russell and Sidney set up last year was *intelligent?* Hah! Fools, trying to reach through a pane of glass for a sweet! You need me, and magic, and a damn large spoonful of luck even to steer clear of the headsman's block, far less become king! And the man who contacted me tonight, greeted me through the candle with the ancient passwords, has more raw power than I've seen in a sorcerer for—well, a long time. You were there, man—I didn't even have to light the candle to receive him—it just burst into flame! Now he's run afoul of something, very possibly James' precious Antaeus Brotherhood, and he's had to fall back to the spot on the Surrey side where there's one of those inexplicable bubbles of indulgence I mentioned to you, in which sorcery is freer. Therefore we will meet him there. Or would you rather return to Holland to pursue the crown on your own, without my help?" The Duke of Monmouth still looked sulky, so Fikee waved the little black box at him. "*And* without my indetectibly forged marriage certificate?"

Monmouth scowled, but shrugged. "Very well, wizard. But let's get *moving,* before your damned frost freezes us solid."

The band moved forward again, toward the bridge.

The boat had been sailing close-hauled, its half-drunk sailors waving their flaring torches more or less in time to their singing, but now the man at the tiller had cut too close into the wind and the sail luffed and fluttered empty; the boat lost its speed, the grotesque faces painted on the great wooden wheels becoming distinguishable as the disks rolled more and more slowly on the wooden axles penetrating the framework that supported the craft, and finally the boat lurched to a stop on the ice, and after a moment began to roll indecisively backward as the sail billowed in reverse.

Burghard, who had been leading Doyle and the ten Antaeus Brotherhood members in a long, curving sprint across the ice behind the screen the wheeled boat provided, caught up with it now, leaped for the rail, caught it, and swung over the gunwale and tumbled into the boat. The drunken mariners, already irate at having lost the wind, turned angrily on this unimposingly slim boarder, but lurched back in confusion when the burly figure of Doyle came vaulting lightly over the rail, all flying mane and beard and cape.

"We're taking command of this vessel," he cried in a voice tight with restrained laughter, for he realized that he'd read about this adventure only a few hours ago. "Burghard, how do you get this thing running again?"

"Stowell," the leader called over the rail, "get the back wheels pushed all the way over and then all of you get in. Everybody's used to seeing this thing tacking around the river—our man won't notice if it follows him."

"It be my boat, though, mate," objected a tubby man in the stern, who scrambled to his feet as the tiller moved slowly over.

Burghard handed him some coins. "Here. We'll not mistreat her, and we'll leave her on the south shore. Oh, and—" he counted out some more coins, "—this is yours too if we can have your masks and torches."

The owner weighed the coins against the obvious determination of the boarders, then shrugged. "Abandon ship, lads," he called to his companions. "And leave the masks and lights—we've got enough here for a whole butt of sack."

The evicted sailors climbed over the gunwales and dropped to the ice cheerfully, and as the last of Burghard's men swung aboard, the sail filled again and the boat began to rock forward.

Burghard, wearing some kind of blue and red toucan mask, worked the tiller and sheet carefully in order to follow but not overtake Romany, and they had got nearly all the way across, and were within thirty yards of the Jeter Lane stairs, when the bounding Romany glanced back for the third time, did a double take, and then skidded to a halt, aware at last that he was being followed.

"He's seen us!" Doyle yelled, but Burghard had already wrenched the tiller all the way over to the left, and the boat heeled, tilting dangerously to port as the two wooden wheels on that side kicked up sprays of shaved ice, then righted itself with a slam and cut sharply to starboard, no longer heading for the stairs but aiming straight at a long section of dock.

Doyle stood up and drew his sword, and then instantly pitched it away, for it was not a sword at all, but a long silver snake looping back to bite him. A moment later his dagger began to squirm strongly out of its sheath, and it took both hands to hold it in. His clothes were undulating in an insane peristalsis, his mask was flapping wildly on his face, and the very hull under his feet was heaving up and down like the ribs of a big, panting animal. Realizing through his panic that he was in the midst of some awful sorcerous focus, he used the hull's next heave as a springboard and catapulted right over the side of the rushing, wriggling boat; he landed on his outstretched hands and curled into a tumble. He rolled several yards and then slid to a stop a second or two after the wheeled boat plowed into the dock, loudly shattering the hull and the mast and pitching members of the Antaeus Brotherhood in all directions like bowling pins.

Doyle sat up, wrenched off his palpitating cat mask and flung it as far as he could, and then he noticed his dagger, which had fallen out of its sheath, crawling toward him like a big inchworm; he kicked it away—and instantly felt an almost crippling disorientation engulf him, for though it bounced away as limber as a length of rubber hose, it clinked each time it hit the ice.

Burghard was up on his feet again only a moment after he hit the ice, and though his face was a grimace of pain he managed to croak, "Up onto the land!" as he forced himself to limp forward.

Flames had begun to lick up brightly here and there from the shattered hull. One of the boat's wheels, wrenched loose from its axle, was rolling slowly around on the ice, its painted

mouth opening and closing spasmodically and its painted eyes
darting about with malign will; and as the flames found and
streaked ravenously up the margins of the sail, the face
painted on it rolled its eyes and crumpled its canvas furiously
as it mouthed unreadable words.

Stowell, his face red as he struggled to stop his scarf from
strangling him, bumped into Doyle on his way to the dock,
and Doyle shook himself, took a deep breath and followed
him. Something had begun to go wrong with the air—it tasted
bad, and burned in Doyle's eyes and nose and lungs, and he
could feel the strength draining out of him.

A litter of wriggling and dancing pieces of broken wood had
congregated in front of the nearest dock ladder, lashing out at
the knees and rolling under the boots of anyone who tried to
get near it—one man had fallen and almost been pounded to
death before Burghard dragged him clear—and so Doyle
simply picked the lurching Stowell up by his belt and collar
and, after two swings to get momentum, used very bit of his
remaining strength to fling the man powerfully upward; then
Doyle fell to his knees and with dimming sight watched the
man hurtle up, his arms and legs waving, and plop lightly onto
the surface of the dock.

The air was astringent now with fumes like sulphur and
chlorine, and Doyle knew that even if the jumping boards
moved aside he wouldn't have the strength to crawl over to the
ladder and climb it. He pitched over on his side and rolled
onto his back, and with no interest he watched Stowell lean
over the edge of the dock, his face lit by the mounting flames,
and reach downward with his sword. Doyle was faintly jealous
that Stowell's sword was straight and solid, while his own had
turned into a leaping eel. Then he stopped thinking about that
and every other thing.

Burghard, still somehow on his feet, staggered into the
middle of the crowd of sticks, and as they cracked viciously at
his knees and cartwheeled up to slam into his crotch and belly,
and as he started to fall he snatched desperately upward and
grabbed the razor-edged foible of the downward extended
sword.

Instantly the sticks backed away from him, making a
frustrated racket of knocking.

Burghard got his feet back under himself to take the weight

off his mangled hand, and he inhaled shudderingly. "To me, Antei!" he fairly screamed.

Longwell crawled forward, one arm covering his head against the savage pounding of the wood pieces, and reached out and grabbed the chain that trailed from Burghard's boot.

The sticks and boards spun away from him.

One by one three other men dragged themselves over to join the chain. The thwarted pieces of lumber—reinforced every moment by new boards, some of them afire, springing away from the burning hulk—skated and whirled toward the still unconnected Doyle. The smaller pieces moved faster, and as they found him and began to rap at his face, Burghard yelled, "Reach him, one of you, quick!"

The man on the end of the chain strained, but couldn't reach Doyle. The man glanced back and saw that the big, skull smasher sized boards were only a few yards away and closing in fast, and so with a hoarse curse he undid the leather restraining loop, drew his dagger, reached out and used the tip to pull Doyle's foot close enough so that he could stab it right through and moor the point firmly in the ice underneath.

Heat spread from Doyle's foot, relaxing his nearly petrified muscles, and finally reached his head, driving out of it the visions of huge, multiplying crystals that had been holding what minimal attention he was still capable of. He sat up on the ice, and as alertness washed hotly through him he became aware of the dagger transfixing his foot and the litter of lumber scuttling away from him to batter a couple of motionless human forms sprawled too far out to have been reached by the Antaeus chain.

"You!" Burghard was yelling. "With the beard! Don't pull your foot free until you've got hold of Friedeman's hand!"

Doyle nodded and inched his way back toward the man with the dagger. "Don't worry," he called to Burghard. "I'm not going to break the connection." He reached Friedeman's free hand and clasped it, and then the man levered the dagger blade loose and drew it out of Doyle's foot. He sheathed it and reached behind himself to join hands with the man who had been gripping his boot chain.

When Burghard said, "Up," the five men rose shakily. Doyle's foot felt like the knife blade was still in it, and when the string of men began shuffling and limping carefully along the foot of the dock toward the ladder he looked back and saw that he was leaving steaming dark stains on the ice and that where his foot had originally been nailed down there was a large irregular dark blot, already iced over.

"Hang onto the man above you, and just use your feet on the ladder," called Burghard, who now stood on the dock, his face visibly pale even in the orange firelight. "We'll pull you up."

In a couple of minutes Doyle and five members of the Antaeus Brotherhood sat or stood swaying unsteadily on the dock, catching their breath, basking in the heat from the burning boat and letting the healing strength spread upward through their boot chains like restoring slugs of brandy.

"He's . . . moved on after swatting us," Burghard panted as he knotted a handkerchief around his cut hand. "We're lucky that he . . . underestimated the amount of time he had, and just shot the quick spell of Malign Animation at us. If he'd taken the time to chant the Deadly Air spell right away . . . "

A man was dashing across the ice toward them. "Ye sons of bitches!" screamed the portly owner of the destroyed boat. He gestured expressively at his unfortunate craft. "I'll have ye all dragged before the magistrates!"

Burghard fumbled awkwardly in a pocket with his good but wrong side hand, yanked out a purse and tossed it. "Our apologies," he shouted as the man caught it. "There is enough there for a new boat and to pay for your time while you find one."

He turned to Doyle and the others. "We lost six men here," he said quietly. "And some of you have sustained injuries that need immediate attention—your foot, sir, is a case in point —and our second greatest armor—ready cash—is gone. It would not be cowardly at this point to fall back to our rooms and . . . patch ourselves up, get some food and sleep, and pursue this matter on the morrow."

Doyle, who had taken off his boot and knotted a section of his scarf around his foot and soaked it in brandy, pulled the boot back on, gritting his teeth against the pain, and then looked up at Burghard. "I've got to go on," he said hoarsely, "if I'm ever to get home. But you're right. You people have done . . . far more than I ever had a right to ask. And I'm terribly sorry about your six men."

He stood up, glad now of the intense cold, for it acted as an anesthetic on his foot.

Longwell shook his head unhappily. "No," he said. "On

the north side of the river I'd have been most willing to forego
the chase and return to our dinner. But now that McHugh and
Kickham and the others are killed—I couldn't savor the port,
knowing that their slayer was at liberty . . . and probably
boasting of his deed.''

"Aye," said Stowell, still fingering his scarf mistrustfully.
"Time enough for food and drink after we've sent this fellow
to hell.''

Burghard's face, haggard as sea-polished driftwood in the
orange light, broke into a hard grin. "So be it. And, sir," he
said, turning to Doyle, "neither trouble nor flatter yourself
with the notion that these men died in aid of you. This is the
work we're paid for, and the considerable danger is the reason
for our considerable pay. And if you hadn't pitched Stowell to
safety, we'd all be lying dead out there. You can walk?''

"I will walk.''

"Very well." Burghard stepped to the edge of the dock. "Is
the payment adequate?" he called to the boat's owner, who
was crouched on the ice watching it burn.

"Oh aye, aye," the man nodded, waving cheerfully. "Ye be
free always to borrow any boat of mine.''

"At least someone is clearing a profit this evening," muttered Burghard bitterly.

The boat, a seething inferno now, rolled over and by slow
degrees fell through the broken and melted ice, and through
the clouds of steam the burning cross beams could be seen to
fall one at a time, like counting fingers.

The innkeeper's eyes narrowed with annoyance when Doyle
ducked under the lintel and stepped into the room, then
widened in surprise when he saw Burghard and the others
follow him in.

"This fellow is with you, Owen?" the innkeeper asked
doubtfully.

"Yes, Boaz," Burghard snapped, "and the Brotherhood
will pay for all damages he may have done. Have you seen
a—''

"The man who fell with me onto the tables," Doyle interrupted. "Where is he?''

"That one? Yes, damn it, he—''

The house trembled, as if a powerful bass organ had begun
playing a dirge in notes too deep to hear, and a high, flat
singing could be faintly heard, seeming to come from a great

distance away. The chain around Doyle's ankle began vibrating strongly. It itched.

"Where is he?" Burghard shouted.

Abruptly a lot of things happened at once. The candles in the wooden chandeliers flared and spouted like Fourth of July fireworks, bouncing bright purple fireballs off the ceiling and casting heavy clouds of a shockingly malodorous smoke, and with a racket of tearing and snapping the tables sprang to pieces, tossing food, dishes, pitchers and diners in all directions, and as Doyle blinked roundabout in the sudden pandemonium he noticed that a long, twisting white funnel like a tornado had appeared over the head of Boaz the innkeeper. Doyle looked at the sprawled diners and saw a similar funnel twisting and swelling over each head. In sudden fright he looked up, but no ectoplasmic larva writhed above him, nor, he ascertained a moment later, over the heads of any of his companions.

It must be the chains, he thought, protecting us from this unholy Pentecost. Glancing down, he saw that his chain was fizzing brightly with gold sparks, and his companions each seemed to be wearing a whole ignited pack of sparklers on the right boot.

The exploded tables hastily reassembled themselves into vaguely anthropoid shapes, their face surfaces bristling with twitching splinters like iron filings on a magnet, and they began stumbling and lurching through the purple-lit smoke, slamming their wooden arms randomly against people, walls and each other, like blind berserkers.

"Circle!" Burghard yelled, and Doyle found himself pushed between Longwell and Stowell as the members of the Antaeus Brotherhood shifted their positions to form a loop. The others had drawn swords and daggers, and though Doyle couldn't see how such mundane weapons could damage adversaries like these, he crouched forward to wrench the sword from the scabbard of a diner who'd been felled on his way to the door.

The white funnels now stretched rapidly upward and all slapped against one point on the ceiling. A big lump of the stuff began forming there. The dozen or so people who were connected by their heads to this spidery unpleasantness had, whether sitting, standing or lying down, ceased all motion, but now they all turned imbecilically calm eyes toward the circle of armed men by the front door. And the ungainly wooden men paused, as if listening, and then, blind no longer, all turned to face the Brotherhood and shuffled toward them with a cautious restraint.

One of them paused in front of Burghard and drew its table leg arm back for a smashing blow, but before it swung Burghard lunged in and poked his sword against the thing's shoulder joint, and the block of wood that was its arm ceased to adhere to the table top that was its chest, and fell off and banged on the floor.

Without conscious thought Doyle leaped forward in a hop-lunge that put his point squarely in the belly of another—and brought tears to his eyes from the pain in his foot—and the thing fell to the ground like an armful of firewood.

In the ensuing mêlée this proved to be the way to deal with the things, and though Stowell was knocked unconscious by a blow from one of them and Doyle's right arm was nearly paralyzed by a blow on the point of the shoulder, in a couple of minutes of leaping, ducking and lunging they'd reduced all of the things except one to inert lumber—the exception was the last one which, when it had found itself alone facing four swords, had in a remarkably human display of dismayed panic, run out the open front door.

Though the purple fireballs had started a small fire or two among the tossed and scattered kindling, the chandeliers had subsided to their normal radiance and the acrid smoke had largely dissipated. "He's on the premises somewhere," Burghard gasped. "Let's try the kitchen—and stay together." He started forward.

"*Wait*," came a chorus of flat voices, followed by a shuffling and knocking as Boaz and a dozen of his luckless patrons were drawn erect by the ectoplasmic umbilicus attached to their heads. Several of them drew swords and daggers, and the rest—including a couple of matronly ladies—picked up heavy, club-length pieces of lumber.

Doyle looked up at the intersection of all the white funnels, and saw that the lump that had grown on the ceiling there was now formed into a huge eyeless face, and the puppet-string tentacles all trailed out of its gaping, flap-lipped mouth.

"Doyle," said all of the people in weird unison, "*gather the remnants of your men and try to find a retreat so obscure that my wrath can't follow.*"

"Right, Burghard," said Doyle, trying hard to keep hysteria from shrilling his voice, "a wizard in a hurry would head for the kitchen—where there'd be fire and boiling water and whatnot all just waiting for him.''

Doyle, Burghard, Longwell and the other remaining member, a short, stocky fellow, made a dash for the kitchen, but were instantly blocked by the innkeeper and diners.

Doyle ducked under a fat lady's swing and managed to rap the board out of her hands with his sword pommel a moment before parrying a sword point that was rushing at his chest. His body automatically lunged forward in a riposte, and only at the last possible instant did he override the reflex and turn his sword to drive the knuckle guard, rather than the lethal point, into the belly of his puppet attacker.

The old lady had danced around behind him, and with a crabapple fist gave Doyle a hard punch in the kidney. He roared with pain and spun, kicking her legs out from under her, and as she tumbled he whirled his blade in a horizontal arc that snicked right through the white snake attached to her head—both ends shriveled away, and the long end snapped up elastically and slapped the ceiling before being slurped like disgusting spaghetti into the now-grinning mouth. The fallen lady began snoring.

Though attacking with concentrated skill and attention, the erstwhile diners were muttering like sleep-walkers; one man who backed Doyle into a corner with a fast and deceptive series of sword thrusts—the instinctive parrying of which made Doyle profoundly thankful that Steerforth Benner had studied fencing—was saying in the most reasonable conversational tone, '' . . . Might simply have asked before throwing it away, that's all I'm claiming, and it seems to me if either of us has a right to be peeved . . . ''

Peeved, he says, thought Doyle desperately as he finally got a bind on the elusive blade and twisted it out of the bemused man's grip.

'' . . . Why it's me, my dear,'' the man went on calmly, aiming a jackhammer kick which Doyle leaped over, ''for it was my most treasured doublet . . . ''

Two more jabbering, placid-faced men were rushing at him with bared swords, and not caring to have an enemy at his rear, Doyle lashed out backhanded at the trolley wire of the man who felt he had a right to be peeved; the blow had no force to it, and rebounded from the white cord, but the man screeched, leaped like a wounded rabbit and then dropped to the floor. Doyle whipped his sword back into line just as the two attackers made their final bounds, swords up and points aimed at Doyle's chest.

Doyle flung himself to the right, parrying that man's blade in a low *quinte*, and let himself keep falling forward into a sort of three-point crouch, catching himself with the fingertips of his right hand spread on the floor as he let his sword rebound from the parry back up into line, the point over his head; and he'd no sooner got the point up than the other man ran onto it, his own sword transfixing the empty air where Doyle's torso had been a second ago.

The first man had recovered and stepped back, ready to drive his point into Doyle's face—"If the damnable cat would just decide whether she wants to be inside," he was saying quietly—and Doyle pulled hard sideways on his sword, toppling the dying man into the way of the thrust. ". . . or outside," the first man continued as his sword chugged deep into his companion's back.

God damn you, Romany, thought Doyle as his cold-bellied apprehension at last ignited into rage, you made me kill one of them. He dragged his sword free and clanked the flat of it against the temple of the man who wished the cat would make up her mind, and as he fell over Doyle snatched up an extinguished but unbroken oil lamp from the floor and pitched it like a football across the flame-lit dining room toward the kitchen door; it knocked the door open as it shattered, and Doyle scrambled over to the nearest fire—which was rushing up a wall and splashing at the ceiling—grabbed a long stick that was burning at one end, and hurled it like a flame-tipped javelin into the kitchen.

He heard the stick clatter on flagstones . . . and he had just decided the move had failed when there was a deep whoosh and an orange flash from the kitchen and the puppet people screamed in perfect unison, like a dozen radios all tuned to the same signal, then dropped their weapons, looked around with expressions of horror, and all but Boaz the innkeeper bolted for the door.

The ectoplasm tentacles dangled limp and unconnected, and a moment later the huge white face tore loose from the ceiling with a loud sucking sound and fell through the smoky air to splat horribly on the floor. Doyle leaped over it and sprinted toward the burning kitchen, closely followed by Burghard and a limping and swearing Longwell. Boaz ran to a shelf of glasses, swept them clanging and shattering to the floor, pulled a cloth-wrapped bundle from the back of the shelf and, untying it with trembling fingers, hurried after them.

Doyle bounded through the kitchen doorway whirling his sword in a wild figure eight in front of him—but Doctor Romany was gone. Doyle skidded to a halt on the dirt floor and looked around at first with caution, then with amazement—for though the kitchen was splashed with smokily blazing oil, he could see that the shelves, benches, tables and even the stone fireplace were all warped, pulled toward the center of the room as though they were forms painted on a taut sheet of rubber that had been pushed far in at the middle.

Burghard piled into Doyle from behind, and Longwell and the raging innkeeper, who was juggling the bell-muzzled flintlock pistol he had unwrapped, bumped into Burghard. Boaz dropped the gun, and it fell muzzle down in a muddy corner.

"Guerlay is dead," Burghard panted. "I *want* this Doctor Romany."

The innkeeper had retrieved his gun and was waving the mud-fouled muzzle in all directions and demanding to know if the Duke of York would reimburse him for the destruction of his inn.

"Aye, damn it," snapped Burghard, "he'll buy you a new one anywhere you please. Give me that before you kill somebody," he added, snatching the gun away. "Where does that doorway go?"

"A hall," answered Boaz grudgingly. "Right to the rooms, left to the stables out back."

"Very well, let's search—"

Suddenly the fires began to burn more furiously, so that instead of flames there was a static radiance, its glare moving up from yellow-orange to white, and for the second time that night Doyle was gasping in baking, oxygen-depleted air.

"*He's doing this from outside!*" Burghard choked. "Run!"

Burghard and Longwell stumbled into the hall. Doyle moved to follow, then remembered the unconscious Stowell, and ran back into the dining room, which was also burning at a ferociously accelerated rate.

Stowell was sitting up, blinking in the white light, and Doyle crossed to him, yanked him upright, and propelled him toward the open front door.

Stowell reeled back, though, when the flaring lintel gave way in a swirl of white sparks and dropped half a ton of tumbling masonry and lumber onto the doorstep.

"No good!" yelled Doyle. "Back to the kitchen!" He grabbed Stowell's shoulder and dragged the dazed man along.
"Look out, it's an oven in here," he said as he braced himself
before entering the incandescent kitchen. Then they lurched
and bumped through, beating out sparks that sprang up on
their clothing and Doyle's beard, and burst at last into the
relative coolness of the hallway beyond. "There should be a
door here," croaked Doyle—then he noticed that the leftward
end of the hall was a slope of smoldering rubble. "Jesus," he
whispered hopelessly.

"Hist!"

Doyle turned toward the sound, and at this point wasn't
very surprised to see the stout innkeeper's head sitting up on
the floor blinking at him. Then he realized that the man was
neck-deep in a hole.

"Hither, you fools!" Boaz cried. "Into the cellar! It connects to a sewer in the next street—though why I should be
saving bastards of the goddamned Antaeus Brotherhood . . ."

Doyle snapped out of his stupor and, pushing the half-
stunned Stowell along in front of him, hurried over to the
trapdoor. Boaz was already down the ladder, and he impatiently guided Stowell's feet onto the rungs as he descended,
followed closely by Doyle, who pulled the trapdoor closed
over them. A moment later all three of them stood on a stone
floor, peering about at the barrels and boxes dimly visible in
the radiance of the two sparkling boot chains.

"French wine I was saving," said the innkeeper shortly,
nodding at a stack of crates. He sighed. "Come this way, past
the onions."

As they left the cellar and made their way down a narrow
stone corridor, Doyle asked, speaking instinctively in a
whisper, "Why did you have this bolt-hole ready?"

"Never you mind why—oh, what the hell. Further on the
sewer's broad enough to row a boat up from the river.
Sometimes it's prudent not to trouble the Customs House
about a taxable shipment . . . and occasionally a patron wants
to leave, but not by a visible door."

Here I go leaving by another invisible door, Doyle thought.

When they'd gone about forty paces down the tunnel the
boot chains dimmed and went out. "We're out of the magic
sphere," Stowell muttered.

"Like enough 'twas the damned chains set the place ablaze," Boaz growled. "But here we are—you can see the moonlight through the grating."

The tunnel floor crowded up against the ceiling below the sewer grating, and Doyle, his knees bent, braced his shoulder against the iron bars. He grinned sideways at Boaz. "Let's hope I'm better at ripping up sewers than crushing pewter mugs." Then his face lost all expression as he strained with all his strength to straighten up.

The fact of the matter, thought the shivering Duke of Monmouth as he stepped closer to the conveniently burning inn, is that I don't truly need these sorcerers—or their damned forged marriage certificate. I've told Fikee that I've every reason to believe that my mother really was documentally married to King Charles, by the Bishop of Lincoln, at Liege. Why doesn't he try to find the *real* marriage certificate?

He pursed his lips—which, to his chagrin, were unattractively chapped—for he knew the answer, and didn't like it. It was plain that Fikee didn't believe Monmouth was the rightful successor to the throne; and therefore his efforts couldn't be interpreted as simple patriotic concern. The sneaking sorcerer must be relying on favors and influence from me when I'm properly crowned, he thought. And I suppose the main favor would be the one he's been agitating for for years: the abandonment of all British interests in Tangier. I wonder, thought Monmouth, why Fikee is so determined to prevent any European power from gaining a toehold in Africa.

He looked toward the artificially tall Fikee, who was standing a few feet away, holding the black box that contained the forgery. "What are we waiting for, wizard?"

"Shut up, can't you?" Fikee snapped, not taking his eyes off the burning building. Suddenly he pointed. "Ah! There!"

A burning man had come bounding around the corner of the building, springing an impossible three yards with each step, hotly pursued by two men who also seemed to be partially afire—at least there was a lot of sparking around their boots.

Fikee started forward just as one of the pursuers flung himself forward in a flying tackle that knocked the burning man off his feet and tumbling through the snow.

A gallant rescue, thought Monmouth. But then the fat man

scrambled over to the stunned and still partially flaming figure, and Monmouth gasped to see him draw a dagger and drive it down at the man's chest—but the blade snapped off, and the two men in the snow fell to wrestling savagely.

Another few steps and I'm at them, thought Fikee as he ran awkwardly toward the prone figures. This may prosper us yet, for though the wizard must be in awful agony lying on the abdicated ground, these interfering men certainly can't kill him with fire or steel—or lead, he added, for he'd just seen the lagging pursuer pull from under his cloak a wide-muzzled pistol.

Burghard knew a gunshot couldn't kill a wizard—especially not inside a magic sphere—any more than Longwell's idiotic dagger thrust, but he'd just seen Doctor Romany reach out and actually grasp Longwell's boot chain—the hand sizzled audibly, and the wizard howled with the pain—and with a wrench pull it right off. There was only an instant in which to distract Doctor Romany from blasting the defenseless Longwell, and Burghard rushed up, shoved the gun's muzzle in Romany's face even as the wizard was opening his mouth to speak some devastating spell, and pulled the trigger.

Doctor Romany's face disintegrated like a kicked sand castle, and he tumbled back onto the blood-sprayed snow.

Both Burghard and Amenophis Fikee froze, staring in astonishment at the sprawled and motionless form, and in that instant the Duke of Monmouth, fearful of being involved in a murder trial when his father the king had forbidden him even to set foot in the country, turned and ran.

Slowly Burghard reached out and knocked the black box out of Fikee's grasp.

When Doyle had gotten to twenty-eight in the thirty-second count that, he figured, would take him to the end of his endurance, the iron frame that had been biting into his shoulder suddenly burst up from its moorings with a metallic clang and a rattle of broken mortar on the cobblestones of the street above. Doyle flung the grating away and hopped out of the sewer. He reached back down and grabbed the innkeeper's wrist and hauled him up onto the pavement, then did the same for Stowell.

"Did you hear some noises while I was straining at that?" he asked Stowell. "I thought I did."

"Aye," gasped Stowell, rubbing his shoulder, "a scream and a shot."

"Let's get back there."

They sprinted back the way they'd come, over the pavement this time, and after a few steps Doyle could feel his ankle chain heating up again. Wearily he dragged the sword out of his belt.

But when they rounded the corner of the burning building it was a played out scene that met their eyes. Burghard and Longwell were sitting in the middle of the street, watching the fire. Burghard was idly tossing and catching a small black box, but it fell forgotten to the cobbles and he leaped to his feet when he saw the sooty trio coming toward him. "How in God's name did you get out?" he cried. "Your wizard pulled down all the doorways a second after we got outside."

"Out through the sewer from the cellar," croaked Doyle, swaying as the evening's full measure of exhaustion began to catch up with him. "Where's Romany?"

"I killed him somehow," said Burghard. "I think he had some allies waiting for him out front here, but they fled when I shot him. We dragged him across the street out of the magical bubble—"

"Did you search him?" Doyle interrupted anxiously, wondering how much longer the gap field might continue, if indeed it hadn't closed already.

"All he had about him was this paper—"

Doyle snatched the damp and darkly stained piece of paper from Burghard, gave it a quick glance, then looked up again. "Where'd you drag his body to?"

"Over yonder under that—" Burghard pointed, then his eyes widened in horror. "My God, he's gone! But I blew his whole *face* off!"

Doyle slumped. "He must have faked it. I don't think they *can* be killed with guns."

"I didn't think so either," said Burghard, "but I *saw* his face blow to bits when I fired Boaz's gun at him! Damn it, I'm not some stripling claiming kills I didn't make! Longwell, you saw—"

"Wait a moment," said Doyle. "The gun that fell in the mud?"

"Aye, that's the one. I'm lucky it didn't burst in my hand, it was so clogged with dirt."

Doyle nodded. A barrelful of mud, he thought, might indeed have given Romany a terrible injury, while a pistol ball would not. It had to do with their aversion to touching the ground.

He opened his mouth to explain it to Burghard, but at that moment all the light went out and Doyle fell away, as it seemed to him, right through the earth and out into starless space on the other side.

After the implosive *thump*, Burghard stared for a few moments at the empty space where Doyle had stood, and at the pile of empty clothes that had flopped and fluttered onto the snow there. Then he looked around.

Longwell walked over to him, craning his neck left and right. "Did you hear a sort of boom that wasn't from the fire?" he asked. "And where'd our mysterious guide go?"

"Back where he came from, evidently," said Burghard. "And I hope it's warmer there." He cocked an eyebrow at Longwell. "Did you recognize the man that was out here waiting for Romany?"

"Matter of fact, Owen, it looked like the gypsy chief, Fikee."

"Hm? Oh, certainly Fikee was here—but I meant the other one."

"No, I didn't get a look at him. Why, who was he?"

"Well, he *looked* like—but he's supposed to be in Holland." He gave Longwell a grin that had a lot of weariness but no mirth in it. "We'll probably never know what, precisely, was going on here tonight."

He stooped and picked up the black wooden box. Stowell trudged up, his boots crunching in the snow. "I shouldn't have left you there, Brian," Burghard told him. "I'm sorry—and glad the bearded man went back for you."

"I don't blame you," said Stowell. "I thought I was beyond rescue myself." He knuckled his eyes. "Hell of a pace. What have you got in the box?"

Burghard tossed it and caught it. "Magical work, I imagine."

He wound up and pitched it through one of the heat-burst windows into the seething ruin.

Hobbling down an alley, trying to see with his one remaining eye, Doctor Romany wept with rage and frustration. He couldn't remember who had hurt him or why, but he knew he was marooned now. And there was a message he needed to give to someone—it was urgent—but the message seemed to have run out of his head along with all the blood that he'd lost before he regained consciousness and scrawled a few basic sustaining cantrips in the snow. If he could have spoken a spell he might have been able to repair himself, but his jaw was shattered and half gone, and the written charms only just managed to keep him alive and conscious.

There was one thing, though, that he knew and was profoundly glad of: the man Doyle was dead. Romany had trapped him inside that inn, and when he'd furtively crawled away from the place where they'd left him for dead, he had looked back and seen the exitless inn burning so thoroughly that he knew nothing inside could still be alive.

His sense of balance was gone, and he was having a rough time walking on his spring-shoes. Well, he thought, I'm already an old ka—after a few decades of deterioration I'll be so light that gravity will hardly have a grip on me anyway, and I'll be able to dispense with the damned shoes. And written spells will sustain me until my face heals and I can speak again. With any luck I should be able to live my way back to 1810.

And, he thought, when 1810 rolls around at last, I'll look up Mr. Brendan Doyle. In fact, in the meantime I think I'll buy that lot where the burning inn stands, and in 1810 I'll take Mr. Doyle there and show him his own ancient, charred skull.

A bubbling rattle that might have been a tortured sort of laughter issued from the lower half of his destroyed face.

After a few more steps he lost his balance again, and lurched against a wall and started to slide to the pavement—then an arm caught him, bore him back up and supported him as he took another step. He turned his head around to let his good eye have a look at his benefactor, and somehow he wasn't surprised to see that it was not a person at all, but a vaguely man-shaped, animated collection of wood that had evidently once been a table. Romany gratefully draped an arm around the stout board that was the thing's shoulder, and without a word, for neither of them was capable of speech, they made their way on down the alley.

CHAPTER 10

"Minerals are food for plants, plants for
animals, animals for men; men will also be food
for other creatures, but not for gods, for their
nature is far removed from ours; it must therefore
be for devils."

—Cardan's *Hyperchen*

DOYLE'S BARE FEET hit a desk after so short a fall that he
barely had to flex his knees to stay upright. He was in a tent,
and as a man suddenly awakened from a nightmare gradually
and with mounting relief recognizes the details of his own
bedroom, Doyle remembered where he'd seen this desk and
litter of papers, candles and statues—he was in Doctor
Romany's gypsy tent. And, he noted as he hopped down from
the desk, he was stark naked; thank God it was hot here.
Clearly he'd returned to 1810.

But how can that be? he wondered. I didn't have a mobile
hook.

He crossed to the tent flap and pulled it slightly open just in
time to see a couple of giant skeletal figures, as faintly luminous as after-images on the retina, running in slow motion
behind the burning tents; they faded to nothing, so quickly
that he wasn't sure he'd even seen them. The only sound, aside
from the quiet crackle of the fires, was incongruously merry
piano and accordion music from the north end of camp.

He let the flap fall shut, then rummaged around in the litter until he found a belted robe and some high-soled sandals, which he put on, a clean scarf to knot around his still bleeding foot, and a scabbarded sword. Feeling a little better equipped, he left the tent.

Footsteps approached from his left. He drew the sword and turned toward them and found himself facing the old gypsy, Damnable Richard, who gaped at him in surprise and then leaped backward, snatching a dagger out of his sash.

Doyle lowered his point to the dirt. "You're in no danger from me, Richard," he said quietly. "I owe you my life . . . as well as several drinks. How's your monkey?"

The gypsy's eyebrows were as high on his forehead as they could be. After several indecisive wobbles his dagger-hand relaxed to his side. "Why . . . very *kushto*, thankee, and all the better for your concern," he said uncertainly. "Uh . . . where's Doctor Romany?"

On the cool evening breeze the music from the north slowed and took on a melancholy tone. "He's gone," said Doyle. "I don't think you'll ever see him again."

Richard nodded, assimilating this, then put his dagger away, pulled his monkey out of a pocket and whispered the news to it. "Thank you," he said finally, looking up at Doyle again. "Now I must go and gather my poor scattered people." He started away, but after a few steps he paused and turned, and by the light of the burning tent Doyle saw his teeth flash in a grin. "I guess you *gorgios* aren't always stupid," he said, then started away again.

The tent Doyle had exited was now burning thoroughly and sending glowing patches of tent fabric whirling up into the clear night sky. Remembering the chamber pot that had shrapnelled over his head, Doyle gingerly felt his hair—but it seemed clean, and it occurred to him that he must have left the befoulment back in 1684 along with the borrowed clothes.

"Ashbless!" someone yelled from away to the right, and it took a moment for Doyle to remember that he was Ashbless. It must be Byron, he thought. Or, he amended, the Byron ka.

"Here, my lord," he called.

Byron came limping up out of the shadows, glaring around and holding his dagger ready. "Here you are," he said. He looked more closely at him. "What are you wearing the robe and odd shoes for?"

"It's . . . a long story," said Doyle, sheathing his sword. "Let's get out of here—I need to find a pair of trousers and a long, strong drink."

"Oh?" Byron blinked. "But what of the fire giants? Have they gone?"

"Yes. Romany consumed them, used them up to fuel a bolt-hole spell of his."

"Spells," Byron said disgustedly, then spat. "Where is he now, then?"

"Gone," said Doyle. "Dead by now, almost certainly."

"Damn. I had hoped to kill him myself." He eyed Doyle suspiciously. "You seem to know an awful lot about it. And how did you manage to lose your trousers in the few minutes since I last saw you?"

"Let's get out of here," Doyle repeated, beginning to shiver.

They walked away, past the burning tent by the tree from which Doyle had broken a limb—only, he realized dazedly, a few minutes ago by local time—and then they set off across the grass beyond, and the streaks of their shadows in front of them were gradually absorbed by the darkness as they left the fire farther and farther behind.

The creature in the dark grass found it easier to crawl than walk through the field, for it could grab weed stalks and pull itself along and only use its feet for kicking off from the ground every now and then to keep itself from settling to the earth; if anyone had been watching, the thing would have looked like some agile crustacean skimming across the sea floor.

Well, thought the thing that had once been indistinguishable from a man, there's the last score settled, the long circle closed, and the man who ruined me is off on his way to be killed by me. I saw the yags extinguished, so I know he's gone. The thing chuckled like dry leaves rattling in the wind. Half an hour ago, it thought, I was afraid he might somehow evade his death, and now he's been dead a hundred and twenty-six years.

It heard voices and the swishing of feet through the grass behind it and to its right, so it ceased all motion, turning over and over as it lost speed until it rocked to a halt against a bush, its arms and legs pointed upward.

"But if my friends will let us stay with them," a man was saying impatiently, "and I tell you again they'd be glad to, then why not?"

Why I believe it's that young lord, thought the thing in the grass. We were going to have him do something for us. That's right, and he was a ka—the original was in Greece. What was his name? And he was to have killed the king. Plots and schemes, half-wit dreams.

"Well," answered someone else dubiously, "they think you're out of the country. How would you explain your presence here?"

There was something about the second voice that profoundly upset the crawler, and it sat up so quickly that it left the ground and hovered for a few moments like a nearly worn out helium balloon, and when it touched down again it kicked strongly and flew twenty feet into the air so as to be able to see.

Two men were walking across the field away from the burning tents, and the slowly descending creature stared in horror at the taller of them. Yes, very tall, it thought, and—Isis!—a full mane and beard that seem to be blond! But by what damnable aid did he get out of that inn? And back to now? *Who is this man Doyle?*

It began flailing and swimming to get back to the ground quicker, for it had to follow him. If there was any spark of purpose left in the deteriorated ka that had once been Doctor Romany, it was to see, finally, Doyle dead.

The induced fever was breaking, and Doctor Romanelli stared angrily at his placidly sleeping patient. Damn you, Romany, he thought, let me know how it proceeds. This fever story won't hold up much longer—I'm going to have to either kill him or let him recover.

The doctor laid his palm on Lord Byron's forehead, and swore softly, for it felt cool. The sleeper shifted, and Romanelli tiptoed hastily out of the room. Sleep on, my lord, he thought; for a little while longer—at least until I hear from my incompetent duplicate. He strode into the disordered room he was using for a workshop, looked hopefully at the lit but inert Candle of Far Speaking, then sighed and let his gaze drift out the open window to where the sun was sinking over the hills beyond Missolonghi. The broad Gulf of Patras was already in shadow, and several fishing boats were plying for home, their triangular sails bellying in the evening breeze.

A sputtering from the table made him whirl and stare at the candle, which had begun to glow more brightly. "Romany!" he called into the flame. "Do you succeed?"

The candle flame was silent, and though it was glowing more brightly every second, it had not taken on the spherical shape.

"Romany!" the wizard repeated, louder now, not caring if he woke Byron. "Shall I kill him now?"

There was no reply. Suddenly the almost blindingly bright candle bent in the middle, like a beckoning finger—Doctor Romanelli grunted in surprise—then it split softly open in the middle and spilled a steaming flood of wax out onto the table top. As the candle folded down to a sizzling puddle Romanelli saw that the whole snaky length of the wick was glowing yellow-white.

Damn me, he thought, that means Romany's candle is at this very moment burning up. His tent must have caught fire. Could he have lost control of the yags? Yes, that must be it—they got too excited, and burned down his camp. There's no way they'll be ready to burn London tomorrow, then; they'll be sated and sluggish for weeks. Romany, you blundering, damned . . . *forgery!*

He waited until the wick stopped glowing and the puddle of wax had begun to scum over as it cooled, and then he went to the closet and unbuckled a trunk and carefully lifted out of it another candle. He unwrapped it, lifted the frosted glass hood of the room's lantern to touch it alight, and in a few moments the new candle's wick bloomed with the magical round flame.

"Master!" Romanelli barked into it.

"Yes, Romany," answered the Master's groaning voice at once. "Are the yags agreeable? Is the toy sufficiently—"

"Damn it, this is Romanelli. Something's gone wrong at the London end. My candle just melted when I tried to contact him—you understand? *His* candle has burned up somehow. I think he must have lost control of the yags. I don't know whether to kill Byron or not."

"Roman—Romanelli? Burned up? Killed? What?"

Romanelli repeated his news several times, until the Master had finally grasped the situation.

"No," the Master said. "No, don't kill Byron. The plan

may still be salvageable. Go to London and find out what's happened.''

"But it will take me at least a month to get to England," Romanelli protested, "and by then—"

"No," the Master interrupted. "Don't travel—go there instantly. Be there tonight."

The last glowing sliver of the sun winked out behind the Patras hills, and there were no more boats out on the gulf. After a pause, "Tonight?" Romanelli echoed in a hoarse whisper. "I . . . I can't *afford* that kind of thing. Magic like that . . . if I'm to be expected to function at my best when I get there . . . "

"Will it *kill* you?" grated the Master's voice out of the flame.

Sweat stood out on Romanelli's forehead. "You know it won't," he said, "quite."

"Then stop wasting time."

The little man walking along Leadenhall Street moved with a brash confidence that didn't suit his appearance, for in the light from occasional windows and doorways that he passed, his clothes looked slept in, and his face, though bright-eyed and tightly grinning, was haggardly lined, and one ear was completely gone.

Many shops had closed for the night, but the new Depilatory Parlor was still spilling light across the cobblestones from its open doors, and the grinning little man entered and strode up to the long counter. There was a bell to ring for service, and he rang it as rapidly as if someone had promised him a shilling for each *ping* he could produce before being forcibly stopped.

A clerk hurried up on the other side of the counter, eyeing the little man carefully. "You want to stop playing with that?" he said loudly.

The ringing ceased. "I wishes to speak with yer employer," the little man announced. "Take me to him."

"If you've come to have some hair removed, you don't need to talk to the boss. I can—"

"The boss I asked for, sonny, and the boss I'll speak to. It's to do with a friend of mine, you see—he sent me here, as it were. He can't travel about because he—" and the man paused to give the clerk a massive wink, "—grows hair, terrible thick, *all over himself*. Eh? You understand? And *don't*, sonny, try to go for yer tranky gun. Take me to the boss."

The clerk blinked and licked his lips. "Uh . . . damn . . . okay, yes. Will you wait while I—no. Uh, will you come this way, please, sir?" He lifted away a hinged section of the counter so the little man could come inside. "Right through here. Now you won't . . . do anything crazy back here, will you?"

"Not me, sonny," the man said, evidently surprised and hurt by the very thought.

The two of them walked through a rear door and down a dim corridor, and were halted at the end of it by a man who stood up from a stool when they approached. "What's this?" he asked, his hand going quickly to a bellpull rope. "Clients aren't allowed back here, Pete, you know that."

"This guy just now walked in," said Pete hastily, "and he says—"

"A friend of mine grows fur all over his body," the little man broke in impatiently. "Now take me to your bloody boss, will you?"

The hall guard gave Pete an accusing look.

Pete shrugged helplessly. "He . . . knew about it somehow. Told me not to go for it."

After a moment of thought the guard let go of the bell rope. "Very well," he said. "Wait here while I tell him." He opened the door behind him and stepped through, shutting it carefully behind him, but the rope hadn't even stopped swinging when he opened it again. "Pete," he said, "back to the shop. You, sir, may follow me."

"Aye aye, skipper." The disheveled little man grinned and stepped smartly forward.

Beyond the door was a narrow carpeted stairway, and at the top was a hallway with several doors visible along it. The next to nearest one was open, and the guard waved toward it. "There's his office," he said, and stepped back. The little man brushed his joke wig hair back with ridiculous daintiness, then walked into the room.

An old man with hard, bright eyes stood up from behind a cluttered desk and pointed to a chair. "Sit down, sir," he said in an impressively deep voice, "and let's take it as given that I am thoroughly armed, shall we? Now I understand you—"

He paused, and looked more closely at his visitor's face. "D-Doyle?" he said wonderingly. His hand darted out and turned up the wick of the lamp on the desk. "My God," he breathed. "It is you! But . . . I see—I must have somehow overestimated Benner's ruthless self-interest. He lied when he said he killed you." His confidence was coming back, but there had been real fear in his face for a moment.

The other man was sitting back, grinning delightedly. "Oh, aye, he lied, right enough. But you might say I *am* dead." He stuck out his tongue and crossed his eyes. "Poisoned."

A bit of the fear was again visible in the old man's eyes, and to cover it he spoke harshly. "Let's not indulge in riddles. What do you mean?"

The grin left the little man's face. "I mean if I throws away me razor I won't be bald much longer." He held up one lumpy hand. "Can ye see the whiskers between me fingers? They've started already." His cheeks accordioned back as he bared all his teeth in a savage smile. "And let's . . . *take it as given*, sir, that I can leave here any time. If I have to flee, this body will stay here, but there'll suddenly be a very scared and confused soul in it—and I'll be miles away."

Darrow went pale. "Jesus, it's you. Very well, no, don't flee, I don't want to do you any harm." He stared hard into the eyes that had been Doyle's. "What did you do with Doyle?"

"I was in yer Steerforth Benner's body, and I'd been in it long enough so's it was furry as a bear; I ate a whole lot o' strychnine and also a drug that makes you see things and act crazy, and then I chewed my tongue up real good—so he'd not have a chance to talk to nobody—and then just switched places with him."

"Good God," Darrow whispered in an awed tone. "That . . . poor son of a bitch . . . " He shook his head. "Well, let the dead bury the dead. I've come a long way to find you—to strike a bargain with you. Damn it, I've rehearsed this conversation in my mind a hundred times, but now I can't think where to begin. Let's see—for one thing, I can cure your hyperpilosity, the all-over fur, any time, and as many times as you please, so from now on you'll be free to take a new body only when you *choose* to—you won't *have* to anymore. But that's not the main item I want to bargain with." He opened a drawer and pulled out a sheet of paper. "Listen to this extract from a book I own. 'It seems,' " he read aloud, " " *a man at another table took exception to some—as I heard the tale later—heathen sentiments the stranger had voiced, and seized the front of the offender's shirt in order the more forcefully to convey his displeasure; the shirt tore, and the man's breast being exposed, it was remarked that the hitherto concealed skin was covered with new whiskers, such as would show on a man's face after not shaving for a couple of days. Mr.—"* Darrow looked up and smiled. "I can't let you know his real name yet. Let's call him Mr. Anonymous. 'Mr. Anonymous,' " he resumed, " 'exclaimed to the company, "I believe it's Dog-Face Joe! Seize him and take off those gloves." *The gloves were promptly pulled off of the struggling man's hands, which proved to be likewise bewhiskered. Mr. Anonymous silenced the uproar and declared that if justice was to be visited on this notorious murderer it would have to be done at once, without involving the slow wheels of the law, and so the man was dragged out into the yard behind the pub, and hanged from a rope which was tied to one of the warehouse cranes.' "* Darrow put the paper down and smiled at the other man.

"An entertaining fiction," pronounced the man in Doyle's body.

"Yes," agreed Darrow, "it's fiction now. But in a few months it will be fact—history." He smiled. "This is going to be a long story, Joe. Would you like some brandy?"

Again Doyle's face grinned. "Don't mind if I do," Amenophis Fikee said.

In the sudden silence Horrabin, his sling still swinging from his violent gesticulations of a few moments before, stared at the shattered corpse on the flagstones beside the table and realized that the fallen beggar lord had put control of the situation back within his reach. He grinned merrily, clapped his painted hands and cried, "He didn't quite make it to the table, did he?" The clown knew he had his audience's attention again, so he reached unhurriedly for a joint of meat on his plate, gnawed it thoughtfully, and then tossed it all the way to the back of the hall, where the shambling derelicts fell upon it with a satisfactory noise of growling and scuffling. "None of you," said the clown quietly, "will ever take anything from me but what I let you have."

He looked up at the remaining beggar lords. Their spider web hammocks were still swaying back and forth across the abyss, though they'd stopped yelling and waving and now just peered cautiously down, their eyes glittering in the smoky red glow from the oil lamps. Horrabin's gaze dropped to the corpse, and then swung to the thief lords sitting at the long table. Miller, the one who had been loudest in the mutinous uproar, avoided meeting his eyes.

"Carrington," Horrabin said softly.

"Aye," said his lieutenant, stepping forward. He still limped from the beating he'd taken in one of the Haymarket brothels, but the bandages were gone, and his look of frustrated anger was tonight especially intense.

"Kill Miller for me."

As the suddenly pale and gasping thief lord kicked his chair back and scrambled to his feet, Carrington drew a pistol from his belt, poked it casually in Miller's direction and fired. The ball struck Miller in the back of the throat through his open mouth, punching out a hole over his collar.

Horrabin spread his hands as the body hit the stones. "You see," he said loudly before the tumult could start up again—then went on more quietly, "I'll feed all of you . . . one way or the other."

The clown smiled. It had been good theater. But where was Doctor Romany? Had all his promises, as Miller had insisted, been lies to manipulate the London thieves into furthering some privately profitable scheme of his own? Horrabin, who knew more than the rest about what was supposed to have happened, was concealing a disquiet greater than Miller's had been. Was the king assassinated yet? If so, why hadn't any of the clown's surface runners reported it? Or was the news being suppressed? *Where was Romany?*

In the silence the unsteady, jarring footsteps from the corridor sounded loud. Horrabin looked up, though without much interest, since it wasn't Romany's twanging step, and his eyes widened in surprise when the newcomer stepped into the hall, for it was Romany after all, but he was wearing high platform boots instead of his spring-shoes.

The clown cast a triumphant glance around the company, then bowed grotesquely to the newcomer. "Ah, your Worship," he piped, "we've been awaiting your arrival with, in a couple of cases," he waved at the two corpses, "*terminal suspense.*"

Then Horrabin's smile faltered and he looked more closely, for the visitor was pale and reeling, and blood was running sluggishly from his nose and ears. "You're . . . Horrabin?" the man croaked. "Take me . . . to Doctor Romany's camp . . . now."

As the clown blinked uncomprehendingly, a voice screeched

from the derelict's corner. "No use going there, Pierre! That whole plan's as dead as Ramses! But I can lead you to the man that wrecked it—and if you can take him and wring him dry, you'll have a better thing than just England dead, Fred!" A few of the penny toss crowd had sufficiently recovered their aplomb to cheer and whistle at this pronouncement.

"Carrington," whispered Horrabin, furious and embarrassed, "get that creature out of here. In fact, kill it." He smiled nervously at Romanelli. "I do apologize, uh, sir. Our . . . democratic policies are sometimes too—"

But Romanelli was staring with almost horrified astonishment at the weightless derelict. "Silence!" he rasped.

"Yes, do shut him up, Carrington," said Horrabin.

"I mean you, clown," said Romanelli. "Get out of here if you can't shut up. You," he added to Carrington, "stay where you are." Then almost reluctantly he turned to the ruin-faced derelict again. "Come here," he said.

The thing flapped and jiggled across the floor and tap-danced to a stop in front of him.

"You're him," Romanelli said wonderingly, "the ka the Master drew eight years ago. But . . . that face wound was taken . . . decades ago, by the look of it. And your weight —you're nearly at the disintegration point. How can this have happened in just eight years? Or no, since I last spoke with you?"

"It's them gates Fikee opened," the thing chittered. "I went through one, and was a long time making my way back. But let's discuss it on the ride, Clyde—the man that knows it all is staying at The Swan With Two Necks in Lad Lane, and if you can take him to Cairo for a thorough sifting, then nothing since 1802 will have been a waste of time." The thing turned its eye on Horrabin. "We'll need six—no, ten—of your biggest and coolest boys, ones smart enough to grab and bind a big man without killing him or denting his precious brain. Oh, and a couple of carriages, and fresh horses."

There was some snickering from the crowd, and Horrabin said, with a not very confident attempt at bravado, "I do not take orders from a damned . . . walking cast-off snakeskin."

Romanelli opened his mouth to contradict him, but the ragged creature in the middle of the floor waved him to silence. "That's nearly exactly what you'll take orders from, clown," it said. "You've done my bidding before, though I can scarcely now remember those evenings of scheming, hang-

ing side by side in the buried bell tower. What I remember
more clearly is waiting for your birth. I knew your father when
he stood no higher than the table there, and I knew him when
he was the tall leader of this thieves' guild, and then I used to
chat with him over a snitched bottle of wine sometimes in the
days after you'd shortened him down again so as to have a
court jester." A couple of the creature's teeth were blown out
of its mouth by the vehemence of its speech, and they spun
away upward like bubbles rising through oil. "It's a terrible
thing to have to sit through one's own foolish speeches again,
knowing they're all wrong while you wait for the clock to
come around again, but I've done it now. I'm the only one in
the world that knows the whole story. I'm the only one worth
taking orders *from*."

"Do as he says," growled Doctor Romanelli.

"Aye," said the bobbing creature. "And when you've got
him, I'll come along to Cairo with you, and after the Master's
finished with him I'll kill whatever's left of him."

Having copied out the cover letter to *The Courier* from
memory, Doyle tossed it onto the stack of manuscript pages
that lay beside Doctor Romany's sheathed sword on the desk.
It hadn't even come as too much of a surprise to him when
he'd realized, after writing down the first few lines of "The
Twelve Hours of the Night," that while his casual scrawl had
remained recognizably his own, his new left-handedness made
his formal handwriting different—though by no means unfamiliar: for it was identical to William Ashbless'. And now
that he'd written the poem out completely he was certain that
if a photographic slide of *this* copy was laid over a slide of the
copy that in 1983 would reside in the British Museum, they
would line up perfectly, with every comma and i-dot of his
version precisely covering those of the original manuscript.

Original manuscript? he thought with a mixture of awe and
unease. This stack of papers here is the original manuscript
. . . it's just newer now than it was when I saw it in 1976. Hah!
I wouldn't have been so impressed to see it then if I'd known I
had made or would make those pen scratches. I wonder when,
where and how it'll pick up the grease marks I remember seeing on the early pages.

Suddenly a thought struck him. My God, he thought, then
if I stay and live out my life as Ashbless—which the universe
pretty clearly means me to do—then *nobody wrote Ashbless'*

poems. I'll copy out his poems from memory, having read them in the 1932 Collected Poems, and my copies will be set in type for the magazines, and they'll use tear sheets from the magazines to assemble the Collected Poems! They're a closed loop, uncreated! I'm just the . . . messenger and caretaker.

He pushed the vertiginous concept away, stood up and went to the window. Lifting the curtain aside, he looked down at the wide yard of the Swan With Two Necks, crowded with post and passenger coaches. I wonder where Byron is, he thought. He should have been able to find any number of bottles of claret by now. I wouldn't mind having a few glassfuls of something, so I could postpone considering certain questions . . . such as what is to become of this Byron ka—he's got to disappear, for I know there's no historical record of him, but here he is talking about looking up old friends tomorrow. So how will he vanish? Do kas wear out? Will he die?

Even as he let the curtain fall there was a knock at the door. He crossed to it. "Who's there?" he asked cautiously.

"Byron, with refreshments," came the cheery reply. "Who did you suppose?"

Doyle undid the chain and let him in. "You must have gone far afield for them."

"I did go over to Cheapside," Byron admitted, limping over to the table and setting a waxed paper bundle down on it, "but with good result." He tore the paper away. "Voila! Hot mutton, lobster salad and a bottle of what is unlikely to be, as the vendor swore it was, a Bordeaux." His face went blank. "Glasses." He looked up at Doyle. "We haven't any."

"Not even a skull to drink it out of," Doyle agreed.

Byron grinned. "You've read my Hours of Idleness!"

"Many times," said Doyle truthfully.

"Well, I'll be damned. In any case, we can pass the bottle back and forth."

Byron glanced around the room, and noticed the stack of poetry on the desk. "Aha!" he cried, snatching it up. "Poesy! Confess, it's your own."

Doyle smiled and shrugged deprecatingly. "It's no one else's."

"May I?"

Doyle waved awkwardly. "Help yourself."

After reading the first several pages—and, Doyle noticed, leaving grease stains on them from having upwrapped the mutton—Byron put the manuscript down and looked at Doyle

speculatively. "Is it your first effort?" He pulled the already
loosened cork out of the bottle neck and took a liberal swig.

"Uh, yes." Doyle took the proffered bottle and drank some
himself.

"Well, you've got a spark, sir, it seems to me—though a lot
of it is damned obscure crinkum-crankum—and God knows in
these times a poet is a worthless thing to be. I prefer the talents
of action—in May I swam the Hellespont, from Sestos to
Abydos, and I'm prouder of that feat than I could be of any
literary achievement."

Doyle grinned. "As a matter of fact, I agree. I'd be more
pleased with myself if I'd made a decent chair, so all the legs
touched the ground at the same time, than I am about having
written that poem." He folded the manuscript, wrapped the
cover letter around it, addressed it, then dripped some hot
candle wax on it for a seal.

Byron nodded sympathetically, started to speak, stopped,
and then quickly asked, "Who *are* you, by the way? I no
longer want to demand any answers, for I became your
lifelong friend when you shot that murderous gypsy who'd
otherwise have ended my story. But I'm damn curious." He
smiled shyly, and for the first time looked his actual age of
only twenty-three years.

Doyle took another long sip of the wine and set the bottle
down on the table. "Well, I'm an American, as you've probably guessed from my accent, and I came . . . here . . . to hear
Samuel Coleridge give a speech, and I ran afoul of this Doctor
Romany fellow—" He paused, for he thought he'd heard
something, a sort of thump, outside the window. Then,
remembering that they were on the third floor, he dismissed it
and went on. "And I lost the party of tourists I was with,
and—" He halted again, beginning to feel the alcohol. "Oh,
hell, Byron, I'll tell you the real story. Give me some more
wine first." Doyle took a long sip and set the bottle down with
exaggerated care. "I was born in—"

With simultaneous crashing explosions of glass from one
side and splinters from the other, the window and the door
burst inward and two big, rough-looking men were rolling to
their feet from the floor. The table went over, spilling the food
and shattering the table and the lamp—and in the sudden
dimness more men were pouring in through the doorway,
stumbling or leaping over the split door, which was hanging at

an angle from one twisted hinge. Blue flames began licking over the oil-splash.

Doyle grabbed one man by the scarf knot, took two steps across the room and then hurled him through the window; the man collided with the frame, and for a moment it seemed he might grab the rope the first man had swung in on, but then his hands and heels disappeared and there was a receding, gasping cry.

Byron had snatched up and drawn Romany's sword, and as two men with raised coshes stepped toward the still off-balance Doyle—and from below, outside, came a multiple crack, and startled yells—Byron kicked forward in a lunge too long to recover from easily and drove three inches of the ex-tended blade into the chest of the man closest to Doyle. "Look out, Ashbless!" he yelled as he wrenched the sword free and tried to straighten up.

The other man, alarmed by this sudden appearance of lethally naked steel, swung his cosh down with all his strength onto Byron's head. There was an ugly hollow smack and Byron fell dead to the floor, the sword clattering away.

To regain his balance Doyle had crouched and grabbed a leg of the desk, and from there he saw Byron's inert form; "*You son of a—*" he roared, straightening and lifting the desk over his head—everything spilled off it, and the envelope for the *Courier* fluttered out the open window—"*bitch!*" he finished, bringing the desk shattering down on the head and upraised arm of the man who'd hit Byron.

The man dropped, and since several of the intruders were busy smothering the fire, Doyle launched himself in a furious charge toward the doorway; two men leaped forward to block his way, but were felled by his massive fists; but as he lurched out into the hall a carefully swung sock full of sand thudded against his skull just behind his right ear, and his forward rush became a sloppy dive to the floor.

Doctor Romanelli eyed the motionless form for a few seconds, waving back the men who had followed Doyle out of the room, then he thrust the weighted sock away in a pocket. "Tie the chloroform rag around his face and get him out of here," he grated, "you incompetent clowns."

"Goddamn, yer Honor," whined the man who picked up Doyle's ankles, "they was ready for us! There's three of us dead, unless Norman survived his fall."

"Where's the other man who was in there?"

"Dead, boss," said the last man to emerge from the room, pulling on a scorched and smoking coat.

"Let's go, then. Down the back stairs." He pressed his hands to his eyes. "Try to stay together, will you do that at least?" he whispered. "You've caused such a pandemonium that I'll have to set a radiating disorientation spell to confuse the pursuit you've certainly roused." He began muttering in a language none of Horrabin's men recognized, and after the first dozen syllables blood began running out from between his fingers. Clumping footsteps sounded from the direction of the front stairs, and the men shifted and glanced at each other uneasily, but a moment later they heard a confused babble of argument, and the footsteps receded. Romanelli ceased speaking and lowered his hands, breathing hoarsely, and a couple of the men with him actually paled to see blood running like tears out of his eyes. "Move, you damned insects," Romanelli croaked, shoving his way to the front of the group and leading them forward.

"What's a pandemonium?" whispered one of the men in the rear.

"It's like a calliope," answered a companion. "I heard one played at the Harmony Fair last summer, when I went there to see my sister's boy play his organ."

"His what?"

"His *organ.*"

"Lord. People pay money to see things like that?"

"*Silence!*" Romanelli hissed. After that they were on the stairs, and gasping and straining too much with their unconscious burden even to want to speak.

It was a chorus of shrill, discordant whistling that finally led Doyle out of his drugged half-dreams. He sat up, shivering with the damp chill in his coffin-shaped box, the lid of which had been taken away, and after rubbing his eyes and taking several deep breaths he realized that the tiny bare room really was rocking, and that he must be aboard a ship. He hoisted a leg outside the box and let his sandalled heel clunk to the floor, and grabbing the sides he levered himself dizzily to his feet. His mouth was still full of the sharp reek of chloroform, and he grimaced and spat as he reeled to the door.

It was locked from the outside, as he'd expected. There was

a small window in the door at the level of his neck, with stout
iron bars instead of glass—which helped explain why the room
was so cold—and, crouching a little to look out of it, he saw a
damp deck that disappeared within a few yards into a wall of
gray fog, and, from out of the close murk, a rope, belt-high
and parallel to the deck, that was evidently moored to the outside of his cabin bulkhead.

The strident whistling seemed to be coming from somewhere only a dozen yards ahead. Summoning all his nerve,
and relying on the probability that his captors wanted to keep
him alive, Doyle yelled, "Cut out that damned noise! Some of
us are trying to sleep!"

Several of the whistles ceased instantly, and the rest faltered
into silence a few moments later, and in spite of himself Doyle
shivered to hear a voice that was almost Doctor Romany's say,
"You—no, you stay here; you—go shut him up. The rest of
you idiots keep playing. If a mere man shouting distracts you,
how do you expect to keep it up when the Shellengeri arrive?"

The eerie whistling started up again, and in a minute or so
Doyle, still resolutely at the window, saw a disorienting thing
—a tiny old man, bundled up in a tarred canvas coat and a
leather hat, was pulling himself along the waist-high rope
toward Doyle, but his legs trailed away upward; it looked like
he was moving underwater. When the weightless crawler had
bumped against the bulkhead and peered in through the little
window, Doyle saw the half-face and single eye and realized
that this was the same street lunatic who had once promised to
take him to a time gap and then had only led him to a vacant
lot and shown him some old charred bones.

"Shout all you . . . please when these . . . people are
through, Lou," the crawler said, "but if you do it again now,
you won't get fed for the rest of the voyage. And you want to
keep up your strength, right, Dwight?" Then the thing shoved
its awful face right at the bars and snarled, "I recommend you
eat—I want there to be some tooth left in you when the
Master's done and turns you over to me for disposal."

Doyle had let go of the fog-wet bars, and now he actually
stepped back, startled by the raw hatred blazing out of that
single eye. "Wait a minute," he muttered, "take it easy. What
did I ever do to—" Then he halted, struck by a grisly suspicion
that instantly became a certainty. "My God, it was the same
lot on the Surrey-side, wasn't it?" he whispered. "And you

couldn't have known I escaped through the cellar . . . for all you knew it was my own skull you were showing me, right? God. And so you survived Burghard's shot of mud . . . but I had that paper that worked as a mobile hook . . . Jesus, you must have simply *lived* your way back here!''

"That's right," chittered the thing that had been Doctor Romany. "And this is my homeward voyage—kas were never meant to survive nearly this long, and damn soon I'll take that last boat ride through the twelve hours of the night—but before I do, you will be, finally and certainly, dead.''

Not unless you're the one who'll meet me in the Woolwich marshes on the twelfth of April in 1846, thought Doyle. "What do you mean, the twelve hours of the night?" he asked cautiously, wondering if this creature had read the poem he'd written out last night.

The thing clinging to the rope grinned. "You'll see it before I do, Stu. It's the course through the Tuaut, the underworld, that the dead sungod Ra follows every night on his dark voyage from sunset to sunrise. Darkness becomes solid there, and hours are a measurement of distance, like sailing on an uncoiled clock face." The thing paused and emitted a thunderous belch that seemed to diminish its body mass by half.

"Quiet down there!" came a shout from out of the fog, loud enough to be heard over the skirling whistles.

"And the dead cluster along the banks of the underworld river," Romany went on in a whisper, "and beg passage on the sungod's boat back to the land of the living, for if they could get aboard they'd share in Ra's restoration to youth and strength. Some even swim out and grab on, but the serpent Apep stretches out . . . oh, very far! . . . and snatches them off and devours them.''

"That's what he—I—was referring to in the poem, then," said Doyle quietly. He looked up and forced a confident smile. "I've already travelled on a river whose milestones are hours," he said; "taken two very long voyages, in fact, and survived. If I wind up on your Tuaut river, I'll bet I pop out the dawn end good as new.''

This statement angered Doctor Romany. "You fool, no-body—''

"We're headed for Egypt, aren't we?" Doyle interrupted.

The single eye blinked. "How did you know that?"

Doyle smiled. "I know all sorts of things. When will we arrive?"

The Romany thing went on frowning for a moment, then it seemed to forget its anger, and it said, almost confidingly, "In a week or ten days, if the gang on the poop deck there manages to raise the Shellengeri—wind elementals, like what Aeolus gave Odysseus."

"Oh." Doyle tried, unsuccessfully, to peer through the fog in the direction of the stern. "Anything like those fire giants that went berserk at Doct—I mean, your camp?"

"Yes yes!" cried the thing, clapping with its bare feet. "Very good. Yes, the two races are cousins. And there are others, the water and earth ones. You should see the earth ones, huge moving cliffs—"

A deafening, air-cleaving whistle—scream, rather, though out of no physical throat—hit the ship with a palpable impact, making every loose board vibrate to blurriness; Doyle leaped away from the window, certain for one unthinking moment that some massive jetliner, a 747 or something, was for some reason attempting a water landing at full throttle very nearby, possibly right on top of them; then he was flung back against the door again as a wall of wind struck from astern, snapped all the sails taut and burst several like a giant punching fist, and the ship's bow went far down and then up again and the vessel surged powerfully forward.

In the few seconds before the ship and all its contents shifted and adjusted to the new velocity, the stern bulkhead pressing against Doyle's back seemed more floor than wall, and when his coffin box clattered across the deck toward him he just lifted his legs away from the deck—no hop required—and let it slam end on where his ankles had been. Then gravity swung back to normal and he pitched forward onto his hands and knees in the box. Over the screaming wind he heard the first high-flung bow wave crash back across the decks.

He scrambled to his feet and grabbed the window bars and, squinting against the steady blast of icy air, peered around for the Romany remnant, but the creature was gone. I hope he went right overboard, he thought—though I guess he wouldn't sink, just come paddling along after us like a big beetle. The ship was slamming along like a bus racing over a plowed field, but Doyle managed to hold onto the window long enough to glimpse a few figures huddled on the poop deck, evidently trying to get down. At least it's dispelled the fog, he thought dazedly as he let go of the bars and slid down to a sitting position, blinking his wind-stung and watering eyes.

As time passed, bringing no abatement of the racket or the cold or the continual bouncing, Doyle was thankful that he was in Benner's body—Doyle's own had been prone to seasickness—though even in this one he was glad he hadn't managed to eat any of the lobster salad poor Byron had bought.

At what must have been about noon a couple of things were pushed through the window bars: a paper-wrapped package, which thumped to the floor and proved to contain salt pork and hard black bread, and a lidded can that fell a few inches and then swung from a little hooked chain; this contained weak beer. Having been snatched away from the food at the Swan, and not eaten before that since lunchtime yesterday, which was longer ago for Doyle than the twenty-four hours that had passed here, he devoured it all with genuine pleasure, even licking the paper wrappings afterward.

About six hours later the procedure was repeated and again he consumed it all. Soon after, it began to get dark—though the wind and the bashing progress of the ship slacked not at all—and he had just gotten around to wondering how he'd sleep, when a couple of blankets were stuffed through the bars.

"Thank you!" he called. "And could I have another beer?"

The room was not absolutely dark, and Doyle managed to improvise a good enough bed in his coffin; and as he was about to climb into it he was surprised to hear the beer can chain rattle as it was drawn up—the sluicing of the beer itself was inaudible over the wind shrilling through the harp of the rigging—and then a clank as it fell back into position, full.

He stood up and hurried over to it, and as he stood braced against the wall trying to drink the sloshing beer without spilling any of it he wondered why he was not too alarmed by his position as captive with torture and death in store. Partially, of course, it was the unthinking self-confidence he'd never entirely been without since finding himself in a body so much better than the one he'd been used to; and the balance of his stubborn optimism was based on being, as he was now willing to concede, William Ashbless, who wouldn't die until '46. Watch yourself there, son, he thought. You can be fairly sure you'll survive, but there's no reason to assume Ashbless won't get thoroughly stomped a time or two.

In spite of his predicament he smiled as he searched for a comfortable position, for he was thinking about Elizabeth Jacqueline Tichy, whom he would somehow marry next year—he'd always thought she looked pretty in her portraits.

The voyage—during which the furious winds never once let up, so that after a couple of days the shambling mariners Doyle could see through his window seemed to have achieved a stunned indifference to them—lasted fifteen days, and in that time Doyle never once saw either Romanelli or the weightless vestige of Doctor Romany. Until an old and overstressed beam in the ceiling of his room developed a long crack on the fourth day, all the captive had done was eat, sleep, peer out the window and try to remember the all too few known facts of Ashbless' visit to Egypt; after the beam split, he occupied his time pulling down a three-foot splinter and trying, with his teeth and nails, to trim a one-foot length of it into something like a dagger. He considered wrenching the beer can from the bars and flattening it to make a tool, but decided that not only would that deprive him of beer for the rest of the trip, but that anything so noticeable would earn him a search when they arrived.

Only once had anything nearly as disquieting as the arrival of the Shellengeri occurred. Sometime before midnight on Saturday, the eleventh night of the voyage, he'd thought he'd heard a wailing over the eternal wind scream, and he'd tried to see out, a trick as difficult as trying to see while riding a motorcycle at seventy miles per hour without goggles. After ten minutes he'd gone back to bed, more than half convinced that the black boat he'd seemed to see, visible because it shone a much deeper black than the waves behind it, had been nothing more than a retinal misfire caused by straining his eyes to see through the blast. After all, what would a boat be doing out there?

CHAPTER 11

". . . Nothing could be more horrible: its head
and shoulders were visible, turning first to one
side, then the other, with a solemn and awful
movement, as if impressed with some dreadful
secret of the deep, which, from its watery grave, it
came upwards to reveal. Such sights became
afterwards frequent, hardly a day passing without
ushering the dead to the contemplation of the living, until at length they passed without observa-
tion."

—E. D. Clarke

ON THE MORNING of the tenth of October Doyle came blearily
awake and realized that he was out on the deck . . . and that
the planks under his bearded cheek were hot, and when he
opened his eyes bright sunlight made him squeeze them shut
again . . . and then it came to him that he could hear talking,
creaking cordage, the slap of water against the gently rocking
hull—the wind had stopped.

"—Drydock *somewhere*," a man's gruff voice was saying,
"though not in this godforsaken outpost."

Another voice said something about Greece.

"Sure, if it'll get to Greece. Every damn seam is leaking,
just about every sail is shredded, the goddamn masts are—"

The second voice, which Doyle now recognized as the one

that was *nearly* identical to Doctor Romany's, interrupted with some brief harshness that shut the other up.

Doyle tried to sit up, but only managed to roll over, for he was tightly bound with thick, tarry-smelling ropes. They're not taking any chances with me, he thought; then he smiled, for he realized that the splintery object biting into his knee was his makeshift wooden dagger, overlooked by whoever had bound him.

"We were none too soon tying him up," said the harsher voice. "He's got a sound constitution—I'd have thought the drug would keep him under until this afternoon, at least."

Though it made his temples throb even more severely, Doyle lifted his head and blinked around. Two men were standing by the ship's rail, staring at him; one seemed to be a pre-time-jump version of Doctor Romany—that would be Romanelli, he thought, the original—and the other was evidently the captain of the ship.

Romanelli was barefoot, and he padded across to Doyle and crouched beside him. "Good morning," he said. "I may want to ask you questions, and we probably won't meet anyone who speaks English, so I'm going to leave the gag off. If you want to yell and make a commotion, though, we can tie it on and conceal it under a burnoose."

Doyle let his head clunk back onto the deck, then closed his eyes and waited until the throbbing abated a little. "Okay," he said, opening them again and blinking up at the empty blue sky beyond the tangle of spars and riggings and reefed sails. "We're in Egypt?"

"Alexandria." Romanelli nodded. "We'll row you ashore, and then it's overland to the Rosetta branch of the Nile, and we'll sail you upriver to Cairo. Savor the view." The sorcerer stood up with a loud popping of the knees and an imperfectly concealed wince. "You men," he called irritably. "The boat's ready? Then get him over the side and into it."

Doyle was lifted up, carried to the rail, and after a hook was snugged in under the rope that went under his arms he was lowered like a bundled-up rug into a rowboat that bobbed and banged against the hull in the emerald water twenty feet below. A sailor in the boat grabbed his bound ankles and guided him down to a sitting position on one of the thwarts while Romanelli descended a rope ladder and, after swinging about for a minute on the end of it, waving a free foot and swearing, did a sort of half-slide into the boat. The sailor helped him to

another thwart and then the last passenger came swinging
wildly down the ladder—it was the Luck of the Surrey-side
Beggars himself, the time-ruined Doctor Romany, with two
big metal spikes tied to his shoes for weight. After placing this
grinning, winking creature on the narrow bow, where it sat
like a trained cormorant, the sailor wiped his hands and sat
down himself, impassively facing Romanelli and Doyle; he
picked up the oars and set to work.

Doyle immediately toppled over against the starboard gunwale, and from this position watched the ship's hull slide past
and eventually give way, as they rounded the high arch of the
bow, to a view of Alexandria, half a mile away across the glittering water.

The city was a disappointment to him—he'd expected the
labyrinthine Oriental city Lawrence Durrell had written about,
but all he saw was a small cluster of dilapidated white
buildings baking in the sun. There were no other ships in the
harbor, and only a few boats lay moored to the weathered
quays.

"That's *Alexandria*?" he asked.

"Not what it used to be," growled Romanelli in a tone that
didn't invite further discussion. The wizard was huddled
against the opposite gunwale, breathing in long wheezes.
What was left of Romany was giggling quietly on the bow.

The man at the oars let the harbor's current slant them to
the left, east of the town, and on a sandy rise Doyle finally saw
some people; three or four figures in Arab robes stood in the
shade of a dusty palm tree, while a number of camels stood
and sat around a section of ruined wall nearby. Doyle wasn't
surprised when the sailor heeled the boat about and aimed the
bow toward the palm tree and Romanelli waved and yelled,
"*Ya Abbas, sabah ixler!*"

One of the robed men was now walking down to the shore.
He waved and called, "*Saghida, ya Romanelli!*"

Doyle eyed the man's lean, sharp-chiseled face and nervously tried to imagine the fellow doing anything just domes-
tically pleasant, like petting a cat. He couldn't.

When the boat was still a few yards from shore the keel
grated on the sandy bottom, stopping the little craft and pitching Doyle forward.

"Ow," he mumbled, his lips brushing the thwart, which
was coldly and saltily wet from the splashing of the oars. A
moment later Romanelli yanked him upright.

"That *hurt?*" asked the wide-eyed bow-croucher with mock alarm. "Sa-a-a-ay—did that *hurt,* Burt?"

The sorcerer had stood up and was barking instructions in Arabic, and two more of the men from under the palm hastened down toward the water, while the first man was already splashing out toward the boat. Romanelli pointed down at Doyle. "*Taghala maghaya nisilu,*" he said, and lean brown arms reached over the gunwale and lifted Doyle out of the boat.

Doyle was tied onto a camel and in spite of the several rest and water stops, by the time they arrived at the little town of El Hamed by the Nile, late in the afternoon, Doyle's legs were distant columns of numbness, only recognizable as his own when they were occasionally lanced with tooth-grinding agony, and his spine felt like a big old dried sunflower stalk that kids had used for a blowgun dart target. When the Arabs untied him and carried him aboard the *dahabeeyeh,* a low, single-masted boat with a little cabin in the back, he was half delirious and muttering, "Beer . . . beer . . ." Fortunately they seemed to recognize the word, and brought him a jug of what was, blessedly and unmistakably, beer. Doyle drained it in several long swallows and fell back across the deck, instantly asleep.

He awoke in darkness when the boat bumped gently against wood and rocked to a stop, and when his captors hoisted him up and sat him on the dock, facing inland, he could see lights only a few hundred yards away to his left.

A man with a lantern stepped down onto the dock. "*Is salam ghalekum, ya Romanelli,*" he said quietly.

"*Wi ghalekum is salam,*" Romanelli answered.

Doyle had been dreading another camel ride, and he sighed with relief when he noticed the silhouette of a real British carriage up on the road behind the man. "Are we in Cairo?" he asked.

"Just past it," Romanelli said shortly. "We're going inland, toward the Karafeh, the necropolis below the Citadel." He barked at the Arabs and obediently they lifted Doyle by his ankles and shoulders and carried him up a set of ancient stone steps to the road and pushed him into the carriage.

A few moments later he was joined by Romanelli, the Romany thing, one of the Arabs and the man who had met them here. Reins snapped and the carriage surged into rattling motion.

Necropolis, thought Doyle unhappily. Excellent. He pressed his knees together as he sat folded up on the floor of the carriage, and was only slightly reassured by the feel of his home-made wooden dagger. He hadn't been aware of the tropical smells of the river until they diminished and were replaced by the fainter but harsher dessicated-stone smell of the desert.

After about two miles of slow travel on a crumbled but serviceable road they stopped, and when Doyle was lifted out and propped upright beside the carriage he stared at the lightless building they'd arrived at, standing alone in the desert waste. The lantern showed an arched doorway, flanked by wide pillars, in a wall otherwise featureless except for a couple of holes that might have been meant to be windows, though they were too small even to poke one's head through. Above, he could dimly see a large dome silhouetted against the stars.

At a nod from Romanelli the Arab who'd accompanied them from the boat pulled a mirror-bright curved dagger from under his robe and sliced through three loops of rope around Doyle's legs. All the rope from his waist down fell to the dusty ground, and Doyle kicked it off his ankles.

"Don't run," said Romanelli wearily. "Abbas would certainly outrun you, and then I'd have to instruct him to sever one of your Achilles tendons."

Doyle nodded, wondering if he'd even be able to walk.

The shrunken ka had taken off its weighted shoes and, gripping the buckles of them, was walking around on its hands, with its legs flailing upward like ribbons tied to a floor heater vent. It grinned upside down at Doyle and said, "Time to go see the moon man, Stan."

"Shut up," Romanelli told it. To Doyle he said, "This way. Come on."

Doyle limped after him toward the door, accompanied by the ka, and when they'd covered half the twenty foot distance to the front door there was a hollowly echoing snap and then the door swung inward and a hooded figure with a lantern was beckoning. Romanelli impatiently waved Doyle and the ka past him into the broad stone hallway and asked a question, in a language that didn't seem to be Arabic this time, as the hooded man closed and re-bolted the door.

The man shrugged and gave a brief answer that seemed neither to surprise nor please Romanelli.

"He's no better," he muttered to the ka as he led the way forward. The man with the lantern followed, and the swinging shadows made the Old Kingdom bas reliefs on the walls, and even the columns of hieroglyphics, seem to move. Doyle noticed that the hall ended a dozen yards ahead at a carefully bricked surface of masonry that was bellied and leaning sharply out toward them, so that the floor extended a good deal farther than the ceiling; as if, he thought, there's an above ground swimming pool on the other side.

"Was you expecting to hear he'd commenced turning summer-salties?" inquired the still-inverted ka.

Romanelli ignored the creature and, turning into an open arch in the left-hand wall, started up a set of steps. Light touched the pitted stair edges from around a corner above, and the man with the lantern remained—gratefully, it seemed to Doyle—below. The three of them climbed to another hall, much shorter than the one downstairs, and this one ended at a balcony that faced the lighted interior of the dome. The trio moved forward to the balcony rail.

Doyle found himself staring out across the inside of a huge sphere, roughly seventy-five feet across, illuminated by a lamp that hung in the precise center, at the same level as the balcony, from a long chain moored to the highest point of the dome. He leaned over the rail and looked down, and was surprised to see four motionless men in a round stone-walled pen at the very bottom of the spherical chamber.

"Greetings, my little friends," came a grinding whisper from the opposite side of the sphere, and Doyle noticed for the first time that there was a man—a very old and withered and twisted man—lying on a couch that was somehow attached to the far wall only a foot or two below the horizontal black line that seemed to be the room's equator. The man lay on the couch, and the couch on the nearly perpendicular wall, with such a convincing appearance of gravity holding them there that Doyle automatically looked around for the edges of the mirror that had to be there . . . but there was no break in the dome's inner surface; couch and man actually hung up there, like some disagreeable wall ornament. And just as Doyle had begun to speculate about how the old man stayed on the evidently nailed-up couch with such an appearance of nonchalance, and where a ladder could be footed to get him up there, there was a squealing of casters and the couch rolled upward a little.

The man on the couch groaned, then leaned over and peered

at the "floor"; the couch now sat right over the equator line. "Moonrise," he said wearily. He lay back again and stared across the sphere at the balcony. "I see Doctors Romanelli and Romany, the latter standing as a clear indictment of my ability to cast a decent ka. I would have thought you would last a century without deteriorating to this point. But who is our giant visitor?"

"His name, I gather, is Brendan Doyle," said Romanelli.

"Good evening, Brendan Doyle," said the man on the wall. "I . . . apologize for not being able to come over and shake hands, but having renounced this present earth, I gravitate instead toward . . . another place. It's an uncomfortable position, and one that we hope to remedy before long. And," he went on, "what has Mr. Doyle got to do with the present débâcle?"

"He did it, yer Honor!" chittered the ka. "He snapped the Byron ka out of the obedience spell we had him under, and he made the yags go crazy, and then when I jumped back to 1684 he followed me and alerted the Antaeus Brotherhood to my presence there—" He'd let go of his shoes in order to gesture, and he floated upward feet first, bumped against the round brick cowl that extended out around the balcony and rolled over it and began floating up toward the top of the dome, "—and they somehow knew that a weapon fouled with dirt could injure me and they shot my face off with a mud-clogged gun—"

"Jutmoop sidskeen efty door?" sputtered the Master.

Romanelli and Doyle, and the ka, who by now was crouching upside-down beside the lamp chain mooring on the ceiling, all stared at him.

The Master squeezed his eyes and mouth tightly shut, then opened them. "Jumped," he said carefully, "to sixteen eighty-four?"

"I believe he did, sir," Romanelli put in hastily. "They used the gates Fikee made—traveling from gate to gate, through time, you understand? This ka," he waved his hand upward, "is obviously too decayed for only eight years of action, and what I've pieced together of his story is consistent."

The Master nodded slowly. "There was something peculiar about the way our Monmouth scheme misfired in 1684." The couch rolled another few inches upward, and though the Master's teeth clenched with pain, one of the motionless figures in the pen below groaned echoingly. Startled, Doyle glanced down at them again, and was not reassured to see that they were wax statues. The Master's eyes opened. "Time travel," he whispered. "And where did Mr. Doyle come from?"

"Some other time," said the ka. "He and a whole party of people appeared through one of the gates, and I managed to capture him, though his companions returned the way they'd come. I had a little time to question him, and—listen—he knows where Tutankhamen's tomb is. He knows lots of things."

The Master nodded and then, horribly, smiled. "It could be that, in this late and sterile age, we've blundered onto the most powerful tool we've ever had. Romanelli, draw some blood from our guest and construct a ka—a full maturation one that will know everything he does. We mustn't take any chances with what he's got in his head—he might kill himself or catch some fever. Do that right now, and then lock him up for the night. Interrogation will commence in the morning."

Ten minutes were wasted in getting the Romany ka down from the ceiling—it could no more scramble down to the balcony than a hamster could scramble up out of a bathtub—but it was finally recovered with a rope, and Romanelli led Doyle back down the stairs.

On the ground floor they entered a room where, in the dim light of a single lamp, the doorkeeper could be seen carefully stirring a long vat of some fishy-smelling fluid.

"Where's the cup of—" Romanelli began, but even as he'd spoken the doorkeeper had pointed at a table against the wall. "Ah." Romanelli crossed to it and carefully lifted a copper cup. "Here," he said, returning to Doyle. "Drink it and save us the trouble of tying you down and administering it through broken teeth."

Doyle took the cup and sniffed the contents dubiously. The stuff had a sharp, chemical reek. Reminding himself that he wasn't slated to die until 1846, he lifted the cup to his blistered lips and downed the drink in one big, gagging gulp.

"God," he wheezed, handing the cup back and trying to blink the fumes out of his eyes.

"Now we'll just impose upon you for a few drops of blood," Romanelli went on, drawing a knife from under his robe.

"Just pop the cork on a vein, Zane," agreed the remnant of

Doctor Romany. The ka was once more holding the buckles of its weighted shoes and walking on its hands.

"Blood?" Doyle asked. "What for?"

"You heard the Master tell us to make a ka of you," Romanelli answered. "Now I'm going to free your hands, but don't do anything idiotic."

Not me, Doyle thought. History says I'll leave Egypt in four months, sane and with all limbs intact. Why should I go out of my way to earn a concussion or a dislocated arm?

Romanelli cut the ropes that had bound Doyle's wrists. "Step over to the tub here," he said. "I'm just going to nick your finger."

Doyle stepped forward, holding his finger out and peering curiously into the pearly liquid. So, he thought, that's where they'll grow an exact duplicate of me. . . .

Oh my God, what if it's the duplicate that gets free and eventually returns to England to die in '46? I could die here without upsetting history.

His tenuous optimism abruptly extinguished, Doyle grabbed for Romanelli's approaching wrist, and though he cut the heel of one hand deeply on the sorcerer's knife, his other hand clamped onto Romanelli's forearm, and with the strength of desperation he wrenched the sorcerer forward and off balance toward the tub; but Doyle winced to see several drops of blood from his cut hand plop into the pearly stuff.

It seemed certain that Romanelli would pitch into the tub, so Doyle whirled, crouching, drew the makeshift dagger from his pant leg and sprang in a wild lunge toward the upside-down ka. It hooted in alarm and let go of the shoe buckles, but before it could float upward Doyle's wooden knife punched into its frail chest.

A blast of chilly and foul-smelling air hit Doyle in the face, and the ka flew backward off the end of the dagger and, visibly shrivelling as all the noxious air whooshed out of it, sailed across the room, rebounded from the wall, started to fly straight up toward the ceiling, then lost speed and stalled.

Romanelli was rolling in agony on the floor beyond the tub, having done an impromptu leap and roll over it without touching it. "Get him," he managed to croak.

The doorkeeper stood between Doyle and the hall door, and Doyle ran straight at him, brandishing the dagger and roaring as loud as he could.

The man leaped out of the way, but not quickly enough;

Doyle clubbed him with the butt end of the weapon and he tumbled to the floor unconscious as Doyle's racing footsteps receded down the hall.

Romanelli was still struggling to get his protective shoes between himself and the torturing floor as, with a sound as soft as the fall of a dead leaf onto a pond, the empty skin and clothes of Doctor Romany settled onto it and didn't move.

The beggars in Thames Street didn't approach the little man who came striding along in the cool twilight, for his ill-fitting clothes, pale, grinning face and wild mop of graying hair all indicated that he'd have no pence to spare, and might well even be mad; though one legless beggar on a wheeled cart did a double take, pushed himself along after the man for a few paces, then coasted to a stop, shook his head uncertainly and then wheeled around to return to his post.

Walking across the open pavement of Billingsgate, the man skirted the little Punch and Judy stage, and he heard the piping voice of Punch exclaim, "Ah, one of the Dolorous Brethren, I do b—" The voice choked off, and the man glanced at the puppet.

He halted and grinned. "Somethin' I can do for you, Punch?" he asked.

The puppet stared at him for several seconds. "Uh, no," it said. "I thought for a moment I—no."

The man shrugged and walked on toward the vacant dock. Soon his worn boot heels were knocking on the weathered wooden decking, and he paused only when he stood right on the splintery lip of the dock.

He stared out across the broad, darkening face of the great river at the first few lights on the Surrey-side, then he laughed quietly and whispered, "Let's just test your . . . stamina, Chinnie." He crouched, leaned forward and, arms over his head, kicked off in a long and fairly shallow dive. There was a splash and spatter, but it was not loud and there was no one nearby.

The ripples were just beginning to subside when his head broke the surface twenty feet farther out. He shook the wet hair out of his face and then trod water for a few moments, breathing in fast, whispered hoots. "Cold as the water through the seventh hour," he muttered. "Ah well—sherry and dry clothes in just a few minutes now." He did a leisurely crawl, punctuated by rest stops during which he floated on his back and stared at the stars, until he was far out in the center of the river, nowhere near any of the few boats and barges that were on the water that evening.

Then he expelled all the air from his lungs in a slow hiss that quickly became bubbles as his head disappeared under the surface.

For nearly a full minute bubbles continued to float up and pop in the lonely center of the river. Then there weren't any more, and the river resumed its featureless smoothness.

It had been a close bout all along, but at last, from his vantage point by the window, old Harry Angelo saw his premier pupil setting up his opponent for the thrust Angelo had recommended for use against a left-handed fencer.

The bout had been going on for more than five minutes without either fencer receiving a touch, and Richard Sheridan, who had strolled over, brandy glass in hand, to join the cluster of spectators, had remarked quietly to the pugilist "Gentleman" Jackson that it was the best display of swordplay he'd seen since Angelo had had his *salle* in the Opéra House in Haymarket.

Angelo's pupil, the prize fighter known as the Admirable Chinnie, had repeatedly disengaged from a feint toward the outside line of *sixte* into a thrust in the *quarte* line, on the other side of his opponent's blade, and his opponent had each time parried it easily, though never managing to land a riposte on Chinnie.

At the age of fifty-four, Harry Angelo had been the unquestioned master of fencing instruction in England ever since his legendary father's retirement a quarter of a century ago, and now he could read his pupil's intention as clearly as if Chinnie had spoken it: another *sixte* feint and then the by now expected disengage—but this time not all the way around the opposing bell guard to the *quarte* line, but instead up *under* the opponent's guard into the unprotected low flank.

Angelo smiled as the *sixte* feint was thrust out—then frowned, for the tipped point just wavered there. The opponent started to make the conditioned *quarte* parry, then noticed that Chinnie's blade was motionless, and so picked it up in a lightning bind that sent his own point corkscrewing in to thud and flex against Chinnie's canvas-jacketed stomach.

Angelo expelled his held breath in a whispered oath; then the Admirable Chinnie staggered back and almost fell over, and several of the spectators rushed to him to hold him up. Chinnie's opponent yanked off his mask and dropped it and his foil on the hardwood floor and exclaimed, "My God, did I hurt you, Chinnie?"

The prize fighter took off his own mask, straightened and shook his head as if to clear it. "No no," he said hoarsely. "Just a bit of trouble catching my breath just now. Right in a sec. Strain of the peculiar posture."

Angelo raised his gray eyebrows. In three years of concentrated instruction this was the first time he'd ever heard the Admirable Chinnie describe the *en guard* position as peculiar.

"Well, we certainly shan't count a point that was made when you were off guard," declared Chinnie's opponent. "Whenever you're ready we'll resume the bout at zero and zero."

Though smiling cheerfully, Chinnie shook his head. "No," he said. "Later. Right now—fresh air."

Old Richard Sheridan helped him to the door, with Angelo striding along beside them, as the rest of the company shrugged and picked up their foils and masks as two couples squared off on opposite sides of the *pistes* painted on the floor. "I trust he's all right," someone muttered.

Out in the hall Chinnie waved the other two men away as the clang and rasp resumed in the *salle*. "I'll be back in after a moment," he said. But when they'd reluctantly gone in, Chinnie hurried down the stairs to the street door, flung it open and sprinted away down the Bond Street pavement.

When he reached Piccadilly he slowed to a walk, taking deep lungfuls of the chilly autumn air, and at the Strand he glanced to his right, toward the river, and whispered, "How ye doin', Chinnie me lad? Cold, ain't it?" Another man on the sidewalk had started toward him as if he recognized him, but drew back, disconcerted, when Chinnie burst into maniacal giggling and did a fast, if inexpert, dance step on the pavement.

He continued muttering to himself all the way down Fleet Street to Cheapside. "Hah!" he exclaimed at one point, bounding into the air. "Good as Benner's, this is. Better! Don't know why it never occurred to me before to grab the West End sort of merchandise."

• • •

The first part of the dream was devoid of horror, and Darrow never remembered until he woke up that he'd been through it many times before.

The fog was so thick that he could see no more than a few yards ahead, and the damp black brick walls on either side were visible only because they were so claustrophobically close. The alley was silent except for an irregular knocking somewhere in the fog overhead, as though an unfastened shutter was swinging in a breeze.

He'd been taking a short cut that should have wound up at Leadenhall Street, but he'd been lost for what seemed like hours in this maze of courts and alleys and zigzagging lanes. He hadn't met a soul yet, but he'd stopped now because he'd heard a low cough from the dimness ahead.

"Hello," he said, and was instantly ashamed of the timidity in his voice. "Hello there!" he went on more strongly. "Perhaps you can help me find my way."

He heard the shuffle of slow steps, and saw a dark form begin to emerge from the wall of mist; then the figure was close enough for him to see the face—and it was Brendan Doyle.

A hand seized Darrow's shoulder and the next thing he knew he was sitting bolt upright in his own bed, clenching his teeth against the despairing cry that in the dream had burst from his lips and resounded flatly in the fog-deadened air: "I'm sorry, Doyle! God, I'm sorry!"

"Jeez, chief," said the young man who'd awakened him, "didn't mean to startle you. But you said to roust you out at six-thirty."

"Right, Pete," Darrow croaked, swinging his legs to the floor and rubbing his eyes. "I'll be in the office. When the fellow I described gets here, send him in, will you?"

"Aye aye."

Darrow stood up, ran his hands through his white hair and then walked down the hall to the office. The first thing he did was pour himself a glass of brandy and drain it in one long swallow. He set the glass down, lowered himself into the chair behind the desk and waited for the liquor to sluice the images of his dream out of his head.

"May the damned dreams go with the body," he whispered, fumbling a cigarette out of a box and lighting it in the lamp flame. He drew the smoke deep into his lungs, leaned back and blew it toward the ranked ledgers on the shelf next to the desk. He considered, then discarded, the idea of doing some more work on his already complicated network of investments. He was getting rich again rapidly, and it was irritating to have to work without computers and calculators.

Soon two sets of boots could be heard ascending the stairs, and in a moment there was a knock on the office door.

"Come in," said Darrow, forcing his voice to sound easy and confident.

The door opened and a tall young man strode in, a smirking grin on his handsome, clean-shaven face. "Here it is, yer Honor," he said, doing a satirical pirouette in the middle of the room.

"Okay, hold still. The doc will go over you in a few minutes, but I wanted to eyeball it myself first. How's it feel walking?"

"Springy as new French steel. You know what surprised me? All the *smells* on the way over here! And I don't think I ever was able to see this well."

"Well, we'll get you a good one too. No headache, stomachache? He's been making a living for years as a prize fighter."

"None atall." The young man poured a brandy for himself, bolted it and refilled the glass.

"Easy on the sauce," said Darrow.

"The wha'?"

"The sauce, the booze—the brandy. Want me to get an ulcer?"

With an injured expression the young man set the glass down. His hand went to his mouth.

"And don't bite the nails, please," Darrow added. "Say, do you . . . ever catch any of the old tenant's thoughts, left behind in the, like, cupboards of his head after his eviction? Uh, do things like dreams ever stay with the old body?"

"Avo—I mean, yes, yer Honor—I believe so. It's not the sort of thing I pay attention to, but sometimes I find myself dreaming of places I've never seen, and I believe it's bits from the lives of the lads I've passed through. No way of knowin' for sure. And," he paused, and his eyebrows drew together, "and sometimes when I'm just driftin' over the line from awake to asleep, I hear . . . well, picture standin' on the forecastle of an emigrant ship, you know, in the middle of the night with all them bunks like bookshelves all over the walls? . . . And imagine that each of those men is talking in his sleep . . . ''

Darrow reached across the desk, took the filled glass and drained it. ''This stomach doesn't matter,'' he said, pushing his chair back and getting to his feet. ''Come on, let's go see the doc.''

Young Fennery Clare, his bare feet still tingling from having stood for a while in the warm pool below the sheet metal manufactory by Execution Dock, waded out from the docks, skirting the Limehouse Hole, and tried to line up the landmarks he'd memorized this morning. It was getting darker by the minute, though, and the two chimneys across the river were completely invisible, while the crane on the third pier downstream of him seemed to have been moved since he saw it last. And though the tide was on its way out again, he was already in up to his waist, and like most Mud Larks he couldn't swim.

Damn that bunch of Irish kids, he thought. If they hadn't been hanging about the Hole here this morning, I could have just picked the sack up and carried it out, for I can thrash any of the local kids. Them Micks would have taken it from me for sure, though, and a stroke of luck like this might come only once in a lifetime: a cloth bag, evidently dropped by one of the workmen who were re-sheathing that big ship here last week, absolutely filled with copper nails!

The very thought of the money he'd get from the rag shop for the haul—eight pence at least, more likely a shilling and some—made the boy's mouth water, and he resolved that if he found it and couldn't work it back up the slope with his feet, he'd risk being swept away and just bend down and pick it up. It would be well worth the risk, for he could live high for several lazy days on a shilling, at the end of which time he'd be ready to do his usual early winter trick of getting caught stealing coal from one of the barges up at Wapping so as to be sent off to the House of Correction, where he'd have a coat and shoes and stockings and regular meals for several months, and not have to wade half-clad out into the cold mud in the winter dawns.

He tensed and the corners of his mouth turned up in a smile, for the toes of his left foot had plunged through the top layer of silt and found cloth. He turned, trying to get his other foot to it without losing his balance.

"Can," croaked a voice from a few yards out in the water, "can someone . . . help me?"

The boy recovered his balance after starting in surprise, and belatedly realized that some of the river sounds that he'd been too absorbed to pay attention to had been the ripple and swish of weak swimming.

There was the spatter of a wet head being shaken. "Hey . . . boy! Is that a boy there? Help me!"

"I can't swim," said Fennery.

"You're standing there, aren't you? The shore's so close?"

"Aye, just behind me."

"Then I can . . . make it myself. Where am I?"

"I'll tell you if you come pick up this sack of nails for me."

The swimmer had been angling toward the boy, and was now close enough to stand on the underwater mud slope. For a few minutes he just stood there as his frame was racked with gasping and choking and retching. Fennery was glad he was upstream of the man.

"God," the man gasped finally. He rinsed his mouth and spat. "I must have . . . swallowed half the Thames. Did you hear an explosion earlier?"

"No, sir," said Fennery. "What blew up?"

"I think a block in Bond Street did. One moment I was—" He gagged and threw up another cupful of river water. "Pah. Lord preserve me. I was fencing at Angelo's, and an instant later I was at the bottom of the Thames with empty lungs. I think it took me five minutes to fight my way to the surface—I don't think anybody who wasn't a trained athlete could have done it—and in spite of clenched teeth and a . . . firm resolve, I tried to breathe the river on the way up. I don't even recall breaking the surface—I think I had fainted, and the cold air revived me."

The boy nodded. "Could you reach down and get me my bag?"

Dazedly obedient, the man bent over, ducked his head under, groped for and found the neck of the bag and yanked it up out of the mud. "Here you go, lad," he said when he'd straightened up. "Lord, I'm weak! Scarce could lift it. And I think I've damaged my ears—voice sounds odd. Where is this?"

"Limehouse, sir," said Fennery gleefully, wading back toward the stairs.

"Limehouse? Then I've been swept much further than I'd thought."

The water was only at Fennery's knees now, and he was able both to hang onto the bag and support the bedraggled swimmer, who was reeling dizzily. "You're an athlete, sir?" the boy asked dubiously, for the shoulder he was supporting felt bony and thin.

"Aye. I'm Adelbert Chinnie."

"What? Not the Admirable Chinnie, the singlestick champion?"

"That's me."

"Why, I saw you in Covent Garden once, fighting Torres the Terrible." They had reached the stairs, and started haltingly up them.

"Summer before last, that was. Yes, he nearly beat me, too."

When they had laboriously gotten up to street level they walked along a cinder path in the shadow of a brick wall for a dozen paces, then rounded the end of it and started across a littered, industrial-looking yard that was lit by a couple of lanterns hung on the wall of a warehouse.

Fennery was glad to be so impressively escorted in this neighborhood, which was one of the most perilous in London. He glanced up at his companion—and halted.

"You stinking liar!" he hissed, all at once fearful of making any noise.

The man seemed to be having difficulty walking. "What?" he asked distractedly.

"You're not the Admirable Chinnie!"

"Of course I am. What the devil do you suppose is wrong with me, though? My whole body feels strange, as though—"

"Chinnie's taller than you, and younger, and muscular. You're some sort of derelict."

The man chuckled weakly. "You young wretch. If there was ever an occasion I'd every right to look like a derelict, this is it. How do you suppose you'd look after swimming up, breathless, from the floor of the river? And I am taller—when shod."

The boy shook his head incredulously. "You've sure gone to hell since that summer. Look, I live just over there, so I'm gonna go, but if you follow that lane it'll get you to Ratcliff

Highway. You ought to be able to get a cab there."

"Thank you, lad." The man began to walk unsteadily in the indicated direction.

"Take care of yourself, eh?" called the boy. "And thanks for helping me with the bag!" His bare feet slapped away into the darkness.

"You're welcome," the man muttered. What was the matter with him? And what actually had happened? Now that he'd had time to catch his breath and consider the problem, the explosion idea made no sense. Had he been waylaid on the way home and tossed into the river, and shock erased the memory of everything since that bout at Angelo's? But no, he never left Angelo's before ten, and the sky in the west wasn't even completely dark yet.

As he was about to round the corner of the warehouse he noticed a window set into the brick just below the lantern, and he glanced into it as he walked past . . . then halted, walked back, and stared into it.

He raised a hand to his face, and was horrified to see the figure in the reflection do the same, for it was not him. The face was not his face.

He leaped away from the glass and looked at his clothing—no, he hadn't noticed it before, one set of wet clothes on a dark night being very much like another, but these weren't any jacket and trousers that ever belonged to Adelbert Chinnie.

For an insane second he wanted to dig his fingers into this face and peel it away; and then he considered the notion that he wasn't and never had been the Admirable Chinnie, but was just a—God knew what, beggar, apparently—who had dreamt it.

He forced himself to walk back to the window and look into it again. The face that peered fearfully out at him was thin, sagging and deeply lined, with, he noticed when he tilted his head back, a network of crazy wrinkles around the eyes, and though the thick tangle of hair was dripping wet, he could see a lot of gray in it. And when he pushed the hair back he nearly burst into sobs, for he had no right ear at all.

"Well, I don't care," he said in a voice as tense as a stressed glass pane. He was so wet, and the body's sensations so unfamiliar to him, that he really didn't know if the wetness around his eyes was tears. "I don't care," he repeated. "I'm Chinnie."

He attempted—and quickly abandoned—a brave smile, but nevertheless squared his narrow shoulders and strode resolutely toward the Ratcliff Highway.

CHAPTER 12

"O death, where is thy victory?"
—The First Epistle of Paul to the Corinthians

WITH THE WAR against France going on, and its attendant embargoes and black markets and rumors of a proposed invasion of England by Napoleon, the financial and mercantile situations in Threadneedle Street were in perpetual turmoil, and a man who was in the right place at the right time with the right commodity could become wealthy in hours, while a fortune that in other times would take decades to lose could now evaporate in one morning at the Royal Exchange. And though only someone who kept an extra sharp eye on the market would have noticed, there was one speculator who had a hand in nearly every area of commerce, and invariably managed to be standing on the winning side of every surprise, disaster and reverse.

Jacob Christopher Dundee, as J. Cochran Darrow now called himself, had only begun his investment career on the twenty-second of October, but within one month he had, by an inspired series of shiftings and reinvestments and possibly extra-legal international currency exchanges, increased his initial capital tremendously. And though his antecedents were of the vaguest, such was the charm of the handsome young Dundee that on the fifth of December the *London Times* announced his engagement to "Claire, daughter of the successful importer Joel Peabody."

In his office over a defunct depilatory parlor in Leadenhall Street, Jacob Dundee irritably waved away a cloud of tobacco smoke that issued from the pipe of his elderly companion, and then squinted again at the notice in the *Times*. "Well, they seem to have spelled all the names correctly, at least," he said. "Though I could have done without the reference to 'the shrewd newcomer on the London market scene.' A low profile is essential in this kind of work—already I've got people watching me and riding along on deals."

The old man glanced curiously at the paper. "Nice girl?"

"Adequate for my purposes," Dundee said impatiently, waving away more smoke.

"Your purposes? And what be they, pray?"

"To have a son," said the young man softly. "A boy that I can set up with a fortune, and a solidly established background, and perfect health. My medical lads say that Claire is as healthy and intelligent a marriageable young lady as can be found in England today."

The old man grinned. "Most engaged young gentlemen look forward to somethin' a little less philo-hosophical, but more fun, eh? And I've heerd this Peabody piece is a comely one. But no doubt you've already ridden around the course a few times, familiarized yerself wi' the turf?"

Dundee reddened. "Well, I—no, I'm not in any—damn it, I'm not a young man—I mean, I am, but all that sort of thing will have to—" He coughed. "Damn it, do you *have* to smoke that stuff? How do you think you got cancer in the first place? If you *need* nicotine, settle for *chewing* tobacco in my presence, okay?"

"*Okay*," said the old man. "Okay, okay, *okay*." He'd only learned the word recently, and still relished it. "Why do you care, anyway? Part of the bargain was a new one any time you like."

"I know." Dundee rubbed his eyes and ran his fingers through his curly brown hair. "It's like a new car, that's all," he muttered. "Until it gets the first dent you worry about everything."

"For such a healthy young sprout yer lookin' distinctly wilted," observed the old man, putting his black clay pipe on the floor and reaching out to snag the brandy decanter instead. He sucked down an awesome amount of it.

"Yeah, I'm not sleeping too well," Dundee admitted. "Dream I keep having . . ."

"You've got to get away from dreams, laddie, get some distance. I suppose I dream all the time, and if I ever paid attention to 'em I'm sure I'd be stark mad right now. I've kind of . . . split off a little bit of me mind to watch the dreams, so I don't have to be bothered."

"That sounds healthy," said Dundee with a despairing nod. "Yeah, that sounds *fine*."

His companion, missing the irony, nodded complacently. "Okay, you'll get used to it. After a couple more jumps you'll pay no more mind to dreams than to the dust your wheels raise on the road behind you."

Dundee poured himself some brandy, added some water from a nearby carafe, and took a sip. "Have you decided where you'll go from," he waved vaguely at the old man, "here?"

"Aye. I think I'll oust Mr. Maturo—yer *Mister Anonymous*. He dines there very frequent, and it ought not to be any trouble sifting the unhinging herbs into his stew some night a week or so hence."

"Maturo? The guy who hangs you? From the account in Robb's *Journals* he sounds like he's about fifty years old."

"Aye, he is, and I won't stay in him more than the necessary week—but I will so enjoy the expression on his face when, in the moment before he kicks that barrel away, he finds *himself* up there standing on it with the rope round his neck, and me in his body grinnin' up at him."

Dundee shuddered. "God rest ye merry, gentlemen," he said.

Down the relatively snow-free gutter in the middle of the street the short man jogged energetically, puffing white clouds like a laboring steam engine as he forced himself to carry the ten-pound box of raisins in one hand at arm's length. After twenty paces he switched the box to his other hand and flailed the now-free one to unstiffen it. His solid shoulders and unfatigued pace were evidence that physical exercise wasn't just a fad he'd taken up this afternoon.

It was only five days before Christmas, and in spite of the snow a number of people were out on the street, bundled up in coats and hats and mufflers, and a couple of boys and a dog were romping about with a sled. Occasionally a costermonger's cart would rattle and jingle past, smoke pluming from the driver's pipe and steam from the horse's nostrils, and the jogger would have to move out of the way. When they came from behind he never seemed to hear the carts until they were almost on top of him, and he'd been shouted at so many times that when he heard another insistent call behind him he just moved aside without looking back.

But the cry was repeated. "Hey, Doyle!"

The short man glanced over his shoulder and then let himself slow to a walk and finally a halt, for a skinny, moustachioed street boy was waving at him and plodding through the street edge snowbank toward him.

"Doyle!" the boy called. "I found your William Ashbless! He had a poem published in this week's *Courier!*"

The man waited until the boy caught up with him. "I'm afraid you've got the wrong fellow," he said. "My name's not Doyle."

The boy blinked and stepped back. "Oh, sorry, I—" He cocked his head. "Sure it is."

"I'd know, wouldn't I? It's not."

Jacky frowned dubiously at him for a moment, then said, "Excuse me if I'm wrong—but don't you have a knife scar running down across your chest below your collar-bone?"

The man's response struck Jacky as peculiar. "Wait a minute!" he gasped, then pressed his palms to his chest. "You know this man?"

"You mean . . . you?" asked Jacky uncertainly. "Yes. What, have you lost your memory?"

"*Who* is he?"

"He's . . . you're Brendan Doyle, a . . . one-time member of Copenhagen Jack's beggar guild. Why, who do you think you are?"

The man watched Jacky carefully. "Adelbert Chinnie."

"What, the prize fighter? But Brendan, he's a lot taller, and younger . . . "

"Until two months ago I was taller and younger." He cocked an eyebrow sternly. "Is this Doyle of yours by any chance a magician?"

Jacky had been staring at the man's head, and now said, unsteadily, "Look at your shoes."

The man did, though he looked up again when he heard a gasp. The boy had gone white, and seemed for some reason to be on the verge of tears. "My God," Jacky whispered, "*you're not bald anymore.*"

It was the man's turn to be mystified. "Uh . . . no . . . "

"Oh, *Brendan* . . . " A couple of tears spilled down Jacky's cold-reddened cheeks. "You poor innocent son of a bitch . . . your friend Ashbless arrived too late."

"What?"

"I wasn't," Jacky sniffed, "talking to you." She wiped her face with the end of her scarf. "I suppose *you* really *are* the Admirable Chinnie."

"Yes, I am—or was. You find that . . . credible?"

"I'm afraid I do. Listen, you and I have got to get together and compare notes. Are you free for a drink?"

"As soon as I deliver this to my boss I'm due for a supper break. It's just around the corner here, Malk's Bakery in St. Martin's Lane. Come on."

Jacky trotted along beside Chinnie, who resumed his exercises. They turned left into St. Martin's Lane and soon arrived at the bakery. Chinnie told Jacky to wait for him, then pushed his way through the gang of little boys that had been drawn by the warm plum pudding smell to cluster around the windows, and disappeared inside.

A few moments later he came out again. "There's a public house down Kyler Lane here where I frequently stop for a pint. Nice people, though they think I'm barmy."

"Ah, it's the Admirable!" the aproned landlord said cheerfully when they pushed open the pub door and stepped into the relative dimness. "With his pal Gentleman Jackson, I perceive."

"A couple of pints of porter, Samuel," said Chinnie, leading Jacky to a booth on the rear. "I got drunk here once," he muttered, "and was fool enough to tell them my secret."

When the mugs of black beer had arrived and been tentatively sipped, Jacky asked, "When—and how—did the body switch occur?"

"*When* was a Sunday two months ago—the fourteenth of October. How . . . " He gulped more of the beer. "Well, I was fencing at Angelo's, and just as I was about to do a particularly clever disengage, I—I suddenly found myself at the bottom of the Thames with no air in my lungs."

Jacky smiled bitterly and nodded. "Yes, that's how he works. Leaving you that way, I guess he wouldn't have to chew the tongue to bits before he left." She looked at the man with some respect. "You *must* be Chinnie—he'd never have left you in that position if it was at all likely you'd survive."

Chinnie drained his mug and signalled for another. "I damn near didn't. Sometimes, lying awake nights in my bed by the bakery oven, I wish I hadn't." He gave Jacky a hard stare. "Now you talk. Who's this *he* you're referring to? Your friend, this Doyle? Is he in my real body?"

"No, Doyle's dead, I'm afraid. He obviously got the same treatment you did, but I can't see *him* swimming up from the Thames bottom. No, it's a . . . magician, I guess . . . known as Dog-Face Joe, who can switch bodies with people at will—and has to frequently because for some reason he starts growing thick fur all over himself as soon as he's in a fresh body."

"Yes!" said Chinnie excitedly, "right! I was all hairy when I climbed out of the river—even had whiskers between my fingers and toes. One of the first things I did was buy a razor and shave most of my body. Thank God it doesn't seem to be growing back."

"I guess it wouldn't, after Joe's moved on. I—"

"So this magician is walking around in my body. I'm going to find him."

Jacky shook her head. "Not after two months, I'm afraid. I've been trying to find him for quite a while, and he *never* stays in any one body for more than a week or two."

"What do you mean? What would he do with it?"

"The same thing he did to poor Doyle's when it started to get furry—get into a position where death is only seconds away, then switch with someone else who's maybe miles distant, and just walk off in the new body while the man he evicted finds himself dying before he even knows where he is. The cast-offs never live long, and I think you're probably the only one to actually survive."

The landlord brought Chinnie a fresh mug of porter. "Th-thank you," Chinnie said, and when the man had returned to the bar he stared at Jacky out of Doyle's eyes. "No," he said firmly. "He wouldn't just abandon that carcass of mine. Listen, I've never been vain, but that was one hell of a fine . . . v-vehicle, in his terms." Chinnie was obviously maintaining his composure only with considerable effort. "Handsome, young, strong, agile . . . "

"—And hairy as an ape—"

"So he'll have to shave then, won't he?" shouted Chinnie loudly enough to make everyone else in the pub turn toward them. There were tolerant chuckles when they realized who it was.

" 'At's right, Admirable," called the host, "shave 'im bald as an egg. But keep the racket down, eh?"

"And," the blushing Chinnie went on more quietly, "there's these places, aren't there, where people go to have hair removed? What's to say he'd not go to one of those?"

"I don't think any of those places really—"

"Do you know? Have you been? You ought to, you know, that m-moustache looks like—" His voice had been rising again but abruptly he stopped, and rubbed his eyes. "I'm sorry, lad. There's tensions involved."

"I know."

For a moment they just sat and drank beer.

"You say you've been looking for him?" said Chinnie. "Why?"

"He killed my fiancé," Jacky said evenly.

"And what'll you do if you find him?"

"Kill him."

"What if he's in my old body?"

"I'll still kill him," said Jacky. "Face it, man, you won't get the body back."

"I'm . . . not resigned to that. What if I find him, and tell you where he is—will you, in return, help me get him to . . . switch back?"

"I can't imagine the circumstances."

"Never mind imagining them. Will you?"

Jacky sighed. "If you can find him, and set it up—sure, if I can be certain of killing him afterward."

"Very well." Chinnie reached across the table and they shook hands. "What's your name?"

"Jacky Snapp, at one-twelve Pye Street, near Westminster Cathedral. What name are you using?"

"Humphrey Bogart. It came to me in a dream I had, the first night I was in this body."

Jacky shrugged. "It might be a name that meant something to Doyle."

"Who cares? Anyway, you can reach me at Malk's Bakery, St. Martin's Lane. And if you find him, will you let me know?"

Jacky hesitated. Why should she take on a partner? Of course a strong companion could be useful, and Joe would certainly be in another body by now, so Chinnie's concern for his ex-body's welfare wouldn't be a hindrance . . . and certainly nobody had a better claim to share in her revenge. "All right," she said finally. "I'll take a partner."

"Good lad!" They shook hands again, then Chinnie glanced at the clock. "I'd better be moving on," he said, getting to his feet and throwing some change on the table. "The yeast is working, and time and dough wait for no man."

Jacky drained her beer and got up too.

They walked together out of the pub, though the landlord tapped Chinnie on the shoulder and, when he paused, said, "You're right about what Jackson's moustache looks like. If you can't get him to shave it off, I advise you to give him an exploding cigar."

The laughter of the patrons followed them out into the street.

On Christmas Eve the taproom at the Guinea and Bun in Crutchedfriars was already fairly crowded by three-thirty in the afternoon. Aromatically steaming cups of hot punch were being handed, free, to each patron after he'd beaten the snow from his hat, hung his cloak or coat on one of the hooks along the south wall and hurried, shivering, over to the bar.

The bartender, an affable balding man called Bob Crank, had poured punch for the last couple of arrivals and now leaned back against the counter and took a sip from his mug of fortified coffee as he glanced around the low-ceilinged room. The crowd seemed to be cheery—as well they ought to be on Christmas Eve—and the logs in the fireplace were set up for a good draft, and wouldn't need attention for an hour or so. Crank knew nearly everyone in the room, and the only patron he might have felt even slightly doubtful of was the old man sitting alone at the table nearest to the fireplace—a crazy-eyed smirking old fellow who, despite the warmth of his position, had his shirt buttoned up to the neck and was holding his glass with gloved hands.

With a bang and a squeak the front door opened, letting a swirl of snow into the entry hall. Crank had poured the cup of punch before looking up, and was holding it out before he recognized the newcomer. "Doug!" he exclaimed when the burly, gray-haired man stepped up to the bar. "Cold out there, is it? Let me," he said, lowering his voice and the cup, "put a bit of flying buttress in that, eh?" He uncorked a brandy bottle and, down behind the bar, topped up the cup.

"Thankee, Crankie."

They both laughed, and Crank stopped laughing first. "Your mates are yonder," he said, nodding toward the fire.

"Ah, so they are." Doug Maturo drained the punch cup and clinked it down on the bar. "Send over a brandy, will you, Crank?"

"Right."

Maturo clumped across to the indicated table and sat down, acknowledging with a grin and a wave the drunken greetings of his friends.

"You bums," he said, helping himself to a stray mug of beer until his brandy would arrive. "Who's minding the shop?"

"The shop can look after itself, Mr. Doug," mumbled one of the men at the table. "Nobody gonna want hub bosses on Christmas Eve."

"Damn right," agreed another. "Tomorrow too, by God. Here's to Christmas!"

They all raised their glasses, but paused when the old man at the next table said, distinctly, "Christmas is for idiots."

Maturo turned around and stared at him, noting with one contemptuously raised eyebrow the effeminate gloves. Crank arrived just then with his brandy, though, so he shrugged and turned back to his companions. He muttered something that set them all laughing, then took a hearty swig of the brandy as the momentary tension relaxed.

"A celebration," the old man went on loudly, "of all that's weakest and most unrealistic in the damned western culture. Show me a man that celebrates Christmas and I'll show you a dewy-eyed bugger that wishes he could still be tucked in every night by his mum."

"Write it all down, sign it 'Iconoclast' and send it to the *Times*, mate," advised Maturo over his shoulder. "And right now stop up your jabbering mouth with drink, before someone stops it less pleasantly."

The old man made an obscene suggestion as to how Maturo would do that.

"I don't need this today," Maturo sighed, pushing back his

chair and standing up. He walked over to the old man and seized him by the shirt-front. "Listen to me, you unpleasant old creature. There's plenty of taverns right nearby that'll provide you with the fight you're looking for, so why don't you tote your wretched old bones thither, eh?"

The old man had started to stand up, but lost his footing and fell back into his chair. His shirt tore, and a button plunked into the cup of punch in front of him.

"Now I suppose you'll want me to pay for your shirt," said Maturo exasperatedly. "Well you can—" Suddenly he stopped talking and peered at the old man's exposed chest. "Holy God, what kind of—"

The old man tore loose from Maturo's momentarily relaxed grip and ran for the door.

"Stop him!" roared Maturo, with such urgency that Crank forgot his never interfere rule and hurled a big jar of pickled pig's feet into the old man's path. It burst with a loud pop and splash, and the old man lost his footing on the wet floor, fell heavily on his hip and slid rolling into a bar stool, which toppled over. Maturo was on him in an instant, and dragged the gasping old fellow to his feet.

"What did he do, Doug?" asked Crank worriedly.

Maturo twisted one of the old man's arms up and forced it down on the bar. "Open your fist, you bastard," he hissed. The fist stayed clenched for a few moments, but sprang open when Maturo began to exert pressure against the locked elbow.

"Jesus, his hand's empty, Doug!" exclaimed Crank with some agitation. "Here we've roughed him up and he didn't take noth—"

"Pull off his glove."

"Damn it, man, we've done enough to—"

"Pull off his glove."

Rolling his eyes unhappily, Crank pinched the fabric at the ends of the thumb and middle finger and jerked the glove off.

The pale, wrinkled hand was completely covered with coarse whiskers.

"It's Dog-Face Joe," Maturo pronounced.

"What?" wailed the flustered Crank. "The werewolf from the kid stories?"

"He's not a werewolf. He's the uncanniest murderer that ever walked this city's streets. Ask Brock over in Kenyon

Court what became of his boy Kenny. Or ask Mrs. Zimmerman—"

"He's the one that did in my brother," said a young man who quickly stood up from a corner table. "Frank was a priest, and ran off from the rectory one day, and didn't recognize me when I found him, and laughed when I told him who I was. But I followed him to where he lived, and a week later a thing they said was an ape leaped from the roof of the place. The busted-up corpse in the street was all covered with fur, but I looked in its mouth and saw the tooth I chipped when Frankie and me was playing sword fights when we was kids."

The captive at the bar laughed. "I remember him. I didn't have too bad a time in his body—though I fear I made a sad shambles of his vow of celibacy."

The young man sprang forward with an inarticulate cry and a raised fist, but Maturo shouldered him back. "What are you going to do, hit him?" Maturo asked. "Justice has got to be done."

"Aye, fetch the police!" someone shouted.

"That's no good either," said Maturo. "By the time he'd even come up for trial he'd be long gone, leaving some innocent poor devil in this carcass." He stared at the young man, then looked around at everyone else. "He's got to be executed," he said carefully. "Now."

Dog-Face Joe began struggling wildly, and at the same moment a number of people leaped to their feet, loudly protesting that they wouldn't be party to a murder. Crank grabbed Maturo's sleeve and said, "Not in here, Doug. No way in here."

"No," Maturo agreed. "But who's with me?"

"John Carroll is," said the young man, stepping forward again.

"Me too," spoke up a hefty, middle-aged matron. "They pulled one o' them apes out of the river at Gravesend, and it was wearin' my Billy's ring on a finger so furry that it couldn't be pulled off—and couldn't have been pulled on, either, after the fur was growed."

One by one three more people walked over and stood beside John Carroll and the woman.

"Good," Maturo said. He turned toward the table he'd leaped up from. "Any of you lads?"

His suddenly sobered friends all shook their heads. "We're none of us the sort to shrink from a scrape, Doug," said one pleadingly, "but helping in a cold-blooded murder . . . we've got families . . ."

"Sure." He looked away from them. "Leave, all of you that are leaving. And fetch a constable if you feel you must—but first consider what sort of thing you'd be freeing. Remember the stories this man and woman just told you, and call to mind the stories I'm sure you've heard already."

Most of the people in the room scrambled for the door, though two more men hung back to join Maturo's group. "Just realized," said one of them, "I was going to leave clean-handed, though damn glad it was being done. That's no way to go."

Maturo clapped a hand over Dog-Face Joe's mouth, then said casually to Crank, "You know, Crankie, I believe I've changed my mind. I'll just take him to the police after all. You understand? The last thing you heard me say was that I was going to take him, alive, to the authorities."

"Got it," said the pale-faced Crank, pouring himself a liberal slug of neat brandy. "Thanks, Doug."

Maturo, assisted by his companions, led the struggling figure toward the back door.

"Uh, Doug?" said Crank in a strained voice. "That's the . . . *back* door you're leaving by?"

"We're going to go over the fence."

The nine vigilantes half-dragged, half-marched their captive outside into the pub's small back lot, and Maturo glanced around at the mounded snow, which in the far corner had nearly buried a derelict beer wagon. A section of the yard wall had been knocked down, doubtless due to the mishandling of some craneful of ironwork by an employee of the forge whose yard adjoined the pub lot. There was no one visible in the forge yard, and the shadow of the unattended crane fell across the pub's back door.

"You," said Maturo, pointing at one of the men with him, "see if there's a length of rope anywhere about that old wagon there. And—where's John Carroll? Ah, there you are—do you think you can climb that crane?"

"If somebody will lend me some gloves I can."

Dog-Face Joe's other glove was wrenched off and the pair was tossed to him, and a moment later he was scrambling over the tumbled and snow-dusted masonry of the gap in the wall.

"There's a rope here," called the man Maturo had sent over to the wagon, "tied around the yoke. It's frozen on, but I think I can get it loose."

"When you do, meet us in the forge yard," Maturo called. To the woman he remarked, "It looks like we may be able to do this properly, and not just hold his head in a horse trough."

In a few minutes the nine people were grouped in a half-circle around a four-foot-tall nail keg on top of which Dog-Face Joe, his head held high, stood on tiptoe, for the rope had proven to be a few inches short, and if he let his heels rest on the barrel top the slip-knot around his neck would be uncomfortably tight.

"If you let me down," Joe said hoarsely, peering down at them over the swell of his cheekbones, "I'll make you all rich. I've kept money from each of my hosts! It's a fortune, and I'll let you people have it all!" He twitched his scarf-bound wrists.

"You said that before," Maturo told him. "And we said no before. Say some prayers, Joe, you're on your way out." Maturo was clearly uneasy about the situation, and he kept squinting up at their captive suspiciously.

"I don't need prayers," said Joe. "My soul's in good hands." His confident words must have been a bluff, though, for an instant later he gave a despairing wail and shrieked, *"Wait a minute! I'm D—"*

The tightening halter choked off any further speech then, for Maturo had kicked the barrel out from under him with such force that it rolled away across the snow-covered pavement as the old man rocked and swung on the end of the suddenly taut rope, his eyes staring with intense supplication out of the darkening face and his mouth forming words that he had no breath to vocalize.

Maturo, who seemed to have dismissed his misgivings now that the deed was done, waited with a faint smile until the grisly pendulum had rotated around to face away from the executioners, toward the yard and the low sun and the still-rolling barrel, and then he leaped onto the shoulders of the dangling man as though to get a piggyback ride.

The snap of the breaking neck was loud in the chilly stillness, and John Carroll turned away and vomited into the snow.

• • •

Doug Maturo entered the dingy office building over whose door could still faintly be seen painted-out letters that spelled DEPILATORY PARLOR, locked the door behind him and walked across the floor through the slanting bars of gray light that came in around the edges of the shutters, past the dusty counter to the dark hallway and the stairs. Halfway up the stairs he became aware of voices on the floor above, and he trod very softly the rest of the way up.

" . . . In Jermyn Street near St. James Square," Dundee was saying. "The rent they're asking is exorbitant, but as you remarked the other day, I do need a better address."

"Honestly you do, Jake," replied a young woman's contralto voice. "And I like the notion of you worrying about rent! What did you say you make every day?"

"Right now an average of nine hundred pounds, but it's an upward geometrical progression—the more I've got, the more I get. By the end of 1811 there'll be no way to calculate it—the time it would take to do all the math would make the figures hopelessly obsolete before you got them."

"What a wizard it is I'm marrying!" the girl exclaimed with a smile in her voice. There was some cooing and giggling, and then she added teasingly, "Not very affectionate, though."

Dundee's laugh sounded, to the man smirking in the dark hall at any rate, forced, and there was no conviction in his voice when he said, "There'll be plenty of that when we're married, Claire. We'd be—betraying the trust your father has in us if we were to . . . misbehave now, here."

The man in the hall stepped quietly back to the stairs, tramped a number of times with increasing force on the top step, then clumped up to Dundee's door and knocked on it.

"Uh . . . yes?" said Dundee. "Who is it?"

The man opened the door and walked in, nodded to Dundee and smiled broadly at the slim blonde girl. "It's Sizzlin' Stan the Immortal Man," he said cheerfully.

Dundee stared bleakly at the tall, burly intruder. He'd never seen this ruddy face before, with its flinty eyes and wiry gray hair, but he knew who it was. "Oh—hello," he said. "I see it all . . . went well."

"Aye, no problem atall atall—matter of fact, I've been doing sprints and bounds on the way here, and I've decided this one has it points—I think I'll stay here a while, your electro-hair-killer devices permitting. And who is this lovely creetur?"

He made a flailing, theatrical bow.

"Uh, Joe," said Dundee, standing up from the couch, "this is Claire Peabody, my fiancée. Claire, this is . . . Joe, a business associate."

Joe bared his even white teeth in a grin. "Pleased to meet you, Miss Claire."

Claire frowned uneasily, not pleased by the undivided attention this man was giving her. "Pleased to meet you, Joe," she said. Suddenly aware that he was staring at her bosom, she frowned more deeply and threw a pleading glance at Dundee.

"Joe," the young man said, "perhaps you could—"

"Isn't that nice," Joe interrupted, smiling more broadly than ever, "we're both . . . *pleased.*"

"Joe," repeated Dundee, "perhaps you could wait in your room. I'll speak with you there presently."

"Sure, Jake," said Joe, turning toward the door. He paused. "Merry Christmas, Miss Claire." There was no reply, and he chuckled almost noiselessly as he closed the door.

Jacky paid her penny at the bar and joined the queue, and after a few minutes, during which she moved one step at a time closer to the back door and the man outside who was periodically shouting, "All right, you've seen it, give someone else a chance," it was her turn to go through the door and join the crowd in the back lot. The snow was all trampled to slushy mud.

Jacky couldn't see anything but the broad back of the man in front of her, but the line was moving, and before long she filed with everyone else through a ragged gap in the brick wall into a larger, paved yard. She could see the crane and the rope now. On the next street over someone was singing snatches of Christmas carols in a drunken baritone.

So what do I do now? she wondered. Go home? Back to the little house in Romford, and school, and eventually some earnest, promising young bank clerk for a husband? Yeah, I suppose so. What else? The thing you came to London to do has been done, though by someone else. Is that what's got you feeling so . . . useless and unmoored and—yes, face it—scared? Yesterday you had a purpose, a reason for living this way, and today you don't. You've got no reason to be Jacky Snapp anymore, but you're not quite Elizabeth Jacqueline Tichy anymore, either. What's to become of you, girl?

She rounded the last loop of the line, and got at last a clear view of the scene. A rope had been tied to the crane boom, and from the end of it swung in the chilly breeze a sack-headed dummy with patches of moth-eaten fur sewn onto the face, hands and feet.

"Yes, friends," said the barker in a hushed voice, "this is where the dreaded man-wolf Dog-Face Joe was brought to justice at last. The effigy you see before you was carefully constructed so as to let you all see exactly the scene the police found here last night."

"The way I heard it," quietly commented the man in front of Jacky to his companion, "he simply had whiskers all over him, like a two-day beard."

"Indeed, my lord?" replied the other man politely.

The line shuffled past the display, which had shifted around to face away from them, exposing a wide, straw-leaking rip in the seat of the trousers. Several people laughed, and Jacky heard one whispered speculation on the circumstances of Dog-Face Joe's capture.

Jacky felt a hysteria kindling deep inside herself. *Are you aware of this, Colin?* she thought. *Can you see this . . . country fair side-show exhibit? You're avenged at last. Isn't that wonderful? And isn't it wonderful of all these people to hang this wonderful memento of the fact? How grand and noble and satisfying it all is.*

She was sobbing before she knew it was coming, and the heavy-set man in front of her took her elbow and led her out of the line to the exit point, a gate leading to the lane that the Guinea and Bun fronted on.

Once they were on the pavement outside, he said, "Parker—my flask."

"Yes, my lord," said the man who had docilely followed them out. He produced a pewter flask from under his coat, unscrewed the top and handed it to him.

"Here you go, lad," said the portly man. "Drink up. Nothing in that silly show is worth tears on such a beautiful Christmas morning."

"Thank you," said Jacky, sniffing and wiping her nose on her sleeve after handing the flask back. "I believe you're right. I don't suppose anything is ever worth tears. Thank you again."

She touched her cap, then shoved her hands in her pockets and strode away down the street at a sturdy pace, for it was a long walk back to Pye Street.

CHAPTER 13

"When the great tragedy was ended, and the last groan had died away by the Bab-el-Azab, Mohammed Ali's Italian physician offered him his congratulations; but the Pasha did not answer, he only asked for drink, and drank a deep draught."

—G. Ebers

MORE THAN SEVEN miles distant across the noon-bright Nile Valley the pyramids stood sharply clear on the horizon, and, seeming to be only a little closer, though just two miles away from the Citadel wall on which the watcher stood, the green-bordered Nile stretched like a polished steel band from north to south. A few wavering pencil strokes of smoke stood up from what he knew was El Roda island, though it was not distinguishable as a separate land mass from this distance, and he could see individual palm trees and minarets and windows of buildings in the old quarter of Cairo on the hither bank. Some of our guests, he thought, the Bahrites, are probably coming through those streets right now. And a splendid parade it no doubt is, too—all the little boys will have stopped work to watch, and the dogs will be barking, and all the mashrebeeyeh lattices of the second-floor harems are sure to be glittering with kohl-darkened eyes peering down at the haughty war lords riding past below. Soon the bejewelled pro-

319

cession will be clear of the old district and will be visible riding this way over the old stone road that transects the mile of desert between old Cairo and the Citadel.

Doctor Romanelli shivered slightly in spite of the heat and turned to the north, squinting at the bristling, tangled maze of whitewashed walls and brightly colored enamelled domes that was the new section of the city, which had grown up like lush riverside vegetation around the highway, called the Mustee, that connected the Citadel with the ancient Harbor of Boolak. The bulk of this afternoon's guests would be riding even now through the crowded Mustee.

He thought he caught a distant wink of glare, as of the sun reflecting on a lance head or polished helmet. Two hundred years ago, he thought, there was a purpose for the army of ex-slaves called the Mamelukes; but in today's Egypt they're an embarrassment that's strangling the country, imposing a crushing and savagely enforced tax on anyone who seems to have money, and strong enough in force of arms to acknowledge no law but their own tastes. We couldn't let them retain that kind of power, especially now that Mohammed Ali is in power and the eyes of the world are watching us, to gauge their own actions by what we do. Independence is within our reach again for the first time in thousands of years, and we can't have it imperilled by a group of local brigands. How fortunate that Ali looks to the Master—through me—as his main advisor!

And if I return to England, he thought as he turned and watched the sweating slaves loading the signal cannon, it will be to disassemble the history of that nation, so that today—a new today—they'll be nothing, probably a possession of France, which we'll also impede. All we've got to do is rediscover the knowledge that died with the Romany ka—and we will before long, either through the completion of our calculations or, still conceivably, the wringing of some vital clue from that wretched ka we managed to draw of Brendan Doyle before he got away from us.

That is a very long shot, though, he thought sourly, remembering last night's interrogation as he walked down the stone steps to the narrow, sun-baked street outside the el-Azab gate.

The ka had been dragged out of its basement cell for the first time in at least a month, and for half an hour hadn't even seemed to hear the questions the Master was putting to it, but just sat on the balcony chewing the end of its filthy beard and springing with little cries away from, evidently, imaginary insects. Finally it had spoken, though not in reply to any question. "I keep trying to stop them," it had muttered, "from getting on the bike, you know? But it's always too late, and they're on the freeway before I can catch them, and I pull over 'cause I don't want to see it. . . . But I *hear* it . . . the clank of the fall, and the grinding slide . . . and the smash of the helmet exploding against the pillar. . . . "

"How did you exit the time stream?" the Master asked, for the fourth time.

"Jacky pulled me out," the ka replied. "He threw a net over the little men and then pulled me into his canoe. . . . "

"No, the *time* stream. How did you exit it?"

"It's all one river, and the mile posts are calendar pages. If your keels be nimble and light, you may get there by candle light. The river is iced-over, you see—weren't you listening when Darrow explained it?—but there's a boat, with faces painted on the wheels, that can sail over the ice—the boat can come alive, and kill you . . . a black boat, blacker than the darkness. . . . "

The Master had fallen into a fit of incoherent rage at this point, and had had to speak through one of the wax *ushabti* figures in the pen on the bottom of the sphere. "Take it away," croaked the voice, "and stop the delivery of food to its cell—we don't need it."

Yes, a long shot, certainly—but still a possibility; after all, there were a couple of interesting hints of *pattern* in its ravings.

In any case, Romanelli reflected as he opened a door that quite soon would be securely locked, we may not even need the Anubis Gates. There will be further bold political strokes like the one that will occur this afternoon, and with as strong a leader as Mohammed Ali taking the Master's council, we might be able to re-establish Egypt even without being able to rewrite history. The question of when to arrange a secret assassination and substitution by a docile ka can be deferred for at least several years.

Before stepping into the hall he glanced up and down the narrow, empty street between the high walls. Quiet right now, he thought.

• • •

The Mustee, at an hour past noon, was at its most crowded, with heavily laden camels pressing stolidly through the throng, and the shouts of the veiled women selling oranges rising in jarring cacophony over the song of the rat catcher—on whose broad-brimmed hat six trained examples of his prey, each wearing a little hat of its own, formed a pyramid—and the yells of the fish and milk vendors and the chanted prayers of the beggars. But the mob parted hastily before the relentless hooves of the procession riding down the center of the street at a relaxed but indomitable walk. In hopes of a tip at the end of the ride, a street boy had taken it upon himself to serve as the—in this case unnecessary—*sais*, or runner-ahead; "*Riglak!*" he would warn some Nubian merchant, whose foot had been snatched out of the way even before the boy called, and "*Uxrug!*" to two ladies from a harem who had already crowded up against a wall and were shrilly and indignantly protesting this usurpation of the street.

But everyone was as eager to see the parade as to get out of its way, and the British *effendis* turned their palm-branch chairs around on the sidewalk in front of the Zawiyah Cafe to keep an uneasy eye on the procession as they took somewhat deeper sips of their drinks, for this was a formal procession of the Mameluke Beys in all their finery. The hot sun glinted on the precious stones that studded their sword hilts and pistol butts, and their colorful robes and feathered turbans and helmets made the rest of the street seem drab by comparison; but in spite of the grandeur of the jewelled weapons and the rich cloths and the gorgeously caparisoned Arabian horses, the most striking aspect of the parade was the lean, hawk-nosed brown faces and the narrowed eyes that remained haughtily above the crowd.

Not least impressive of the faces was the helmeted, black-bearded one that belonged to an impostor; and though many of the people who scurried out of the way or peered down from windows knew the cobbler Eshvlis, whose place of business was a niche in the outside wall of a mosque two blocks away, none of them recognized him in the gold-chased armor of the Mameluke Bey Ameen.

And none of them knew that even in his daily routine of repairing shoes Eshvlis was an impostor—that, before choosing that name and dying his hair and beard black, he had been called Brendan Doyle.

Over the past few months Doyle had got used to being Eshvlis, but he was far from confident in this role he'd assumed today, and he averted his face whenever he noticed one of his patrons in the crowd. The impersonation that he'd agreed to so cheerfully this morning was beginning to make him nervous—was it, he wondered, a crime to attend the Pasha's banquet by arriving disguised as one of the invited guests? Probably. If his friend Ameen hadn't been counting on the success of the deception, Doyle would have spurred the borrowed horse out of the parade, divested himself of the sword, daggers and fine clothes, and sneaked back to his cobbler's niche to enjoy the show from a comfortable distance.

He glanced at his niche as they rode past it, and, although he had booked passage out of the country on a ship that would weigh anchor tomorrow, he was surprised and angry to see another cobbler perched there in a nest of dangling shoes. Absent one morning, he thought bitterly, and the competition moves in like rats.

Up ahead was the square where he'd first encountered Ameen. Doyle smiled grimly, remembering that hot October morning, which had begun to go wrong when Hassan Bey's shoe buckle broke off during a meeting with the British governor.

The humiliating misfortune had caused the immediate termination of the interview, and Hassan and his brothers-in-law Ameen and Hathi had left the Citadel and ridden back toward their boat at Boolak, but in this square by the Mustee there had occurred a further disaster: the burly beggar known as Eshvlis, whose large, wood-framed placard proclaimed him a deaf-mute, was a little slow in scrambling to his feet and getting out of the Mamelukes' way, and a projecting nail on his placard caught in a fold of Hassan's embroidered robe and tore a wide rent in it, exposing the outraged Mameluke's thigh.

Hassan had roared a blasphemous curse, reached around and snatched the ivory inlaid hilt of his sword, and in one lightning motion drew the yard of gleaming steel and whirled it in a torso-splitting arc at the beggar.

But quick as a mongoose Doyle had dropped to all fours in the dust, so that though the blade shattered his begging sign, it flashed harmlessly over him, missing the top of his head by several inches—and before the surprised Mameluke could raise the sword again, Doyle sprang up at him, seized the grip of one of the horseman's daggers and wrenched it free, and with it parried the weaker return stroke of the great sword.

Hathi had moved then, with a sort of indolent swiftness, reining his horse back and lifting the barrel of his sheathed rifle to hip level; and even as Ameen's eyes widened with the realization of what Hathi was about to do, and he rode forward with a shout, Hathi pulled the trigger.

With a bang that echoed around the square the rifle had recoiled out of the sheath; Hathi's battle-trained horse hadn't jumped, but shook its head and flapped its lips in the sudden burst of smoke. Doyle finished a backward somersault face down on the paving stones, and a glistening red hole torn in the back of his robe quickly disappeared as flowing blood soaked the fabric.

"You villains!" Ameen had shouted then. "He was a *beggar*." His voice conveyed the point that a beggar was not only no sword-worthy opponent but, in the Moslem view of things, an actual representative of Allah, with the job of demanding the alms every true believer was bound by duty to give.

The street took a jog to the left now, and beyond the shadowed shoulder of a building Doyle could see, still a mile away, the minarets and sheer stone walls of the Citadel seeming to loom halfway to the sky on the top of the precipitous Mukattam Hill, and though the occasion that brought the Mamelukes to the fortress was nominally social—the appointment of Mohammed Ali's son as a pashalik—the forbidding aspect of the tall edifice made Doyle glad that he and his companions were so well armed.

Ameen had assured him this morning that the mass arrest he expected, and was secretly fleeing to evade, would not take place at this banquet. "Relax, Eshvlis," he had told Doyle as he drew the straps tight on the last of his trunks and peered out the window at the baggage-laden camels on the street below, "Ali is not insane. Though he will—and soon, I believe—curtail the unreasonable power of the Mamelukes, he'd never dare try to arrest all four hundred and eighty of the Beys as a lot, and while they're armed. I think the real purpose of this banquet is to count his foes, make sure they're all in the city, so that sometime tonight, before dawn, he can drag them drunk and unarmed out of their beds on some charge or other. Not that we don't deserve exactly such treatment, as you with

your bullet scar would be, if you weren't so polite, the first to
aver. But I am off for Syria this afternoon, and you are returning to your Eshvlis identity right after the banquet and
leaving Cairo tomorrow morning, and so you and I will escape
the net.''

Ameen had made it sound perfectly safe. . . . And Doyle
owed him his life, for it had been Ameen who had ordered
Doyle's bleeding body to be picked up and taken to the
Moristan of Ka'aloon for medical attention, and two months
later got him well started in the cobbling trade by demanding
that Hassan pay him a hundred gold pieces for the repair of
the broken shoe buckle. The torn robe had never been alluded
to, and Hassan probably considered it paid for—by the two
holes, entry and exit, in the cobbler's hide.

Doyle frowned, and for just a moment wondered why none
of these events were even hinted at in the Bailey biography of
Ashbless. After all, they were just the sort of thing that would
make a poet's biography interesting: a brief career as a beggar,
shot through the side by a Mameluke warlord, attending a
royal banquet in disguise—and then he smiled, for of course
he couldn't tell Bailey these things, because Doyle was going
to read the biography some day. And would you, he asked
himself, have gone anywhere near that square if you'd known
you'd be shot there that day?

Well, at least I know that Ashbless does leave Egypt on the
Fowler, bound for England, tomorrow morning, so even
though I never got around to researching Cairo in 1811, there
can't be too many more surprises I'll neglect to tell Bailey
about. I guess I won't, for example, be recaptured by
Romanelli, who has now, I hear, got himself set up as
Mohammed Ali's personal physician. I don't think he'd
recognize me now anyway, with the black dyed hair, the deep
tan and all the new furrows and lines in my face that are the
legacy of a long convalescence without anesthesia. At least this
body's still got both ears.   •

At the parade ground in front of the Citadel the ranks of
mainland Mamelukes were joined by the Bahrite Beys, and for
fifteen hot minutes—during which Eshvlis sweated into the
appallingly expensive borrowed robe and let Ameen's horse
follow Hathi's, who rode just ahead of him—all but one of the
four hundred and eighty Mameluke Beys, the tribe of one-time
slaves that had risen to absolute control of the country, and

had in recent years fallen only a little from that zenith, paraded in colorful, barbaric splendor under the empty blue sky of Egypt.

Ameen's agile and powerful mare, Melboos, pranced proudly along, tossing her head sometimes, and in general making her rider seem to be what he was not, a competent horseman. She was a fine animal, and had been Ameen's proudest possession, but the impersonation had demanded that he leave her behind.

It suddenly occurred to Doyle that he'd miss Ameen, who'd been the only one in Cairo who knew Eshvlis was not really a deaf-mute. Schooled in Vienna, the young Bey had learned other goals and perspectives than the traditional war and glory ones of the Mamelukes, and through many long afternoons Ameen had stood beside the cobbler's niche and talked to him in English about history and politics and religion—though they'd always been careful to cease speaking if a customer crowded close enough to hear their low-pitched conversation, for Ameen had heard that the Pasha was offering a reward for any information about a big, English-speaking fugitive.

Now several ranks of the Pasha's Albanian mercenaries rode up, bristling with swords and maces and pistols, and rifles taller than themselves, and looking, to Eshvlis at least, ridiculous in their pleated white skirts and extra-tall turbans.

The Albanians rode down a set of steps into a narrow street leading up the steep slope to the Citadel, and the ranks of the Mamelukes followed them into it as the Bab-el-Azab gate at the far end of the sunken street slowly swung open.

In spite of the fact that they were now out of sight of the spectators, the Mamelukes maintained their stately pace, though the Albanians galloped rowdily ahead toward the open gate.

Doyle stared curiously around at the twenty-foot-deep ascending trench through which they were marching; it was certainly part of the Citadel's fortifications, for there were only a few stout doors in the solid stone walls on either side, and the windows, though many, were vertical slits just wide enough to poke a gun barrel through.

Now fifty yards ahead, the galloping Albanian mercenaries had reached the Bab-el-Azab gate . . . and Doyle's eyes widened in surprise to see, when the last of them was inside the Citadel, the gate begin to close. He hunched around in the saddle to look behind, and saw that the distant entrance to the walled street was blocked by more of the mercenaries. Even as he watched, the front row of them dropped to their knees and every one of them raised a long rifle and sighted along the barrel.

As he took a breath to yell an alarm a cannon boomed and spurted a stain of gray smoke into the blue sky, and an instant later the street erupted with deafening and continuous gunfire from in front and behind and from every slit window, and the air chirped and twanged with the whipping flight of dozens of bullets every second, and dust and stone chips burst from the walls as churning smoke burned in eyes and throats and obscured any view of the foe.

The ranks of Mamelukes broke apart like a row of Japanese lanterns struck by fire hoses. Most of the Beys were slammed off their horses in the first couple of seconds, although even the ones who managed to draw their weapons had no visible enemy to attack except the clot of Albanians at the far end of the street. But the several Mamelukes—including, Doyle dazedly noticed, Hassan—who tried to charge at them were punched down by the ceaseless spray of lead before they'd taken five paces.

Though he'd felt several sharp tugs at his robe, after four whole seconds Doyle wasn't hit yet, and to judge by the way Melboos sprang forward over a pile of the slain when a wall exploded by her flank, neither was she. Doyle's cry of "God damn it, over the wall, horse!" was lost in the tumult, but the horse bounded ahead, scrambling and leaping over the heaped corpses that twitched as bullets thudded into them. A spent ricochet struck Doyle a solid knock above his left ear, and while he reeled in the lunging saddle three shots hit him almost simultaneously—one nicked his right arm bicep, one plowed a long furrow down his left thigh, and the third tore shallowly across his belly, helping him hang on by making him jack-knife forward onto the horse's neck—and then Melboos was climbing the highest hill of corpses, at what he been the front of the procession, and from the top of it she vaulted up toward the rim of the wall, still an unmerciful eight feet above.

Doyle felt the catapulting power of her jump, and through smoke-stung eyes saw the wall rim loom closer—then he could see over it in the weightless moment of apogee. In an instant, he knew, gravity would tumble them back down into the raking crossfire—but the horse got her fore hooves onto the rim agile as a cat, replaced them with her hind hooves, and a moment later they were falling, all right, but outside the wall.

The horse fell head-first and Doyle rolled helplessly
backward after having got a glimpse of a moat fifty feet
below, and then he was plummeting unsupported downward,
blinking in horror at the moat rushing up at him with shocking
velocity.

The duration of the fall was torture, and twice on the way
down Doyle emptied his lungs and sucked in a fresh breath to
hold, though the eventual impact punched all the air out of
him anyway, and banged his hands and knees against the
stones at the bottom of the moat. As he rebounded, his feet
swung back under him and he forced his legs to kick, propelling him back up through twenty-five feet of thickly swirling bubbles.

He rolled to the surface like something loosened from the
bottom of a pot of boiling water, and then began thrashing
weakly toward the high coping, where a man obviously interrupted in the process of urinating into the moat gaped at him
for a moment and then rearranged his robes and fled.

"Filthy damn slob!" Doyle sobbed after him.

As soon as the fugitive cobbler had dragged his trembling
and bleeding body out of the now dirtier than ever moat, he
pulled off Ameen's robes and weapons and tossed them—except for the sword, which he wrapped up in the unrolled turban and hung onto—in all directions, confident that the street
beggars would make off with them. He found a nearby patch
of sun-baked, powdery dirt and, naked except for his
loincloth, rolled in it until he was dry—though far from clean.
The bundled sword, he thought, would pass for a crutch inherited from a diseased ancestor.

"Melboos!" exclaimed a couple of shopkeepers who'd
observed the whole performance, and until Doyle remembered
that the word meant "clothed in divinity," frenzied to
madness by the perception of Allah, he thought they somehow
knew the name of the horse, which had clambered out of the
moat and was now being eyed avariciously by several members
of the ragharin, the Egyptian gypsies.

"Yes, take her!" Doyle croaked. "Avo, chals!"

Though the day was hot, he shivered as he ran across the
road and down a narrow lane, moving through alternate
brightness and shade as he passed beneath the occasional wide
cloths strung from building to building. It was only after he
sat down in a recessed doorway and lowered his face into his

hands that he realized he'd been weeping ever since he crawled out of the moat. He lifted his head and tried to stop it.

Laid like multiple exposures over the narrow, tan-colored street scene in front of him were images of the dozen seconds in the street of the Bab-el-Azab; now they demanded, almost audibly, his attention. He saw for the first time—his brain having only stored it unregarded before—the spray of blood and dust and bits of cloth exploding away from a horse and rider who were jigging violently in a particularly intense moment of the crossfire, both of them dead but kept upright and animate by the ceaseless upward-slanting blasts from either side . . . one quick glimpse of a face behind one of the gun barrels poking out of the wall, a face calmly intent on doing a moderately difficult job well . . . one Mameluke Bey, blinded and dying from a cross shot that had punched in one temple and out the other, standing on the pavement and swinging furious sword strokes at a blank section of wall during the few seconds between his horse's death and his own. . . .

Doyle wailed and pressed his forehead against the gritty stone of the doorway, provoking another exclamation of "Melboos!" from a boy carrying a water bag down the lane.

Doyle couldn't hear very much over the ringing in his ears, but he saw the boy lope out of the street and flatten himself against the far wall, and a moment later a dozen white-skirted Albanian mercenaries rode down the lane, scrutinizing every person; and each of the twelve stared hard at the prodigiously dirty old beggar with awful mud-caked sores on his arm and leg and belly, sobbing and hugging a stick in a doorway. A couple of the mercenaries laughed, and one threw a coin at the wretch, but none of them stopped.

When they'd ridden around the next corner, Doyle picked up the coin, stood up, and waved to the water boy, who trotted over and let him have a drink from the neck of the goatskin. Though warm and fetid, the water rinsed the taste of gunpowder out of his head, and made the horrid new memories recede enough that he could think of something else.

Well, Ameen, he thought dizzily, you were right on two counts—Ali sure enough did intend to sharply curtail the inordinate power of the Mamelukes, and he sure enough didn't attempt to arrest four hundred and eighty fully armed Mameluke Beys—but you were wrong in thinking it was therefore safe to go to the banquet.

He was still shivering and sweating, and his arm was bleeding as freely as ever. I need clothes and medical attention, he thought—and maybe just a bit of revenge. There was a Mameluke place down by the Nile, the summer house of Mustapha Bey, where Mustapha's sons and wives would be idling the day away. Doyle set off in that direction. He had some news and a proposal for them.

Though the sun had just set behind the Mukattam Hills, and just above the eastern horizon the moon stood out on the deep blue velvet of the sky like the print of an ash-dusted penny, the tops of the pyramids across the valley still shone with the ruddy gold of direct sunlight, and the colored lanterns on the ungainly wagon leaving the old quarter of the city were, for the next hour or so at least, more decorative than functional.

The gay ribbons and bells with which the wagon was lavishly adorned struck an incongruous note to the expressions of the six men who rode on it—their tight-lipped faces were set in hard lines of weariness, grief and, more than anything else, rage too deep to be vented by any speech or gestures. And in spite of its festive appearance, a sharp-eyed palace guard would have stopped them, for the rear wheels, which were most heavily disguised with woven garlands, cut a surprisingly deep pair of tracks in the dust, while the front wheels almost skated over it, and the wide carpet that flared out from the wagon's stern and trailed on the ground seemed to be concealing something—but no guard would see it, for the six horses harnessed to it turned right on the old road to the Karafeh, the necropolis, rather than bearing left on the new one that ran to the Citadel.

"Yeminak," said the man who rode up on the carpet-concealed hump of the wagon, just under the wide parasol, and the man at the reins obediently turned the horse off onto a path that slanted away to the right. "Slow now. I'll know it when I see it." He carefully scanned the tombs and headstones scattered haphazardly over the low hills. "There," he said finally. "That place with the dome there. And just as I said, Tewfik, there don't seem to be any guards. They certainly expect retaliation from the remaining Mamelukes, but they don't expect it here."

"I wanting more attacking the Citadel, professor," growled the man at the reins. "Having head of Ali rest forever in public toilet if could I. But orders of him coming from this magic man I know. Him we killing certainly."

"I hope you're right," said Doyle. "I hope Romanelli's there too."

"Yes." Tewfik eyed the building that squatted in the dusk a hundred yards away. "Here?"

"You know these things better than I do. I'd say we should be close enough so that we can ride in right after the door's blown."

"But not so they see us make ready." Tewfik nodded decisively. "Here."

Doyle shrugged and climbed down, very carefully, for one arm was in a sling. He glanced up the slight rise at the building, and was chilled to see the doorkeeper—probably the same one he'd clubbed four months before—standing out front and watching them. "Hurry," he said quietly. "They see us."

"Is no harm from at distance of us," said Tewfik, lifting a long pole from a slot in the wagon. He quickly stripped the ribbons from the length of it and then yanked a huge baby's-face mask off the end of it. The pole now terminated in a thick wooden disk. "She be loaded already, only needing to be shove down tight again." He tossed back a flap of the carpet covering the wagon's central hump, exposing the yawning muzzle of a cannon, and rattled the disk-headed pole all the way down inside the barrel and bumped it twice, hard, against the ball at the bottom. "Good." He drew it back out in three quick jerks and dropped it on the ground, then turned to the four others and barked something in Arabic.

One of them lit a cigar from a lantern swinging at the rear of the wagon and then strolled away puffing great clouds of smoke, engrossed, to all appearances, by the view of the Citadel a mile to the north. Another of the young Mamelukes flipped the carpet away from the breech end of the concealed cannon and began energetically whirling a ratcheted crank that slowly raised the breech and lowered the muzzle. Doyle glanced up the rise to see what the doorkeeper was making of all this, and saw the man hurry back inside and close the door.

"Hurry," Doyle repeated.

The man by the breech ceased his cranking and called to the man with the cigar.

"Hurry, goddammit!" whispered Doyle shrilly, for the ground had begun to vibrate as if a note too deep to hear had been struck on some vast subterranean organ, and the cool evening air was suddenly sharp with a smell like garbage. He bent down and hastily set about unbuckling one of his borrowed shoes.

The man with the cigar began sprinting back toward the cannon but tumbled to the ground when a beam of green light lanced from the top of the dome and struck him. At the same time, the barrel of the carpet-draped cannon began, incredibly and with a loud squealing, to *bend* upward.

Doyle got his shoe off, flung it away and drew a dagger and, just as the beam flashed across the intervening ground toward the cannon, jabbed the dagger point into his bare heel and then slammed his foot to the ground.

Then they were all in the sickly green radiance, choking in a stench of wetly rotting vegetation, and Tewfik and the three other young Mamelukes dropped limply to the ground.

Against resistance, Doyle reached up and slapped a hand against the hot cannon barrel, and with more squealing and an agonizing increase in the heat of the metal it began to bend down straight again. With slow, wading steps he shambled toward the breech of the cannon, trailing his blistering fingertips along the barrel and being careful to drag his bleeding foot through the dirt—maintain the connection, he kept dazedly telling himself—and when he got there he unhooked one of the colored lanterns and crushed it against the powder-primed vent.

The paper lantern flared, caught fire, went out, and then a smoldering bit of the wick fell into the vent.

A moment later he was staring up into the darkening sky, wondering why he was lying flat on his back and why his face stung so, and wishing someone would answer at least a couple of the dozen telephones that were all ringing at once. He rolled his head and looked at what had, a few seconds ago, been Tewfik. There was still some bulk within the agitated heap of clothing, but most of the glistening, crab-like pieces into which Tewfik's flesh had broken up had struggled free and were crawling away in random curlicues across the dirt. Doyle spasmed away in horror from the nearest of them and came up in a tense crouch, whimpering and scrabbling at the hilt of his borrowed sword and looking around wildly.

Smoke was still spilling up from the muzzle of the cannon, which was no longer concealed amid the wreckage of the makeshift wagon, and at the top of the rise the silhouette of the building had changed: the broad curve of the dome was shattered open like the shell of a huge egg. Doyle thought he could hear shouting, but with his abused ears he couldn't be sure.

He drew his sword and ran awkwardly toward the door of the building, and when it opened he was only a dozen yards away and closing fast. He collided hard with the man in the doorway, and in his stunned state was not even surprised when the man's head and right arm broke clean off; when they thudded on the floor he realized they were made of wax.

Three more of the wax men were just inside the doorway, two of them stumbling back as their disabled companion rebounded into them. Doyle parried a sword cut from the third and riposted with a punch of the hilt into the wax face, snapping the nose off and denting the cheek; and he saw that a line had appeared in the thing's neck, so he hit it in the face again, with more force, and the head of this one too cracked free and rolled away.

The two undamaged ones stepped back and raised their weapons, while the two others knelt on the floor groping for their heads. A panicky shouting echoed down from upstairs, in words that didn't seem to be Arabic, and the two whole wax men turned and ran ponderously down the hall toward the stairs.

Doyle followed. Someone else was shouting upstairs now, definitely in Arabic, and his voice sounded more anguished and defensive than personally scared. Doyle caught the words for I don't know and immune and magic.

At the foot of the stairs he kicked off his remaining shoe and padded silently up, holding Ameen's sword well out in front of him. Above he could hear gasps and grunts of effort, and feet scuffing on a gravelly floor, and it belatedly dawned on him what the emergency must be.

His eyes narrowed and a grin deepened the lines in his cheeks. Yes, he thought, let's see if we can't accomplish that—cut the title right out from under Neil Armstrong.

At the top of the stairs he peered around the corner, down the short corridor toward the inward-facing balcony. It was as he'd expected: the only light in the chamber was the dusk grayness coming in through the gaping hole. The sweating doorkeeper was standing on the right side of the balcony—the left side had been torn loose by the shot, and was swinging free—and he was hastily knotting a rope around one of the railing bars. The left wall of the corridor had collapsed, and Doyle could see the two wax men crouched out on the roof of the ground floor, leaning over the curved rim of the hole to peer down into the chamber; and even as Doyle watched, they leaned forward into the yawning gap where the eastern quarter of the dome had been and began pushing downward on something that evidently wanted to move up.

Having moored the end of the rope, the doorkeeper was pulling more of the line in, from some point below and to the left—against considerable resistance—and tying off all the slack he managed to get. Obviously he was trying to shorten the line.

Doyle waited until the man had drawn in another yard of line, and, before he could tie a knot in it, bounded up behind him, crouched, hooked his good hand under the man's belt and hoisted him up, over and out past the balcony rail. For a moment the surprised doorkeeper held onto the line as he fell, and there was a rusty squealing of casters, then he lost his grip and tumbled to the rubble-littered floor of the chamber. The line snapped taut. There was a choked-off scream from nearby, and an empty, wheeled couch skated down the bowl-shaped wall and banged against the pile of broken masonry at the bottom.

Doyle whirled and ran out onto the roof through the hole in the corridor wall and, ignoring for the moment the twitching thing dangling at the end of the nearly horizontal rope, delivered a kick and a sword poke to the off-balance wax men, tumbling both of them, too, down into the round chamber.

Reluctant to face the man he knew he must kill, he stared for a moment down into the chamber. The doorkeeper had sat up and was rocking back and forth holding his leg, which was apparently broken, and the two wax men, one of whom had predictably lost his head, were crawling aimlessly over the rubble. Doyle supposed there was a door down there, but with any luck at all it would be buried under the shattered stones that had been the eastern quarter of the dome.

"Ah, Doyle!" came a voice from behind him, in an urbane tone that must have sorely taxed the self-control of the speaker. "You and I have a lot to discuss!"

The Master was swinging back and forth twenty feet away, supported by a rope knotted under his arms, but he was hanging *straight out*, with the rope roughly parallel to the roof. Behind him Doyle could see the moon, still low in the eastern sky. The Master had to strain his head back to look "up" at Doyle. The effect was as if he were a man-shaped kite in a strong wind, or as if he and Doyle were confronting each other through a mirror tilted 45 degrees.

"We have nothing to discuss," said Doyle coldly. He raised Ameen's sword over his head one-handed, and sighted at a point on the taut rope.

"I can bring back Rebecca for you," said the Master, quietly but distinctly.

Doyle exhaled sharply, as though he'd been punched in the stomach, and he stepped back and lowered the sword. "Wh—what did you say?"

Though his position must have been painful, the Master uncovered his teeth in a smile as he slowly rotated on the end of the rope. "I can save Rebecca—prevent her from dying. Through the time gaps which I caused to be opened and Darrow discovered. You can help. We'll prevent them from getting on the motorcycle."

The sword clattered onto the roof tiles and Doyle sank to his knees. His face was now level with the Master's twenty feet away, and he stared in helpless fascination into the old man's eyes, which seemed to shine with a terribly intense blackness.

"How . . . can you know about . . . Rebecca?" he gasped.

"Don't you remember the ka we drew of you, son? The blood that fell into the tub? We grew a duplicate of you from it. It hasn't been a great deal of use to us as far as getting any consistent and coherent information—it seems to be insane, which might or might not mean that you tend that way—but we have happened to learn, a bit at a time, a lot about you."

"This is a bluff," said Doyle carefully. "You can't change history. I've seen that that's true. And Rebecca . . . died."

"A ka of her died. It wasn't the real Rebecca that fell off your motorcycle. We'll go into the future and get some of her blood, grow a ka, and then switch them at some point, let the ka go die as you remember, and then the real Rebecca can come back here with you and," the Master smiled again, "change her name to Elizabeth Jacqueline Tichy."

Ashbless slowly and wonderingly shook his head. I really think I'm going to do it, he thought. I believe I'll actually reel him in and save him. My God, I thought he was only going to offer me money. "But there's already an Elizabeth Tichy —somewhere."

"She dies and is replaced by Rebecca."

"Oh. Yeah." Doyle took hold of the rope. Sorry, Tewfik, he thought. Sorry, Byron. Sorry, Miss Tichy. Sorry, Ashbless, but it looks like you live out the rest of your life as a slave of this creature. And sorry, Becca—God knows this isn't any way you'd have chosen it.

With a good deal more ease than the doorkeeper, Ashbless drew in a yard of the rope. As he tried to knot it with one hand, he glanced once more at the Master's face, and the smile on it was not only triumphant, contemptuous and smug, but imbecilic too.

That glimpse of idiocy in the supposedly all-knowing Master was like cold water on a fevered forehead. Jesus, Doyle thought, was I really going to buy Rebecca back with the death of the Tichy girl, whom I've never even met? "No," he said conversationally. He let go of the rope and it snapped back out with a twang and an evidently agonizing jerk against the Master's shoulders.

"You'll be saving Rebecca's life, Doyle," croaked the wincing Master. "And your own sanity—you're going mad, you know that—and the facilities for the insane aren't very nice here, remember."

Ashbless turned away, snatched up the sword and as he and the Master both screamed he swung it in a hard overhead wood-chopping stroke that not only snapped the taut rope but shattered the blade and a roof tile.

Still screaming, the Master receded rapidly away, as though he were lying in the bed of an invisible truck that was trying to beat the zero-to-sixty record. Then he was out past the roof edge and picking up more speed, skimming away twenty feet or so above the ground. He was silhouetted against the moon, so Ashbless could see him clearly even in the deepening dusk.

"Enjoy it in the stinking madhouse, Doyle!" roared a voice from the pit below Ashbless' feet. "Eating excrement and being buggered by the guards, that's what's in store for you, boy! It's true, Romanelli jumped ahead and looked! And listen, we *already* rescued Rebecca, Romanelli's got her, but now that she's no good for barter I'll tell you what *she* can look forward to. . . ."

As the voice raved on, Ashbless realized that it was the Master speaking through the one wax man that still had a head. The Master himself was just a dot on the face of the moon now, slowly shrinking. After a minute or two the voice from the pit, which was still dilating upon the defilements in store for Rebecca, and how much she'd eventually come to relish them, abruptly choked and ceased. Either the wax speaking apparatus had broken down or the Master was out of range.

Ashbless shambled back through the hole in the wall and lurched down the stairs. When he reached the ground floor hall he saw someone start out of a dark doorway on his right and then, hearing his approach, scramble back inside; but Ashbless didn't even look into the room as he passed it.

When he got outside he glanced around. The horses had suffered the same disintegrative fate as Mustapha's sons, so Ashbless set out, barefoot, to walk the five and a half miles to the Harbor of Boolak. His boat didn't leave until dawn, so it didn't matter that he walked very slowly, pausing every few steps to glance fearfully up at the rising full moon.

A few minutes after Ashbless had shambled away out of sight a wild-eyed, dirty, bearded face peeked out of the doorway and blinked at the darkening funeral plain.

"See what you've done, Darrow?" the man was muttering. "Perfectly safe, you said! I remember you saying it—'It is perfectly safe, Doyle.' Hell, you might as well have let Treff come along. He couldn't have made things any worse. I've got to get back to the river, see if I can't swim back up to when everything was all right."

And the Ashbless ka tiptoed out into the evening air and stood looking around uncertainly, for he couldn't exactly recall where the river was or what it was called, though he did know he'd seen a number of branches of it. Then he remembered that one could get to it anywhere, so he chose a direction at random and strode away, a jerky but confident smile on his face.

CHAPTER 14

"Sisters, weave the web of death;
Sisters, cease, the work is done."
                                    —Thomas Gray

ONCE AGAIN HE was trying to find his way out of the maze of fog-choked alleys; and though Darrow—in the dream he could never remember his new name—had groped several miles through the snaky, doubling-back and sometimes simply dead end lanes and alleys, he still hadn't come to a street wide enough to wheel a cart through, much less the broad, well-trafficked pavement of Leadenhall Street. Finally he stopped, and heard, as he always did at this point in the dream, a slow, irregular knocking somewhere in the thick fog overhead; and then a second or two later a shuffling of footsteps nearby.

"Hello," he said timidly; then, more confidently, "hello there! Perhaps you can help me find my way."

The footsteps rasped closer across the fog-damp grittiness of the cobblestones, and a dark blur in the fog became recognizable as a ragged man.

As always, Darrow recoiled in mind-numbing fear when he realized it was Brendan Doyle. "Jesus, Doyle," he screamed, "I'm sorry, stay away please, oh God . . . " He'd have run back up the alley, but his legs wouldn't move.

Doyle smiled and pointed upward, into the fog.

Helplessly, Darrow looked up—and then put his entire soul

into a shriek so loud that it woke him.

He crouched motionless on the bed until, with considerable relief, he recognized the furniture in the dim room, and realized he was in his own bed. Once again it had just been a dream. His hand darted out, seized the neck of the brandy decanter on the bedside table, tipped the thing upside-down to expel the glass stopper, and then he righted it and brought it to his lips.

The door to Claire's room snapped open and she hurried across the room toward Dundee's bed, frowning sleepily through her disordered hair. "What in *hell* is the matter, Jacob?"

"Muscle cramp . . . (gulp) . . . in my back." He clanked the decanter back down on the table.

"You and your muscle cramps!" She sat down on the bed. "I'm your *wife*, Jacob, you don't have to lie to me. I know it's a nightmare. You always yell, 'I'm sorry, Doyle!' when you come crashing awake. Go ahead and *tell* me about it—who's Doyle? Did he have something to do with you getting so wealthy?"

Dundee took a breath, then let it out. "It's just muscle cramps, Claire. I'm sorry I woke you up."

She pursed her lips. "Is the cramp gone now?"

Dundee groped for the stopper and poked it back into the decanter neck. "Yes. You can go back to bed."

She leaned forward and kissed him lightly. "Maybe I'll stay here with you for a little while."

"I don't think—" he began hastily, but was interrupted by a knock at the hall door.

A muffled voice asked, "Are you all right, sir?"

"Yes, Joe, no problem," Dundee called. "Just couldn't sleep."

"I could bring you a cup of rum coffee if you'd like, sir."

"No thank you, Joe, I—" Dundee hesitated, glanced at his wife, then said, "Thank you, Joe, yes, that might help."

Footsteps receded away down the carpeted hall, and Claire stood up.

Knowing she wouldn't take him up on it now, Dundee raised his eyebrows and said, "I thought you were going to stay here for a bit."

Claire's mouth was a straight line. "You know how I feel about Joe." She strode back into her own room and closed the door.

Dundee stood up, clawed the hair back from his forehead and crossed to the window. He pulled the curtain aside and stared down at the broad curve of St. James Street, the uniformly elegant housefronts all palely lit in amber by the flickering street lights. The sky was less black toward the east—it would be dawn soon, a clear Sunday in March.

Yes, my dear, he thought bleakly, I do know how you feel about Joe. But I certainly can't explain to you why I need to support him and keep him around. I wish to hell he'd get a new body, though, so I could tell you I fired him and hired this new guy—but he likes Maturo's body, and I don't dare try to force him. After all, he's going to be my partner long, long after you've died of old age, my dear . . . after I've taken the best of our sons, and then our grandsons, and then great-grandsons, getting richer and buying more and more during my successive stays in each descendant's body, until by the time 1983 rolls around again I will be the secret owner of all the world's important corporations. I'll own whole cities —whole countries. And after 1983, when old J. Cochran Darrow disappears, I'll be able to come out of hiding, step out from behind the screen of corporate links and overlaps and figureheads and front men, and I'll damn well no exaggeration rule the goddamn world.

If I can keep Joe happy.

So you see, my poor bride of two months—during which time I still haven't been able to consummate the marriage and set to work on the second generation of the Dundee line —you're replaceable. Joe's not.

The richest man in London sighed, let the curtain fall back across the window and sat down on the bed to wait for his rum coffee.

In the pantry Joe the butler had climbed up onto the counter—for though he'd been able to touch the ground without pain ever since he ceased practicing high level magic nine years ago, he seemed to be able to think better when slightly elevated—and he was slowly sifting his fingers through a bowl of gray-green powder.

I've learned a great deal from the nervous young master, he thought. I've learned that having a lot of money is more fun than not having a lot of money, and that once you've got it, it tends to grow all by itself, like a fire.

He's got a lot of it. And he's got a truly beautiful young

wife who may as well be his sister, and who hates the way old
Joe looks at her . . . though it seems to me somebody ought to
look at her, aye, and do more than look. She'll turn to vinegar
in the cask if she's not tapped.

Yessir, young Dundee, thought Joe, you'd still be a dying
old man if it weren't for me—and what do I get in return for
setting you up? Employment as a *butler*. It's not fair as it
stands right now. Things aren't balanced. But I've got a solution to everyone's problems right here in this bowl. Miss
Claire's handsome young husband will become much more affectionate, and poor old butler Joe will commit suicide.
Everybody will be happy.

Except, of course, the one who's in Joe's body when it hits
the pavement.

He reached up to a shelf, took down a jar of ground cinnamon, and shook a lot of it over the powder in the bowl. He
put the jar down and stirred the mixture with his fingers, then
tapped it all into a big mug, added a hearty slug of rum, and
then hopped to the floor, lifted the now ready pot of coffee
and filled the mug with the steaming black brew.

He stirred it with a spoon as he walked down the hall and up
the stairs. When he rapped quietly at Dundee's door, Dundee
told him to come in and set it on the table. Joe did, and then
stepped back respectfully.

Dundee seemed preoccupied, and a faint frown rippled his
unlined brow. "You ever notice, Joe," he asked, mechanically
picking up the mug, "that it always takes a little more trouble
to get something than the thing was really worth?"

Joe considered it. "Better than taking a lot of trouble and
getting nothing."

Dundee sipped the coffee. He didn't seem to have heard
Joe. "There's so much weariness and fatigue in it all. For
every action there is an equal . . . stupefaction. No, that might
be bearable—it's *greater* than the action. What's in this?"

"Cinnamon. If you don't like it I could make another cup
without."

"No, it's all right." Dundee stirred it with the spoon and
took another sip.

Joe waited for a while, but Dundee didn't seem to have any
further instructions, so he left the room and closed the door
quietly.

●   ●   ●

"Hey, Snapp? That you?"

Jacky looked around. A stocky little dark-haired man sprinted lightly up to her from the other side of the street.

"Who's that?" asked Jacky, not sounding interested.

"Humphrey Bogart, remember? Adelbert Chinnie, Doyle." The man grinned excitedly. "I've been walking up and down this damn street for an hour, trying to find you."

"What for?"

"My body—my *real* body—I've found it! The fellow that's in it has grown a little moustache and he dresses and walks different, but it's me!"

Jacky sighed. "It doesn't matter anymore, Humphrey. The body-switching man was caught and killed three months ago. So even if this person you've found really is in your old body—which is damned unlikely; he'd never fail twice in a row to kill the discarded host—there's no conceivable way you can switch with him. There's nobody around anymore that knows how to do the trick." She shook her head wearily. "Sorry. Now if you'll excuse me . . . "

The grin had fallen from Chinnie's face. "He's *dead?* Did—did you kill him? God damn it, you promised me—"

"No, I didn't kill him. A crowd in an East End pub did. I heard about it next day." She started to walk on.

"Wait a moment," said Chinnie desperately. "You *heard* about it, you say. Have many people heard about it?"

Jacky stopped and said, with exaggerated patience, "Yes. Everybody—except you."

"Right!" said Chinnie, beginning to get excited again. "If I was the body-switching man I'd do the same thing."

"What do you mean?"

"Listen, I went looking for depilatory shops, remember I said I would? Places where they take hair off so it won't grow back. And I learned that there was one in Leadenhall Street where the people really could do it, something to do with electricity. The place closed down last October, but that doesn't mean the process was lost. Hell, the body-changer might have bought the place. Anyway, if I was him, and now had the option of being able to stay in a body without turning into an orang-outang, why, I'd let myself be recognized, and caught, and then just as I was falling through the gallows trap, I'd switch into another body. Let 'em all think they'd killed me so they'd call off the hunt."

Jacky slowly walked back to where Chinnie stood. "Right," she said softly, "I like it so far. But what's all this about your old body? He'd already moved on out of it—when he was hanged he was a skinny old man."

"I don't know. Maybe he put someone else in my body just to hold it while he went off to get killed, and then he switched back into it. Or maybe—yes—maybe he's placing wealthy but elderly people in young bodies for tremendous fees. Or maybe any number of things. It's getting hold of the hair-killing trick that made it all possible."

"This person in your old body," Jacky said, "what's he doing? How's he situated?"

"He's living high. Offices in Jermyn Street, big house in St. James with servants and everything."

Jacky nodded, feeling the old excitement building in her again. "That fits well enough with your idea. It could be an old man that paid Dog-Face Joe to make him young and healthy again—or it could be Joe himself. Let's go have a look at that house in St. James."

"Why, but," sputtered the disconcerted doorman, "you said, sir, that it would be an hour at least before you'd be needing the carriage. Yustin's just gone off in it for a spot of supper. Ought certainly to be back in a—"

"Yustin's fired," rasped Dundee harshly, his face looking, in the lamplight, as drawn and pinched as an old man's. He strode away down the sidewalk, the heels of his elegant boots tocking against the cobbles like the works of an old clock.

"Sir!" the doorman called after him. "It's late to be walking unaccompanied! If you'd wait a few minutes—"

"I'll be all right," Dundee answered without pausing or turning around. He reached inside his coat and touched the butt of one of the pair of miniature pocket pistols he'd had specially made for him by the Haymarket gunsmith Joseph Egg. Though no bigger than a bulldog pipe with the stem pulled out, each of the guns fired a .35 caliber ball from a charge detonated by a thing Dundee called a percussion cap, which he'd diagrammed for the fascinated gunsmith.

On a sudden impulse he turned left a block sooner than he usually did. I'll walk halfway down this block, he thought, and then cross to St. James through the service alley. I'll come out just across the street from my house, and if that loafer I've seen hanging about is still there I'll shake an explanation out of him—and if he tries any funny business he'll be the first man in history to be killed by a percussion cap pistol.

In the fog the street lamps were just shifting yellow blurs, and tiny drops of moisture began to collect on Dundee's little moustache. He scratched it irritably. You're awfully short-tempered these days, he told himself. That poor devil you shouted at in the conference room back there probably won't do business with you now, and those patents and factories he has to sell will be damn useful in a decade or two. Oh hell—wait and buy 'em from his heirs.

He paused when he turned into the service alley. Well, he thought, as long as you're sneaking, you may as well do it right. He took off his boots, held them both in his left hand and then padded noiselessly down the dim alley. His right hand rested on the knob grip of one of the Egg pistols.

Suddenly Dundee froze—he'd heard whispering up ahead.

He drew the pistol out of its little holster and tiptoed forward, probing the fog with the two-inch barrel.

Two floors overhead someone rattled a window latch and Dundee nearly fired—and then nearly dropped—the gun, for abruptly, totally and without any warning he had remembered the last part of his recurring nightmare, the part he'd never been able to recall after he woke up. With photographic clarity he'd seen the thing that in the dream had made the random knocking sound in the fog overhead, the thing the corpse-figure of Doyle had pointed at.

It was the body of J. Cochran Darrow dangling from a rope tied around its neck, its booted feet knocking against the wall like the devil's own wind chime, and its head, twisted into a posture exclusive to hanged men, staring down at him with a rictus grin that seemed to bare every single one of the yellow teeth.

His gun hand was shaking now, and he was more aware of the clammy chill of the air, as though he'd shed an overcoat. Ahead he could see a brightening stain of yellow light, for he was nearly through to the St. James sidewalk, and a street lamp stood only a few yards from the alley mouth.

There was more whispering from in front of him, and now he could see two vague silhouettes standing just inside the alley.

He raised the gun and said, clearly, "Don't move, either of you."

Both figures exclaimed in surprise and leaped out onto the

sidewalk. As Dundee stepped forward out of the alley to keep
them both covered he let his boots clop to the pavement and
drew his other pistol. "Jump like that again and I'll kill both
of you," he said calmly. "Now I want an explanation, fast, of
what you're doing here and why you've—"

He'd been looking at the younger of the two ragged lurkers,
but now he glanced at the other.

And the color drained from his features and was instantly
replaced by sweat as cold as the fog, for he recognized the
man's face. It was Brendan Doyle's.

At the same instant Chinnie realized who it was behind the
pistols. "Face to face at last," he whispered through clenched
teeth. "We're going to change places, you and I . . . " He took
a step toward Dundee.

The gunshot had a flat sound in the thick fog, like someone
slapping a board against a brick wall. Dundee began sobbing
as Adelbert Chinnie stepped back and then sat down on the
sidewalk. "God, I'm sorry, Doyle!" Dundee wailed. "But
you should stay dead!" .

The other gun wobbled toward Jacky, but before it could
train on her she lunged forward and brought the chopping
edge of her hand down hard on Dundee's wrist. The little gun
clattered onto the pavement and she dove for it.

Dundee, jolted out of his hysteria by the sharp pain in his
wrist, was right on top of her.

Jacky grabbed the gun just as Dundee's weight slammed her
onto her knees and his right forearm hooked around under her
chin; his free hand was scrabbling at her wrist, but weakly
—her blow must have numbed it. From the opposite side of
the street came the sound of a window breaking, but both of
the gasping combatants were too busy to look up; Jacky was
fighting to get her legs under her and keep air passing through
her constricted throat, and Dundee was striving with
considerably more strength to prevent those things. Jacky
couldn't raise the gun without pitching face down onto the
pavement. The pulse in her head sounded to her like labored
strokes of a pickaxe through frozen topsoil.

"Lead the dead back to me, will you, boy?" Dundee was
whispering harshly. "I'll send you across that river yourself."

In a last desperate gambit Jacky suddenly bent her arm and
rolled hard to the left. For a moment her gun hand was free,
and she swung the barrel toward Dundee, who had fallen back
and now snatched for the gun, missed it, and instead grabbed

her shirt collar and kneed her with all his strength; but the blow that he thought would jackknife his opponent in oblivious agony only jolted Jacky, and didn't prevent her from pressing the stubby barrel of the pistol against the bridge of Dundee's nose, and pulling the trigger.

The shot was even more muffled than the previous one had been. Dundee relaxed his hold on Jacky's collar, evidently in order to give his full attention to doing a sort of gargled imitation of a rattlesnake. A moment later he was limp, staring at her with two bulging eyes, between which a neat round hole had been punched. A gleaming crescent of blood collected on the lower edge, then spilled in a line across the forehead.

"All of ye smug bastards!" came a loud cry from across the street. Jacky sat up. "Ye've won, ye heartless sons of bitches," shouted the voice from the fog, and it seemed to Jacky to be coming from higher than street level. "Ye've driven old Joe to the point where he'd rather be dead than take yer smarmy ways any longer. May it trouble what shreds of conscience—"

"Joe!" called a quiet voice. "Are you drunk? What the devil are you shouting about? Stop it this instant!"

Jacky knew she should run away before the racket attracted a police officer, but besides being very shaky she was curious about the invisible drama across the street.

"I broke this here window, Miss Claire," said the man's voice. "And I reckon it'll cost ye something to get the front walkway cleaned tomorrow. Write up a bill for it all and send it to me in hell, ye teasing bitch!"

"Joe," said the lady's voice, louder now. "I order you to—oh my God!"

Jacky wondered, Did he jump? an instant before she heard the solid crack and thudding of something impacting hard onto the pavement.

Then Jacky's attention was distracted by Dundee's corpse.

It had sat up.

The blind eyes were blinking, and an expression of abysmal horror was forming on the blood-streaked face. One of Dundee's hands wobbled up, awkward as a rusty hinge, and groped at his punctured face. For a moment it seemed to be trying to get up; then it shuddered and collapsed, and its last exhalation seemed to go on forever.

Jacky got up and ran.

CHAPTER 15

"He whispered, 'And a river lies
Between the dusk and dawning skies . . .' "
—William Ashbless

THOUGH THE LIGHTERMEN and bargemen on the Thames had another half hour of April sunlight to work in, the inhabitants of the St. Giles rookery had seen the sun set an hour ago behind the tall, ragged old buildings that were their drab and stultifyingly close horizon, and nearly every one of the unmatched windows of Rat's Castle glowed with light.

Standing out in the alley by one of the building's side doors, Len Carrington impatiently answered one more objection from the party of six men that was about to leave for Fleet Street. "You'll do it because it's the very last such errand you'll ever run for them, and because if you didn't it would tip them off, and we want to hit them with no warning—and also because once you fetch this fellow for them they'll be so absorbed with him that we'll be able to kill them both with no trouble."

"Is by any chance this lad we're going to fetch the same one that pitched Norman out the window at the Swan With Two Necks?" asked one of the men.

Carrington pursed his lips, for he'd hoped they wouldn't make that connection. "Yes—but you mishandled that abduction—"

"And they seem to have *mishandled* hangin' onto him," the man added.

"—And this time you'll take him quiet," Carrington went on sternly. Then he grinned. "And if we all do our parts correctly, there'll be a real celebration in Rat's Castle tonight."

"Amen to that," whispered another of the men. "Let's off—he'll be at his silly book meeting by now."

The six men padded away down the alley and Carrington went back inside. The huge old kitchen was empty at the moment, and lit only by the dull red glow of the hearth. He dragged the door closed behind him and the room was quiet, except for the faint sound of distant wailing and grunting. He sat down on a bench and hooked a jug of cool beer down from a shelf.

He took one long swallow, then re-corked the jug, put it back and stood up. He'd better be getting back to the front room; it wouldn't do to let the clown wonder what had delayed him.

As he walked toward the inner door he passed the drain, and the wailing and groaning were louder. He paused and peered with distaste down into the black hole that led to the deep cellars and the subterranean river. I wonder, he thought, what's got Horrabin's Mistakes so riled up this evening. Maybe old Dungy was right, and the things are able to read minds a little, and they're aware of our imminent mutiny tonight. He cocked his head, listening for the basso profundo voice of Big Biter, who was the only one of the Mistakes anyone would pay any attention to, but he didn't hear him. Good boy, Carrington thought nervously—if you sense any part of our plans, keep it behind the portcullis of your appalling teeth.

He groped around for the wooden plug, found it under a pile of potato peelings, and fitted it over the drain hole, effectively silencing, up here at least, the noise from the deep cellars.

He opened the door to the hallway just as Horrabin's fluty voice called from the front room, "Carrington! Where in hell are you?"

"Right here, yer Worship," Carrington said, striding forward and forcing his voice to sound relaxed. "Just stopped in the kitchen for a sip of beer." He stepped unhurriedly into the room.

The clown, looking like a huge spider perversely made of

ribbon candy, was penduluming rapidly back and forth in his swing, while Romany or Romanelli or whatever his name was this week was reclining in his high wheeled cart that looked like nothing so much as a baby's perambulator, the snapping glow of St. Elmo's Fire flickering around his tortured frame even more brightly now than it had five minutes ago.

"I assume they're off?" asked Horrabin.

"They are."

"And instructed not to bungle it this time?" put in Romanelli.

Carrington gave the man a cold look. "They got him for you that time and they'll get him for you this time."

Romanelli scowled, then made his face relax, as though he just didn't have the spare energy to resent the insubordination. "Go downstairs to the old hospital," he said. "Make sure they've got everything ready."

"Aye aye." Carrington hurried out of the room and his boots could be heard clumping along the hall and then tapping down the long flight of stone steps.

"Why don't you go too?" croaked Romanelli to the clown.

"I just got here!" the clown protested. "And there's a couple of things you and I have to straighten out. Now I had an agreement with your ka: I was to—"

"He's dead and you have no agreement with me. Go."

After a pause Horrabin reached out and snared his stilts, thrashed out of his swing and onto them, and stood wobbling in the center of the floor. "You're pretty damn sure of—"

"Go," Romanelli repeated. He had closed his eyes, and his face looked like a thin rag that someone had draped over some stones to dry in the sun and forgotten forever.

The knocking of Horrabin's stilt-poles receded away.

Romanelli's mouth fell open and a deep sigh echoed in and out of his chest.

His time was getting damned short—he only weighed thirty pounds now, but he knew he wasn't as strong as the Master had been; he would lose his hold on the unnaturally maintained components of his body, and simply break down or fly to bits, long before the zero gravity point was reached. There'd be no big dive to the moon for him.

He shuddered, trying to remember how many sorcerers had been both strong enough and contra-natural enough—the two qualities were tremendously difficult to hold onto at the same time, like trying to press the positive ends of two lodestones together—to build up that weird lunar attraction which in extreme cases, such as the Master's, could become a fiercely drawing force far, far greater than could be explained by the actual physical gravity of the moon. There had been that Turk, Ibrahim, who had finally had himself encased to the knees in solid stone in a high-walled courtyard several miles outside of Damascus, and used to charge fortunes to tell fortunes—he'd only do it when the moon was overhead, and his hair and arms were dangling straight up, an effect that mightily impressed his customers—until one man, not pleased with his augury, had drawn a scimitar and chopped right through both of Ibrahim's knees, and the truncated screaming body had shot away upward into the sky. And there was a brief mention in one of the lost books of the apocryphal *Clementine Recognitions* of a very old magician who had just floated off the ground one afternoon in Tyana, and was visible in the sky for days, gesticulating and crying, before he drifted too far away to be seen anymore. Obviously there was some truth in the very old stories of the once inhabited moon having become, through some long-forgotten but transcendent perversity, the monument and archetype and fitfully living embodiment of desolation.

Romanelli remembered that he had been overseeing the disagreeable task of clearing out the street below the Bab-el-Azab when he'd heard the hollow knock of a cannon shot from away to the south. He had tensed, ready to call out the Albanians to repel a revenge raid by sons of the murdered Mameluke Beys, but there were no further sounds of gunfire, and when he climbed to the battlements he hadn't seen any troops massing on the darkening plain. It wasn't until later that night that he heard one of the fellahin talking about an old man who had been seen by many to fly over the old quarter of Cairo just at dusk. . . . He'd rushed back to the Master's house and found it broken, and empty except for some damaged *ushabtis* and the injured doorkeeper. . . .

From the doorkeeper he'd learned that the man who had done this was the Brendan Doyle who'd escaped from them back in October, and the next day he'd discovered that Doyle had left Egypt aboard the England-bound *Fowler*, having booked passage under the name William Ashbless. Romanelli had abandoned his post as Mohammed Ali's physician and taken the next ship for England and, by whistling on the stern until his lips were numb and the very captain had ordered him to stop it, several times managed to summon a couple of the Shellengeri for a few hours—the voyage wasn't nearly as quick as the trip south in the Chillico had been, but Romanelli did manage to step off his ship onto a London dock on Sunday, the day before yesterday, while this Ashbless-Doyle person's ship hadn't arrived until this morning.

And Doctor Romanelli had kept busy during his forty-eight hours of lead time. He'd learned that under the Ashbless name his quarry was expected to appear at, of all things, a literary gathering in the offices of the publisher John Murray, and Romanelli had browbeaten the sorcerer-clown Horrabin into having some of his swinish thugs follow Ashbless everywhere he went, and to abduct him and bring him back here to Rat's Castle after he left Murray's offices.

And when they've brought him here, thought Romanelli as the weary breaths trudged up and down his throat, I will simply wring him dry. I'll learn from him enough about the time jumping to do it myself, and I'll jump back to when I was healthy and tell my younger self how to do things differently, so that on Monday the second of April, 1811, I am not a trembling, bleeding, far overextended wreck.

He opened his bloodshot eyes and glanced up at the clock that sat on a doll-crowded shelf just below the niche where old Dungy's head was perched. Quarter to nine. In another hour or so, he told himself, Horrabin's hoodlums will bring Ashbless to me, and we'll adjourn to the subterranean hospital.

As the cab rattled past St. Paul's Cathedral William Ashbless peered out at the dark square on the west side of the huge church and remembered begging there as Dumb Tom. I never, he thought, get to use my voice. Dumb Tom was mute, and so of necessity was Eshvlis the cobbler, and though William Ashbless will be a voluble poet, he'll only be copying from memory poems he read and memorized long ago.

His mood was a blend of relief, anticipation and vague disappointment. It was certainly pleasant to be back in England again, free at last of all that hellish magic, and able to look forward to meeting, as he knew he would, Byron, Coleridge, Shelley, Keats, Wordsworth and the rest of the gang—but now that he was, irrevocably, Ashbless, and had wandered

back into the scope of the Bailey biography, there could be no
more major surprises for him; he'd already read his own life
story.

He still half wished that the test he'd thought up during the
month-long voyage of the *Fowler* had turned out negative. It
had occurred to him that if the universe was dead set on his
being Ashbless it would have to get busy and do two things. It
would have to have seen to it that the manuscript of "The
Twelve Hours of the Night," which he'd last seen on the desk
in that room at the Swan With Two Necks, was somehow conveyed to the *Courier* office in time to have been published in
December; and it would have to make sure the *Fowler* arrived
in London in time for him to attend the gathering at John
Murray's, and meet Coleridge again, on the second of April.
Both were unalterable facts in the life of the Ashbless he'd
studied, and if either one didn't happen, then he might still be
able to be his own man, with the capacity for chosen action,
able to feel hope and fear.

But when he'd gone to the Swan this afternoon and asked
them if they were holding any mail for William Ashbless,
they'd told him he owed postage on three items. These had
proven to be a letter of acceptance from the *Courier*, together
with a check for three pounds; the December 15 issue of the
paper, with the poem printed in it; and a letter from John
Murray, dated the twenty-fifth of March, inviting Ashbless to
an informal gathering at the publisher's office a week
later—tonight.

It was settled. He was Ashbless.

And it wouldn't be dull—for one thing, there were some
pieces of the story he would be interested to watch unfold.
Where, for example, is Elizabeth Jacqueline Tichy, my wife to
be? I'll presently tell Bailey that I first met her way back in
September of last year. I wonder why I'll say that. And of
course the final question is: who is it that will meet me in the
Woolwich marshes on the twelfth of April in 1846, stab me
through the stomach and leave my body to be found more
than a month later? And how in hell will I make myself keep
that appointment?

The cab had slanted to the right, past the Old Bailey onto
Fleet Street, and now drew to a stop at number 32, a narrow,
pleasant-looking building with lights glowing behind the curtains. Ashbless stepped down, paid the driver, and as the cab
clopped and jingled away into the night he took a deep breath,

glanced up and down the street—noticing a beggar boy slouching in his direction—and then knocked on the door.

After a few moments there was the snap of a bolt being drawn back and the door was opened by a sandy-haired man with a glass in his hand; and in spite of the haircut, beard-trim and respectable clothes that Ashbless had spent most of his three pounds on, the man stepped back uncertainly when he got a look at the huge bronzed visitor.

"Uh . . . yes?" he said.

"My name is Ashbless. Are you John Murray?"

"Oh? Yes, yes, do come in. Yes, I'm Murray. You gave me a start—if there is such a thing as a typical poet, sir, may I say you don't look anything like him. Would you care for a glass of port?"

"I'd love it." Ashbless stepped into the entry hall and waited while Murray re-bolted the door.

"There's a beggar boy been hanging round out front," Murray explained apologetically. "Tried to sneak in earlier." He straightened, had a gulp of his port and then gingerly stepped past his guest. "Right this way. I'm glad you were able to come—we're lucky enough to have Samuel Coleridge with us this evening."

Ashbless grinned and followed. "I knew we would."

Jacky had timidly started forward when she saw the stranger climb out of the cab, but before she could think of what to say, the man had knocked and been admitted into the house by that ill-tempered Murray. She walked back to the lightless recessed doorway she'd been crouching in during the past hour.

That's certainly the man Brendan Doyle described, she thought. Murray wasn't just talking through his hat to that *Times* columnist when he said he had reason to believe that the controversial new poet William Ashbless would be a guest at his Monday night gathering.

So how do I get to *talk* to the man? she wondered. I owe poor old Brendan Doyle that much—to convey the sad news of his death to this friend of his. I guess I'll just have to wait here until he comes out, and then catch him before he can get into a cab.

Though Jacky hadn't slept since killing Dundee—and, by extension, Dog-Face Joe—two nights ago, she'd begun having hallucinations, as if her dreams were impatient to get at her. Huge shadows seemed to rush toward her, but after she flinched away there'd be nothing there; and she kept hearing . . . not the sound, not even the echo, but a sort of after reverberation in the air of a vast iron door slamming down over the sky. It hadn't begun yet, for it was still early in the evening, but she was wearily certain that in a few hours she'd begin to wonder why it wasn't dawn yet . . . and long before five o'clock the uneasy wondering would deepen to a panicked conviction that something really had shut down over the sky, and she'd never again see the sun.

She'd once visited the Magdalen Hospital for insane women—"Maudlin," as it was known in the streets—and she had vowed to kill herself rather than be committed there, if the options should ever become as narrow as that.

Tonight she was pretty sure they'd become that narrow.

Her only remaining intentions were to meet Ashbless, break to him the news about Doyle, and then do The Admirable's Dive, swim out to the middle of the Thames and empty her lungs and sink to the bottom.

She shivered—for it had just occurred to her that subjectively her fears were justified: for her there wouldn't be any dawn.

As far as the professional purposes of the gathering went, Coleridge and Ashbless were disappointments to Murray. When the publisher strolled over to the corner of the book-lined room where the two of them were talking, and managed first to enter the conversation and then to change the subject to a proposal of publication for each of them, neither one looked eager; which puzzled Murray, for Coleridge was in financial ruin, his family having to be supported on the charity of friends, and Ashbless was a raw novice who ought to have been delighted at the prospect of getting such a good publisher so quickly.

"A translation of Goethe's *Faust*?" said Coleridge doubtfully. When his attention had been distracted from the subject he and Ashbless were discussing, the animation had left his face, and now he looked old and ill again. "I don't know," he said. "Though Goethe is a genius whose work—especially *that* work—it would be a privilege and a challenge to translate, I'm afraid that my own philosophy is so much . . . at odds with his that such an undertaking would . . . compromise us both. I do have many essays. . . ."

"Yes," said Murray, "we'll certainly have to discuss publication of your essays sometime. But what do you think, Mr. Ashbless, of the idea of publishing a volume of your own verse?"

"Well," Ashbless began. You can't, Murray, he thought helplessly, for it happens that Ashbless' first book will be published by Cawthorn this May. Sorry—but that's history for you. "At the moment," he said, "the 'Twelve Hours' is all I have. Let's wait and see if I manage to write any others."

Murray forced a smile. "Right. Though I may not have a space in my schedule when you're ready. You gentlemen will excuse me?" He returned to the group by the table.

"I'm afraid I shall really have to be excused as well," said Coleridge, putting down his scarcely tasted glass of port and massaging his gray forehead. "I feel one of my headaches coming on, and they make dull company of me. The walk home may even cure it."

"Why not take a cab?" Ashbless asked, walking with him toward the door.

"Oh . . . I like to walk," Coleridge answered, a little shamefacedly, and Ashbless realized that the man didn't have cab fare.

"Tell you what," Ashbless said casually. "I've about had my fill here, and I don't particularly like walking. Perhaps I could give you a lift."

Coleridge brightened, then asked cautiously, "But in which direction are you going?"

"Oh," Ashbless said with a careless wave, "I'm heading in all directions. Where are you staying?"

"Hudson's Hotel, in Covent Garden. If it isn't an inconvenience . . . "

"Not at all. I'll go make excuses to Mr. Murray, and fetch our hats and coats."

A few minutes later they were being let out the front door, and Murray leaned out and scowled at the vagrant lad who was still loitering a few doors away.

"Thank you, Mr. Ashbless, for seeing our friend home."

"It's no trouble—and I believe I see a cab now. Hey! Taxi!"

The cab driver didn't understand the call, but the waving arm was a clear enough summons. He slanted his vehicle in toward them and Murray bade them goodnight, closed the door and re-bolted it.

The cab had just rocked to a halt when there came a cry of, "Mr. Ashbless! Wait a moment!" and the ragged boy came dashing up.

My God, thought Ashbless as the boy's face was lit for a moment by the street lamp, it's Jacky. He's shorter than he used to be; no, that's right, I'm taller. "Yes?"

Jacky stopped in front of them. "Excuse me for interrupting," she panted, "but I'm afraid I've got some bad news about a friend we have in common."

Ashbless stared at Jacky in the light from the curtained window at his back. The months have dealt harshly with him, Ashbless thought. The kid looks starved and exhausted and . . . somehow, in spite of those things, even a trifle more effeminate than he used to. Poor devil.

"I really think," said Coleridge awkwardly, "that a walk would be restorative. I—"

"No," protested Ashbless. "This damp fog would do you no good, and I'd like to hear more of your thoughts on the Logos. I'm sure this lad—"

"Does anybody want the bloody cab?" called the driver, twitching his whip impatiently.

"Yeah, let's all three hop in," said Ashbless, opening the door. "And maybe after we see Mr. Coleridge home, young man, you'll let me buy you some dinner."

"I'll ride along," said Jacky, scrambling in, "but I'll have to . . . decline your kind offer of dinner. I've got . . . an appointment on the river to keep."

"Don't we all?" grinned Ashbless, helping Coleridge in and then climbing in himself. "Driver! Hudson's Hotel, please, Covent Garden!" He slammed the door and the overloaded cab lurched back out into traffic.

The carriage that Jacky had seen waiting near Murray's got under way too, following the cab at a distance of a dozen yards, though not even the cab driver noticed it.

"So what friend and what bad news?" asked Ashbless, who had wedged his tall frame into the corner by the port window.

"You . . . knew a man named Brendan Doyle, I think," said Jacky.

Ashbless raised his eyebrows. "Knew him pretty damn well, yes. Why?"

"He's dead. I'm sorry. I knew him myself, briefly, and I liked him. He was trying to find you before he died—he thought you'd help him, and you do seem to be as generous as he said. You just . . . arrived too late." There was real grief in Jacky's voice.

The cab halted at the Chancery Lane intersection, and Jacky reached for the door handle. "I'd better leave. This isn't getting me any closer to the river. Good to have met you both."

Alarmed by the flatness of Jacky's voice, and suddenly guessing the nature of the river appointment, Ashbless closed his hand firmly over Jacky's and held the door shut. "Wait."

The driver seemed to be having some difficulty getting the cab going again—it sounded as if he jumped to the pavement and punched the horse—but eventually they got moving again, and Ashbless released Jacky's hand.

"He's not dead, Jacky," he said quietly. "Later I'll tell you how I know—right now just take my word for it. And I don't care if you saw his corpse. As you know," and Ashbless winked, "there *are* cases where that's not conclusive evidence." Jacky's eyes widened with comprehension, and Ashbless smiled and sat back as much as he could. "In any case! Mr. Coleridge and I were discussing the concept of the Logos. What are your thoughts on the subject?"

It was Coleridge's turn to raise his eyebrows in surprise at asking a grimy street urchin such a question; and his eyebrows climbed even higher when Jacky answered.

"Well," said Jacky, not too disconcerted by the conversational change of gears, "it seems to me that there's something about the Logos, as defined by St. John, that parallels Plato's idea of absolutes: the eternal, constant forms that material things are sort of imperfect copies of. Some of the pre-Socratic philosophers, in fact—"

She was interrupted by a fist abruptly poking in through the open window and pressing the muzzle of a pistol against her upper lip. She could feel the coldness of the metal right through her false moustache. Another arm had snaked in through the other window at the same moment and was holding a pistol against Ashbless' eye.

"No one moves," said a harsh voice, and a lean, squinting face grinned in at them through Jacky's window. " 'Ello, Squire," he said to Ashbless, who was too jammed in to make a move even if he could think of one. "Not gonna be pitchin' anybody through a winder this time, eh? 'Pologize to break in on yer pretty talk, but we're takin' a detour—to Rat's Castle."

To his own surprise, Ashbless realized that his breathless feeling was as much elation as it was fear. By God, he thought, you never know when you'll come across a chapter Bailey missed. "I'm pretty sure it's me you want," he said carefully, blinking against the muzzle. "Let these two go and I'll promise to go quiet."

"Yer fair makin' me weep with yer heroicals, sport." The man poked lightly with the gun, rocking Ashbless' head back. "Now shut the hole, eh?"

The cab made a right turn onto Drury Lane, and though the new driver almost had the starboard wheel spinning in midair as he wrenched the vehicle around the corner, the two men crouching outside on the step bars never flinched or lowered their guns.

"I'm not sure I follow this," said Coleridge, who had shut his eyes and was rubbing his temples. "Are we to be robbed, or killed? Or both?"

"Probably both," said Jacky evenly, "though I think their boss would be more interested in stealing your soul than your purse."

"They can't steal that unless you've lost it already," said Coleridge calmly. "Perhaps the time would be best spent if each of us . . . shored up his claim to possession of one." He composed his pudgy features into a placid blankness and let his hands fall into his lap.

The cab paused at Broad Street, then moved rapidly across. The clatter and jingle of the cab sounded louder now, for the lane was much narrower north of Broad Street.

After a few moments Jacky sniffed. "We're in the St. Giles rookery, sure enough," she muttered jerkily, as though she couldn't get enough air into her lungs. "I can smell the trash fires."

"The man said shut up," her guard reminded her, giving her a poke in the moustache. She obediently remained silent, afraid that another such would knock the thing off.

At last the cab halted and the two armed hijackers hopped down and opened the doors. "Out," said one of them.

The three passengers unbent themselves from the cramped interior and climbed out. Coleridge promptly sat down on the step bar, held his head and moaned; evidently the headache was getting worse. Ashbless glanced bleakly up at the huge, ragged building they'd arrived at.

Partially brick—brick in every degree of size, shade and

age—and half-timbered, the structure was linked to the dark bulks of other buildings at every level by flimsy bridges and ratlines, and was pierced by windows in such an uneven pattern that they couldn't, it seemed to him, reflect the arrangement of floors inside. Jacky just stared down at the wet mud between her boots, and breathed deeply.

Len Carrington hurried out of the well-lighted open doorway and surveyed the scene. "All go smoothly?" he asked the driver, who was still perched up on the bench.

"Aye. By yer leave I'll take this back to Fleet Street before the real cabbie can report it missing."

"Right. Go."

The whip snapped and the cab rolled forward, for there was no room to turn it around. Carrington stared at the captives. "That's our man," he said, pointing at Ashbless, "and that's . . . what was the name, haven't seen him in a while . . . Jacky Snapp!—whose involvement in this I'll want explained . . . but who's the sick old bastard?"

The hijackers shrugged, so Ashbless said quietly, "He's Samuel Taylor Coleridge, a very famous writer, and you'll be buying more trouble than you can afford if you kill him."

"Don't tell us what we—" began one of the hijackers, but Carrington shut him up with a wave.

"Get 'em all inside," he said. "And quickly—the police *have* been known to come this deep into the rookery."

The captives were marched at gunpoint into the large front room, and for the first time that night Ashbless felt the icy emptiness and despairing inner wail of real fear, for Doctor Romanelli was there, reclining in some sort of wheeled crib and staring at him with wrathful recognition.

"Bind him," the sorcerer croaked, "and take him downstairs to the hospital. Hurry." The St. Elmo's fire was flickering wildly now, and popped every time he pronounced a hard consonant.

Ashbless leaped at the man to his right and with the whole weight and strength of his body punched him in the throat; the man went straight over backward and his reflexive shot exploded the face of the clock on the wall. Ashbless had just gotten his balance back and was about to whirl and grab Jacky and Coleridge when his left leg was abruptly slammed out from under him and he landed awkwardly on the floor.

The scene stopped being a moving mix of impressions for him, and he could only perceive things one at a time: his new trousers had a gaping, blood-wet hole blown out in the left knee; his ears were ringing from the bang of a second gunshot; blood, and bits of bloody cloth and bone, were spattered on the wall and floor in front of him; his left leg, which was extended straight out in front of him, was bent sideways at the knee.

"I still want you to bind him," rasped Romanelli. "And put a tourniquet on his thigh—I want him to last a while."

Ashbless lost consciousness when Carrington and the gunman grabbed him under the arms and yanked him upright.

Three minutes later the room was empty except for Coleridge, who was sitting pale-faced in Horrabin's swing with his eyes closed, and one of Carrington's men, a rat-faced young man named Jenkin who was embarrassed at having been posted as guard over such a harmless old fellow. Jenkin looked around the room curiously, noting the fresh blood puddle and the shattered clock, and wondered exactly what had happened here before Carrington had called him in. He'd seen three people being taken out of the room as he hurried in, and only one of them was walking, but everything had seemed to be under control; Jenkin had thought when he heard the two shots that it was the start of the mutiny, but evidently that would have to wait for a bit.

He started violently when he heard a step in the hall, and then sighed with relief to see Carrington enter the room.

"They got tea hot in the kitchen?" Carrington growled.

"Aye, chief," replied the mystified Jenkin.

"Fetch a pot and a cup—and sugar."

Jenkin rolled his eyes but obeyed. When he got back with it Carrington had him set it on a table, then went to one of the higher shelves and took down a brown glass bottle. He uncorked it and shook several splashes of a sharp-smelling liquid into the tea. "Throw a lot of the sugar in, too," he whispered to Jenkin.

Jenkin did, and jerked a thumb inquiringly toward Coleridge.

Carrington nodded.

Jenkin drew the thumb across his neck and raised his eyebrows.

Carrington shook his head and whispered, "No, it's laudanum. Opium, you know? It'll just put him to sleep, and then you'll stash him in Dungy's old room. And when we've got rid of the clown and the wizard we'll take him down the underground river and dump him by the Adelphi somewhere. He won't remember where this is. Extra trouble, but after the publicity the papers stirred up over the murder of that Dundee fellow Saturday, we don't dare kill a well-known goddamn writer.'' He poured a cup of the tea and carried it across to Coleridge. "Here you go, sir," he said gently. "A bit of hot tea will help."

"Medicine," Coleridge wheezed. "I need my . . . "

"The medicine's in the tea," said Carrington reassuringly. "Drink up."

Coleridge drank the cup empty in four swallows. "More . . . please . . . "

"That's plenty for now." He took the empty cup back to the table. "He'll sleep till noon with that dose," he told Jenkin. "I'll dump the pot before somebody else finds it. Be quick about getting our friend here down to Dungy's room if you don't want to carry him there."

Jenkin lowered his voice and asked, "When do we . . . ?"

"Soon now, though we're one man short—that Ashbless bastard punched Murphy in the throat, and smashed everything from his chin to his collarbone. Dead before he hit the floor."

"Who is this Ashbless?"

"I don't know—but it's luck for us that he seems tough; their lordships will need a bit of time to wreck him. But he won't last forever and we've got to take them while they're busy with him, so get moving."

Jenkin crossed to the swing, helped Coleridge up and hustled him out of the room.

Carrington, his face looking leaner than ever with tension, took the teapot to the front door and dumped it out on the steps, then bolted the door, tossed the teapot into a chair and glanced around. It certainly wouldn't do to let any inquisitive police officer see the place like this. He dragged a couple of little rugs over from the hall and flung them over the broken glass and the smeared pool of blood.

He straightened and shook his head wonderingly, remembering the quickness of Ashbless' strike at Murphy. Who the hell was the man? And why was he out riding in the mismatched company of an evidently well-known writer and a beggar boy, like Jacky Snapp?

Some of the color left Carrington's face, and very carefully he conjured in his mind an image of Jacky Snapp . . . and then compared it to a face he'd seen six months ago, on the afternoon old Dungy and Ahmed the Hindoo Beggar had tried to kill Horrabin and escape down the underground river.

Brother and sister? A boy masquerading as a girl? Or just a coincidental likeness? Carrington was going to find out.

He hurried to the hall, wrenched open the stairwell door and began hastily skipping down the first of the four flights of stairs, each one more ancient than the one above it, that bottomed out in the deep cellars.

Now that it looked pretty certain that she'd be killed before dawn, Jacky's intended suicide seemed to her like the gesture of a vain and affected lunatic. Maudlin indeed! She was locked in the nearest to the stairs of a row of low-roofed cages, and the sounds made by the occupants of the other cages made her glad that the nearest wall torch was dozens of yards away along the hall, and was kept low fluttering by the cold stale-smelling breeze from the underground watercourse; for though the roars and growls and wails, and the wet slitherings, the rustling of heavy, scaled limbs being shifted and the rattle of claws on the stone floor might have led her to believe she was sharing the accommodations with an exotic menagerie, she also heard, obviously linked with those sounds, quick whispers and muted laughter and, from one of the farther cages, a low voice monotonously reciting nursery rhymes.

After she'd been sitting in the cage about five minutes she was brought bolt upright by a harsh scream—and as it died away in sobbing and coughing she recognized the voice of William Ashbless. "All right, you bastards," she heard Ashbless say, spitting the words out like pieces of teeth, "you want it, you can buy it. I'll tell you—" His voice broke off and the scream was wrenched out of him again. The sound seemed to Jacky to come from some distance to her right, amplified by the tunnels.

"You're in the position," grated a voice, "to buy yourself a quick death. Nothing else. Buy now before we add more tax."

"God damn it," gasped Ashbless, "I'm not going to—"

Once more the full-throated scream abraded the stones of the tunnel walls.

The creatures in the neighboring cages were muttering and shifting uneasily, evidently upset by the noise.

Jacky heard footsteps on the stairs and looked up. A tall

man had stepped out of the stairway door and was walking quickly in this direction, and as he passed the mounted torch he yanked it off the wall without breaking stride—and Jacky cowered back in her cage, for the newcomer was Len Carrington.

She hunched up and hid her face on her crossed arms as Carrington's boot heels knocked closer and closer. He's going to check on how they're doing with Ashbless, she told herself. Keep your head down and he'll walk right on by.

Tears began running out of her eyes and she began to sob, very softly, when the knocking steps stopped directly in front of her.

"Hello there, Jacky," crooned Carrington's voice. "I've got a question or two for you. Look at me."

She kept her head down.

"God damn it, you little sod, I said look at me!" Carrington shouted, shoving the torch in through the bars and whacking the flaming end against Jacky's shin.

Burning oil had splashed on her trousers and she had to leap up to slap it out. She wound up on her hands and knees on the floor of the cage, face to face through the bars with Carrington.

Another scream from Ashbless batted echoes up and down the halls, and when it had died away Carrington chuckled. "Oh, there's a resemblance, all right," he said, softly but with cold satisfaction. "Now listen to me, boy—I want to know who that girl was that I met upstairs here, who sent me off to the Haymarket to be nearly killed six months ago."

"I swear to God, sir," gasped Jacky, "I don't—"

With a snarl of impatience Carrington thrust the torch through the bars again, but before he could do anything with it, two green, long-fingered hands gripped the bars that divided Jacky's cage from the next one, and Carrington found himself staring into the wide-mouthed, huge-eyed reptilian face of one of Horrabin's Mistakes. "Leave her alone," the thing said very clearly.

Carrington blinked and withdrew the torch. "Her?" He peered closely at Jacky, who had scooted back to the rear of the cage and was sobbing again. After several seconds, "Oh, well now," he said in an almost choked voice, as if he'd swallowed a tablespoonful of honey just before speaking. "Oh, yes yes yes." He dug in his pocket, fumbled out a ring of keys and shoved one into the cage lock, snapped the bolt back and pulled the door open so fast that the ring of keys was set banging against the iron door frame.

Horrabin's voice echoed up the hall from the direction of the hospital: "I'm afraid he's dead, your Worship," the clown fluted.

Carrington grimaced in frustration and started to close the cage.

"There's still a heartbeat," came Romanelli's voice. "Get the ammonia spirits over here, he's still got a good half hour left in him, and I need some answers."

"Hang in there, Ashbless," Carrington whispered, yanking the door back again. He reached in, grabbed Jacky by the upper arm and dragged her out. She was struggling, and he slapped her across the face hard enough to unfocus her eyes. "Come on," he said, and marched his dazed captive down another hall and through the arch that led to the wide, downward sloping cellar.

A dozen armed men waited on the other side of the arch, and one of them sprinted over to Carrington. "Now, chief?" the man asked tensely.

"What?" snapped Carrington. "No, not yet—there's still plenty of sand in Ashbless' hourglass. I'll be back soon; I'm taking Jacky here to the deep end to collect on a long-standing debt."

The man gaped at him.

Carrington smiled, pinched the corner of Jacky's moustache and ripped it off. "Old Jacky's been a girl all along."

"Wh—you mean you—not now, chief! Put her back in the cage and save her for dessert! My God, we've got things to do here, you can't—"

"I'll be back in plenty of time." He shoved Jacky forward, out across the floor, and she tripped over the lid of one of the sunken cells, and fell.

"Please, chief!" the man insisted, catching Carrington's arm as he went to pick her up. "For one thing, you can't go down into the deep end by yourself! All the Fugitive Mistakes live down there, and—"

Carrington dropped the torch, spun and drove his fist into the man's belly, and the man sat down hard and rolled over on his side. Carrington looked up at the rest of the men. "I'll be back," he said, "in plenty of time. Is that clear?"

"Sure, chief," a couple of them muttered uncomfortably.

"Fine." He picked up the torch and hoisted Jacky to her

feet and walked away from the lighted end of the vast chamber, down the increasing incline into the darkness. His torch flickered in a damp breeze from below, and lit only the wet stones of the ancient pavement right around them; whatever walls and ceiling there might have been were lost in the solid blackness.

After they'd been walking down the slope for several minutes, and each of them had twice slipped on the wet and ever-steeper paving stones and done short, sitting slides, and the wall torches by the entry arch were not even a faint glow over the hump of the floor behind and above them anymore, Carrington tripped Jacky, knelt beside her and shoved the butt of the torch into a wide patch of mud between two of the flagstones.

"Be nice and I'll kill you quick afterward," he said with an affectionate grin.

Jacky drew her legs back and kicked at him—he blocked it easily with his forearm, but as her heels rebounded they knocked the torch loose; it rolled away downward, picked up speed, began cartwheeling and then abruptly went out far below with a wet sizzle.

"Want the lights out, eh?" said Carrington in the now absolute darkness. He seized her shoulders and knelt on her knees to hold her down. "That's fine—I like shy girls."

Jacky was weeping hopelessly as Carrington shifted his position above her; he paused for a long several seconds, and then jerked and began making a peculiar muffled groaning. He shifted again, his hand scrabbling weakly at her face, and a moment later he lurched off of her and she heard a sound like a pitcher of water slowly being poured out; and when she caught a smell like heated copper she realized that it was blood splashing on the stones.

Because she'd been crying she hadn't heard the things approach, but now she heard them whispering around her. "You greedy pig," giggled one, "you've wasted it all."

"So lick the stones," came the hissed reply.

Jacky started to get up, but something that felt like a hand holding a live lobster pushed her back down. "Not so fast," said another voice. "You've got to come deeper with us—to the bottom shore—we'll put you in the boat and push you out, and you can be our offering to the serpent Apep."

"Take her without her eyes," whispered another of them. "She promised them to my sister and me."

Jacky didn't begin screaming until she felt spidery fingers groping at her face.

What he found in the cages pretty much confirmed Coleridge's suspicion that he was having another opium dream—albeit an extraordinarily vivid one.

When the pain of his headache and stomach cramps had receded a while ago he'd found himself in a dark room with no recollection of how he'd arrived there, and when he sat up on the bed and reached for his watch and couldn't even find the table—and noticed how profoundly dark the room was—he realized he was not at his room at Hudson's Hotel; and after standing up and blind-man's-bluffing his way around the tiny chamber, he'd realized he wasn't in John Morgan's house either, or Basil Montagu's, or any other place he'd ever been before. Eventually he'd found the door, and opened it, and for a full minute just stood in the doorway, staring up and down the dimly torchlit stairwell, whose architecture he recognized as debased provincial Roman, and listening to the distant wails and roarings that he didn't recognize at all.

This Fuseli-esque scene, together with the familiar—though extra strong this time—balloon-headed feeling and the warm looseness in his joints, made him certain that he had once again taken too strong a dose of laudanum and was hallucinating.

In Xanadu, he'd thought wryly, did STC a morbid dungeon world decree.

After a while he had wandered out onto the stairwell landing. The folk notion that a house explored in a dream symbolically represented one's mind had always struck him as having a grain of truth in it, and while in many dreams he had explored the upper floors of his mind house, he'd never before seen the catacombs beneath. The nightmare noises were coming from below, so, bravely curious about what sort of monsters might inhabit the deepest levels of his mind, he carefully picked his way down the ancient steps.

Despite a moderate apprehension about what he might run into, he was pleased with himself for conjuring up such a detailed fantasy. Not only were the weathered stones of the stairwell done in painstaking chiaroscuro detail, and the scuffing of his shoes producing a faint echo, but the cold air rushing up from below was dank and stale and smelled of mold, mildew, seaweed and—yes, that was it—a zoological garden.

It had grown darker as he'd descended, and when he reached the bottom of the stairs he was in an absolute blackness relieved only by occasional faint flickerings that might have been distant torchlight reflected around more than one corner, or might just have been the random star patterns provided by a bored retina.

He had walked slowly out across the uneven floor in what seemed to be the direction the groaning and cawing came from, but when he'd still been a few yards short of finding the cages he'd been frozen by an echoing scream that had as much weariness and hopelessness as agony in it. And what was *that*? he'd wondered. My ambition, fettered and all but starved by my sloth? No, that's misleading; more likely it's the embodiment of my duties—not the least of which is talent—ignored by me and imprisoned in this bottommost oubliette of my mind.

Now he continued forward, and in a moment he felt the cold bars of the nearest cage. Something slapped heavily on the floor within, then there was a sound like a wet mop being slowly dragged over stones, and presently Coleridge realized that the intermittent breeze on his hand was the breath of something.

"Hello, man," it said in a profoundly deep voice.

"Hello," said Coleridge nervously. After a bewildered pause he said, "You're locked up?"

"We are . . . all locked up," assented the unseen thing, and there were grunts and chirps of agreement from other cages on each side.

"Are you, then," muttered Coleridge, mostly to himself, "vices that I have actually managed to shackle? I wouldn't have thought there were any."

"Free us," said the thing. "The key is in the lock of the cage at the end."

"Or are you," Coleridge went on, "as is more likely, strengths, virtues I've been too lazy to exercise, warped by long confinement and inattention down here?"

"I don't know . . . these things, man. Free us."

"And would not a twisted strength be a thing more to be feared than an atrophied vice? No, my friend, I think I'd be wise to leave you caged. I must have had good reason to make these bars so solid." He started to turn away.

"You cannot just ignore us."

Coleridge paused. "Can't I?" he asked thoughtfully. "That might be true. Certainly no valid answer is ever gained by excluding any factors of the problem; that was the Puritans' error. But surely these cages represent a—rare!—manifestation of my will, my control. I must already have taken you into account."

"Free us and be sure."

Coleridge stood pondering it in the darkness for a full minute; then, "I don't see how I can not," he whispered, and groped his way to the last cage, where Carrington's key ring still dangled from the lock on the open cage door.

The harsh ammonia fumes dragged Ashbless back to consciousness—and the horrible little mud-floored, torch-lit room—one more time.

After the last ammonia-enforced revival he'd found that he was able to remove himself from the tortured body tied down on the table, or, more accurately, to sink so far down into the fever dream depths of his head that he felt Romanelli's desperate surgeries only as distant tugs and jars, the way a deep swimmer can faintly feel agitations on the surface.

It had been a welcome change, but in this new moment of clarity he realized that he was dying. While none of the injuries Romanelli had inflicted were instantly fatal, Ashbless would have needed the attentions of a 1983 Intensive Care ward to achieve even a qualified recovery.

He blinked up at the near wall through his good eye, noting without even any wonder the row of four-inch tall toy men along a shelf above the water pump, then rolled his head and stared into the weirdly lit face of Romanelli. I guess this is an alternate world after all, he thought with a cold remoteness. Ashbless dies in 1811 here. Well, he'll die silent, too. I don't think, Romanelli, that you could extrapolate the location of a future gap by learning what I know about previous ones—but I'm not going to give you the chance. You can die here with me.

"You're overdoing it," came Horrabin's Mickey Mouse voice from behind him. "It's not as easy or quick as just ripping open a crate. You're just killing him."

"He may think that too," gasped Romanelli. The sorcerer stood in an evidently painful net of miniature lightning bolts.

"But listen to me, Ashbless—you won't die until I let you. I could cut your head off—and I may—and still keep you alive in it by magic. You probably imagine you'll be dead by dawn. Let me assure you I can prolong your death agonies *decades*."

The doorway was directly behind the two magicians, and Ashbless forced himself not to move his eye or show any reaction when he saw the monstrous forms appear in it and steal silently forward into the dim room. Whatever they are, he thought, I hope they're real, and kill us all.

But there was a flicker of motion on the shelf above the pump—one of the little dolls twitched, pointed its tiny arm and shrilled, "The Mistakes are loose!"

Horrabin spun on one stilt like a compass and, poking out his tongue until it touched his nose, produced a piercing two-tone whistle that jarred Ashbless' remaining teeth. At the same moment Romanelli took a deep breath—it sounded like an open umbrella being dragged down a chimney—and then barked three syllables and flung his bloodstained hands out, palms forward.

One of the Mistakes, a long, lithe furry thing with huge ears and nostrils but no eyes, launched itself in a cat-like leap at Horrabin, but thudded against a barrier and tumbled back to splash in the mud of the wet floor.

"Get . . . rid of them," sobbed Romanelli. Blood was welling freely from his nose and ears. "I can't do . . . another one of these."

Half a dozen of the Mistakes, including one amphibian giant with an underslung lower jaw and multiple ranks of wedge-shaped teeth, were noisily hitting and clawing at the barrier.

"Open little holes along the floor," said Horrabin tensely. "My Spoonsize Boys will make 'em glad to get back in their cages."

"I . . . can't," Romanelli said in a faint whine. "If I try to alter it . . . it will just . . . break." Blood had begun running from his eyes like tears. "I'm . . . falling to pieces."

"Look at the clown's trousies," boomed the thing with all the teeth.

Horrabin automatically glanced down at himself, and saw by the torchlight that his baggy white pantaloons were spattered with mud from the furry Mistake's splash in the puddle.

"Mud goes through," the creature bellowed, prying up a fist-sized stone from the floor and flinging it.

The stone thudded into Horrabin's belly, and he reeled gasping on his stilts until two more struck him, one on his polka dot ruffled wrist and one on his white forehead, and he folded backward, his face a mask of horrified wrath, to sit down with a loud splat in the mud.

The Spoonsize Boys bounded down from their shelf like oversized crickets, drawing their tiny swords in midair, splashed and tumbled in the mud and then bounded through the barrier, stabbing the ankles and swarming up the legs of the Mistakes.

Romanelli folded Ashbless' ruined leg back and belted the ankle to the thigh, then, with an effort that crumbled the teeth between his hard-clenched jaws, the sorcerer lifted the dying poet and lurched across the floor to the far archway.

Every step down the hall produced further snaps and internal burstings, but Romanelli plodded on, the breath shrieking in and out of him, as crashes and shouts erupted from the hospital behind them, to the archway that led into the descending cellar.

Carrington's men, huddled against the wall below one of the torches, had been getting increasingly impatient for the return of their chief, and swearing to each other in whispers that they would damn well go in there without him, but they blanched and stepped back when the grisly spectacle of Romanelli and his burden walked in through the arch and passed them.

"Jesus," whispered one of them, fingering the grip of a dagger, "shouldn't we go after him and kill him?"

"What are you, blind?" growled one of his fellows. "He's dead already. Let's go get the clown."

They had just started toward the arch when a gang of the Mistakes burst hopping and slithering through, hotly pursued by a leaping swarm of the Spoonsize Boys.

Ashbless had, despite all the chemical and sorcerous consciousness maintainers, sunk into a semi-comatose state from which he roused only for moments at a time. At one point he was vaguely aware that he was being carried down a steep incline; at another he noticed that his bearer was mindlessly and in a bubbling voice singing some jolly little song; then things became confused: there was a lot of yelling behind them, and by the light of his bearer's personal electrical storm he saw a thing like a huge toad wearing a three-cornered hat bound past on one side while a six-legged dog with a man's head galloped by on the other, and then the air was full of leaping bugs which weren't bugs at all but tiny angry men waving little swords.

Then his bearer had stumbled, and everyone was tumbling down the increasingly steep slope, and the last thing Ashbless glimpsed before losing consciousness one more time puzzled him even through his death-fog: he saw Jacky's face, streaked with tears and shorn of its moustache, staring at him in surprise as he rolled past.

The sparking, flickering thing that tumbled against Jacky collided with the Eyeless Sisters too and sent them spinning away into the darkness, chittering in disappointment, and Jacky scrambled to her hands and knees in time to see that the blue-flashing thing was a man, and that William Ashbless, evidently dead, was sliding down the slope right behind him; then Jacky ducked her head and dug her fingers and toes into the mud between the stones, for a rush of barking and mewling forms, invisible in the darkness, spilled heavily past and over her, closely followed by a horde of what felt and sounded like large locusts. A few moments later the Hell's circus rush was receding below her, and she began crawling back up the slope.

There were noises from above too, faint screams and shouts and maniacal laughter that echoed weirdly through the cavern, and she wondered dazedly what madness had struck Rat's Castle this night.

After many minutes she felt the floor level out beneath her, and looking up she saw the distant torches and the archway. Carrington's men no longer lurked there and whatever the action was, it was taking place somewhere else, so Jacky got up and ran madly toward the light.

When she'd got there she crouched panting for several minutes in the semicircle of wonderful yellow light, enjoying the delusion of safety it gave her, like the King's X in the games of tag she'd played not that many years ago, and it was with reluctance that she finally got up and stepped through the arch and into darkness again.

She could hear nervous voices from the direction of the dock, so she padded silently up the corridor that led to the ascending stairway, but halted when she heard voices there too.

Guards, she thought—Carrington's men, probably, making sure nothing gets out of this ant's nest.

She decided to go back and hide somewhere until the guards returned to the surface, and then swim down the waterway to the Thames, and she'd just turned and started back when the steady shouting doubled in volume and a dim, reflected glow sprang up in the corridor. It quickly waxed brighter, as if men with torches were just about to appear around a corner ahead. Jacky looked around in panic, hoping to see a doorway she might duck into, but there was none. She flattened herself against a wall.

The yelling grew louder still, and she could hear a fast wooden knocking, and then from out of one of the farther tunnels burst Horrabin, completely ablaze and running on his stilts, flanked and followed by what seemed to be a horde of bounding, chittering rats; a moment later his pursuers skidded around the same corner and came bounding after him, flinging rocks and baying like hounds.

Jacky looked back at the stairs, and dimly saw two men crouching just outside the archway, aiming some sort of guns at the approaching rout. No help in that direction, she thought. In desperation she flung herself down against the wall with one arm over her face, in the faint hope of being mistaken for a corpse by all parties.

The two guns went off with one prolonged roar and a flash that brightened the tunnel for a full second, and as stone chips flew from the walls and ceiling, the burning clown rocked to a stop—but caught his balance, evidently unhurt by the blasts; their impact did, though, stop him long enough for his bestial pursuers to catch up with him.

A number of the Spoonsize Boys and their foot-tall counterparts had been blown away by the sprays of shot, but the survivors turned and flung themselves into the faces of the ravening Mistakes, who had knocked the flaming, screaming clown over against the wall and were tearing at his legs with mudstained claws. The miniature men leaped right in past the talons of the Mistakes and drove their little swords into eyes and throats and ears, totally careless of their own survival; but the Mistakes were fighting to the death and were willing to risk the blades of the Spoonsize Boys, and a scorching, in order to get close enough to Horrabin to take a bite out of any reachable part of him with muddied teeth, or to pull one of the stilts farther out from under him.

The lunatic spectacle was taking place only a few yards in front of Jacky, and she couldn't help lifting her head a little to watch. The blackened, whimpering clown wasn't burning as brightly as before, but there was still enough flame to see some individual struggles: Jacky saw one of the Mistakes, a poodle-sized thing with tentacles all over it and both eyes ruined by the homunculi's swords, latch a toothy mouth onto Horrabin's clutching right hand, and, with a horrible snapping, bite most of it off; and a couple of things like unshelled snails, dying under the fierce attentions of a dozen of the little men, had got in between the wall and the left stilt, and managed with their last, expiring efforts to push it out past the supporting point, so that the clown came crashing down onto them; most of the light went out when Horrabin hit the floor, so that all Jacky could see was a heaving, tortured mass of dying shapes, and all she could hear was an ever-weaker chorus of gasps, crunchings, whimpers and long, rattling exhalations. A nasty smell like burning garbage choked the tunnel.

Jacky got up and ran past the mass of death, deeper into the maze, and after twenty paces in the darkness she lost her footing and tumbled, and when she slid to a dazed stop a hand closed firmly on her wrist.

She writhed around, wondering if she had the strength left to strangle something, but she halted when she heard her unseen companion's voice. "I say, excuse me, Sir Thought or Whimsy or Fugitive Virtue, but could you possibly direct me to the waking levels of my mind?"

Ashbless had been dimly aware for some time that he was lying in the bottom of a boat that was being weakly rowed by Doctor Romanelli, but he came fully awake one more time when he noticed that the surface he was lying on had changed. The last time he'd been aware of it, it had been hard, angular wood, but now it seemed to be soft leather stretched loosely over some kind of flexible ribs. He opened his eye and was mildly surprised to find that he could see, though there was no light. The boat was passing through a vast ruinous hall, along the walls of which stood upright sarcophagi that shone with an intense blackness.

He heard Romanelli gasp, and looked in his direction. The gaunt sorcerer too shone in the anti-light; he was staring in awe at something over Ashbless' shoulder. Ashbless dragged an elbow under himself and managed to turn his head, and

saw several tall, dim figures standing at the stern, and a little
shrine in the center of the boat, encircled by a snake with its
tail in its mouth, and in the shrine stood a man-high disk that
blazed so darkly with the radiant blackness that it hurt
Ashbless' eye, and he had to look away; though he thought he
had seen dimly the pattern of a kephera beetle inscribed on the
disk.

When he could see again he noticed that Romanelli was
smiling with relief, and that tears were slicking his eroded
cheeks. "The boat of Ra," he was whispering, "the Sektet
boat, in which the sun journeys through the twelve hours of
the night, from sunset to dawn! I'm in it—and at dawn, when
we emerge into the world again, I'll sail in the Atet boat, the
boat of the morning sky, and I'll be restored!"

Too ruined to care, Ashbless slumped back down onto the
leather—beneath which, he noticed, he could hear a pulse
beat. The wailing that he'd seemed to be hearing all night was
louder now, and had a supplicating tone. He rolled his head
and looked out over the low gunwale to the bank of the river
and saw vague forms stretching out their arms toward the boat
as it passed; and when it had passed them he could hear their
despairing weeping. There were poles standing in the bank at
intervals—marking the hours, he thought—with snakes' heads
stuck on the top of them, and as the boat passed each one it
became, just for an instant, a bowed human head.

Ashbless sat up, and noticed for the first time that the boat
was a huge snake, broadened in the middle like an exaggerated
cobra's hood, and that at both stern and bow it tapered up in a
long neck to a living serpent's head.

This is the poem, he thought—the twelve hours of the night.
This is what I was writing about. I'm in the boat that only
dead men see.

He sensed that the disk was alive—no, very dead, but
aware—but that it was uninterested in the two stowaways. The
tall figures in the stern, which seemed to be men with the heads
of animals and birds, also ignored them. Ashbless slumped
back again.

After a time the boat floated through a dim gate flanked by
two sarcophagi as tall as telephone poles, and the shore figures
on the other side were screaming and shifting from side to side
along the shore and over their frightened cries he could hear a
slow metallic slithering. "*Apep!*" the ghosts were shouting.
"*Apep!*" And then he saw a shape of blackness rising, and

realized it was the head of a serpent so vast that it dwarfed
their freakish boat. Man-shaped forms dangled from its jaws,
but it shook its ponderous head, sending them spinning away,
and arched slowly forward over the river.

"The serpent Apep," whispered Romanelli, "whose body
lies in the deep realms of the *keku samu* where pure darkness
becomes an impenetrable solid. It senses that there is a soul on
this boat that . . . doesn't qualify for emergence into the
dawn." Romanelli was smiling. "But I don't need you any
longer anyway."

Unable even to prop himself up on his elbow anymore,
Ashbless watched the absolutely black head blot out every
other thing above him. The air became bitterly cold as the
thing bent down closer, and when it opened its vast jaws he
thought he could see negative stars shining in a remote distance, as if Apep's mouth was the gateway to a universe of absolute cold and the absence of light.

Ashbless shut his eye and commended his soul into the care
of any benign god there might still somewhere be.

A thin screaming drew his attention outward again, and he
looked up for what he hoped would be the last time . . . and
saw the disintegrating figure of Doctor Romanelli falling upward into the vast maw.

Just to be sure, Jacky stared into the dark west, where the
broad Thames curled to the south past Whitehall before
straightening out westward, and then she looked east again.

She smiled with relief. Yes, the sky was definitely paling.
She could see the dark arches of Blackfriars Bridge against the
tenuous pre-dawn glow.

She relaxed and sat back on the low stone wall, aware now
that it was chilly out on the mud bank above the Adelphi
Arches. She pulled her coat closer about her shoulders and
began shivering. Hopeless as this vigil is, she thought, I'll
nevertheless wait here until somewhat after dawn to see if
Ashbless might drift out here—it's just conceivable that he
wasn't dead when he fell past me in the deep cellar, and that he
reached the subterranean river and was well along it before the
dreadful . . . solidification began.

She shuddered and glanced for reassurance at the waxing
eastern light, and then allowed herself to remember the ascent
from the deep cellars.

She had taken Coleridge's hand and cautiously begun to

pick her way back up the lightless corridor when she noticed the silence. Not only had the distant wailing stopped, but the subtly complex resonances in the air, the echoes of the perpetual breeze through all the cubic miles of subterranean corridors and chambers below them, had ceased.

She'd pressed against the right-hand wall as they went past the place where she knew Horrabin's corpse lay—and she nearly screamed when a startlingly deep voice spoke to them out of the darkness.

"This is not a place for people, my friends," it said.

"Uh . . . right," squeaked Jacky. "We're leaving."

She heard a heaving and thudding—and several metallic clinkings—and when the voice spoke again, it was from over her head. "I'll escort you," it said heavily. "Even dying from the pinpricks of the clown's little men, Big Biter is a protector few would care to cross."

"You'll . . . escort us?" asked Jacky incredulously.

"Yes." The thing sighed ponderously. "I owe it to your companion, who freed my brothers and sisters and me and gave us the chance to revenge ourselves on our maker before we died." Jacky had noticed that the thing's voice was not echoing, as though they stood in a room instead of a tunnel. "Make haste," Big Biter said, moving forward, "the darkness is hardening."

The peculiar trio made their way to the stairs and plodded up them. At the first landing Coleridge wanted to rest, but Big Biter told him there wasn't time; the creature picked Coleridge up and they continued.

"Don't hang behind," their escort cautioned Jacky.

"I won't," Jacky assured it, for she realized that now there was no sound or echo from the corridor they'd vacated, or even from the flight of stairs they'd just ascended. What was it the eyeless Sisters had said to her half a year ago? *The darkness is hardening, like thick mud, and we want to be away when it turns as solid as the stones . . . we mustn't be caught forever in the stones that are hardened night!* Jacky made sure she matched Big Biter's pace, and was glad he moved so quickly.

When they finally got to the top and stepped into the bright torchlight of the kitchen hallway in Rat's Castle, a couple of Carrington's men took a step toward them, then took two steps back when they saw the creature that was carrying

Coleridge in its heavy arms. Jacky looked up at Big Biter and almost recoiled herself.

Their escort was an amphibious giant, with long black catfish tentacles around its face like a caricatured beard and hair, and eyes like glass paperweights, and a pig-like snout, but by far his most striking feature was his mouth: it was a twelve-inch slash across his face, which he could barely close because of the rows of huge teeth in it. He wore an ancient coat, the front of which was shredded and wet with red blood.

"These vermin won't interfere with you," Big Biter said quietly. "Come on."

He set Coleridge down and walked with them to the front door. "Go now," he said. "Quickly. I'll watch until you're out of sight, but I've got to get back down the stairs before the darkness hardens completely."

"All right," said Jacky, gratefully breathing the relatively fresh pre-dawn air of Buckeridge Street. "And thank you for—"

"I did it for your friend," rumbled Big Biter. "Now go."

Jacky nodded and hustled Coleridge outside and down the dark street.

They'd made it back to Hudson's Hotel without mishap, and when they'd gotten into Coleridge's room Jacky had flopped him onto the bed. The man was asleep before Jacky had gotten to the hall and gently closed the door behind her. She'd seen the laudanum bottle on the bedside table, and she believed she understood now why Carrington's restraining measures had proven ineffective on the elderly poet. How could Carrington have known what a tremendous tolerance for opium Coleridge had developed?

Then she had walked down to the Thames, by the Adelphi Arches' where the subterranean tributary emptied into the river, on the chance that Ashbless, or whatever remained of him, might emerge from the tunnel.

The sky was a bright steely blue in the east now, and a tattered string of clouds above the horizon had begun to smolder and glow. The sun would appear at any moment.

There was a turbulence in the water in the still deep shadows below the arches, and Jacky glanced down just in time to see a ghostly, semi-transparent boat surge out. As it emerged into the dawn grayness it became simultaneously incandescent and more transparent, and it receded away toward the eastern horizon at such a speed that Jacky was momentarily certain it was only a hallucination born of total exhaustion; but a split second later she became aware of two things: the first red sliver of the rising sun had appeared over the distant London skyline, and a man was splashing about in the water a dozen feet out from the bank, having apparently fallen through the ghost boat when it became insubstantial.

Jacky leaped to her feet, for she recognized the man, who was now swimming a little dazedly toward shore.

"Mr. Ashbless!" she shouted. "Over here!"

Just as the snake boat had passed between the two poles—each supporting a pharaoh-bearded head—that flanked the last archway, Ashbless felt a tremendous swelling heat burst up inside himself, stunning the beleaguered shred that was his consciousness, and until he splashed into the icy Thames he was blissfully sure that this was death.

When he'd thrashed to the surface and shaken the long hair out of his eyes it occurred to him that he once again *had* hair, and two eyes. He held up first one hand, and then the other, in front of his face, and grinned to see all fingers present, all skin unbroken.

The restoration Doctor Romanelli had hoped for in vain had happened to him—when the sun was resurrected and made whole and alive again at dawn, Ashbless had been allowed—God knew why—to partake in it.

He'd just begun to swim in toward shore when he heard a call. He paused, squinting at the shadowed shore, then recognized the person sitting on the wall, waved, and resumed his stroke.

The water was surging and swashing around the Adelphi Arches, and when he stood up in the shallows and splashed his way up onto the mud bank he saw why: the subterranean waterway had stopped flowing into the Thames, as completely as if a huge valve had been closed somewhere—and now that the immediate backwash had abated, the river was flowing past Ashbless' point of exit as smoothly as it swept past the rest of the bank. A few river birds had swooped down to peer inquisitively at the churned-up mud that was swirling away downstream.

He looked up at the thin figure perched on the wall. "Hello, Jacky," he called. "Coleridge got out too, I think."

"Yes, sir," said Jacky.

"And," said Ashbless, climbing up the bank, "I daresay he won't remember anything he saw last night."

"Well," said Jacky, mystified, as the dripping, bearded giant scrambled up the slope and hoisted himself up to sit next to her on the wall, "as a matter of fact, he may not." She peered closely at him. "I thought you were dead when you slid past me down there. Your . . . eyes, and . . ."

"Yes," said Ashbless gently. "I was dying—but there was magic loose last night, not all of it malign." It was his turn to peer at her. "You found time to shave?"

"Oh!" Jacky rubbed her bare upper lip. "It . . . the moustache . . . was singed off."

"Good Lord. I'm glad to see you made it out, anyway." Ashbless leaned back, closing his eyes and taking a deep breath. "I'm going to sit here," he said, "until the sun's high enough to dry me off."

Jacky cocked an eyebrow. "You'll die of the chill—which seems at least a waste, after surviving the . . . condensed works of Dante."

He grinned without opening his eyes, and shook his head. "Ashbless has got lots of things to do before he dies."

"Oh? Such as what?"

Ashbless shrugged. "Well . . . get married, for one thing. Fifth of next month, as a matter of fact."

Jacky tossed her head carelessly. "That's nice. To whom?"

"A girl named Elizabeth Jacqueline Tichy. Pretty girl. Never met her, but I've seen a picture of her."

Jacky's eyebrows went up. "Who?"

Ashbless repeated the name.

Her face twitched irresolutely between a piqued smile and a frown. "You've never met her? So how can you be so damn sure she'll have you?"

"I know she will, Jacky me lad. You might say she hasn't any choice."

"Is that a fact now," said Jacky angrily. "I suppose it's your broad shoulders and fair hair that will . . . render her incapable of resisting you, eh? Or no, don't tell me—it's your poetry, isn't it? Sure, you're going to read her a few verses of your incomprehensible damned 'Twelve Hours,' aren't you, and she'll figure since she can't understand it, it must be . . . Art, right? Why, you arrogant son of a bitch . . ."

Ashbless had opened his eyes in astonishment and sat up. "Damn it, Jacky, what's the matter with you? Lord, I didn't say I was going to *rape* her, I—"

"Oh, no! No, you're just going to give her the once in a lifetime chance to—what, consort?—with a *real* poet. What a bit of luck for her!"

"What in hell are you raving about, lad? I only said—"

Jacky leaped to her feet on the wall and planted her fists on her hips. "Meet Elizabeth Tichy!"

Ashbless blinked up at her. "What do you mean? Do you know her? Oh my God, that's right, you *do* know her, don't you? Listen, I didn't mean—"

"Damn you!" Jacky brushed her hair out with her fingers. "*I'm* Elizabeth Jacqueline Tichy!"

Ashbless laughed uneasily—then did a double take. "Holy God. Are . . . are you *really*?"

"It's one of the perhaps four things I'm sure of, Ashbless."

He flapped his hands in dismay. "Damn me, I'm sorry, Ja—Miss Tichy. I thought you were just . . . good old Jacky, my buddy from the old days at Captain Jack's house. I never dreamed that all this time you—"

"You were never at Captain Jack's house," said Jacky. Almost pleadingly she added, "I mean, were you?"

"In a way I was. You see, I—" He halted. "What do you say we discuss this over breakfast?"

Jacky was frowning again, but after a pause she nodded. "All right, but only because poor Doyle thought so highly of you. And it doesn't mean I'm conceding anything, you understand?" She grinned, then caught herself and frowned sternly. "Come on, I know a place in St. Martin's Lane where they'll even let you sit by the fire."

She hopped down from the wall as Ashbless stood up, and together they walked away, still bickering, north toward the Strand in the clear dawn light.

EPILOGUE—APRIL 12, 1846

" 'Tis not too late to seek a newer world.
Push off, and sitting well in order smite
The sounding furrows; for my purpose holds
To sail beyond the sunset, and the baths
Of all the western stars, until I die."
                                    —Alfred, Lord Tennyson

AFTER STANDING IN his doorway for nearly a quarter of an hour, staring out across the gray, hummocked expanse of the Woolwich marshes that stretched for several miles under the rain-threatening sky, William Ashbless nearly took off his coat and went back inside. The fire was drawing well, after all, and he had not entirely killed the bottle of Glenlivet last night. Then he frowned, tucked his cap lower over his bone-white hair, touched the pommel of the sword he'd strapped on for the occasion, and drew the door closed behind him. No, I owe it to Jacky, he thought as he trudged down his steps. She met her own appointment so . . . gallantly, seven years ago.

During the last couple of solitary years, Ashbless had fretfully noticed that his memory of Jacky's face had disappeared—the damned portraits had looked fine when they were new and she was still alive to supplement them, but recently it had seemed to him that they hadn't ever caught her with her real smile on. But today, he realized, he could remember her as clearly as if she'd just that morning taken the coach into

London; her affectionately sarcastic grin, her occasional snap-
pishness, and the gamin, Leslie Caron prettiness that, to his
mind, she had kept right up until her death of a fever at the
age of forty-seven. Probably, he thought as he crossed the
highway and started out along the marsh path—which he'd
morbidly watched appear over the last couple of seasons,
knowing he would this day walk it—probably I remember her
so well today because today I join her.

The path rose and fell over the hilly marshes, but when the
river came into view after ten minutes of brisk walking, his
step was still springy and he wasn't panting at all, for he'd
been exercising and studying fencing now for years, determined at least to seriously injure whoever it might prove to be
that was destined to kill him.

I'll wait here, he decided, standing on a low rise that
overlooked the willow-fringed Thames bank fifty yards away.
They'll find my body closer to the bank, but I'd like to get a
long, clear look at my murderer first.

And who on earth, he wondered, will it turn out to be?

He noticed that he was trembling, and he sat down and took
several deep breaths. Take it easy, old lad, he told himself.
You've known for thirty-five long and mainly happy years
that this day was coming.

He leaned back and stared up at the turbulent gray clouds.
And most of your friends are dead now, he thought. Byron
went—of a fever, too—in Missolonghi twenty-some years ago,
and Coleridge bit the dust in 1834. Ashbless smiled and
wondered, not for the first time, how much of some of Coleridge's very late poems—particularly "Limbo" and "Ne Plus
Ultra"—might have derived some of their imagery from his
dimly remembered experiences that night in the early April of
1811. Certain lines made Ashbless curious: "No such sweet
sights doth Limbo den immure, Wall'd round, and made a
spirit-jail secure, By the mere horror of blank Naught-at-
all . . ." and "Sole Positive of Night! Antipathist of Light!
. . . Condensed blackness and abysmal storm . . ."

He rubbed his eyes and stood up—and froze, and his chest
went icy hollow, for a rowboat had been moored to one of the
willows while he'd been looking away, and a tall, burly man
was climbing sturdily up the slope, a sheathed sword swinging
on his right hip. Interesting, Ashbless thought nervously—a
lefty like myself.

Okay, he told himself, now stay calm. Remember, the

wound in the belly is the only one they'll find on you, so don't bother with the epee-type parries, that protect the arms, legs and head—only parry thrusts to the body . . . while knowing, of course, that there's one coming that you'll fail to parry.

His right hand fluttered over his stomach, and he wondered which patch of presently healthy skin would soon be parted to admit several inches of cold steel.

In an hour it'll be done, he thought. Try to brave out this last hour as well as Jacky did. For she knew it was coming too . . . knew it ever since that night in 1815 when you got drunk enough to give in to her demands to know the date and circumstances of her death.

Ashbless squared his shoulders and stepped off the crest of the rise and walked down the path toward the river to meet his murderer halfway.

The man looked up, and seemed startled to see Ashbless coming toward him. I wonder what our quarrel will be, thought Ashbless. At least he isn't young—his beard looks as white as mine. He's been in foreign parts, too, judging by that tan. His face does look vaguely familiar, though.

When they were still a dozen yards apart Ashbless stopped. "Good morning," he called, and he was proud of how steady his voice was.

The other man blinked and grinned craftily, and Ashbless realized with a chill that the man was insane. "You're him," the stranger said in a cracked voice. "Ain't you?"

"I'm who?"

"Doyle. Brendan Doyle."

Ashbless answered, in a tone that concealed his surprise, "Yes . . . but it's a name I haven't used for thirty-five years. Why? Do we know each other?"

"I know you. And," he said, drawing his sword, "I've come to kill you."

"I guessed," said Ashbless quietly, stepping back and drawing his own blade from its sheath. The wind whispered in the tall grasses. "Any use asking why?"

"You know why," the other man replied, lunging fast as a whiplash on the word know; Ashbless managed to parry it with a wild outside flail in sixte, but he forgot to riposte.

"I really don't know why," he gasped, trying to get a firm footing on the muddy ground.

"It's because," the man said as he launched a quick feint and disengage that Ashbless barely avoided with a screeching circular parry, "while *you're* alive," the man's sword sped up out of the bind and darted in at Ashbless' chest, so that Ashbless had to hop back out of distance, "I *can't* be." As he recovered from his lunge his blade flicked sideways at Ashbless' forearm, and Ashbless felt the edge cut right through his jacket and shirt and grate against the bone.

Ashbless was so stunned that he almost forgot to parry the next lunge. But this is wrong, he thought bewilderedly, I know I won't be found with a wounded arm!

And then he laughed, for he'd figured it out.

"Yield now or die," Ashbless called almost merrily to his opponent.

"It's you that's to die," the tanned man muttered, starting a lunge and then abruptly halting halfway through it, so as to provoke Ashbless into a premature parry; but Ashbless didn't fall for it, and caught the end of his opponent's blade with the forte of his own, and lunged forward with a strong bind that drove his point corkscrewing in to poke, and then deeply stab, the tanned man's belly. He felt the narrow blade stop and constrictedly flex against the spine.

The man sat down on the wet grass, clutching himself with hands already slick with blood. "Quick," he gasped, pale under his tan, "me be you."

Ashbless just stared down at him, his exhilaration suddenly gone.

"Come on," grated the man on the ground, dropping his sword and beginning to crawl. "Do the trick. Switch."

Ashbless stepped back.

His opponent crawled forward for a yard or two, then fell forward onto the grass.

Several minutes went by before Ashbless moved, and when he did it was to kneel beside the body, which had stopped breathing, and lay his hand gently on the dead man's shoulder.

If there is any reward after death, he thought, for such creatures as you, I'll bet you've earned it. God knows how you made your way back to England from Cairo, and how you found me. Maybe you were drawn back to me, very like the way ghosts are supposed to be drawn to the place where they died. Well, you get to share, a little bit at least, in my biography: you provide the corpse.

Eventually Ashbless wiped his sword clean on an uprooted tuft of grass, and then stood up to sheathe it; and he tore off a strip of his scarf and knotted it around his cut forearm. The chilly spring breeze blew all thoughts of the past out of his mind, and with a sense of adventure he hadn't known in decades he walked on down the path to the moored boat, leaving behind him the ka which Doctor Romanelli had made of him so many years ago.

It's unknown, whatever happens to me from here on out, he thought with a smoldering elation as he untied the rope. No book I ever read can give me any hint. It may be that I'll capsize the boat and drown within five minutes, or it may be I'll live another twenty years!

He climbed in and fitted the thole pins into the oarlocks, and after three strong strokes he was well out onto the face of the river. And as he rowed on, toward whatever might prove to be the true destiny of the man who'd been Brendan Doyle and Dumb Tom and Eshvlis the cobbler and William Ashbless, and was not any of them any longer, he regaled the river birds with every Beatles song he could remember . . . except *Yesterday*.